MW01492336

The One-Donkey Solution

A Satire

Richard Bulliet

iUniverse, Inc.
Bloomington

The One-Donkey Solution
A Satire

iUniverse books may be ordered through booksellers or by contacting:

iUniverse
1663 Liberty Drive
Bloomington, IN 47403
www.iuniverse.com
1-800-Authors (1-800-288-4677)

ISBN: 9781462000128 (sc)
ISBN: 9781462000135 (ebk)

Printed in the United States of America

iUniverse rev. date: 4/13/2011

PROLOGUE

The gray donkey picks its way up the arid mountainside along a crag-shadowed path strewn with loose rocks. The cloudless summer sky casts outlines in sharp relief: boulders, big rocks, small stones … more stones. The old man sits sideways on the donkey rhythmically tapping its haunch with a stick.

"Ya'fur. Donkey. Tell me, will it rain tomorrow?" He waits half expectantly. "Tell me, Donkey. Don't be silent like that."

The old man wears a striped wool burnoose. Its hood, which he'll need by day's end when a brisk wind will blow through the mountain passes, hangs slackly from his shoulders. A single twist of white cotton around a black skullcap shields the crown of his head from the sun. He squints at the distant point where the mountainsides come together in a vee. The entrance to the first pass. Two more beyond that and he is home.

"So tell me, Ya'fur. Good donkey, Ya'fur. Will the king's wife bear him a son this year?"

A speckled lizard scurries from beneath a rock kicked by the donkey's hoof. The old man thinks about the mint tea that Fritz, his young German guest, will prepare for him when he reaches his stone hut.

"Listen to me, Donkey. The sheikhs of the Ouled Muhammad and the Ouled Hassan want me to tell them who has the right to water their herds first at the well of Mu'nis. What should I say?"

"Give it to the Ouled Hassan," says the donkey.

THE ISLAND OF hYDRA, GREECE—2005

"Praise the Lord! Jesus the Christ will someday return and ride in glory into Jerusalem mounted on a donkey, lowly and humble. The Bible says so explicitly! Anything else is lies." Pastor Steve—the name he insists on to the annoyance of his fellow conferees—thinks to pour a fresh round of retsina but encounters a glass too far when he gets to Monika Farber at the end of the table and slops wine onto her mussel shell-strewn plate instead. She grabs the bottle before all is lost and tops her glass off.

The portly professor at the head of the table, whom everyone will remember as being less pompous drunk than sober, rises unsteadily from his chair. The glass he holds up is tippy but not actually losing its contents. "I offer a toast to the donkey of Jesus ..."

"Here! Here!" seconds a lean Scotsman named Douglas Greeley.

"And to the donkey of the Moshiach ..." He nods to the muscular man in a black skullcap whom they have taken to calling the Rabbi. The Rabbi slightly raises his glass of sparkling water to acknowledge the inclusion of the Jews.

"And to the donkey of the Mahdi—something for our absent Muslim friends."

"Boo! Hiss!" cries Pastor Steve.

"May all of the Messiahs come in peace."

"To the Messiahs and to peace," echoes the drunken company.

"Wait, I'm not done. And may they all come at the same time." No response. "What I mean is, if we're going to think e-cu-men-i-cal-ly"—a hard word to enunciate under the circumstances—"we can't very well have one come and not the others because that would mean that one religion is true and the others aren't."

"The Bible says ..." begins Pastor Steve.

The professor overrides him. "The Bible applies to them all. Messiahs ride donkeys. Some traditions even say that the donkey the Messiah is going to ride is descended from the donkey that Jesus rode, and the donkey that Moses rode, and the donkey that Abraham rode. One magnificent donkey family. And as the world's expert on donkey traditions ..."

"The world's leading ass, you say?" Monika Farber's sharp German accent cuts through the noise of the taverna.

The professor presses on. "... I want to propose the three-donkey solution. The Christian, Jewish, and Muslim Messiahs all come at the same time. Each of them finds himself a donkey descended from the donkeys of his predecessors. Then they race each other into Jerusalem. Whoever gets to the Temple first—or if the Israelis haven't rebuilt the Temple, to the Western Wall of the old Temple—is not only the true Messiah, but his followers get to claim Jerusalem once and for all for themselves."

"Jesus' donkey the winner by a nose!" snorts Pastor Steve.

"Oh, I say," laughs Douglas Greeley. "A bit much."

"But why not?" says Farber. "I'll go along with the three-donkey solution. It makes as much sense as the two-state solution or the one-state solution that everyone gabbles on about."

"Friends! Colleagues!" says the Rabbi with his hands raised to calm the commotion. "As the only Israeli at this table or at this conference, I want to say officially that a three-donkey solution is such a bad idea that it would be better for the Moshiach to stay away."

"Not your choice!" cries Pastor Steve. "The world is in God's hands. No one can know the hour or the day, but the day cometh and the hour is at hand."

"What does that mean?" says Farber caustically. "Continue, Rabbi. You have the floor. But first more retsina for the rest of us." She refills all of the glasses without spilling a drop.

"Thank you, Professor Farber." The Rabbi stands. The proposer of the three-donkey solution plops down on his chair. "Under the three-donkey solution just proposed to us by the learned Professor Constantine, I see mobs of Christians, and mobs of Jews, and mobs of Muslims lining the road to Jerusalem cheering their Messiah on. Some throw palm leaves, some throw stones. People make bets. Quarrels break out. Each Messiah goads his donkey to push and shove the other two donkeys off the road. They're neck and neck and neck going through the Damascus Gate. Rumors flash that the Jew is ahead, or the Muslim is ahead. Quarrels turn into fistfights. The Western Wall is in sight. The Messiahs look crazed and sweaty. The fistfights explode into riots. Pandemonium engulfs the Messiahs before any of them can win the race, and Jerusalem becomes a slaughterhouse. In other words, the three-donkey solution is no solution at all. It's Armageddon."

Greeley, who is busy pouring himself yet another glass of wine, seems not to have followed the speech. "What I don't understand is how the Messiahs find their donkeys. I have hundreds of donkeys at my sanctuary, and the Messiah is welcome to any of them. But how will he know which one to choose?"

"The donkey finds the Messiah, not the other way around," says Professor Constantine, slurring his words.

"No, the disciples go out and get one for him. Says so in the gospels," says Pastor Steve.

The professor casts him an annoyed look. "The only reason the donkey is there for the disciples to get is because it knows who

Jesus is and has arranged to be there." *Ignoramus*, he adds under his breath.

Greeley doesn't want to let go of his problem. "Look here, if all three donkeys are related, they should be living as a family. Donkeys like to live in families. So each Messiah would have to come to the same place to pick up his animal."

"Too many details," declares Monika Farber with Teutonic decisiveness. "I agree with the Rabbi. The three-donkey solution can never work."

An inebriated lull ensues until Professor Constantine once again propels his aging body to its feet and raises a nearly empty glass. "In that case, I propose a toast to the one-donkey solution."

"What's the one-donkey solution?" asks the Rabbi amiably.

"The one-donkey solution fits the traditions just as well. It says that there is only one donkey for all three Messiahs. There has always been only one donkey. The donkey of Muhammad was exactly the same animal as the donkey of Jesus, which was exactly the same animal as the donkey of Moses, which was exactly the same donkey as the donkey of Abraham, ad infinitum. So when the End Times are at hand, it will be the animal of the one and only true Messiah."

"An immortal donkey, then?" ventures the Rabbi skeptically.

"The alpha and the omega. A donkey that's been there since Creation and will be there at the Eschaton. All hail the immortal donkey!" No one responds.

"He's bonkers," says Greeley to Monika Farber.

The Rabbi steps to the swaying professor's side and puts an arm around his shoulder. "Time to get you back to the hotel, Professor."

The party gathers its belongings while the waitress processes their several credit cards.

"What time tomorrow?" asks Pastor Steve as if already contemplating his hangover.

"Nine sharp," says Farber. "One more half day and the first ever International Conference on Donkeys and Mules will be history."

"Praise the Lord!"

Greeley trails the group to the door still musing about the three-donkey solution to Pastor Steve. "You know, if there were a family of donkeys special to the Messiahs, it might be possible to identify it. Perhaps they have some kind of sign."

"DNA," replies Pastor Steve in a suddenly serious voice. "Modern science. They would have to be different from regular donkeys, and that would have to show up in their DNA."

"I don't know about that," replies Greeley vaguely. "I thought maybe a sign, like a notch in the ear or maybe a color pattern."

The fresh Mediterranean air revives the professor. Releasing himself from the steadying hand of the Rabbi he moves alongside the comely Monika Farber and ventures an arm around her waist.

"I've told you once, Paul, not to touch me," she whispers. "This is the second time. Once more and you will feel pain you will never forget."

"Sorry," mumbles the professor. "Didn't mean anything."

EIGHT YEARS LATER
A GIRL AND A BOY

A waifish young woman huddles in a doorway in a southern German city. She is dressed in jeans and a hooded fleece jacket that keeps her black hair from blowing in the cold wind. She presses the lowest buzzer, the one next to the business card of Professor Doktor Monika Farber. She presses a second time, and a third. She holds the button down with fierce thumb. Giving up on the buzzer, she puts her hands on her hips and glares at the door. Then she starts to pummel it rhythmically with the heels of both palms. Her acrylic fingernails are checked magenta-and-black.

As her assault on the door makes a natural progression to kicking, a man saunters up to the same doorway. He is well over a foot taller than she, and perhaps ten years older. *"Kann ich Ihnen helfen?"*

"I don't understand German," she replies with a truculence better directed at the door.

"I said: May I help you?"

"Help me what?"

"Help you break down the door."

"Is this your house?"

"No, it is where my professor has her flat."

She surveys the tall man's appearance. "Aren't you too old to be a student?"

"I followed a crooked path."

"Is that something you normally say in German? Crooked path?"

"*Krummen Weg*? No, I'm trying to speak colorful English. Am I succeeding?"

"Maybe. I don't think I've ever said 'crooked path,' but my father might."

"Good. I learned English from a Canadian in Belgium. He drank immense quantities of triple beer and believed in colorful language. He also taught me how to polish and set gems."

"You are a jeweler?"

"I never got that good. My crooked path took me instead to foreign lands to buy and sell stones."

"I'm getting cold. Shall we break the door down? I've come a long way to see Professor Farber, and if she's not going to be home, I want to leave a note on her desk."

"You could leave it on her door. Or I could deliver it."

"It might blow away, or you might forget. It's better to break into her flat and leave it on her desk."

"Then by all means leave it on her desk. If you'll stand aside …"

"Don't you need my help?"

"Not to unlock the door." He produces a ring of keys from his pocket.

"Your professor gives you the key to her flat?"

"Yes."

"Are you sleeping with her?"

"No. There's no chemistry. By the way, my name is Fritz."

"I'm Toots."

The door opens and they enter.

"Professor Farber's desk is in the room on the left."

"Why do you have a big round tattoo on your neck?"

"Some professors fancy that their instruction leaves a lifelong mark on their students. Professor Farber prefers a more tangible mark."

"She had you tattooed?"

"A story for another time."

Toots looks around the appallingly orderly study. The largest portraits on a shelf of silver-framed photographs show three men and a woman, all in uniforms. Toots considers asking a pointed question and then thinks better of it.

Fritz sits at the professor's desk and extracts a blank sheet of paper from the center drawer. "If you tell me what you want to say, I'll write it in German."

Toots looks at him askance. "Professor Farber is fluent in English. My father attended a conference with her in Greece. Why are you trying to find out what I intend to put in my note?"

Fritz is unperturbed. "Because Professor Farber has disappeared. I have not seen her for three weeks. The university is not in session so the administration has no concern. The police take no interest either. Nothing out of the ordinary appears in her mail, either here or at her office. But then you arrive. As her loyal and concerned student, how could I not be interested in what you want to say to her?"

"You're thinking a ransom note? Dear Professor Farber, when you read this, be advised that unless you pay us one million euros, we will … we will what? You see, it doesn't make sense. The kidnapper can't send a ransom note to the kidnappee."

"That wasn't what I had in mind."

"What did you have in mind?"

"Nothing, I suppose. I'm just concerned about her, and I thought you might know something."

"Something I would put in a note."

"Doesn't sound very plausible, does it."

Toots relishes her small victory. "My note will contain my name and mobile number and will remind her of meeting my father at an International Conference on Donkeys and Mules. It will conclude by asking her to call me as soon as possible. Would you like to put all that in German?"

Fritz makes no reply.

"You're not yourself a donkey specialist, are you?"

"No, not at all. Aside from one particular donkey that I happen to be on conversational terms with ..."

"So to speak."

"... I have neither personal insight nor scholarly expertise on the subject."

"Have you ever heard of the Donkey Genome Project? The DGP?"

"No."

"Do you know if Professor Farber has had any dealings with the DGP?"

"No."

Sitting at the desk, Fritz's head is on Toots' level. They stare, or better, gaze at one another for a long time. There is chemistry.

"Would you like to see the rest of the flat?"

Toots blushes. "Yes, why not?"

Fritz takes her hand and guides her from the study to the bedroom.

*   *   *

Hours elapse—or days, no one is counting—before wakefulness and a temporary satisfaction of appetites converge enough to permit a resumption of non-intimate conversation.

"Why do you have checked fingernails?"

"They are an assertion of self in the face of my daily chore of milking donkeys."

"You milk donkeys?"

"I do. Daddy maintains a sanctuary for donkeys in Scotland. We sell the milk. Daddy is the reason I came here. A sinister group that goes by the name of the Donkey Genome Project is harassing him."

"Are you under the impression that I am buying this, Toots?"

Toots sits up in outrage. "Would a woman in love lie to her lover?"

"Happens all the time."

She hits him with a pillow. "I'll have you know that the DGP is making mysterious demands, and it is a very secretive organization. Daddy is worried that they have designs on our donkeys. So I am searching them out. I started here because Daddy has many times told me that when the day comes that I decide I want to know the secrets of donkeys, and not just milk them, there are two people I can turn to: Professor Monika Farber at the University of Erlangen and Professor Paul Constantine at Harvard. There was also a third, an Israeli, but he couldn't remember his name."

"I'm sorry I don't know the secrets of donkeys."

Toots caresses his thigh. "It may be your only fault. That and the tattoo. But since you can't help me, I must now tear myself from your arms and proceed on to Harvard."

"Don't go, Toots. It will be a waste of time better spent with me. Professor Farber has spoken of Professor Constantine more than once. He is old, pedantic, and inappropriately flirtatious. In a word—her word—an asshole. So your trip to Harvard is likely to be expensive and fruitless."

"You underestimate my resourcefulness."

Fritz looks around at the signs of their lovemaking. "Perhaps I do."

CAMBRIDGE, MASSACHUSETTS

The mind of the aging scholar immersed in a reverie idles slowly, running on fumes of self-regard and memories of old television shows.

The name is Constantine. Paul Constantine. I'm an asinologist. An assman. (That's a joke.) Not one of your horse-faced English girlies on a crusade to save that last lonely donkey from some Italian butcher's sausage grinder. Nope, that's not me. I'm a real assman. I know the history. The deep history. The unsuspected history. Never forget: Prolegomenon to the Study of the Ass as a Religious and Sexual Symbol *came first in the Society for the History of Animal Husbandry's book prize competition. Never forget that. Harvard received an endowment for Asinine Studies from a rancher who also gave a few mil for cancer research? Who got the job? No competition. I'm Paul Constantine, Professor of Asinine Studies in Harvard's Department of Symbology.*

Looking between his brown wingtips propped on his desk. Gazing at late winter snowflakes drifting down on Harvard Yard. He hears the creak of his door opening. He swivels his chair with studied slowness. It's a woman. A compact five feet of sturdy female encased in a yellow slicker and rain hat that make her look like a walking fire hydrant.

Constantine's reverie dissipates.

"Professor Constantine?"

"Yes."

"I need your help."

"Get in line, Toots. Everybody wants a bite from the Harvard genius apple. Do I know you? Are you in one of my classes?"

She shrugs off the question. "I was warned that you were difficult. A complete asshole according to someone whose name I won't mention. So don't think that rudeness will drive me away."

Insults are nothing new. Constantine is used to the jealous gibes of assman wanna-bes. "*Asshole*, Toots, is a linguistic accident. A conflation of *ass*, meaning donkey, and *arse*, meaning backside. Came about when the pronunciation distinction between the two words disappeared in American dialect. Shakespeare knew the difference. Never used the word *arse*. It was filthy. But calling a person an *ass*, or a *jackass*—meaning, of course, the male animal, that is to say, the animal possessed of a jack, which was the old way of saying possessed of a dick—was okay. Meant that the person was funny-stupid. Nowadays it's 'asshole' that means funny-stupid. Go figure."

"I was also warned that you were a pedant." Her voice is seductively deep and mellifluous. "A professors' professor they called you. And not in the nice sense of the phrase ... if there is a nice sense. Nevertheless, I need you. I'm told there are only two people in the world who know the secrets of donkeys."

"Don't tell me. I'm guessing your informant identified the other one as that acidulous valkyrie in Erlangen, the vastly overrated Monika Farber. Don't believe a word of it. Monika Farber is a sham. She couldn't tell her ass from ..."

"Professor Farber has disappeared. I traveled to Erlangen first. It's closer to St. Andrew's, and my need was urgent. No one had seen her for weeks. But no one seemed to miss her, except for her student, Fritz Messiassohn. Fritz was a lost child. A spiritual innocent. I took pity on him."

"Did you tell him to transfer to Harvard? I wouldn't mind having another student to pass my erudition on to."

"Fritz and I fell in love. Our passion was intense. We did not speak about erudition. He told me about life in the mountains of Morocco amidst the rocks under the blue, blue sky. He showed me how the tribesmen make love. It tore my soul to leave him. But my mission came first. I am here because of my father."

Constantine throws her a shrewd-genius look honed to perfection over countless Faculty Club lunches. "Let me guess. You say you're from St. Andrew's. That makes your father a professor at the university? Nooo. A golf instructor? Nooo." He waits a beat. "Then possibly the proprietor of Ass Isle, Scotland's largest donkey sanctuary?"

He savors her look of astonishment. As well as her transformation from fireplug to fetchingly elfin young lady effected by slow removal of the yellow slicker and hat, a down vest, several sweaters, and a twelve-foot knit scarf in the Campbell tartan.

"You are amazing, Professor Constantine. I am indeed Victoria Greeley. My father is Douglas Greeley, the Master of Ass Isle. We give refuge to three hundred and fifty donkeys, each of whom would have met certain death had we not rescued them."

Professors trade in brutal truths. "Face it, Toots. Donkeys are becoming extinct. And personally, I don't give a damn. They're no longer needed, and I'm not the sort of masochist who would want one as a pet. But I met your father once in Greece at the infamous First International Conference on Donkeys and Mules on the island of Hydra. I respect him. He's not your run-of-the-mill know-nothing donkey rescuer. No disrespect to you intended. He favored the conference with several commendable bits of donkey lore. I recall in particular his illustrated presentation proving that the dunce cap is an English borrowing of the naughty French schoolboy's *cap d'âne*, or 'donkey head,' but with a tall conical shape instead of big ears. Do you want to know what the tall conical shape represents?"

"I already know. He's my father."

"Your loss. I tell the story really well. My students love it. But be that as it may, I presume he sent you to seek me out."

Her heavy black eyebrows shoot up in alarm. "No, I came on my own initiative. He must not know that I'm here. I fear they might kill him if they found out."

"Who might kill him?"

"The agents. The agents of the DGP, the Donkey Genome Project."

"The Donkey Genome Project? I've never heard of it."

"We hadn't either until rumors spread from the other donkey refuges. The DGP operates in the dark recesses of the scientific world. We don't even know where it is located. They offered to buy DNA samples of all of our donkeys, but father refused. He believes—we both believe—that the donkeys we have saved from abandonment or the sausage grinder should be spared further exploitation."

"Giving someone a few hairs from each donkey in the interest of science doesn't sound like exploitation to me."

The girl's eyes flare with passion. "The question is why are they collecting donkey DNA samples? What sort of vile experimentation or perverse use of the donkey genome have they in mind? I quail to think about it."

Stripped now of her knee-high black boots and bib overalls, she looks positively alluring in a brown leather miniskirt, black torso-hugging top, and black stockings. Paul Constantine steps from behind his desk. The teary-eyed girl glides across the room in her stocking feet. She comes in daughterly fashion into his arms. He looks down ... way down ... at her gleaming black hair nestled against the bottom button of his tweed vest. Something deep inside him says that he must help this poor waif if at all possible. He disentangles himself with a supreme exertion of will.

"Please sit down, Miss Greeley. Victoria, if I may."

She sinks into a deep leather chair and tucks her legs beneath her. "My nickname is Toots, actually. I thought you knew." A flip of her head sends her raven tresses shimmering. "They told me that despite being a pedant and well past your prime you might be willing to help a poor, lost girl."

A flash of insight tells the professor that he has fallen for her wiles. It may be too late to back out, but it's not too late to assert a steely professionalism.

"Tell me, Toots honey, what exactly do you know about the Donkey Genome Project?"

"As you're aware, Britain leads the world in donkey rescue. Virtually every donkey in the country is sheltered in a donkey sanctuary. British kindness toward our fellow animals knows no bounds. From Jeremy Bentham to Peter Singer, our finest minds have taught us that it is our duty to reduce their suffering whenever possible." (*Peter Singer is an Australian*, thinks Constantine, but he suppresses his natural urge to interrupt.) "The DGP agents are unquestionably foreign because they exhibit no humane concern for the donkeys. They have visited every sanctuary and asked them all for samples. A sample from every single animal. Most complied, but Ye Olde Donkey Hospice in Gloucestershire refused. A few days later, poor Mrs. Codrington was run down by an articulated lorry while locking her bicycle to the lamppost in front of The Snout and Coxcomb. Killed, she was. In the confusion following her death, unknown persons, doubtless the agents of the DGP, stealthily entered ye olde hospice and plucked hair samples from each of the donkeys. Professor Constantine"—she ardently grabs his wrist—"I'm afraid my father will be killed too. But I have nowhere to turn. They are mysterious people with an evil purpose. They'll stop at nothing. Yet all I know about them is on this business card. They gave it to my father when he said he would get back to them about providing the DNA samples. It doesn't have an address. Only a hand-written mobile phone number, the letters DGP, and a picture."

She releases his wrist and extracts a card from the bosom of her jersey. Her fingernails are gleaming checkerboards of magenta and black. He glances at the picture. Pulchritudinous distractions abruptly flee his mind.

"I know this image," he murmurs. "And I am one of the very few who know its deep significance."

"What does it signify?"

"It signifies that the world of genetics and the world of religious symbolism are colliding. Like two continents borne along willy-nilly on tectonic plates. In the second century of the Christian era this image was scratched onto a wall in Rome. The building collapsed; the wall was buried. Only to be unearthed by an archaeologist in 1857. Father Grapelli. Soon afterward he fell into his own excavation and died. They said he had been drinking, but I suspect …"

"Please, Professor. The image."

"Yes, the image. It shows a man with a donkey's head crucified on a T-shaped cross. And there in front of him is another man and three words scratched in Greek: ALEXAMENOS CEBETE THEON 'Alexamenos worships God'."

"But what does that tell us?"

"That tells us that your DGP agents may be on the track of the greatest riddle of all time. A riddle so potent that solving it could bring on the end of the world." She gasps and heaves forward her jersey-encased bosom. The movement draws Constantine's gaze. "I shouldn't tell you the answer to the riddle. After all, I have only just now met you."

"But it may save my father's life."

"Indeed it may. But still …" A second heave of her bosom erases his remaining sense of caution. "Let me ask you a question. After Jesus Christ was crucified, what became of the donkey that carried him into Jerusalem?"

Toots looks puzzled. The professor notes that puzzlement becomes her. "I have no idea."

"It's a trick question."

"What's the answer?"

Though they are far from any listeners, Constantine feels obliged to whisper in her ear. A spot of perfume dabbed behind its lobe makes him woozy as he leans toward her, but he finds the strength to carry on.

"Legend says that it wandered off and eventually died in northern Italy. An alleged relic is preserved in Genoa. But what I, Paul Constantine, and perhaps three other people, know is that Jesus' donkey never died. It is still alive. Hiding somewhere in plain sight."

Her gasp of astonishment causes spiders to run up and down Constantine's spine. She presses her dainty fist against her mouth.

"Not only is the donkey alive, but whoever finds it first, be they Christians, Muslims, or Jews, will produce the next Messiah … and possibly trigger Armageddon."

ERLANGEN, GERMANY

10:45 AM. Joseph Snow and Jessie Zayyat credit their police driver, Dieter, with making good time from Munich. But now is the slow part, taking apart Professor Monika Farber's life one piece of paper at a time. Jessie works the professor's desk, Joseph her bookcases.

"She's meticulous, I'll say that for her," says Jessie as she looks at folders of rent and utilities bills, credit card statements, and tax calculations organized by month and subdivided by pastel-colored plastic tabs. Copies of student papers bearing corrective marks and blunt evaluative comments. Jessie's German is minimal, but who can't figure out what *Dummkopf!* means? "She writes small and doesn't tolerate numbskulls."

Joseph from the other side of the austere study. "Obsessive, if you ask me. Her books are shelved by field and then alphabetically by author and by date of publication if there are several by the same person. Some family photographs here too, I would guess. Someone seems to have been an SS officer. And here's a woman wearing some kind of uniform. Family background like that must be a tough thing for a German girl to grow up with these days."

A hatless man in black windbreaker and trousers appears at the open doorway. Dieter, their driver. "*Kann ich Ihnen helfen?*"

"*Helfen?* No thanks, Dieter, we don't need any help. Go get a beer if you want. This will take us a couple of hours." The man in black turns away. POLIZEI is written on the back of his jacket.

"You shouldn't tell a policeman to drink on duty, Joseph." A critical frown does not look natural on Jessie's normally sunny young face.

"That's just your SDA talking. You think I shouldn't encourage him to drink a beer off duty either."

"Well, you shouldn't. Bavarians drink far too much beer. That's a simple fact. And don't go on about my SDA. I'm tired of it. You're LDS, and if you had any respect for the faith you were brought up in, you wouldn't encourage drinking either."

Joseph and Jessie can pursue their religious argument on autopilot while carrying out any sort of Agency work, including rifling through a missing professor's belongings. Repeated allusion to their same-but-different backgrounds levels the gap in seniority between them.

"The Snow family has been Mormon for too many generations, Jessie, for us to get ants in our pants if someone we know drinks a beer or a cup of coffee."

"I know you didn't say that at your intake interview, Joseph. You just let them assume that you were a good Mormon boy. That's how lax screening was before 9/11."

"I suppose you informed the panel that your father was a Hell's Angel before he saw the Seventh-day Adventist light?"

"I most certainly did. Unlike certain Jack Mormons I know, SDAs don't prevaricate."

"Neither do Latter Day Saints. And don't call me a Jack Mormon. I'm a Snow, and Erastus Snow was sent as an apostle to Arizona. Snowflake, Arizona is named after us. Us and the Flakes."

"As if you've never told me this before."

"Jack Mormons aren't baptized. That's definitional. But I was baptized, and I take our rules seriously."

"All the rules?"

"What? You're talking about my drinking Coke now? There is a legitimate difference of opinion on that."

"Not the way we SDAs look at it. Caffeine is caffeine. Hold on a minute, Joseph, I think I've found something."

Joseph crosses the room and looks over her shoulder as she opens up a saddle-stitched lavender notebook and runs her finger down the first page. "What in the hell is that?"

"I haven't a clue. Six columns. The one on the left is obviously for dates. Earliest date over two years ago. But these others? No headings. Check marks in this one. And these doohickeys here seem to be icons of some kind. Over here are some more numerals."

"Looks like nothing higher than a 5."

"So a rating system maybe?" Jessie flips pages. "If we knew what the columns stood for …"

"Second one from the right has some names."

"But mostly *Unb.* or an icon or ditto marks. I bet *Unb.* is *Unbekannt.* 'Unknown.'" In the kingdom of Americans who don't know German, the woman who took one semester in college is queen.

Jessie turns more pages until the entries stop.

Joseph points with a felt-tip pen. "Look at the last name listed in the second from the right column. 'Ali-Akbar.' That has to be our man."

"You think? It's just a compound first name. No last name. There must be a lot of Iranian Ali-Akbars."

"In the coded notebooks of German professors who are on our watch list? What do you want, a photo-ID? That's him. That's him, I tell you. Damn our intel is good! They put her on the list because they suspected she was hooked up with an Iranian terrorist. And here he is."

"But that still doesn't tell us what the notebook is about or what the stuff in these columns means."

"We'll put the German police on it. Let them do their share of strategic cooperation. Maybe Dieter knows."

Jessie riffles through the blank pages and stops at a business card in the crease. "How about this?"

Joseph reads over her shoulder. "Madam Dominique Raven. *Sexschule?*"

*   *   *

The neighborhood is post-war residential, the street drably commercial. The door of the three-story brick building at the address stated on the Sexschule business card is painted green. It opens to their ring.

Dominique Raven is tall. Joseph at five-eleven (his bald head and round shoulders make him look shorter) looks up to her.

Dominique Raven is stately. Her softly draped, calf-length blue dress, padded at the shoulder and plunging at the neckline, makes Jessie feel dowdy in the gray pantsuit she wears to seem older. Dieter ogles her over the agents' shoulders until they discover she is fluent in English and tell him to wait outside.

Jessie takes the lead. "Can we speak someplace in private, Ms Raven?"

"My hallway is private enough for me," (Dominique looks at Jessie's card) "Fräulein Zayyat. But if you and your gentleman friend,"(a glance at Joseph's card) "Herr Snow, wish to sign up for our services, you will have your privacy absolutely guaranteed."

"What services would those be, Ms Raven?"

"For you, Fräulein, self-assertiveness. Much needed. For Herr Snow, I should imagine learning how to gain release from anxiety by accepting a submissive role. But I'm sure that is not what you have in mind. When you arrive in the company of a German policeman and carry identification from the American government, I must assume you're not here for personal reasons, however much you both could benefit."

"We found your business card in a notebook belonging to Dr. Monika Farber. We'd like to know whether you are acquainted with Dr. Farber."

"But you are not from the police or the judiciary. And you are Americans. Whatever makes you think I am going to answer your questions? My business depends on absolute discretion."

Joseph intervenes. "I assure you, Miss Raven, we can call on your German police whenever we like. So it would be easier to get this over with now."

Domique Raven smiles teasingly. "Call on my German police? Would that be our Polizeipräsident? My dear friend Willi? Or perhaps Reinhard? My very beloved Kommandant? Come back when you decide. Until then, I have a business to manage. Good day."

Back at the car, Joseph commandeers the front passenger seat. Neither agent can find anything to say.

"*Nach München?*" queries Dieter.

"Yes, Dieter, we're going back to Munich," says Jessie from the rear.

Joseph turns his head and puts his left arm holding the lavender notebook on the seatback to make it easier to talk to his junior colleague. "We'll put the Germans to work on this as soon as we get back. If they find something, we'll get a search warrant and go back to that … that woman's sex school."

"Isn't it ridiculous that we don't know German, Joseph? I feel so … so limited in what I can do in this country."

"It's not ridiculous, Jessie. The Germans we care about all know English. The important thing is that you know Arabic and I know Persian. Those are the languages of global Islamic terrorism. Osama bin Laden doesn't send Germans to fly airplanes into skyscrapers."

"Mohammed Atta studied in Hamburg."

"I wasn't being literal."

Dieter glances from the road to the lavender notebook. "*Das Buch. Es ist ein Orgasmusbuch.*"

"What's he saying?" asks Joseph.

"I didn't get it," replies a blushing Jessie as she settles back in her seat and looks out the window at the dormant hops fields.

"I didn't either," says Joseph turning back toward the windshield.

The Munich CIA station lies behind a steel door on the third floor of the U.S. consulate. It consists of three rooms: One contains electronic equipment, supply cabinets, combination locked files, and an oversize state-of-the-art shredder. A second has the desks of Station Chief Joseph Snow and his junior colleague Jessie Zayyat. They face a wall mostly covered by a whiteboard below portrait photos of President Barack Hossein Obama and Agency Director Leon Panetta. Another wall contains a one-way window onto the third room, where individuals of interest are interviewed.

As liaison between the CIA and the Bundespolizei, the German federal police force charged with border control and counterterrorism, Karl Müller is neither a person of interest nor a full colleague. So he is sitting on the uncomfortable guest chair alongside Joseph's desk as he reports his findings about Dominique Raven and the lavender notebook.

"I'm disgusted," says Jessie looking down at her desk. "I don't want to hear any more." Joseph's owlish face is unreadable.

"It is not typical, Ms Zayyat," explains Müller in a pleading overtone as if apologizing for his nation. "Most Germans do not keep written records of their orgasms. But I have checked with the police in Erlangen, and it is indeed a requirement of Madam Raven's establishment. She trains women to be dominatrixes. If you want details …"

Jessie shakes her head. "I most certainly do not want details. Suicide bombings and wholesale murders I can deal with, but perversion creeps me out. Just tell us what we need to know."

"As you wish. Fräulein Professor Doktor Monika Farber has had numerous … what should I call them?"

"Relationships," says Jessie.

Officer Müller's conscientious expression brightens. "Just as you say, 'relationships.' Numerous relationships. Three of the men have Muslim names, one of which is Ali-Akbar. This Ali-Akbar, if it is always the same person, is named four times. He rates between a 3 and a 4 in performance. On page eighteen, in the third column, the one devoted to *bemerkungen* or 'comments,' the second mention of Ali-Akbar is accompanied by the name Ahmadinejad, which is, of course, the name of the president of Iran. On the line just below it come the numerals 313. Two pages later, in the comments column accompanying the fourth Ali-Akbar entry, come the letters YA'FUR and just below them the letters UFAIR. That is all we have found that relates to your inquiry." Officer Müller flips to another page of his notebook. "As for the professor herself, she flew from Germany to Morocco four weeks ago and has not reentered the country."

"That we know, Herr Müller," says Joseph. "Our Rabat station has informed us that after seventeen days in Morocco, she flew to Tehran. But that is no concern of the Bundespolizei. So let me thank you for this report. We will pursue matters from here."

The German officer rises from his chair with his hat tucked under his arm and takes his leave with just the slightest clicking of his heels.

"Now we do what we do best," chortles Joseph once they are alone. "We are American intelligence. We know how to connect the dots, and we start with UFAIR."

"An airline," volunteers Jessie looking at her computer screen. "UF is the IATA code for Ukrainian-Mediterranean Airlines. They were barred from operating in Europe for safety violations, but now they seem to be back in business. They connect Boryspil International Airport in Kiev with airports in the Middle East, including Tehran, Beirut, and Damascus."

"Bingo! Each one a terror center."

"But here's the downside. Their website uses the abbreviation UM Air instead of the UF code assigned by IATA."

"Close enough. Ali-Akbar and Professor Farber probably stuck with UF for concealment. Let's see where this takes us." Joseph writes UF Air on the whiteboard with a red dry marker and underlines it. "Assuming we know the airline, what do we make of 313? A flight number? A date?"

"If it's a date, it must be for some other year. The entry in the notebook comes after March 13th."

"After March 13th, yes. But before March 31st. Make a note of this, Jessie. Europeans usually list the day before the month, and March has 31 days."

"But it could also be a flight number. We'll have to run it through the FAA database. The UM website doesn't give flight numbers."

Joseph is writing and underlining the names <u>Ali-Akbar (Baktiari?)</u> and <u>Monika Farber</u> on the whiteboard. "So perhaps something happened on March 31st ... ."

"Or is going to happen on March 31st of next year."

"... very good ... happened, or is planned to happen," he writes as he speaks. "Something that ties one or the other of these two people to a Ukrainian Mediterranean Airlines flight, conceivably flight number 313." With a blue marker he draws dotted lines interrupted with question marks. "We'll do a search of the master terrorism file and check with the Israelis."

"Here's what I'm getting so far for YA'FUR," says Jessie. "The apostrophe in the middle means that it's almost certainly Arabic, and in Arabic it has three meanings. It's the name of a neighborhood in Damascus, also spelled Yafour; the name of a tribe in northern Yemen; and the name of—get this one—the Prophet Muhammad's donkey."

Joseph snickers. "I guess we don't have to worry about the last one. So we have two possibilities, Syria and northern Yemen. Both hot zones. Let's assume that the person who planned whatever went down, or is scheduled to go down, with UF Air on March 31st comes from either Damascus or Yemen."

Jessie's computer screen reflects her intense expression. "Or maybe just stays there. I've found a Hotel Yafour in Damascus."

"Or maybe just stays there, then. How about this? Maybe the hotel is where Iranian Revolutionary Guards hang out when they're on assignment teaching terrorism to Hizbullah. The Mossad will tell us. They have a book on all these creeps." Joseph is busy writing on the whiteboard and drawing lines. "This is great, Jessie. This is what connecting the dots is all about."

ASS ISLE, SCOTLAND

A grotesque turreted hulk of Victorian gingerbread architecture looms in the growing dusk. A U-shaped assemblage of low sheds adjoins the mansion's south side, but Paul Constantine can discern no other buildings as the motorboat approaches a wooden pier projecting from the stony shoreline. He steps gingerly out of the tippy vessel that has transported them from the St. Andrew's Old Course golf links. The yellow hydrant version of Toots Greeley secures the boat to the pier. A barren expanse of rocks, withered grass, and scrubby bushes presents itself as the very portrait of windswept winter desolation. The waves of the North Sea splash noisily against the stones behind him.

"I don't see any donkeys, Toots."

"When the wind is from the west, they shelter on the lee side of the island," she says as she helps the boatman unload suitcases and boxes of supplies and carry them up the path.

Thirty meters away a painfully thin, shawl-wrapped man with a hollow chest and stooped shoulders beckons from the warmly lit portal of the mansion. As he draws near, Constantine observes that Douglas Greeley has aged greatly in the years since the donkey conference. Yet his voice is the hearty baritone he remembers singing Scots ballads during late hours at the tavernas of Hydra.

"Professor Constantine, how good to see you again. Welcome to Ass Isle. The trip out from the land must have chilled you. Take a nip of whiskey."

Constantine accepts the quart bottle proffered by the cadaverous Greeley and sucks down the top inch and a half.

"Good draught, my friend. A proper Scottish hello. Now step inside out of the wind. Toots, take the professor's suitcases up to the north guestroom."

"Yes, father." Despite her size, Toots hefts Constantine's suitcase, roll-aboard bag, and computer case quite easily as she trips nimbly up the stairs ascending from the cavernous entrance hall.

"Toots is strong for her height. Comes from hiking across the moors and milking the jennies."

"You milk your donkeys?"

"Oh, yes. It's a major source of income. Our only competition is in Belgium, the Asinerie du Pays des Collines at the Château des Mottes. Between us we sell about 1500 liters a year."

"For cheese?"

"Cosmetics, actually. As you know better than I, regular bathing in ass's milk was Cleopatra's legendary beauty secret. So it's no surprise that today's most ravishing women still swear by it. It's what gives Toots her creamy complexion: high levels of protein, phospholipids, and ceramide 3 along with sixty times the vitamin C of cow's milk. Sixty times! Amazing, isn't it? Many of our donkeys are old and worn out, like me. But some still enjoy a robust sex life. So we have fifteen to twenty jennies in milk at any one time."

The old man's monologue is delivered over his shoulder as Constantine trails him past timbered walls adorned with stag heads and antique edged weapons and into a wood-paneled study where a fire crackles briskly on a great stone hearth. Constantine takes the capacious easy chair his host urges upon him and watches the old man settle painfully onto a thick foam donut placed on the straight chair facing it.

"Hemorrhoid operation, Professor Constantine."

"Please, call me Paul."

"And I'm Douglas. As I was saying, worst thing in the world a hemorrhoid operation. Avoid it at all costs."

"I'm sorry to hear you are in pain, though I trust you are otherwise well. Your daughter had led me to fear the worst."

"Toots is a dear and has been my only companion for all these years since her mother died. But she became needlessly alarmed at the report of Mrs. Codrington's demise. While she was away, the Donkey Genome Project people paid me a second visit, and I decided to give them the samples they wanted. In return for a generous financial contribution to our rescue efforts, I might add."

His voice quavers. His words sound uncertain.

"Did you find out more about them?" asks Constantine.

Toots enters the room and seats herself on the leather ottoman beside her father's chair. Her face is grim. Constantine decides that grimness becomes her.

"What they told me is that a research team at the University of Salamanca completed decoding the donkey genome six months ago."

"Yes, I read about that in *Donkey Science Monthly*."

"They further said that the decoding opened up the possibility of answering some long unresolved questions. Merely historical in most cases: For example, whether any of today's donkey breeds descend from crosses between the true asses of North Africa and the several half-ass species of Asia. You'll recall the debate about whether the word 'mule' in the Bible refers to a cross between a horse and an ass or an ass and a half-ass. That sort of thing. But the DGP is apparently interested primarily in what makes mules sterile. Such a marvelous animal, the mule: the size of its horse dam with the endurance and strength of its jackass sire. There have been occasional reports, of course, of jackasses mating with mares and producing fertile mules. I'm sure you remember the case of 'Old Beck' in Texas in the 1920s. She gave

31

birth to a mule daughter named 'Kit'. But no one has proved that this is generally possible. The DGP hope that DNA screening will establish whether some asses may in fact have this ability to produce true-breeding mule offspring."

"And if they do?"

"There are parts of the world, they told me, where mules, unlike asses, are still immensely valuable as work animals. Being able to breed them true could be an economic boon. Needless to say, it would also be a milestone in evolutionary research since no one has ever managed to create a true-breeding new species."

Constantine reaches for the glass that his host has refilled with whisky and quaffs its life-restoring contents as he reflects on the plausibility of what he is hearing. Breeding fertile mules hardly seems important enough to justify collecting a DNA sample from every donkey in Britain. And certainly not important enough for him to have traveled across the Atlantic with a cute but dotty girl.

Suddenly Toots stands up and cocks her grim-faced head at him. "Professor Constantine, would you be so kind as to come to the kitchen with me and help bring in some food." She gives a suggestive nod.

Constantine responds with a wink. "Why of course, Toots. To the kitchen we go. Lead the way."

What is he expecting? A surreptitious kiss on the cheek? A great bulging haggis on the kitchen table? He doesn't know, but for some reason his heart is racing.

"Professor Constantine," Toots says as soon as they are out of range of the study, "they have gotten to my father. They have hurt him. He has never had a hemorrhoid problem in his life. He eats oatmeal three times a day."

"You think they . . ?"

"I'm certain of it. He seems to have aged ten years while I have been gone."

"I see. But we can't let him know what we suspect."

"I agree. He has his pride. It would be too humiliating."

"You should talk to him privately and see what more you can find out. I will pursue a different line of inquiry, the image of the crucified donkey."

Back in the study and partaking of a succulent spread of smoked salmon, goat cheese, and oat-cakes, Constantine reminisces about the Hydra donkey conference to distract Greeley from the ache in his fundament.

"Do you remember that imperious German woman, Monika Farber?"

"Of course I remember her," he chuckles. "One of the most beautiful women I've ever seen. You were quite taken with her. Called her the 'Grand Teuton'. As I recall, however, the feeling was not reciprocated."

Embarrassing memory brings a frown to Constantine's face. "I would not have allowed my head to be turned if I had known what she was going to say in her review of my *Prolegomenon to the Study of the Ass as a Religious and Sexual Symbol* for *The Journal of Equine History*. It's clear to me in retrospect that she has made her way in the academic world through sexual allure rather than true scholarship."

"I'm not so sure, Professor Constantine. I recall her being quite knowledgeable. Particularly in comparison with that arrogant ass—if you'll pardon the expression—from Columbia University who gave the so-called keynote speech."

"We're in full agreement on that. I mention the unbearable Farber, Douglas, because she seems to have disappeared. Toots thinks it is related to the DGP."

The old man's face is blank. "What possible connection could she have had with them? She's an anthropologist, not a geneticist."

"Do you recall any conversations on Hydra relating to one special donkey?"

He searches his memory. "No, I don't believe so. What donkey?"

"A special donkey. The donkey of Jesus, say."

"Donkey of Jesus? I don't think so, though I remember it was mentioned in one of the papers."

"Yes it was. That's how the matter came up. The paper dealing with the crucified man with the donkey's head. The same image that is on the DGP business card."

"Yes, yes that's it!" The returning memory enlivens his drawn features. "A woman from the University of Tennessee—can't remember her name—suggested that the crucified assman wasn't meant to be Jesus but the Egyptian god Set, lord of the underworld. No question about the Egyptians representing Set as a donkey, of course, or of the spread of various Egyptian cults in Rome at the time the image was scratched on the wall. But where does crucifixion fit in? Set wasn't crucified. I certainly wasn't convinced by her proposal of a hitherto unknown sect of Sethists. A real god like Set is hardly going to let himself be crucified."

"The way Jesus did," says Constantine with a wry smile.

The old man is flustered. "Well, I say! I didn't mean to be disrespectful. I hope you're not one of those believing Christians."

"Don't worry, Douglas. I'm just making a joke. But back to Hydra. Do you remember that one night, after dinner, a bunch of us were drinking wine and we got into a discussion about the three-donkey solution and the one-donkey solution?"

Greeley searches his memory. "Yes, yes," he says at length. "It's coming back to me. Someone—I believe it may even have been you—proposed that since the Christians, Jews, and Muslims all believed in a Messiah coming at the end of time riding on a donkey, the one that showed up first would preempt the other two. So logically all three Messiahs would have to appear simultaneously, which raised the question of whether they would fight over the same donkey or whether each would have his own donkey. Very amusing what a few glasses of wine can inspire."

Constantine smiles. The debate had been as raucous as it was silly. At least in everyone's mind but his own. Farber and Greeley had been there, and the secretive Israeli they all referred to as the

Rabbi because of his skullcap. Had there also been a fifth? Ah yes, how could he forget? Pastor Steve, the evangelical Protestant who had once been the lieutenant governor of some southern state before going to prison for bribery and finding Jesus in his jail cell. What a line of baloney he had fed to anyone who would listen.

"Tell me if I have this right," said Greeley. "The three-donkey solution, as I recall, visualized Christian, Jewish, and Muslim Messiahs heading for Jerusalem at the same time, each on his sacred donkey."

"That's right. Three mobs of followers cheering them on as they try to shoulder one another off the road. And the donkeys, of course, following tradition, all belonging to the same family lineage as the donkeys of Abraham, Moses, Jesus, and Muhammad. As an alternative I proposed the one-donkey solution, which maintained that when the Messiah comes, he will be riding not on just any old donkey descended from the earlier animals, but on the one and only sacred donkey, the immortal steed of all the Semitic Messiahs. If that's the right scenario, whichever bunch of zealots gets their hands on the one sacred donkey will be in a position to receive the true Messiah."

Douglas Greeley gives a weak laugh. "Quite. Quite. I remember. What a ridiculous idea. We were all drunk as pirates. A remarkable conference that was. Remarkable." He picks up his whisky glass and empties it.

Constantine waits for the penny to drop, but the old man shows no sign of making the connection between the genetic explorations of the DGP and the three-donkey/one-donkey debate. So be it.

*   *   *

At seven the next morning, according to his custom, Paul Constantine stands in front of the high porcelain sink in the guest room, gazes into the mirror, and assesses the effect of his night's sleep on his bodily person. The bed had been moderately comfortable, but as was so often the case in recent years, he had spent much of the fitful night dozing in an armchair. And now his eyes are bloodshot from drinking half a bottle of Douglas Greeley's whiskey. He observes that the forehead furrows and jowl lines that on good days he feels add distinction to his visage are deeper than usual. He splashes water on his face and uses his fingers to stroke into place the unruly white strands of his eyebrows, then does the same to the wisps of gray hair marking the boundary of what was once a luxuriant brown hairline.

On the whole, the person staring back at him from the mirror strikes him, as it does every day, as a fine specimen of sixty-three-year-old masculinity. To be sure, a twenty-, maybe a thirty-, or even a forty-, pound reduction in weight could improve the picture, and the white hair in the pubic region has anhedonistic implications. But Paul Constantine's penchant for self-absorption seldom progresses far down the path of self-criticism.

Once dressed, he makes his way down the grand staircase and follows various breakfast-type sounds to the overlarge kitchen where Toots greets him with a winning smile and serves him oatmeal, eggs, sausage, toast, rough-cut orange marmalade, and a savory portion of haggis. For herself, she slices a sesame seed bagel purchased at Logan airport on their departure from Boston and puts it in the oven to toast.

"We must talk," she remarks matter-of-factly. "But not here." She hums a scrap of tune and watches Constantine eat. When her bagel is ready, she spreads it thinly with sticky marmite from a tiny brown bottle.

ST. ANDREWS OLD COURSE

They bundle up and exit the house into a cold wind. The diminutive Toots, once again tricked out as a yellow hydrant, precedes the baby-stepping professor down to the pier and rings a stanchion-mounted bell to summon the boatman from the far shore. Alighting on the mainland adrip with salt spray, they hike up a cliff and through the rough beside the fairway until they are standing arm-in-arm on the tiny stone Swilcan Bridge that arches a frozen burn winding across St. Andrew's Old Course. The fairway grass is withered. Patches of frost make crescents in the numerous traps. The cold is biting.

"Now we can talk," says Toots.

"You didn't want to talk at breakfast. Were you afraid someone might overhear us?"

"No. Father was still asleep. It's just that I very much like this spot as a place to talk. It's so picturesque, so romantic. Tourists love to have their picture taken here with the clubhouse in the background. Don't you just love the view?"

The elfin allure that had made the professor forget his hangover at the breakfast table has not survived well either the biting wind or the return of the fire hydrant costume. Constantine determines to make their talk as brief as possible.

"As I suspected, Professor, the three men who paid the second visit to my father were not the same as the first lot. Yet they knew that he had negotiated over the phone with the DGP and had agreed to supply them with the DNA samples. They demanded that he hand the samples over to them. When father refused to cooperate, one of them brutally sodomized him with a broom handle until he relented and gave them the samples. The man said he had learned this interrogation method in Iraq as an interrogator for the CIA. But father is sure from their accents and beards that they were not Americans, just as he is sure from the accents of the DGP that they *are* Americans."

"Does he have any clue as to who brutalized him?"

"Yes. And then again, no. The young one who did the deed boasted that his punishment would teach Daddy never to stand in the way of the *See-Sad-Oh-Seize-Da*. Unfortunately, Daddy has no idea what that signifies."

"He is sure of those words, though?"

"Yes, quite sure. He says he will never forget them. What do they mean?"

"I have an idea, but I don't wish to be hasty. It would be best if we discuss it someplace where the wind does not blow our words away."

"That's fine. We can go. I just wanted you to see this darling little bridge while you were visiting in St. Andrew's. If we head into town, we can take the opportunity to explore one other clue I uncovered. The boatman who ferried the men to and from the island told me he saw them later in the day eating at the Drouthy Neebors Pub on South Street."

Despite his recent hearty breakfast, the thought of warm food energizes the frigid assman. "Then it is to the Drouthy Neebors that we must repair to make inquiries. That is, if you're fully ready to depart this charming spot."

Half an hour later Constantine's fork is venting steam from a toasty chicken pie while Toots, minus her yellow outer gear, stands at the bar warming her hands on a cup of tea and chatting up the waitress. Her smile as she returns to the table tells the professor that she has gotten somewhere with her inquiries.

"Agnes remembers the men. They had dark hair, foreign accents, and two-week-old beards. And they didn't order alcohol although it was that time of day. The oldest of the three was their leader. He ordered fish and chips. So did the youngest, who was cute and had wild eyes. The third ordered vegetarian beans with rice."

"Did she overhear what they talked about? Did they mention Ass Isle or your father?"

"She did not hear anything. They spoke softly, and she is always discreet with customers. However, the one who ordered the rice and beans asked her for something called 'sumac'. Whatever it was he wanted, she told him they didn't have any."

"Aha!" exclaims Constantine. "My hunch is right! They are Iranians."

Toots arches a comely eyebrow. "How do you know that?"

"Iranians sprinkle ground sumac bobs on their rice. It gives it a slightly lemony taste. Other people don't do this."

"What about people who have been to Iran and picked up the habit? And what's a 'sumac bob'?"

"The berries of the sumac bush are called bobs."

"Don't you sometimes get bored being a pedant?"

"Let me finish. The sounds *See-Sad-Oh-Seize-Da* aren't words. They're the number three hundred and thirteen in Persian. *See-Sad* is 'three hundred,' *Oh* is 'and' …"

"I suppose *Seize-Da* is 'thirteen.'"

"Precisely. Which leads inescapably to the conclusion that the DGP and the Three-Thirteen are rivals in a race to collect donkey DNA samples."

"Surely we already knew that. The question in my mind is who exactly are the Three-Thirteen? They're the ones who hurt Daddy and must be held to account."

"They're Iranians. I just said."

"Yes, but beyond that. They wouldn't be calling themselves the Three-Thirteen if the number didn't signify something."

"Now you're asking me for two miracles of erudition in a row. Maybe 313 is the number of Persians it took to kill 300 Spartans at the battle of Thermopylae."

"Is that a joke? The Persian army numbered in the hundreds of thousands and included ninjas. I saw the movie."

"Which generally follows what Herodotus says ... except for the ninjas. But maybe Herodotus lied. After all, he was a Greek."

"What are you saying now? Greeks are liars? Or are you suggesting that some Iranian nationalist group ..."

"I'm just talking nonsense, Toots. Riffing. You've heard of Holocaust denial? Maybe the Iranians are into Herodotus denial too. Same thing. Maybe they're Iranian fanatics trying to rewrite history to pursue their terrorist ends."

"Why are you talking nonsense? I'm sure 313 means something special, and I need your help."

"I'm just being whimsical. Like you."

"Really. Do you think I could ever be whimsical about my Daddy being sodomized? You wouldn't be joking if you had had a broomstick shoved up your ass."

Constantine screws his face into an expression of remorse. "I'm sorry. You're absolutely right. Totally inappropriate. But I have a suggestion. I could make a phone call to the head of the university's Iranian Studies Center. St. Andrew's is well known in this field. Though I don't know the Director personally, he will certainly have heard of me. The upper reaches of academia form a small and intimate world. If there are Iranians in town, he is sure to know about them."

Still chuckling to himself about the 313 vanquishing the 300, Constantine finishes off his chicken pie while Toots busies herself with her mobile phone. She holds it momentarily to her head and then hands it across the table.

Constantine advances the phone gingerly to his ear. "Hello? This is Paul Constantine. I'm the Professor of Asinine Studies in the Department of Symbology at Harvard University. To whom am I connected?"

"How are you doing, Professor Constantine?" replies a stilted voice in a refined English accent. "This is Professor Mohammed Reza Nasseri. I'm the Director of the St. Andrew's Iranian Studies Center. I have been waiting for your call. There are some men in my room who want to meet you."

"How could you have been waiting for my call? I don't believe we've ever met, and since I'm not here to visit the university, you surely had no way of knowing I was in town."

"Quite. But the three gentlemen who are with me now in my room assured me that you were here. St. Andrew's being a small place, they persuaded me that if an American professor with Iranian interests should happen to be around, he would sooner or later get in touch with me."

"How very peculiar." He covers the phone and whispers to Toots that the Three-Thirteen are on the other end of the line. "Three men, you say. If they have a broom or a broom handle with them, I should be very careful not to annoy them."

"No, no broom. They persuaded me with an automatic."

"An automatic what?"

"An automatic pistol. A gun. They've been holding me at gunpoint for the past two hours."

"Why have they been doing that?"

"To make sure that whenever you called I would tell you what they want me to tell you."

"And what is that?"

"They want you to come to my office and meet with them. They say you should bring along the donkey girl, whatever that means."

Five minutes suffice to see Constantine and Toots along cobbled lanes from the Drouthy Neebors to Professor Nasseri's office in the university library. The three dark-haired men waiting

41

for them fit the description given by Agnes, the waitress: one older, one young with wild eyes, and one in the middle. All have facial hair on the borderline between short beard and unshaven neglect. The bespectacled, round-faced Professor Nasseri, a man who looks as though under normal circumstances he would be of a cheerful demeanor, is sitting anxiously behind his desk. The others are standing.

"Professor Constantine," says the oldest of the Three-Thirteen trio, "I am Asef. I have a proposition for you. As you know, we are collecting DNA samples from donkeys. You may even know why. You may also be aware that there is another group doing the same thing, and presumably for the same reason. They call themselves the Donkey Genome Project. We think they are dangerous fanatics. But whether they are or not, competition on this matter is something we cannot allow to continue. Unfortunately, however, the people going around representing the Donkey Genome Project are obviously Americans. This poses a problem for us because no member of our organization is likely ever to get a visa to go to the United States. So here is my proposition: When you return to Harvard, you will find out who operates the Donkey Genome Project, and you will find a way to bring its operations to an end. Our headquarters in Tehran has informed us that for some reason not divulged to us you are uniquely placed to investigate critical donkey matters."

Constantine fixes his interlocutor with the disdainful gaze of a world authority on something. "You are asking me to do this or else what? I am a prominent professor at the world's most famous university. I don't believe you either will or can do anything to get me to follow your orders."

"That brings me to the second part of my proposition. While you are pursuing your mission, Miss Greeley will remain with us and her father on Ass Isle. They will be completely isolated from the mainland. If she tries to leave, we will harm her. If she eludes us and succeeds in leaving, we will harm her father. If you don't come up with satisfactory results in five weeks time, we will harm both of them. I'm not saying how they will be harmed, but you already know the sort of excess my young colleague Said here is capable of. Finally, if either you or she attempts to contact the police or any other authority, we will harm both of them. You may not think we can tell whether such a contact has been attempted, but I assure you that we have the technical means at our disposal."

Toots is clinging to the professor's arm. He feels her fingers tighten. "So you have a knife to cut the telephone line with. The pinnacle of sophisticated technology."

"Believe what you want."

"I believe you are making a mistake in relying on a broken down old professor's lust for a pretty young thing. I will not deny that Toots stimulates the jaded imagination, but I'm long past the age of chivalric gestures."

"So you claim."

"Besides which, suppose five weeks is not enough time. After all, I'm not a youthful daredevil symbologist like my colleague Dr. Langdon, who sometimes keeps going night and day with neither food nor sleep."

"You will keep Miss Greeley informed of your progress by e-mail. We will be monitoring all activity on her computer. If you are making progress, we will consider extending the deadline."

"But how will I know that Miss Greeley and her father are safe?"

"You will have to take my word on that."

"Then it is no deal. I must be regularly reassured of their safety."

"Do you have a plan for doing that? We can hardly allow you to phone up and chat privately or send an inspector."

"I'm a much more subtle person than that, Asef, and I do have a plan. I happen to have with me on a flash drive the unfinished manuscript of my new book on donkeys. Toots will read one chapter each week and send me a report on her reactions. Included in the first sentence of each report will be a secret key word, different for each chapter. When I see the word, I will know that it's Toots who has written the report."

Toots releases his arm and puts her hands on her hips. "You colossal jerk! First you call me a pretty young thing, which I do not take as a compliment. And now you're trying to force me to read your stupid book."

"Toots, I'm trying to keep you out of harm's way. That's all. As it happens this means improvising with the resources immediately to hand. I was planning to leave the file of the manuscript with your father anyway. I think he would enjoy your reading it aloud to him."

"Exactly as I said. Daddy and I are in deadly peril, and all you can think of is forcing me to read your book."

"Well, in a sense, yes. But under my proposal reading the book becomes a way of making sure you're safe."

"What if I finish the book, and you still haven't done anything about the DGP?"

"I'll just have to make sure that doesn't happen, won't I? The draft only has five chapters so it should come out just right."

Having bemusedly followed the exchange between the professor and the donkey girl, Asef retakes control. "I accept your plan. Where is the flash drive?"

"Here." He pulls a small drive shaped like a yellow taxi out of his pocket.

"And what are the secret words?"

"I'll tell them to Toots tomorrow when she sees me off at the airport."

Toots is sulking. "I don't want to see you off at the airport. I don't want to read your stupid book. And I don't want to be put under house arrest by these foreigners who hurt my father. I asked you to come here to Scotland to help solve a problem. Now you're becoming a part of the problem."

"Now, now, now. Don't be childish. You wanted me to find out who the DGP were, and that's exactly what Asef wants me to do too. I don't see what your problem is."

"You are my problem because you're leaving us in Asef's hands, and Asef has a gun."

*   *   *

The Three-Thirteen trio sit on a bank of seats in the check-in area of Edinburgh airport. Across from them sit Toots and the professor, who have barely spoken for the past twenty-four hours. Silence during the boat trip back to Ass Isle. Silence during a light smoked herring dinner. A night of fitful sleep. Then more silence over a meager toast and coffee breakfast. And on the boat-ride back to town. And on the bus to the airport.

Constantine reaches into his jacket pocket and produces the taxi-shaped flash drive. "There's only one file on this so you won't have any trouble finding the manuscript." Toots sulkily accepts the drive. "My *Prolegomenon to the Study of the Ass as a Religious and Sexual Symbol*, which is the book I earned my tenure with, was not a popular success. It sold 244 copies, 50 of which I bought myself. So what I have written here is the popular version of the true donkey secrets that I didn't dare mention in my academic work. No footnotes, just fabulous, groundbreaking scholarship packaged for an educated lay reader like yourself. I'm sure you will enjoy it."

"I'm sure I won't."

Constantine puts his head to her ear and again gains a whiff of her perfume. "Take note of the original scholarly title," he whispers. "It's mentioned in the Preface. The capitalized words in that title are the codewords you need to mention in the first sentence of your reports. You must follow the same sequence as in the title, the first capitalized word for the first chapter, the second for the second, and so forth."

"What does 'prolegomenon' mean?" she whispers back.

"It means 'introduction'."

"Why didn't you say 'introduction'? Likable people use words other people know."

"Am I to assume from that that you don't like me?"

"I despise you."

"Nevertheless, you are stuck with me."

"That, I'm sorry to say, is correct. But I shouldn't be stuck with your stinky prose."

"So change it. I don't mind editorial suggestions."

Toots does not reply. Presently Paul Constantine rises from his seat, says good-by to the stony-faced girl, nods to the Three-Thirteen trio, and heads for the gate. Once airborne he ponders whether he really does think Toots is nothing but a pretty, whimsical young thing. And if so, what that means in terms of contacting the DGP.

TOOTS WRITES

3:30 A.M. Back in Cambridge and indulging his jet-lagged body with a breakfast of poached eggs and canned corned beef hash, Paul Constantine opens the attachment to a just-received e-mail from Toots. The text is familiar, but he can't stop himself from reading it again.

Richard Bulliet

YA'FUR, THE MESSIANIC DONKEY

by

Paul Constantine, Ph.D.
Professor of Asinine Studies
Department of Symbology
Harvard University

CHAPTER ONE

My name is Ya'fur, and I'm a donkey. Think about that.
Donkeys don't write memoirs, but I am writing mine. So obviously
I'm not your ordinary donkey. I'm a special donkey. The question
this autobiography will answer is: How special?

I'll start at the beginning, or what I believe might possibly
have been the beginning. I wasn't even in existence at the real
beginning, of course. So I'm just surmising how things might
have gone. For the longest time, you should realize, I never really
thought about there being a beginning, that is, a first day in my
life and in Ufair's. Ufair, by the way, is sort of like me, but also
different. I like to talk but he never says much. Which is okay.
After all, we're donkeys. We walk around, eat grass, get the urge,
mate, let people shower attention on us, walk around some more.
It's a satisfying life. For donkeys. Even for donkeys that never
die.

When I first sensed a connection with what human beings were thinking and feeling, and later when I made the acquaintance of a person I could actually talk to from time to time, I realized that Ufair and I weren't like other donkeys. But I didn't wonder why until I heard someone tell the story of that guy Job. Listening to it, it occurred to me that if Satan and God could sit down together and make a bet on how faithful Job would be if Satan really messed with him, they could just as well have made a wager about us. So here's my story about what might have happened at the beginning with me and Ufair.

I'm making it up, you realize, but it seems about right.

Once upon a time, maybe when God had just finished creating heaven and earth and all, he was taking a break. And who do you suppose was hanging out with him? That's right, Satan. Or whatever you want to call God's negative counterpart—Lucifer, Set, Iblis, Typhon, Ahriman. Whatever. At that time, Satan was God's right-hand angel, so to speak. And he also probably needed some rest because God had given him a lot of chores to do during the days of creation.

So they get to talking, and God looks at everything he's created and says, "You know what, Satan? It's all good. Every bit of it." And just like later, when God boasts about how faithful his servant Job is, Satan asks, "How do you know it's good? You haven't tested it."

"It doesn't need a test," says God. "And anyway, a test wouldn't make any sense. The people I've made have free will so they obviously will do a lot of bad things. It's the overall pattern that's good."

"Even mosquitoes?"

"You know, people are always going to ask that. But yes, even the mosquitoes. You're an angel, but that doesn't mean you can see the big picture the way I can."

Satan, who's a wily sort, reflects on this. "I understand. I didn't mean any disrespect. Of course, you're God and I'm not. But what if there were something outside the big picture? Something that is part of creation, but you didn't create it."

"Like what?"

"*Like maybe you let me create something. You know, on my own, sort of. Of course, not really on my own, because you would have to permit it.*"

"*What would you create?*"

"*I don't know. I'm just thinking abstractly.*"

"*You want to mess with my creation, don't you?*"

"*No, not at all. I love your creation. You've done a wonderful job. I just want to test it to prove how good it really is. See how it copes with something that isn't part of it. A perfect creation shouldn't have any trouble dealing with something out of the ordinary.*"

Does this make God testy? Probably not. After all, he's God. "*My creation would have no trouble at all dealing with something out of the ordinary,*" *he says. But Satan's challenge has made him think.*

"*You're sure? I mean, divine foreknowledge may not extend to things that are outside the big picture.*"

"*Yes, I'm sure.*"

"*So why don't we do the test?*"

"*Now you're trying to manipulate me.*"

"*I'm not. No one can manipulate God. I'm trying to help you.*"

"*If I let you create something, you have to do it the same way I did. You set something going, but you don't interfere with whatever happens to it or whatever it does. If you create living beings, they have to have free will. And you can't make a wandering asteroid or something like that that will wreak random havoc. I've already made plans for a few game-changers like that. I don't want any copycat stuff.*"

"*Agreed. At least in principle. But what I have in mind also has to fit in, if you know what I mean. It will have to look and act like it's a normal part of creation or else it won't have any impact. Fitting in isn't the same thing as being a copycat creation.*"

"*I can tell you have something specific in mind, Satan. You have to tell me what you're going to create before you do it, or it's no deal.*"

"*Fair enough. You're the boss. My plan is to create two immortal donkeys, one named Ya'fur and the other named Ufair.*"

"Ordinary donkeys? I mean, except for the immortality?"

"Pretty much ordinary. They'll be free to think for themselves and do whatever they're inclined to do. No special program. No interference on my part. I guess they should also be able to talk if they find someone who can understand them."

"What else? What's the catch?"

"Each of them will represent an aspect of male sexuality."

"Like they're living symbols?"

"Yeah, unless they decide to become more than symbols. It's up to them. Ya'fur will be the positive aspect of maleness and Ufair the negative."

"You're picking donkeys, I suppose, because I've given them disproportionately the biggest penises of any animals."

"Precisely. You did get a bit carried away."

God chuckles. "It's part of the big picture ... so to speak. So what exactly will they do? Just existing as a symbol of something seems like a pretty passive test of creation."

"As I said, I don't know what they'll do. That's why it's a test. But I assume that in time they'll figure something out."

God smiles. "Okay. Let's do it. Maybe it will keep creation from getting boring."

And that is the story I made up to explain how Ufair and I came into being. It couldn't be literally true, of course. I mean the part about the day of rest after the creation. I took that from what some rabbi wrote a couple of thousand years ago. If it were true, I'm sure I would remember either the age of the dinosaurs or riding out the big flood on Noah's ark. Which I don't. But it's as good a story as any made up by humans.

The first thing I actually remember is hanging out with the herd, and then sensing that people were having these weird thoughts about me. Or about us. I mean, us donkeys. Not just me and Ufair. Home was the desert on either side of the Nile River. Or rather, it was the grasslands that later became deserts when they stopped getting enough rain around six thousand years ago.

We donkeys are designed to live in deserts so when most animals migrated south or north, we stayed put. This meant that whole bunches of people who developed weird fixations on cows or bulls or rams migrated north or south along with the animals, though some of them gathered in the marshes by the river, where they could fixate on hippos and ibises. People liked to fixate in those days. Come to think of it, they still do.

What I'm getting at is that people in those days spent most of their time hanging out. They hadn't learned to work all the time growing stuff yet. While they were hanging out, they spent a lot of time telling each other animal stories since animals were the most interesting things around. And wouldn't you know, when they told stories about us donkeys, they nine times out of ten involved our dongs. That's what I call a fixation.

I'm not necessarily saying that the people who lived around the Nile and in the deserts were penis-crazy. Since I'm just a donkey, that's not my place. Besides which, my penis is three feet long so I don't have any of the anxieties that I sensed so many of the humans having. But even then I thought it was bizarre that they took it into their heads to cut off that little fleshy skin that covered up the tips of their penises. I know they made up stories later on to explain why they did that, but they were doing it for a long time before they thought up the stories. They even thought of a way to do it with little girls, though that made even less sense than it did with the little boys.

But I digress. The point is that back then, about as early as I can remember, I'm sensing what people are feeling and thinking. And I'm sensing that they're imagining a powerful god with a huge penis who lives out in the desert. They call him Set, which a long time later I came to realize sounded like it was short for Satan. They think he's red and has a donkey's head and hooves. And they're imagining that us donkeys symbolize that god, though it strikes them that it's more civilized to draw us with a stiff, straight, split-end tail and huge erect ears than to draw our dongs. I think the ears and tails were like stand-ins for something they thought was too special to draw, namely, as I say, our dongs.

The good part of all this was that they stopped hunting us and started to treat us nice and give us a lot to eat. In return, we carried their pots and bundles around on our backs, which was no biggie because we're naturally strong and don't mind carrying stuff. Carrying people on our backs came a lot later and was more of a chore, except that Ufair and I found that we could connect mentally with a rider much better than we could with people who were just standing around.

The bad part came when they got the idea that they could get some of Set's strength by tying one of us up, slitting his throat, and barbecuing him. They never chose me or Ufair for this, which I first thought was because we were lucky. It was only much later that I realized it was because we can't be killed. For that matter, we can't even be seen if we don't want to be.

I should also say that killing and eating animals because they were symbols of gods was a very big deal all the way around in those days. Bulls, rams, even pigs, got the treatment just as often as we did. But they were killed for different gods. Except for the pigs, who lived in the swamps along the river. They were killed in Set's name, too. I never understood why, but maybe it was because they had such large litters and sort of penis-like noses that they kept snuffling the ground with. In any case, people thought they had sex power, and that was the big deal about Set.

Then one day things began to change. I don't know why, but I suspect Ufair was involved. A bunch of people started saying that Set was a bad god, and they came up with strange curses like, "May Set penetrate your wife with his giant penis." I didn't understand what was going on because I knew that Set from the very beginning was only a figment of their storytelling. Why switch from calling him a god to calling him a demon? It was like they went from thinking that penis-power was good to thinking it was bad. Frankly, in my opinion, you can argue that either way. But most of the people who lived along the Nile became anti-Set fanatics and fixated instead on a sacred bull. They knocked the heads off Set's statues and scratched out the faces of donkeys wherever they saw them painted. And they said it was unclean to eat donkeys or pigs because they were the animals of Set.

Politics came into it too. The farmers in the valley said that the nomads in the desert were still Set-worshippers, which was more or less true. The nomads didn't see any reason to get rid of their big herds of donkeys, and they kept up the various donkey rituals that they had thought up over the centuries. They had special ceremonies for eating donkeys and pigs, they swore oaths on the sacred donkey, and so forth. Then eventually, Egyptian magicians devised spells to conjure up Set's demons. They'd cut off the head of some poor donkey, put it in a pentagram, and mutter a lot of mumbo-jumbo. This may have been Ufair's idea, I don't know.

In any case, one thing led to another, and pretty soon I found myself hanging out with the nomads and traveling with them when they took their donkey herds and migrated out of Egypt to what they later called the Holy Land, and even past there into Mesopotamia. That's where I first found out that I could hold conversations with a special person who had gotten in touch with his inner donkey. (That's a joke.) I'll talk about that in my next chapter.

To: Professor Constantine
From: Toots Greeley
Subject: Comments on your first chapter

If you think these pages form a suitable prolegomenon to Ya'fur's memoir, you are mistaken. The reader doesn't have any idea what you are trying to do. The story is absurd. Moreover, anyone with any religious sensibility is going to be offended. Reducing donkeys, one of the most lovable and threatened of all God's creatures, to crude caricatures represented by their genitalia is puerile. I read this to my father, and he was equally offended.

Also I don't like the title. Try thinking of something like *Our Friend Ya'fur.*

As you will notice, I have taken the liberty of changing some of your pedantic language to normal conversational English. If you ever publish this, don't feel you have to credit me for unpaid editorial services.

The Three-Thirteen people have settled into the house. The middle one, Moosa, has taken over the cooking. I really like Persian food, at least the way Moosa makes it. Also, I think all three of them are genuinely sorry that Said sodomized Daddy. Apparently, Said is a little bit crazy. They are more than slightly eager to hear about your progress tracking down the DGP. They seem to see them not just as rivals, but as actual enemies. They trade off keeping watch down by the pier as if they think they're going to be attacked.

I will write again in a week.

Toots

PROFESSOR DOKTOR MONIKA FARBER

Four hours after Paul Constantine finishes his eggs and hash and eight-and-a-half time zones to the east an Iranian-built Soren sedan with the rear windows blacked out discharges a tall, chador-clad woman and three burly men in front of a villa in north Tehran. When the woman pauses to look at the city spread out below the villa, the men brusquely shoulder her forward and usher her into the building. At the top of a broad flight of marble stairs they enter a spacious room with windows overlooking a winter-dulled garden. They leave her alone to select a seat among the several chairs encircling a carved teak coffee table.

The woman removes and folds her chador and seats herself on an ornate chair upholstered in gold brocade. A gray, buttoned-up, thigh-length jacket, worn over blue jeans, conceals her shapely figure, but not the lush waves of her shoulder-length blonde hair or the striking lines of her face. Makeup, were she wearing any, would only diminish her natural beauty.

The door opens to admit one of her escorts along with a trim man in a dark suit. He has short hair graying slightly at the temples and sports a neatly maintained five-day growth of facial hair. His suit, worn tieless with a white shirt buttoned at the neck, is superior in cut and quality to the similar outfits of the burly escort and the skinny, bespectacled junior aide who sidles in behind them both and takes up his station beside the door.

"Put on your *hejab*!" barks the burly escort in Persian.

"Your father is a dog. And you are a donkey prick," replies the woman in fluent Persian.

The well dressed man gestures for the escort, whose face is quickly reddening, to leave the room.

"Please remain seated, Doctor Monika." The professor has given no sign of rising. "With your permission, I will sit also."

"Whatever you wish. It's your house."

Her interlocutor sits. "You speak Persian very well."

"I speak Persian perfectly."

"Yet you have chosen not to answer any of the questions that have been politely put to you during your two days here as our guest."

"As you know perfectly well, I did not refuse to answer questions. I only set conditions on my answering them. I came to this country of my own free will to inform you about things you want to know. I assure you that I am both able and willing to answer your questions precisely. But I will answer them only in the presence of President Ahmadinejad himself after we have been properly introduced, and I have shaken hands with him."

The man is unruffled. "That will not be possible, of course. But I am the Chief of Staff of the President. My name is …"

"Esfandiar Rahim Mashaei. I know exactly who you are. And I recognize that if I were to relax my conditions and shake hands and speak with anyone other than President Ahmadinejad personally, it would be with you. After all, if I am not mistaken, your daughter is married to the president's son, you enjoy the president's complete confidence, and you are the chief of the Three-Thirteen."

"I am so honored, Madam, in all those particulars. However, I can no more easily accede to the conditions you have proposed than the President can. You may not be familiar with our religious customs, but I cannot shake hands with a woman I am not related to, especially a foreign woman. Neither, of course, can the President."

"I understand your customs perfectly. It is you who do not understand mine. No handshake, no information."

Her interlocutor nods to his youthful aide, who comes silently forward and offers the woman to partake of the bowl of apples and bananas and the dish of pistachios on the coffee table.

"Bring tea, Jamsheed," says the Chief of Staff. The slender man slips out of the room. "As you seem to be aware of our customs, you will perhaps understand the compromise that I am going to propose. We have discussed this over the past two days. I would like to offer you a temporary marriage, a *seegheh*."

"With you, or with the President."

He tilts his head deferentially. "Whichever you prefer."

"So once this *seegheh* is agreed to, my new husband will be able to shake my hand and talk to me in private. Is that correct?"

"That is correct."

"Or, if he so chooses, force me to have sexual intercourse with him as a dutiful wife? What positions does the president favor?"

"Needless to say, that would not be called for. It is true that our religion finds this institution a commendable device for addressing the urges men experience. But it is often used simply to ease social contact, as in this case. The *seegheh* contract can be as brief as you wish. Let us say, half an hour, depending on how much information you have to impart."

Jamsheed returns with a tray bearing a teapot, two cups on saucers, and a bowl of sugar cubes. He fills one cup and deposits two sugar cubes in it in response to Professor Farber's two lifted fingers. She takes several sips while Jamsheed serves the Chief of Staff.

"Half an hour should be enough time for sexual intercourse. Though in your case, Mr. Mashaei, a minute or two might be sufficient."

The slightest of smiles shapes his fine lips. "By being in this room with you while you are uncovered, Doctor Monika, I am already generously consenting to a breach in our rules. So you should think twice before insulting me." He sips his tea.

"Thank you for the warning."

"Not a warning. Just a comment. Let us return to the handshake. You must understand that a *seegheh* in the form I am proposing has nothing to do with sexual intercourse. It simply permits a man to talk privately to a woman he is not otherwise related to. And indeed to shake her hand, if that is what the two of them desire. A professor, for example, might contract a temporary marriage with his female students. Or a cleric with a woman who comes to him for counsel."

"I understand. The man isn't obligated to have intercourse with his *seegheh*. But he can if he wants to. Meanwhile, everyone knows that the woman in question has surrendered her body to him, at least in principle. And usually without his other wife or wives being aware of it."

"Her status in the relationship would only be known if the *seegheh* were publicly acknowledged. However, it can just as easily be a private, oral contract. The two of us agree, let us say, hypothetically, to be married for half an hour. No one knows about it. We shake hands. We talk. You answer my questions. At the end of the time, the marriage is over and you fly back to Germany. Everything is entirely private."

"Except that as a woman I cannot contract another *seegheh* until I have had three successive menstrual periods. To assure paternity in case I have become pregnant. From the handshake, perhaps. Hypothetically."

"Technically that may be true. But I must repeat that there's no question of sexual relations in the proposal that I am advancing to you. I'm simply trying to facilitate the handshake that you so obstinately require."

"It *may* be true? You mean I *can* legitimately contract another *seegheh* in less than three months?"

"If a condom is used, yes. It is a recent ruling."

"I despise condoms."

"Then if you are sterile or past menopause, you are also excused from the three-month waiting period. But I would suppose you fall into neither category."

Professor Farber looks up from her tea in mock surprise. "Are you asking my age, Mr. Mashaei? How very impolite."

"I have no interest in your age, Madam," replies the presidential Chief of Staff with a hint of exasperation. Let us just assume that you would indeed be required to observe the three-month waiting period. Surely that would not be a problem. You're not Iranian, you're not Shi'ite, you don't live in this country. As a practical matter, you would have neither need nor opportunity to contract another *seegheh*."

"How little you know of me, Mr. Mashaei. Haven't you wondered why I speak Persian so well? I have contracted four *seegheh* marriages with Iranians in Germany; and when I get home, I have my eye on another gentleman who is much more attractive than your little president, and even handsomer than you."

The Chief of Staff frowns. "I hadn't realized that you were one of those promiscuous Western women."

"But surely I am not, Mr. Mashaei. For if entering into a temporary marriage were a sign of Western promiscuity, then many of Iran's leaders, perhaps even you yourself, would be as guilty of moral degeneracy as, say, the American president Bill Clinton. We are talking here about Eastern promiscuity. As you said, it is a question of urges."

"Madam, should I gather from all of this unpleasant sexual obfuscation you are not going to agree to a *seegheh*?"

"No, I am not. A simple handshake—no gloves—is all I require."

"But for us a simple handshake, as you call it, is religiously equivalent to having illicit sexual intercourse."

"Now you're the one gratuitously bringing sexual intercourse into the discussion. Isn't that interesting?"

The Chief of Staff places his teacup on the table and pauses before responding. "You are aware, I am sure, that there are alternative ways to find out what you claim you are eager to tell us."

Professor Farber's face brightens. "Torture! We finally get around to it. I have read so much about the horrors of Evin Prison. So far all I have suffered from has been too few towels in the guesthouse bathroom and meals no longer hot when they are delivered. Even your questioners have been generally polite."

"I am glad to hear this. We have done our best to treat you as a respected guest even though we made no effort to bring you here and would not now be talking to you if you yourself had not insisted that you are in possession of important information. Your behavior, let me say, is quite baffling. Nevertheless, hospitality toward the guest is the hallmark of our Iranian culture. But that does not mean that it is going to continue indefinitely."

"Of course it doesn't. What could be more boring? However, before we go down the torture road, I should tell you a little more about myself, Mr. Mashaei. About my family. It is obvious that your intelligence people have been derelict in checking my background. One of my grandfathers worked as a concentration camp guard during World War II. The other was a Gestapo investigator. I remember them only in very old age, but I know that both my mother and my father were physically and psychologically abused as children. This came to form a bond between them. They met while working as interrogators for Stasi, the East German Ministry of State Security. I am sure you have heard of it. You might not believe this, but I vividly remember dinner table discussions about the relative merits of different torture techniques. Discretion prevents me from speaking about my parents' behavior toward me. I will leave that to your imagination. Let me just say that I am quite looking forward to learning how you inflict pain here in Iran."

The ashen-faced Chief of Staff is silent. His aide looks frightened. "Is what you say true, Madam?" he says eventually.

"Do you want to see my scars? Are you curious about that? Do you still believe that a *seegheh* between us would be limited to a handshake? You are such a young chickie, Mr. Mashaei. If I recall, you were once the head of the National Cultural Organization. Such a civilized job. I wonder whether you are even qualified to talk about using torture to extract information. I can see it in your face. You've never watched … ."

"Madam, this is not an appropriate discussion. You are shocking this young man."

"You can tell your assistant to leave the room."

"No, no. I can't be alone with you. We will both leave. You are a revolting and degenerate woman."

"But alluring?" She shakes her shimmering blonde tresses as she speaks to their retreating backs. "Beautiful?"

*   *   *

Two hours pass before the door reopens to again admit the Chief of Staff, this time accompanied by a turbaned cleric wearing blue-tinted rimless spectacles and a heavy brown cloak over a white gown. Behind him is the President of the Islamic Republic of Iran, and still farther behind is the aide Jamsheed. Mahmoud Ahmadinejad is unprepossessing with his short stature, narrow face, and signature ill-fitting jacket, but his eyes are alive with curiosity and his manner completely relaxed.

"Mr. President, this is Professor Doctor Monika Farber of the University of Erlangen," says his Chief of Staff.

Monika stands, smiles, and steps forward with her hand delicately outstretched. The three men cringe backward.

"Please resume your seat, Doctor Monika," says the president. "We are still far from any handshaking."

Ahmadinejad sits on the forward edge of the chair nearest the professor and leans toward her. "You have told my friend Rahim some remarkable things, Doctor Monika. Whether they are true or whether you just enjoy making fun of our religion is unimportant. Moreover, I don't care whether you are a virgin or a seasoned prostitute. You told the security examiner at the airport that you had information about the donkey of the Mahdi."

"Ya'fur."

"Why do you think we care about this donkey?"

"I am reliably informed, Mr. President, that you are a messianist, as is Mr. Mashaei and the other members of the Three-Thirteen. You all share a conviction that the Hidden Imam, the twelfth successor to Muhammad's son-in-law Ali, will very soon return to human society and reveal himself as the Mahdi after living in occlusion since the late ninth century of the Christian calendar. When he reappears, he will inaugurate an era of perfect governance and global peace that will culminate in the end of the world and the salvation of the pious. Just as the Prophet Muhammad had 313 warriors with him at the first battle he fought against the unbelieving Meccans, so the Hidden Imam when he returns as the Mahdi, or the Master of the Hour, will have 313 agents to do his bidding. It is a token of the imminence of the Mahdi's return, you believe, that the Three-Thirteen know who they are and are all alive today."

The President sits up straight in his chair and glances at his Chief of Staff. "This is remarkable. Only a verty few Iranians know these things, and those people outside of Iran who hear rumors of them dismiss them as fantasies. How did you learn the truth, if you don't mind telling me?"

"I don't at all mind telling you. I had a *seegheh* with one of the Three-Thirteen, obviously. His name is Ali-Akbar Baktiari."

"And he divulged these things to you? A foreign woman?"

Professor Farber smiles. "He has learned to obey me," she says lasciviously. "He enjoys obeying me."

The president shells a pistachio and pops it into his mouth. "I see. I understand. Let us proceed. What more do you know?"

"You are searching for Ya'fur, an animal that is either a donkey or is visibly indistinguishable from a donkey. The name is a guess, but it is what the world's leading ass historian, a professor at Harvard, has proposed. The historically known Ya'fur was the

Prophet Muhammad's donkey. It supposedly committed suicide when Muhammad died leaving only his mule Duldul for the originator of your Shi'ite faith, his son-in-law and cousin Ali ibn Abi Talib, to inherit and ride on.

"But sacred donkeys are either immortal or have incredibly long lives. So the belief has spread in recent years among evangelical Christians that the donkey of Jesus, or should I say the Ya'fur of Jesus, is alive but in occlusion, just like your Hidden Imam. Consequently, since your Mahdi is expected to manifest himself riding on a donkey, and it would be absurd for him to ride on an ordinary donkey, the Three-Thirteen have been assigned to search for the lost Ya'fur, whom they expect to identify from its anomalous DNA."

"You do indeed seem to know everything, Madam. Do you also know where Ya'fur can be found?"

"Yes, I do."

"Am I right in presuming that this is the information you refuse to reveal without a handshake?"

Monika nods.

"And am I similarly right in presuming that you are unlikely to divulge what you know under physical coercion?"

Monika smiles and stretches out her hand. The President makes no move to take it. Instead he looks at the silent cleric with the blue-tinted spectacles.

"We have decided that our colleague from the clergy will be the one to shake your hand. There will be no need of a *seegheh*."

Monika looks over at the mullah, who nods slightly in acknowledgement. "Honored Pilgrim, I am humbled by your willingness to shake my hand, but I must ask you a question first. Are you a *mojtahed*?"

"Yes, Madam."

"So unlike your President and Mr. Mashaei, you are theologically qualified to declare a new religious policy when an unprecedented situation arises?"

"That is correct."

"So you could decide, for example, without acquiring any religious blame, that in this particular very unusual instance you might permit yourself to act in accordance with the Hanafi legal understanding of contact between the sexes instead of Shi'ite law and thus shake my hand with a clear conscience. It that correct?"

"That is precisely my intention, Madam."

"Then I respectfully decline the offer. You must understand. My condition for cooperating in your search for Ya'fur is not a handshake per se, but being witness to your deeply pious president bowing to my authority."

"Enough!" says Ahmadinejad sharply. "The matter at hand transcends the law." He abruptly stands and extends his hand. "It is a pleasure to make your acquaintance, Madam," he says stiffly.

Monika Farber takes his hand with a gleam in her eye and firmly shakes it. "The pleasure is all mine, Mr. President." Their hands part. "Ya'fur is in Morocco. I know where to find him. I have been to the village."

Esfandiar Mashaei looks startled. "Morocco? But that is not possible."

The professor accords him a derisive glance. "Because the Parsee seer you visit in Quetta to consult about the future has not mentioned Morocco?"

"You know about Rahim's trips to Pakistan too?" says Ahmadinejad in wonderment.

"I told you. I know everything."

Mashaei reddens. "The Parsee has visions of Ya'fur, and in the visions he hears English being spoken, not Arabic. Zoroastrian belief is very much like ours in these matters. They call their Mahdi the Sayoshant, and they believe that before he comes, the world will be beset by a great demon, who will be killed by the hero Keresaspa. This is just like our belief that Jesus will kill the demon Dajjal before the Mahdi comes. So we take the Parsee's visions very seriously."

"Having a vision of a sacred donkey is one thing. Actually listening to a conversation between a sheikh and his donkey in the high reaches of the Anti-Atlas Mountains is another."

"You have done this? You have heard the donkey speak?"

"Not me personally. But my student Fritz Messiassohn has. He is the only one who can identify which of the donkeys in the village is the right one. It will be necessary to bring him with us. If the Three-Thirteen can manage to find him, I will guide the expedition and guarantee his obedience."

The President ventures a thin smile of satisfaction.

BALEINE TONTONMACOUTE

Paul Constantine silently opens the door and gazes at the back of the private detective. Her bare feet are splayed on her desk, buttercup yellow toenails against dark brown skin. Early spring sunshine pours through the dirty window replacing the late season snowy haze of two weeks earlier.

"I hear you," she says sharply without turning around. "Don't think you can sneak up on Baleine. I hear your footsteps all the way from the elevator. They tell me that you are an old white guy, six-foot-two, 250 pounds, deeply insecure in his masculinity." She takes her feet from the desk, swivels in her chair, and fixes him with a penetrating and distinctly hostile gaze.

"That's remarkable," stammers Constantine.

"Baleine is nothing if not remarkable," she replies.

"You determined all that from the sound of my footsteps?"

"From the sound of your footsteps and the security camera feed on my computer."

"But the insecure masculinity?"

"All old white guys believe they are insecure in their masculinity, whether they actually are or not."

It is not easy to impress a Harvard professor, but Constantine is impressed. "I went to several agencies looking for a confidential investigator who could also offer me personal protection. Your name came up. Yet you'll excuse me if I say you don't look like a bodyguard."

"Baleine is not a bodyguard. She investigates, she protects, she drives. The protection she offers is of a higher quality than mere bodyguarding. Tell me this, old white guy, what is the best defense?"

"A good offense?" he ventures.

"Correct. And what kind of person scares Americans more than any other?"

Constantine is at a loss.

"You know, but you can't bring it to mind. So I'll tell you. It's not Rocco Three-Fingers from New Jersey with the white necktie, slick hair, and baseball bat. Why not? Because he's a cliché. That's why not. And it's not Tyrone from uptown with the bling, the pimpmobile, and the straight razor. That's another cliché. You talk to me about the buzz cut white guy in the black suit with the dark glasses and the coiled wire coming out of his ear? Same thing. Cliché. And don't even think about no ninjas or yakuzas. Or Gary Busey-type rednecks grinning like Jack Nicholson and carrying chain saws. You can't scare people nowadays with clichés. We've all seen too many movies. So what really scares Americans, makes them think twice before doing something? I'll tell you. What scares them is a seriously overweight Haitian woman with fake hair, a mean attitude, and a really harsh tongue. And that's what you get with Baleine Tontonmacoute. Baleine protects you by being herself. Now isn't that what you want, old white guy?"

"Well, I guess perhaps ..."

"You 'guess perhaps'? I was right on with the masculinity thing, wasn't I? And don't give me any of that white man crazy-eye racist look. If anyone is going to be doing any harassing on this job, it's going to be me. When do you want me to start work?"

"Tomorrow morning at nine? If that's convenient."

"Where."

"Widener Library, Study Q on the top floor. The library is in ..."

"I know where your library is. I used to protect Larry Summers when he was president over there. But I couldn't save him from himself."

"Should we talk about payment?"

"No. You pay whatever I charge. Now go away. I'm very busy."

He turns to leave but pauses in the doorway and looks back. "My name is Paul Constantine. I'm the professor of …"

Her derisive laughter drives him into the hallway. Her office door clicks shut behind him.

*   *   *

To make his study a safer place to work, Constantine has dragooned three students into erecting a double row of bookcases across the middle of the room leaving at one end an opening half-concealed by a bamboo bead curtain. His desk by the window on the far side of the bookcases is invisible to anyone entering the study from the hallway. What a visitor encounters instead is a large receptionist's desk and Baleine Tontonmacoute working behind a computer screen. The Haitian detective is wearing an orange T-shirt that reads YOU ARE BEGINNING TO DAMAGE MY CALM. A brown pit bull is curled on a cushion in a basket beside the desk. It looks up when Constantine arrives after his nine o'clock class.

Baleine looks down at the dog. "Don't worry about the old white guy, Baby Dog. If he behaves, you won't have to hurt him."

An hour later, as he sits at his desk pondering the best strategy for tracking down the DGP, Constantine hears the study door open. He creeps to the bookcase barrier. Through a crack between books he can make out the form of his symbological colleague Robert Langdon. He holds his breath and listens.

"May I help you?"

"I'm Robert Langdon. I'm here to see Professor Constantine."

"The professor is not seeing anyone."

"I'm his colleague."

"Anyone. Good day."

"We are members of the same department."

"Do you support the establishment of a program in Haitian studies here at Harvard?"

"No. And what does that have to do with anything?"

"People who support the program get to see the professor."

"Since when? I've never even heard of a plan for a program on Haiti."

"If you're not here on Haitian matters, what is your business with the Professor?"

"I will tell him that in person."

"You will tell him that in person when Baby Dog here wins the right to vote."

"You can tell him I want to consult him about what I think is a hidden donkey image in a painting by Leonardo da Vinci."

"Doesn't everyone. I'll tell him. Now go away. I'm very busy."

When the door shuts, Constantine sticks his head through the bead curtain. "Excellent! You are a gem, Baleine."

"What kind of gem? A Pearl? A Ruby? An Opal? All names white folk give their black servants. Call me a gem again, and I'll file a harassment complaint. I have very delicate feelings. You have to appreciate that. Now leave me alone. I'm very busy."

TOOTS WRITES AGAIN

When Toots' second report arrives, Constantine realizes that he has been home for almost two weeks and has spent most of his time nursing his jet lag and providing for his own safety. His suddenly reawakened awareness of the Three-Thirteen thugs encamped on Ass Isle features Toots at her most fetching rather than the grumpy young woman he took leave of in Edinburgh. He resolves to proceed at an early opportunity to perusing the data on equid DNA research pulled from the Internet by the surprisingly resourceful Baleine Tontonmacoute. Just as soon as he has read what Toots has to say about his manuscript.

CHAPTER TWO

Out of Africa. What was it like to move from our homeland into new lands that had never known us? Not as amazing as it might have been if we hadn't been donkeys. Deserts, plants, the people herding us: all pretty much the same. But there was one big difference. The new place had a lot of not-quite-donkeys. Later people called them onagers, hemiones, and half-asses; but we just saw them as bigger and more ornery versions of ourselves.

As for the fillies among them, they were definitely attractive and something of a challenge. Those of us who stood up to the challenge, foremost among them yours truly, found that the foals we sired looked more like us than like them. But the people could tell the difference. They called the ones with mixed blood mules. They also proclaimed that our ability to impregnate a different species was a sure sign of our penis-power. Later, when horses came into the region, they said the same when it turned out we could make mules with them too. Unfortunately, some of the onagers and the mules got folded into the sacred ritual thing and ended up as barbecue on an altar. But most didn't because they preferred to stay away from people and roam around the desert in the wild.

This is kind of boring so now I'm going to jump ahead. I mentioned earlier that once people started riding us, Ufair and I sometimes developed a rapport with the rider. It was hit or miss, but I hit the jackpot when I became the property of a man named Abraham. Abraham was a guy who was full of unanswerable questions and had a hard time settling down. We started out from somewhere in the east (I don't remember exactly where) and I carried him back toward the west where the donkey-herders who had come from Egypt kept to the old ways better than they did in Abraham's homeland. Abraham settled down with them but kept in touch with his relatives back east.

It's funny how Abraham and I came to realize that we could understand each other. In fact, talk to each other. It was not until after he had settled in Canaan, when I had already been carrying him on my back for years. My recollection of the first time is that Abraham and I were alone together and he was complaining out loud about not having any children. His greatest desire was to have a big family like his cousins had, but somehow he and his wife hadn't been able to manage it. Probably the reason I could understand what he was saying, or perhaps just thinking, was that he was basically having a maleness problem. My specialty. So I just happened to say to him that he might try having a kid with his wife's servant. It sounded, I'm sure, like *heehaw, heehaw, heehaw*, but I could tell that in his mind he was understanding my meaning. So he asked his wife's permission, because he was always very considerate of her, and lo and behold, her servant Hagar became pregnant. And after that his wife Sarah became pregnant too.

The story that came to be told later made Abraham and Sarah so old that her pregnancy sounded like a miracle, though no one commented on Abraham's still being able to get it up at a hundred years of age. As I said, it's a maleness thing. In point of fact, however, as a living symbol of maleness, I've known plenty of cases where a couple who can't have kids adopt one, and then the wife becomes pregnant. It's just not that unusual. But it laid the foundation for something that was unusual, which I was also involved in.

Let me set the stage. Abraham's people were very much into blood sacrifice, which was hardly surprising since they originally came from Egypt. I've already mentioned that they had rituals for sacrificing the Set animals, donkeys and pigs. But they also had a ritual for sacrificing little children, preferably first-born sons, if times got hard. They had the nutty idea that the god watching over them would be so impressed if they cut a little boy's throat on an altar that he would strike down their enemies, or cause it to rain, or save their crops from the locusts. I thought this was pretty disgusting, though not as disgusting as cutting a donkey's throat on an altar.

One day, Abraham gets it into his head that God has ordered him to sacrifice his little son. No special crisis, just an ordinary day. He wakes up one morning and thinks, "I do believe God wants me to slit my son's throat." The tricky thing is that God hasn't specified which son to kill. So Abraham calls the two boys, Ishmael and Isaac, together, saddles me up, and we all head up the mountainside to where there's an altar. The kids don't know exactly what's going on, but they know enough about how dad does things to figure out that he's planning a sacrifice. However, he hasn't brought an animal with him. Though I can't talk to them the way I can with their father, I can sense them thinking, "Hmm, I wonder if dad knows what he's doing."

As for me, I know exactly what Abraham has in mind, and I am appalled. These are great little kids, and there's no conceivable need to kill one of them. But when I mention this to Abraham while we're going up the mountain, he just says that God is testing his faith. Trying to find out who he loves more, his sons or God. And since at some level this is no more wacky than thousands of other things I'd seen people do, I decide to keep quiet. I tell myself it's not my business. But then suddenly we're there, the boys are getting anxious and asking questions, and old Abraham is at the altar sharpening his knife.

Feeling very uncomfortable with what's about to go down, I'm thinking of getting out of there. But what happens? I look around and see a ram with its horns caught in some bushes. Now I've known a lot of sheep and they are undoubtedly stupid, but I'd never seen one that couldn't eat grass and manage his horns at the same time. So I put two and two together and say, "Abraham, why don't you sacrifice that sheep over there? I think it's been sent by God." To this day I feel guilty about that poor sheep, and I might not have said what I said if it had been a donkey stuck in the bushes. Subliminally I think I was afraid that Abraham would come to his senses about sacrificing a son and try to sacrifice me instead. Whatever the case, Abraham followed my suggestion and everything came out okay.

In later times, I should add, the descendants of Ishmael and the descendants of Isaac quarreled, and each family claimed that their ancestor was the one God asked Abraham to sacrifice. As if that made any difference since no one actually got sacrificed. What was more important than this disagreement about who was supposed to have gotten his throat slit on the altar was that both families declared that since Abraham had been willing to sacrifice his son, it proved that he loved God more than anything. As a result, his descendants resolved never again to sacrifice a child. Abraham's more distant cousins didn't all go along with this, but Abraham's immediate descendants became famous for saying no to that horrible custom.

Why am I telling this story? Because it's well known, obviously, and because my own part in it never gets talked about. But there's another reason too. A long time later, I became the donkey of a man named Moses, whom I could talk to the way I could talk to Abraham. I'll tell you all about Moses later on. What I want to talk about now is that when Moses set down in writing the laws of his people, one of them prohibited the descendants of Abraham—they called themselves the Israelites—from sacrificing their first-born donkey. Their first-born cow or sheep? Barbecue time. But not the first-born donkey. Instead, they were supposed to substitute a sheep for the donkey; and if they didn't, they were supposed to break the little donkey's neck. You have to understand that this is entirely different from slitting its throat: no barbecue. You see, other laws banned Abraham's people from eating blood, and the blood couldn't be drained from the little donkey's body if it died from having its neck broken.

Those food laws involved not just a ban on blood, but also a ban on eating animals that did not have two toes (we have one) and did not chew the cud (we don't chew the cud; it's a disgusting practice). What this amounted to was a ban on eating us donkeys, so the ban on sacrificing our first-born was a matter of consistency. Even so, what a change it was. Worshippers of Set had always before sacrificed and eaten donkeys. Those Egyptians who considered Set a demon, on the other hand, banned eating his two animals, the donkey and the pig. So here were the Israelites, who belonged to a much bigger group of nomads who all started out worshipping Set and his donkey, copying the food bans of the anti-Set Egyptians. Go figure. My explanation is that somehow—maybe it was Moses' idea; I'm not sure—they decided to follow laws that would distinguish them from all their cousins. They didn't sacrifice children because of the Abraham incident, and now they swore off sacrificing donkeys even though they still were so obsessed with them that they killed the first-born if they couldn't find a sheep to sacrifice in its place.

The food ban also applied to pigs, of course, so later on people who either loved pork or hated it yammered on endlessly about what the ban meant. But unlike the Egyptians, the Israelites didn't keep any pigs. Not only did I never see any in Canaan what weren't wild, but Moses didn't proclaim a law about not sacrificing the first-born pig. So there's no question that all this food and sacrifice business was primarily about us donkeys. Did it mean donkeys became less sacred or more sacred? I'll get into this later on. For now, I'll just leave that question hanging because I want to say a bit about Ufair.

What can I say about Ufair? I always know where he is, but we seldom hang out; and when we do, we don't talk much. Frankly, I find Ufair grumpy, sometimes to the point of being scary. But during the period I'm talking about, between Abraham and Moses, Ufair was off on his own. He had found out that when humans get drunk, the men with the biggest masculinity issues get horny and rowdy and then get into fights. This appealed to Ufair so much that he went north into Turkey and Greece with people who began making wine in those regions. In Egypt people mostly drank beer instead of wine and didn't get super-drunk. They did grow grapes, though, and the donkey-herders who migrated out of Egypt, the Israelites and their cousins, were big wine-drinkers. I remember Moses getting a little tipsy once and singing: "He ties his foal to the vine, And his donkey's colt to the choice vine; He washes his garments in wine, And his robes in the blood of grapes."

But I digress. That had nothing to do with Ufair because he had already headed north with a herd of donkeys the wine makers kept to carry their grapes around. To make a long story short, Ufair made a sort of mind-meld with a guy named Dionysos and his fat old buddy Silenos. They started a drunkenness cult that sometimes got really wild. Naked ladies going crazy and tearing voyeurs limb from limb. Just the sort of thing Ufair got off on. The Dionysiacs drew pictures of their god riding a donkey with a big erection, and their initial ideas about Silenos identified him with a donkey-headed demon from Egypt. Unfortunately, only Ufair can tell this story in detail. I just picked up bits and pieces. The only reason I mention it here is because it shows how complicated things could get when people associated us donkeys with both good and bad, gods and demons. I'll talk a lot more about this later.

To: Professor Constantine
From: Toots Greeley
Subject: Report on chapter two

Now we're getting to the heart of your story, and it's about time. A lot of this sounds sort of familiar from what I know about Jewish beliefs, but I think they interpret the things you are writing about differently. Nevertheless, you're entitled to your opinion.

Asef has become quite a dear. And my father has been counseling Said about his personal life. A neighbor sexually abused him when he was twelve, and it happened again when he was in the army in the Baseej Corps. I think that is where his mean streak comes from. Today I very much doubt any of the three will ever harm us, but don't use this as an excuse to ignore your mission. I may just be suffering from Stockholm syndrome. That's where kidnap victims bond with the people holding them. I'm sure a collector of trivia like yourself could tell me exactly why it has Stockholm in its name, but I don't care and I'm not asking.

You will see that I have done more editing, but don't bother to thank me.

I'll write again in a week.

Toots

Paul Constantine muses over Toots' final comments. *The 1973 robbery of the Kreditbanken on Norrmalmstorg square in Stockholm,* he thinks. *Any symbologist knows that. Why is it that people like Toots find my knowledge distasteful but go all aflutter when Langdon comes up with some arcane fact? No matter, it's time to start on the DGP. The sooner I finish that job, the sooner I can explain things to Toots face to face.*

He steps into his outer office. "Baleine, I don't suppose you have ever heard of the role of the red heifer in Jewish religion."

Baleine fixes him with a Medusa look. "Would that be the same red heifer referred to in Numbers, chapter 19?

> *Speak unto the children of Israel, that they bring thee a red heifer without spot, wherein is no blemish, and upon which never came yoke:*
>
> *And ye shall give her unto Eleazar the priest, that he may bring her forth without the camp, and one shall slay her before his face:*
>
> *And Eleazar the priest shall take of her blood with his finger, and sprinkle of her blood directly before the tabernacle of the congregation seven times:*
>
> *And one shall burn the heifer in his sight; her skin, and her flesh, and her blood, with her dung, shall he burn:*
>
> *And the priest shall take cedar wood, and hyssop, and scarlet, and cast it into the midst of the burning of the heifer.*

That the one?"

Constantine receives her words like a slap on the face. "Yes, we seem to have the same beast in mind." Uncertain how to proceed, he cautiously asks, "You don't … you don't happen to have the entire Bible memorized, do you?"

"No, I do not, though I don't see how that is any of your business."

"Then how do you know about the red heifer?"

"You hire Baleine to detect for you, Baleine detects. That's my job. That means I do a web search for information relating DNA research to animals in the Bible. Voilà. Red heifer. There been no end of postings about evangelical Christian projects to breed a red heifer. They want to give it to the Israelis so they'll have the blood the priest is supposed to dab his fingers in when they start having temple rituals again. That, of course, depending on first blowing up the Dome of the Rock and the al-Aqsa Mosque to make room for a new temple. Sure to piss off the Muslims. But until that temple gets built, Jesus can't come again."

"Yes, yes, I know all that. In fact, that's what I wanted to tell you about."

"Well, since I already know it, maybe you can go back to your desk and let me work."

Constantine turns away and then turns back. "Just one thing, Baleine, did you happen to notice which evangelicals are working on breeding the red heifer?"

She hands him a piece of paper. "Five projects. Here are the details. First three are using traditional breeding techniques. Other two involved with DNA."

Constantine looks at the list. "The DNA ones are in Hannibal, Missouri and Greensboro, North Carolina. I imagine the DGP comes from one of those two."

You are quick on the uptake, aren't you, says Baleine to herself as she returns her attention to her computer screen. "In case you're interested, the man leading the project in Missouri gives financial support to a megachurch in St. Louis. The one in North Carolina, run by a man name of Ray Bob Krumlake, has a daughter who's a geneticist. She's married to a TV preacher who advertises himself as Pastor Steve Klingbeil on his website."

"Pastor Steve? That charlatan?"

"Baleine thought you'd find that interesting."

Constantine looks again at the list. "It seems to me, as I think about it now, that Krumlake Farm in North Carolina is probably where the Donkey Genome Project is located."

Baleine gives Baby Dog a knowing look.

ESCAPE FROM ASS ISLE

Douglas Greeley stands on his doorstep and sniffs the almost still evening air. "Smell that, Toots? The wind's backing to the northeast. That means the donkeys will be joining us. I believe I'll go out and sleep with them tonight. It's been some time."

"Do you really feel up to it, Daddy? I don't like your being out in the cold all night"

"Toots, dear, you know I'm never cold with the donkeys. They don't let me get cold. And I will enjoy their company better than that of our Iranian guests. Their presence in the house is beginning to weigh on me."

"Okay, but be sure to take your heavy blankets and your whisky. I'll come out and check on you."

Greeley blesses his worried daughter with a tender smile. "You know I would never forget my whisky. But thank you for reminding me. I'll be just outside. So if you think I'm overdoing it, Toots dear, do come out and check on me. The donkeys will enjoy seeing you."

They step back into the house and shut the door. Toots fidgets in the entrance hall while her father makes his preparations. Soon a familiar donkey smell seeping around the mansion's ill-fitted windows and doors tells her that the herd is making its way from the northeast side of the island toward the sheds on the south side of the house. It pleases her that as part of the regular chores she has kept up during the Three-Thirteen occupation she put fresh straw in the sheds earlier in the day. Presently her father reappears in a heavy ulster overcoat, a deerstalker hat with the earflaps tied below his chin, and an armload of blankets. A large bottle of whisky protrudes from the pocket of the overcoat. He gives his daughter a peck on the forehead. "Good night, dear." He opens the front door and steps out into the growing dark. There is a definite breeze from the northeast now.

"Where is your father going?" asks Asef, who has silently made an appearance in the entrance hall.

"He's going to sleep tonight with the donkeys. He does that sometimes when they come up here to the house."

Asef thinks of Said standing watch at the pier and decides that there's no reason to deny the old man the comfort of his donkeys. Moosa appears from the kitchen and announces that dinner is ready.

A celery hater since childhood, Toots has been won over by Moosa's special stew, a concoction of celery, mutton, and onions flavored with mint, parsley, lime juice, and sugar. Plus his magnificent fluffy Persian rice. She regrets that her father has retired early leaving her alone with the Iranians, but she is not uncomfortable being alone with them. "Moosa, this is marvelous as usual." The Three-Thirteen cook grins his response. He is missing a tooth. "I really do want the recipe."

"I'll get Moosa to give me the details and write it out for you," says Asef. "Moosa's English is the speaking kind only. And I'll include the other recipes you've said you wanted. It will be our going away gift."

"Going away?"

"We received a message today from our headquarters. Our assignment to collect DNA samples is over. We will be leaving in two days to join the hunt for someone named Ifritis. But we will miss being here. You and your father treat guests very well. As Iranians we value that."

"You're the ones who have treated us well, Asef. You cook and clean up, and you stay out of the way."

"Thank you. We have tried not to be a burden. But you must remember, Miss Greeley, that if harming you and your father had become necessary, we would not have hesitated. So you have been very generous in not looking on us as prison guards."

"But actually, you and Said and Moosa have been very nice. Except, of course, for that awful thing Said did to Daddy. That was unforgivable, but we won't think about it. After you leave, will I be free to tell the professor that he doesn't have to track down the DGP?"

Asef thinks. "I'd rather you didn't," he says slowly. "Professor Constantine is obviously a lazy, vain person who can benefit from being forced to care about others. Once he thinks you are safe, he will do nothing. That is not good for him, and it is not good for us since we still think the DGP are bad people and would like to see them removed from the picture."

"Maybe they're personally nice, like you, Asef. After all, you're bad people too, aren't you?"

"We follow orders, Miss Greeley. We were ordered to hold you and your father. Now we're ordered to capture Ifritis and carry him to Tehran. I don't think this makes us bad."

"Maybe not, but I'd hate to be Ifritis. Where will you be searching for him?"

"A place in Germany called Erlangen."

Toots freezes. "Erlangen? When you say Ifritis, Asef, do you mean Fritz?"

"Is Fritz the right pronunciation? I've only seen it written in Persian."

Toots is suddenly steamed. "Yes Fritz is the right pronunciation! And he happens to be my boyfriend!"

"Maybe not. I believe Fritz is a common German name. There must be many people with that name in Erlangen."

"But only one who's studying with a specialist on donkeys. You can't go and kidnap Fritz, Asef. I forbid it."

The Three-Thirteen leader looks at her kindly. "You see, Miss Greeley? That is the problem with seeing us as friends. We are not your friends. We are holding you prisoner. And now that I know about your Fritz, I will have to ensure that after we leave you won't warn him that we're coming after him."

"Ensure that I won't warn him? Just how do you expect to do that?" Asef's look is no longer kind. Toots takes it in slowly. "You'd kill me? I can't believe that."

"Only with the deepest regret, I assure you."

Panic wells up from Toots' midsection. "Asef, that's absurd."

"Why?"

Toots can't think of a reason. "My father," she says at last. "He knows nothing about Fritz. I never tell him about my love life."

"That is what you say. But I will have to determine that for myself."

Suddenly there is the sound of the front door opening and a few seconds later Said bursts into the dining room. "A rubber boat is coming!" he says breathlessly. "Five men dressed in black. They are paddling like a trained team."

"Weapons?" says Asef coolly.

"Slung on their backs. They look like Uzis."

"How long until they get here?"

"Depends on the donkeys. They're all around the house. They'll have to find their way around them if they don't want them to make noise. Ten minutes maybe."

Asef ponders. "And us with one pistol." He looks at Moosa and Said's expectant faces, then at Toots. "Miss Greeley, get your father and go upstairs. Moosa, go with her."

"My father will be safe with the donkeys, Asef. The men who are coming will never see him. And if they are from the DGP, they probably won't do any harm to the animals."

"I want the two of you together."

Toots looks hard at Asef's stony face. "You're thinking that if the DGP break in, you'll order Moosa to kill us, aren't you? To keep me from warning Fritz."

"Go find your father, Miss Greeley."

"What if I show you where Daddy keeps his shotguns? Will you let us live?"

"How many shotguns?"

"Three. One of them is automatic."

Asef thinks for half a minute then barks out orders. "Said, you know how to blockade the front and back doors. Do it and then block the doors to the entrance hall. We'll defend there and in the old man's study." He hands the pistol to Moosa. "Moosa, go upstairs and take a position at a window where you have a clear shot at anyone coming to the front door. Lock Miss Greeley in her room. We'll leave the old man outside for now. Now, you, Miss Greeley, show me the shotguns."

Toots leads Asef to her father's study and fishes two small keys out of an ornamental jar on his desk. She inserts one in the keyhole of a wooden panel to the left of the fireplace and opens her father's gun cabinet. The three shotguns inside are secured in place by a small chain that yields to Toots' application of the second key. She pulls out a drawer. "Here's the ammunition."

"Thank you, Miss Greeley. Now go upstairs with Moosa and go into your room."

"Are you going to kill me?"

"I will decide that later. Now please hurry."

Standing at the bottom of the stairs Toots sees Said struggling to slide a huge antique armoire into a position blocking access to the entrance hall from the dining room. Moosa prods her gently. She can now hear sounds of stamping and agitation coming from the donkey herd outside. As soon as Moosa turns the key to lock her in her room, she goes to the northwest window overlooking the narrow strait between the island and the mainland. In the dim light of an early moon she can see nothing moving on the barren slope leading down to the shore. A gunshot rings out from not far away. Moosa's pistol. Going to her closet she pulls out the black foul weather gear she uses instead of her stylish yellows when she tends the donkeys. Automatic weapons fire comes in bursts from several directions. A shotgun bellows a response. Then a second. In moments she is bundled up and climbing out the window, which had originally been designed to facilitate escape from fire by people on the upper floors of the mansion. She slides on her rear down the inclined slate roof to an iron ladder jutting up over the eave at the back of the house. The gunshots she hears are still coming from the front of the house. She climbs onto the ladder and silently makes her way down.

In the entrance hall, Asef takes an occasional shot through a narrow window at a moving shadow outside. He hears Said doing the same in the study. But after the first flurry of shots, the men outside have lessened their fire. Then somewhere glass breaks. A muffled boom comes from the direction of the kitchen. A first slight whiff of tear gas alerts his nose. "Said!" he yells through the doorway into the study. "Cover your face! They're using tear gas!" He thinks about the girl upstairs and whether he should give Moosa the order ... but decides that the time hasn't come yet.

Toots snakes her way through the milling donkey herd and finds her father without difficulty. She rouses him by shaking his shoulder. "Daddy, are you awake enough to hear me?" Her father nods. "The DGP are attacking the house. I gave Asef your shotguns, but I don't think they will be enough. I'm leaving to warn my boyfriend in Germany. You remember I told you about Fritz? For some reason the Three-Thirteen are after him. You just stay here and hide with the donkeys. When it's safe to come out, tell Professor Constantine what has happened. The DGP are bad people, and he should find them and stop them if he can." A fresh burst of automatic weapons fire and responding shotgun blasts seem to focus her father's attention. Toots no longer hears Moosa's pistol. "I have to go now. Remember, stay here and hide until it's safe to come out.

The way to the pier is open, but Toots takes an indirect route in case a guard has been left at the boat. She crouches in the shadows and studies the area around the pier as gunfire continues back at the house. Seeing nothing, she creeps to the pier and pulls out the rowboat stored beneath it. Moments later she is all but invisible on the dark water rowing stealthily toward the golf course landing.

YAFOURI THE TERRORIST

Adnan Yafouri has felt uneasy ever since landing in Amman airport on his flight from Dubai. After two weeks in China buying socks and costume jewelry at the gigantic market in Yiwu, he had expected to feel relief at getting back to the Arab world. There had been a throng of traders in Yiwu from every part of the Arab world, of course, but eventually one longs to get home. All he has left on his schedule now is to present some Chinese perfumes and lotions to his wife's sister, who has a home in the Fourth Circle neighborhood, and then take a taxi to Damascus. Yet he still has this uneasy feeling. The red-haired European woman who stood behind him in the passport line checked in at the same hotel. Fine. She has to stay someplace. But in the room adjoining his? With a shared balcony divided only by a chin-high concrete partition? He thinks about the notorious Israeli assassination in a hotel in Dubai. Is somebody stalking him? Why would they?

He unpacks and takes the elevator to the mezzanine level where the restaurants are. He takes his time perusing first one menu and then another as if undecided about which cuisine to try. Soon he sees the redheaded woman getting out of the elevator. Now she is with two European men, one with a walrus mustache and the other wearing a sweatshirt with OHIO STATE 36 lettered on its front. Adnan makes a second round of menu reading and observes that the trio seems to be similarly undecided about where to eat. Eventually he enters the Bamboo Pavilion and lets a waiter seat him at a table near the windows. Five minutes pass. The redhead and her two companions enter and get shown to a table across the room.

Adnan finds he is perspiring despite the air conditioning. Is he being targeted? A serving of spring rolls arrives. He eats one and coughs. He coughs hard. He beckons the waiter over. "Could you direct me to the men's room?" he stammers between coughs. "And bring a pitcher of water to my table?"

On entering he has noted that the men's room is near the door of the restaurant. But it is also in the line of sight from the redhead's table. Holding his fist to his mouth in a seeming effort to stifle a cough, he passes by the restroom and strides out of the restaurant. He walks briskly to the escalator heading down to the lobby level and runs down the stairs. The street entrance is only a few meters away. Through the tall windows he sees three taxis waiting. He heads for the revolving door with a calm yet hurried step. He is through the door and signaling for a taxi. The driver leans over his steering wheel to turn the key in his ignition, but before he can put the car in motion a black SUV pulls into the entrance drive and cuts him off.

Adnan feels paralyzed. The door of the SUV slides back. A European man steps out. Suddenly he feels a presence behind him. He catches a glimpse of the man with the Ohio State sweatshirt a moment before he is pushed forcefully toward the car. The man standing by the door grabs his arm and pulls him forward. Another man inside reaches out to help. Panic is stripping Adnan of his will to resist. In a matter of moments he is seated in the vehicle and a hood has descended over his head. He hears some scuffling, a voice yelling in Arabic, and then the vehicle is under way. He is in their power.

*   *   *

Joseph Snow and Jessie Zayyat are waiting for news in their Munich office. Their liaison from the Mossad, an Israeli of American birth named Ben Halprin, is listening intently to his mobile phone. Presently he smiles and disconnects.

"They've got him." Joseph and Jessie beam with pleasure. "He bolted at the hotel, but the team was ready. They'll have him on the plane to Bucharest in about fifteen minutes."

"I wish we could be there for the first interrogation," says Joseph. "He's our catch. Jessie and I put it together. Connected the dots."

Ben Halprin smiles. "You did indeed. Congratulations. He may be a big fish. Once you gave us the word Yafour and the number 313, his name popped out; but before that he was completely under our radar. You'll have to the get the details from him, but our first analysis indicates that he uses his trips to China as a cover for contacting al-Qaeda operatives. They use Yiwu because it attracts hundreds of Arab small businessmen, and the Chinese surveillance is lax. They just don't get the War on Terror. All they care about are Uighur separatists. Arabs come and go as they please. Anything to export consumer goods even if the result is a car bomb at an embassy."

"Who would have thought," says Jessie, "that 313 would turn out to be a bank account number?"

"That's our guess, but we're pretty sure about it. This Adnan Yafouri is very clever. If you go from a base-10 to a base-2 system, 313 becomes 100111001. The first four digits are used for Syrian banks. When we identify exactly which bank the account is in, we'll pass it on to you."

"We appreciate that."

"That's why we have teamwork. You guys connect the dots, and we fill in the details of the picture once they're connected."

"Enough self-congratulation, you two," says Joseph. "We have work to do. You picked up the guy we wanted, and now it's our job to pick up what's-his-name."

"Fritz Messiassohn. Small potatoes compared with Yafouri, but we've been cooling it with field operations in Germany ever since that one that went sour last year."

"Let's not even talk about it. The Germans can be such sticklers on some things. In any case, we shouldn't have any problem with this Fritz. By fortunate coincidence, Jessie and I already have good contacts with the police in Erlangen."

"Don't treat him roughly. We want him to be a happy camper when we get him. He's not a terrorist. Probably not even a criminal. But we're pretty sure he does have information about illegal donations to an Israeli politician."

"Happy to help you out, Ben. But I hate to see you guys diverting effort from the War on Terror for small fry like Fritz. We've got over half a million people in a whole slew of agencies working on counter-terrorism, and you're just a little country out there on the front lines."

Ben sighs. "We do our best, but sometimes the political heat forces us to take on an irrelevant job."

"Don't worry about it. Once we nab him and turn him over to you, Jessie and I are off to Romania to work on interrogating Yafouri. I just hope they haven't gotten all of his secrets out of him before we get there."

"Good luck on that. Judging from what we've put together on him, my guess is that he will spend a good long time denying he has any connection whatsoever with al-Qaeda."

Joseph smiles. "Maybe so, but we're the CIA, and getting people to tell us what we want to hear is what we're good at."

"Okay, I'll let you get at it." Rising to leave, Halprin takes a look at the maze of words and arrows on the whiteboard. "Is that how you spotted Yafouri? Pretty impressive."

Joseph beams and holds the door.

*   *   *

Pastor Steve Klingbeil crunches up the gravel drive to Krumlake Farm in a white Porsche. Ray Bob Krumlake hefts his corpulent fifty-year-old body out of a rocking chair on the front verandah and gives his minister a vigorous handshake accompanied by a fat man's one-arm hug. "Pastor Steve, welcome as always. Come on inside. I'll get you a lemonade."

Pastor Steve removes his wide-brimmed straw hat and whisks it at some road dust on his white pants leg. "I've told you you oughta get that drive paved. We're in the twenty-first century, Ray Bob, and you're still living in the nineteenth."

Ray Bob has heard this before. "Say what you like, Reverend, but I paid for my genius daughter to set up the best DNA lab between the Potomac and the Pee Dee. And that was before you married her and before we started in on that red heifer. Sounds pretty twenty-first century to me."

"Indeed it is, Ray Bob. What's a little dust compared with preparing for Jesus' return? Praise the Lord."

Pastor Steve looks about the living room and settles himself into an easy chair underneath a fine-looking framed print of Mary holding her blessed son on her knee. He puts his hat on a side table and then moves it to the floor to make room when Ray Bob lumbers back from the kitchen carrying a tall glass of lemonade with a sprig of mint on its rim. "Is it cool enough for you, Reverend? I can crank up the AC."

"Don't touch a thing, Ray Bob. We shouldn't get ourselves dependent on the AC so early in the season."

"Easy for you to say, Reverend, bein' thin as a rail." Ray Bob plops down on a butt-sprung leather sofa facing Pastor Steve's easy chair. "But us old full-bodied types need the relief. I've been having a real hard time sleeping."

"Now don't you go calling yourself old, Ray Bob. I know for a fact that you're five years younger than I am, and I'm certainly not old. Your problem is that you can't stay away from the biscuits and gravy and the hush puppies and the peach cobbler. It ain't healthy to be as big as you are."

"Amen. That's what J.M. tells me whenever he's home."

"Well, sir, now that you mention J.M., you'd better fill me in. He's the reason I drove all the way out here."

Ray Bob fishes the printout of an e-mail from a manila folder on the sofa beside him. Then he takes his reading glasses out of his shirt pocket and fits them around his ears. "I'll read it aloud to you because there's a part where J.M. talks about his mother, God rest her soul, that I'd prefer to keep private."

"Whatever you say, Ray Bob."

"Okay, here goes: 'Dear Pa, I'm writing from that island in Scotland you sent us to. You were right about there being Eye-ranian terrorists holed up there. We had us a gunfight, but thank the Lord, none of us was hurt. They's all dead, though. We buried them in a paddock they have for their donkeys. Once the ground gets stamped down, I don't think anyone will ever find them. We also buried the guns and some other stuff that we don't want to get caught with. Sending that gear over in that crate of Bibles worked great, but now that the action's over, we're covering our tracks as best as we can. The main thing I want to say, though, is that after the fight, we found a drunk old man hunkering down with the donkeys. His name's Douglas Greeley, if that means anything to you.'"

"My gracious!" exclaims Pastor Steve. "Douglas Greeley. I met him at a conference. Must have been almost ten years ago."

Ray Bob resumes: "'He's the one who owns this donkey park, though why he put it way up here in the north is a mystery to me. And I guess to the donkeys too. Once he sobered up, he told us a little about the Eye-ranians. As you and Pastor Steve thought, they're doing the same thing we are, looking for Jesus' donkey. He also had a copy of part of a unpublished book about the donkey. Written he says by some Harvard professor, though it didn't seem like professor writing in the pages I read. When we leave here, I'll put it in the mail for you.'"

"The professor must be Paul Constantine," says Pastor Steve.

Ray Bob gives him the annoyed glance of someone who hates being interrupted. "'Greeley also said that his daughter, who escaped while we were having our set-to with the Eye-ranians, is on her way to Germany to warn some boyfriend that the Eye-ranians are after him. I don't know what that's all about, and Greeley didn't know either. But the daughter apparently spent a lot of time talking with the Eye-ranians so I suspect she may know more about what they're up to than her daddy does.' Then here comes the private part about J.M.'s mother." Ray Bob runs his finger down the page. "And now here's the end. 'Let me know what else you want me and the boys to do before we come home. If you think it's important, we can go over to Germany and pick up that girl. Greeley told us what city she's heading for and what her boyfriend's name is. That's all for now. Your loving son, J.M.'"

"You've got a fine boy there, Ray Bob, a fine boy."

"I'm pretty proud of him. Going into the service really made a man of him."

"Indeed it did, and it gave him the training he needed to do the Lord's work. So what I want you to tell him when you write back is that his idea of going on to Germany and talking to Greeley's daughter is a good one. But he shouldn't get anyone killed or arrested. He's got to play it smart and keep his head down. Once he has her, he should stick her someplace, maybe in a hotel, and wait for my instructions. I might have to fly over myself and talk to her."

Ray Bob looks unconvinced. "Seems to me you're asking J.M to go to a lot of trouble and risk for not very much, Reverend?"

"That's because you're not looking at the big picture, Ray Bob. You should stick to your stockbreeding and let me do the strategic thinking. J.M. mentioning the Harvard professor has made me think. It's possible that we've been following the wrong angle on preparing for Jesus' return. Once I get a look at his book and figure out what the Eye-ranians want with her boyfriend, I reckon I'll know for sure. Remember, Ray Bob, the Last Days are coming fast, and we want to be prepared to receive our Savior."

"Amen, Reverend."

"The Lord be praised."

*   *   *

The Rabbi stands on the penthouse porch and looks out over the high-rise apartment buildings of Petah Tikva toward distant Tel Aviv. The setting sun filtered through a thin layer of clouds bathes the scene in a rosy glow.

"You think they bought it?" asks the cabinet minister, who is a fellow dinner guest.

"I'm pretty sure they did. They are the CIA, after all. Point them toward someone and say that he's a terrorist and they'll spend months making the poor sod miserable."

"Is this Adnan Yafouri really guilty of anything?"

"He buys cheap Chinese goods for a group of shopkeepers in the Suq al-Hamidiya in Damascus. It's likely that he's profiting from an unreasonable mark-up in prices and covering it with fake invoices. And if not, we've had a set of invoices made to back up that story."

"A far cry from terrorism."

"True. But it's in the interest of the greater good. The last thing we want is the CIA paying attention to the German student Fritz, which they would be bound to do if we showed real interest in kidnapping him."

"Very clever."

"Thank you."

"You should be a member of the Mossad and not just an advisor."

Their host, a militantly secular Zionist professor from the left side of the political spectrum, joins them on the porch. "Miriam says that dinner is ready. We're having her special lamb and eggplant dish."

The three men turn and go into the apartment.

Douglas Greeley Writes

Hi, Paul (Toots tells me that's the way you're supposed to start an e-mail)

I am finally free to contact you. So much has happened that I scarce know where to start. Five Americans employed by the DGP landed on my island and besieged the house with automatic weapons. They killed the Iranians, but fortunately the donkeys came through unscathed. Toots escaped in the turmoil, and I assume that she is on her way to Germany to warn her boyfriend Fritz that the Three-Thirteen are after him. Why, I have no idea. She only spoke to me for a few seconds while I was out communing with the donkeys, and I was not at my most receptive.

The DGP team, whose leader is called J.M., stayed on for four days. They buried the Iranians and cooked me some very good food. Have you ever heard of grits? It's a kind of porridge but quite different from oatmeal. They had it every morning, and it is quite good with butter. In going through the house they found both copies of your book manuscript. Mine was pristine, but Toots had made all sorts of edits on hers and saved them on one of those tiny memory devices. Quite sensible edits, I must say. She's rather good with words. Be that as it may, they impounded my copy, and I believe they intend to send it to their leader when the opportunity presents.

I would like to say that given the difficult circumstances we've lived through, everything seems to have been properly sorted. But actually I am quite worried about Toots. If her boyfriend is in danger, she is too. So please, if she should happen to contact you—she took her laptop with her—let me know immediately. She's a dear girl, and I could not bear to see anything happen to her.

I am attaching—that is, I think I'm attaching if I understood Toots' instructions correctly—her edited versions of your chapters three and four. It's been quite laborious entering her changes, but I'm sure that's what she would want me to do. I'll send the last chapter when I've entered those changes. Do let me know if the attachment comes through.

Sincerely,
Douglas

CHAPTER THREE

Obviously I have to talk about an important person like Moses, but in truth, he and I were only close for a brief period. We had a parting of the ways. (As opposed to a parting of the Red Sea.) It all started fine. I had stuck around in Canaan and hung out with various members of Abraham's family, some of whom were way out there, by the way. Dreaming of a ladder coming down from Heaven, for example. But I had a hankering to see what was happening back in Egypt so I formed a bond with this guy Moses and took him back there on my back. It was a homecoming for both of us because Moses had grown up there. But now that he was back, all he could think about was forcing the Pharaoh to let the descendants of Abraham and the ladder-to-Heaven guy leave Egypt.

I didn't care much one way or another about his project, but I became very excited when I learned that it was going to come down to a contest between Moses and the Egyptian magicians who served Pharaoh. I knew those magicians relied on their ability to summon the powers of Set. But of course Moses, as an Israelite, was someone they considered—and for that matter I considered—to be a confirmed servant and devotee of Set. So it looked like a balanced contest.

One thing you should keep in mind when you visualize the contest is that both sides not only were calling on the power of Set, but all of the participants fit the Egyptian stereotype of a magician. Like most mumbo-jumbo organizations, they were like a guild and had strict rules and procedures. What I mean by this is that Moses didn't look at all the way he did later after he had been living in the desert for a bunch of years. He was distinctly on the roly-poly side and wore a kilt. And he shaved his head and his face smooth every day. That, in fact, was why everyone called him Moses. People today don't seem to remember that the word for "razor" in Arabic is *moosa*, which is also the Arabic for Moses. At the time I'm talking about, he was regularly known among the Israelites as The Razor, or sometimes Moses the Razor (Moosa Moosa), because they were a shabby, unkempt people who were given to long beards and straggly hair. As you can imagine, Moses did not consider it a friendly nickname as I found out during some of our conversations about self-esteem issues. His core problem in this area, however, was that he stammered so badly he could scarcely say abracadabra.

Anyway, I went with him to a series of these magic contests. The first set the tone. The way it got told later is that Moses had a rod that turned into a snake when he threw it on the ground. And then the rods of the king's magicians turned into snakes too. But Moses' snake ate up the magicians' snakes. I know you're probably laughing if you haven't already read the story, but what can I tell you? My big rod is bigger and more powerful than your big rod. I mean really. What could be more Set-like? Being a donkey with a bigger rod than anybody in the palace, it was so ridiculous to witness this sort of contest that I'm not even going to spell out what really happened. As the story relates, however, The Razor won the first round, even though the magicians were almost able to match him. Then similar things happened over the next few rounds. The magicians called on Set to match what Moses was doing, but they always came up a little bit short, if you catch my drift. The magicians, I might add, were very impressed. The way they saw it, calling on Set as chief of the demons just didn't have the force of calling on him as a god. That was why in later centuries they spread the rumor that Moses was a Set worshipper who kept the head of a donkey hidden in the fancy portable shrine he had built called the Ark of the Covenant.

Back in the palace, Pharaoh stupidly kept doubling down on his loser magicians, even after it became clear that they couldn't match The Razor's feats. But every time he refused to set the Israelites free, Moses upped the ante. That's when I started to have doubts about him. Frogs, locusts, blood in the Nile: good tricks and appropriate to the situation. They shook everybody up. But killing the Egyptians' first-born sons? This guy was supposed to be channeling the karma of Abraham, but Abraham's big deal was precisely not killing his son.

Nevertheless, I must admit it worked. After that, drowning Pharaoh's army in the Red Sea was just a straightforward military decision. So I decided maybe I was just too softhearted to appreciate The Razor's edge. (Sorry, I couldn't resist.)

I kept my opinions more or less to myself and was still with Moses when he led the folks out into the desert. We were still talking, but he knew I was not happy. What was he going to do to me anyway? I was immortal, though he didn't know this, and he couldn't complain about me to anyone because it wasn't in his interest to have people know that he sometimes talked to his donkey.

The upshot of all this is that when he made his famous trips up into the mountain, he left me behind. He didn't trust me. As a result, I never saw the burning bush or his receiving the tablets or any of that stuff. Instead, I was back in camp watching people melt down their jewelry to make a golden calf and then dance around it. Good solid Egyptian ritual dancing, I must say. I'd seen it for hundreds of years, and I had a lot of respect for cattle worship.

Suddenly Moses shows up after being away for days, and he's furious. "I've been talking to God, and you've been worshipping a golden calf!" He's stammering so bad he can barely get the words out. Then he storms off, secretly recruits a gang of thugs from his parents' tribe, and orders them to kill all the calf worshippers. Except for his brother Aaron, whom he had left in charge and who should have been the one to take the blame.

The bloodbath was the last straw for me. I had been willing to stretch my moral standards when he killed the Egyptian children, but these were his own kin. He had told them back in Egypt that God had sent him to save them from slavery, and he had passed a whole slew of miracles to make it happen. But now he was having them slaughtered. They would have been better off if they had stayed in Egypt and continued to make bricks without straw. I was completely disgusted. It even crossed my mind that bloody Ufair might somehow have taken my place in Moses' mind. However, when I reached out to sense where Ufair was, I found that he was in Crete appearing to people in the persona of a donkey-headed demon and stirring up big trouble in the aftermath of a huge volcano explosion on the island of Thera. Minoan civilization never really recovered. Nor did I back in Sinai. I decided to let the Israelites go their own way, and I headed toward Canaan.

When I got there, I found out that being a prophet and riding a donkey had become something of a fad all the way from Moab down into Arabia. Since there was only one of me, I knew that most of these prophets only imagined they were talking to their donkeys; but I was happy to see the high esteem they were according to my asinine fellows. Besides, if people believed that these wild-eyed loners riding around the desert on donkeys were prophets, what was wrong with that?

Occasionally I ran into some crazy long-beard I could communicate with, but they were mostly low-potential types until I met a weird duck named Balaam. At first Balaam was just a garden variety prophet who barely understood me, but one day the king of Moab, named Balak, sent a delegation to ask him to go out and curse the Israelites, who were getting set to invade the country. Balaam consulted with me, and I told him it was a bad idea. So he said no. But King Balak nagged him until he agreed to ride out and confront the Israelites, with the proviso that he wouldn't utter any curses unless God authorized him to.

This was a dumb compromise that couldn't possibly have a good outcome, but Balaam saddled me up and we set off down the road. Balaam says, "Let's go curse the Israelites, Donkey," and that gets me riled up because I've already told him it's a bad idea. So I swerve off the road and the idiot beats me with a stick. Again it's, "Let's go curse the Israelites, Donkey," and I swerve again and mash his foot against a wall. Pow! He's after me again with the stick. When he tries the same stunt a third time, I just sit down and chew him out.

Now here's the stupid part. Folks are watching, and understandably Balaam is getting more and more upset by what I'm doing. So what does he do? He tells them that I'm talking to him—they can't understand donkey talk—and that I can see an angel of the Lord standing on the path with a fiery sword protecting the Israelites, who have God's blessing. He can't see the angel, he tells them, but I can. Well, this is like a bombshell. It's one thing to have crazy prophets roaming around on their donkeys, but never before has one of them actually repeated what his donkey is saying to him. It had always been a secret between me and whoever I was with, and the prophets who rode other donkeys never heard anything except hee-haw. But now everyone is convinced that Balaam is a real prophet—not that I'm a real prophetic donkey, mind you—and they want him even more to curse the Israelites. King Balak implores him three more times, and each time he blesses the invaders instead of cursing them, and for this he gets remembered in the Israelites' legends while I get relegated to the category of the Bible's only talking animal.

CHAPTER FOUR

To start with, let me say straight out that even though I knew Jesus and carried him into Jerusalem, I was not his donkey. I was his mother's donkey. Her son's followers succeeded in getting most of her life story deleted from their scripture, but it was quite remarkable. At the age of three she was presented at the Temple in Jerusalem and was dedicated by her parents as a Temple virgin. This lasted until she was fourteen, which was the age at which Temple virgins were sent back to their families. But Mary refused to accept a future that would inevitably bring her virginity to an end. So the Temple authorities summoned all of the eligible men in Jerusalem to see which of them had the most propitious rod. (Again this rod business!) It turned out that when they compared rods, a dove perched on the end of Joseph's, and this meant that he had to take Mary into his household. He didn't want to do this because he was an old man who already had kids, and he worried about the neighbors snickering behind his back. In fact, he had actually tried to conceal his rod. But he was given no choice.

Sometime later he went off to do his carpentry work in another town, and while he was away, Mary learned from her communion with God that she was pregnant. I should mention that I wasn't in the picture yet. When I got to know her, she was already pregnant. Joseph acquired me to carry her to Bethlehem to have her baby. Once we were together, however, we very quickly did our mind-meld, or whatever you want to call it, and I found her conviction that she was still a virgin quite compelling. It's true that as a symbol of maleness I felt somewhat marginalized. But on the other hand, pairing a virgin with a donkey did not seem outlandish to people in those days. I think people thought it symbolized female purity triumphing over male horniness just as the image of the virgin and the unicorn—guess what the horn symbolized—did later on after us donkeys had been superseded by horses and lost our status as paragons of maleness.

In any case, I was there when Jesus was born simply because I was Mary's ride, not because Isaiah had said, "The ox knows its owner, and the ass its master's crib." The Isaiah line is just typical of how everything that happened in Jesus' life was interpreted in terms of some earlier prophecy, no matter how obscure. Not only was I there in Bethlehem, but as I mentally shared Mary's pain I probably realized more than anybody else how much more special it is to conceive and give birth as a virgin than to be the baby the virgin gives birth to. It's not that I didn't like baby Jesus, but he was just a human baby, and human babies aren't very different from one another.

Mary, of course, loved her little son and became panicky when she heard that Herod Archelaus, the ruler, planned to do to the baby boys in Judaea what Moses the Razor had done to the first-born of the Egyptians. To calm her down, I told her that I was very familiar with the route to Egypt and I would take her and Jesus there, which I did. It really felt like we were a holy family: Mary, Jesus, and me. Along the way we had a bunch of adventures, but they were mostly forgotten, except for the time we met some maidens weeping in a cemetery. Mary asked them what their problem was, and instead of answering, they invited us all to their home. When we got there, what did we find? Standing in the living room was their brother, who had been transformed into a donkey (an ordinary donkey) by witchcraft and was eating hay out of a basket instead of arranging good marriages for his poor sisters. Needless to say, it was Ufair who was behind this skullduggery. While a lot of the things he did led to bloodshed, he also liked to perpetrate really nasty jokes. In this case, once everything was explained to Mary, she put baby Jesus on the donkey's back, and he immediately changed back into a man.

After that miracle and a few others like it, Mary became completely committed to her son's specialness. It was, "My son, the Messiah, raises the dead," "My son, the Messiah, heals the sick," "My son, the Messiah, brings a new law." Very monotonous for those of us who were around her all the time. Not untrue, but monotonous.

As for Jesus, he usually walked. To tell the truth, I think he consciously avoided me. He knew I could understand what was going on in his mind and that I was able to talk, but I think he also knew that I had hung out with Moses and Abraham, and he wanted to do his own thing. He was afraid I would nag him about what his predecessors had done. Which I never would have done, but I could understand his concern. So I didn't press matters. Mary needed someone sympathetic to talk to about her son, so that became my job.

Then one day she says that I have to go out and give Jesus a ride into Jerusalem. I told her I didn't think that was a good idea, but she insisted. It seems this old dude Zechariah had written a poem that said:

> Rejoice greatly, O daughter of Zion!
> Shout aloud, O daughter of Jerusalem!
> Lo, your king comes to you;
> triumphant and victorious is he,
> humble and riding on an ass,
> on a colt the foal of an ass.

Mary had convinced Jesus that when he came to Jerusalem, he had to be riding on a donkey the way Zechariah had prophesied; and Jesus, like a good son, had told her that when he got close to the city, he would send his disciples out to find a young donkey that had never been ridden.

As soon as I heard this plan, I knew I had to do something. It didn't seem to have occurred to anyone that if a grown man leaps on a young donkey that has never been ridden, the poor animal is not going to be happy and is not going to go where the rider wants him to go. Assuming he is willing to carry him at all. So I trotted off to intercept the disciples and let them see me in the form of an innocent young donkey. This made them happy, and the person they mistakenly took to be my owner couldn't have cared less who rode on me. They took me to Jesus, and there we were going into Jerusalem together.

Once he was on my back, you understand, there was no way he could avoid connecting with me mentally. So that was my one opportunity to sense what kind of Messiah he was. What did I conclude? He was a less self-centered than Abraham, less brutal than Moses, and less stupid than Balaam. On the other hand, he knew he was walking into a trap and didn't do anything to avoid it. And there was nothing I could do either. He had barely started his career, and now it was racing to an end.

After he was crucified, I stayed with Mary for a while to comfort her. But eventually I had enough of moaning and crying and wandered off.

One footnote to the above: I was particularly annoyed by the word "humble" in Zechariah's prophecy. I knew Zechariah, of course, and he never would have used that word in talking to me. The fact is he fell under the sway of popular opinion. When Abraham and Moses rode on donkeys, no one said it had anything to do with being humble. And when King David gave orders that his son Solomon should be mounted on the king's personal mule—one of those crosses between a real donkey and an onager—to ride to the place where he would be anointed king, no one talked about it having anything to do with humility. It was only when horses began to show up in large numbers—David had only a few—that the idea spread that horses were aristocratic and donkeys were humble. Baloney! What horses were good for was war, something we donkeys were never much attracted to. But not even the prettiest horse has ever been able to communicate mentally with a human the way Ufair and I can. Donkeys had prestige in the good old pre-horse days because the two of us set examples that made people believe that donkeys in general had spiritual powers. And because of our big dongs, of course. Damn horses came along and spoiled all of that, and Zechariah didn't have the guts to go against the tide.

Just wanted to get that off my chest.

She does edit well, thinks Paul Constantine. *And she may be in danger. Time to act.*

"Baleine, are we ready to leave?"

Baleine Tontonmacoute sticks her head through the bead curtain separating her desk from his. "Town car I rented been waiting at the gas station on Mass Ave for the last two hours. You're the one who's holding things up."

"And you're sure you know where we're going."

"Don't even ask."

"Krumlake Farm outside of Greensboro, North Carolina."

Baleine grabs his briefcase and the handle of his roll-aboard and stalks off without a word. *Old white guy pays my salary*, she thinks to herself. *I do all the work.*

TOOTS AND FRITZ

Toots and Fritz are basking in the cuddly aftermath of early morning lovemaking. Dust motes diffuse the first rays of sunlight peeping over the windowsill. The third floor of the Hotel Paganelli on the Riva della Schiavoni in Venice is their final trysting site after a road-trip south from Erlangen in Fritz's canary yellow 2000 Opel Speedster. Short driving days and long loving nights had kept Toots' anxiety level in check, but Fritz's lack of concern about his situation had been a constant source of underlying concern.

Nor had the trip been free of tense moments. On day two, Fritz's roommate Hans called his mobile to tell him that some scary foreigners with scruffy beards had come looking for him. Not knowing whether he should or not, Hans had eventually told them that Fritz was driving down to Venice to participate in an Ironman Triathlon competition. Was that all right? Fritz told him it was fine. When Toots urged him to be more careful about giving out information, he persuaded her with the gentlest of caresses that as he had nothing to hide, he had nothing to worry about.

On day three, Fritz explained his name. His father's family came from the village of Willendorf in southern Austria. It was there in 1908, during the building of a railroad along the Danube

107

River through the hilly Wachau valley, that a 25,000-year-old stone statuette was found depicting an obese naked woman with pendulous breasts. Some local historians, taking note of an old but now defunct tradition of putting on a Passion Play every five years in Willendorf, put about the story that Willendorfers were heir to the world's oldest spiritual tradition.

One year—Fritz didn't know how long ago—an ancestor named Wolfgang had been chosen to play the part of Jesus in the Willendorf Passion Play. He had proved to be the most moving Jesus anyone could remember, and his aura of holiness did not dissipate when the performances ended. As a consequence, until the end of his life, people in the village called him Wolfgang the Messiah. And his son, a person of similarly reverential character, they called Heribert, the Messiah's son, or Messiassohn in German. Fritz said he wasn't sure he believed the story, but Toots thought it was charming. Just as everything about Fritz was totally charming and lovable, including his unshakable calm.

On day four, Hans phoned to tell Fritz that two Americans, a man and a woman with credentials from the American Consulate in Munich, had come by looking for him. He just thought Fritz would want to know that he had told the two about the Venice competition. Toots resisted the urge to chasten her lover about allowing Hans to tell everyone where he was headed and instead asked him, for the nth time, about the conspicuous tattoo on his neck: a blue circle with the words ACADEMIAE FRIDERICO ALEXANDRINAE SIGILLVM surrounding the busts of two men in eighteenth century dress.

"It's the seal of my university. Professor Farber requires it of any of her students who reach the fourth year of study."

"That's a strange thing for a professor to require."

"Professor Farber is known for having many strange requirements. For some, studded dog collars and pierced nipples. But for me, only this. I've been favored in that respect."

"Why is that? Are you her best student?"

"No. She has never said so. I learn and enjoy learning, but I don't actually feel much of an urge toward scholarship."

"Then why are you studying with her?"

"She wanted me. I was with a group of her students in a beer hall talking about my travels to buy gemstones: lapis lazuli from Badakhshan in Afghanistan, amethyst from Ouro Preto in Brazil, tanzanite from Mererani in Tanzania. When the professor showed up, I was talking about buying ammonites in Morocco. After listening for a while, she took me aside and ordered me to become her student."

"Ordered you or invited you?"

"I would say ordered me. Professor Farber doesn't invite."

"And you agreed."

"I had no reason not to. I had been traveling for years— growing in wisdom and stature as I like to describe it—but I had never settled down. Nor had I wanted to. However, when she promised to give me a doctoral degree and find me a permanent teaching job if I became her student, the idea seemed right, at least momentarily. My whole life I have followed what has seemed right at the time. It's as if I have a moral compass inside me."

"So studying seemed right, but not studying donkeys."

"No. Professor Farber is an anthropologist whose specialty is the donkey-herding tribes of Somalia. She wanted me to study the mountain people of Morocco, where I lived for a couple of years. That's what she has planned for my dissertation. In fact, she intends to go there with me once I pass my seminar requirements."

"She's going with you? Isn't that a bit strange for a professor? It sounds like she has a crush on you."

"A crush?"

"You know, she's hot for your body."

Fritz laughed. "Professor Farber's style is to make people hot for her body, not the other way around. Most of her students have dreams about her making them her sex slaves."

Toots frowned. "But you don't?"

"No. She is a beautiful woman, but she is hard. Gentleness is what appeals to me."

"When you met me, I was trying to kick down a door. Doesn't that mean that I'm hard?"

"Professor Farber is hard in her mind."

"My mind isn't hard?"

"Not at all."

"Are you saying that I'm soft in the head?"

"Not that either. You're just teasing. What you are is lovable, and what I am is love."

Toots smiled and looked at her watch. Two more hours before the time they'd set for finding an inn. *Tonight I will show him what love really is.*

Day five was spent entirely in bed except for breakfast and a late lunch.

On day six, Hans called to tell Fritz that another American has come looking for him. This one young and rough looking. Short haircut like a soldier. And he knew nothing about the Americans who had come looking for him earlier. He also asked whether Fritz was traveling with a petite girl. Naturally, Hans had confirmed this though he hadn't mentioned it to the others who had come looking. They hadn't asked.

And now it is early in the morning on the seventh day. They have only twenty-four hours left before Fritz splashes into the Venice lagoon to begin the competition.

Toots is sitting cross-legged on the bed clad only in sweatpants. "Fritz, I think you are in danger. The foreigners who came to see Hans are almost certainly Iranians from the Three-Thirteen, and they've had plenty of time to get to Venice. As for the Americans, they sound like CIA or FBI or something. Why don't you pull out of the competition and stay here with me? Hans didn't know where we would be staying so no one can find us here."

"No. The competition is something I want to do. I've trained for it. It feels right. If we start to hide, when will we ever stop? Even when the competition starts, I'll be hard to spot. There will be so many people." Toots looks forlorn. "Besides, Toots, I have a feeling that this is where I am meant to be and what I am meant to do. I can't explain it, but as I've told you, it's a feeling I've had again and again in my life. Something inside me tells me what I should be doing. And tomorrow what I should be doing is competing in the Venice-to-Trieste Ironman Triathlon."

"There'll be what, a hundred athletes?"

"More than that. Many more. It is a popular event. This is my third time."

"What I'm thinking is that if these people who Hans talked to don't know what you look like, or have just seen a photograph, maybe we can disguise you. It will make you a little bit safer."

"How can I swim and ride and run wearing a disguise?"

Toots ponders the problem. "Let's shave your head. They'll be looking for someone with beautiful curly hair. Are you willing to do that?"

"To please you, Toots, yes. It will also make my swim cap fit closer."

"And you can wear your warm-up jacket with the collar pulled up so no one can see your tattoo until you actually start swimming."

"If that's what you want."

Toots is bent over studying the map of the race. "You mean it when you say you'll do whatever I want to keep you safe?"

He gives her a kiss on the forehead. "Whatever pleases you."

"Well, it looks like the final marathon segment goes very near an airport, the Friuli Venezia Giulia Airport. If you don't insist on finishing the last few miles, you could leave the route here"—she points at a road junction—"and meet me at the airport. You give me your passport and I can go on ahead and buy some plane tickets."

"Where to?"

"I don't know. I'll have to look at the flight board to see what's available. How long will it take for you to get there."

Fritz studies the map. "I should get there about six hours after the start, which is at 7:00. That makes 12:45. So get the tickets for 1:30."

"You're sure?"

"Sure of the time, or sure of the plan?"

"Both."

"Then yes to both. Hopefully that makes you happy, and in my experience a happy girl is a girl who wants to make love all day long."

"Yes, I'm happy," murmurs Toots as Fritz blankets her slender torso with his well-muscled chest and eases down her sweatpants."

*   *   *

6:45 AM. Toots has already departed. Fritz unzips his warm-up jacket to reveal a black-and-gold wetsuit. A gold swimming cap partially covers his freshly balded head. With the hair removed from his neck, his tattoo stands out more sharply than ever against his pale skin. Being six-foot-three he has little trouble scanning the packed crowd of athletes and wellwishers. The Three-Thirteen are not hard to spot: two muscular men in wet suits accompanied by a mullah in black turban and cloak over a white gown. Fritz averts his face and works his way to the end of the starting line farthest from where they are standing.

Fritz is sure he has not been spotted when with scores of others he splashes into the chill and polluted Venice lagoon at precisely 7:00 AM. He hangs back from the lead group of swimmers and holds his position on the edge of the field away from the Iranians. His long, sinewy arms pull him easily along despite foot-high waves stirred up by a wind from the north. Two kilometers into the swim he sees one of the Iranians angling in his direction with fast, choppy strokes. There is a baleful gleam of recognition in his eye. *But he is kicking too much*, thinks Fritz. *Maybe he hasn't done an Ironman before and doesn't realize that he should be swimming with his arms to save his legs for the bicycle and marathon. If I can beat him to the bicycles, I can put him away.* Fritz increases his stroke rate and looks at the looming Italian mainland now less than a kilometer ahead.

The Iranian splashes ashore slightly ahead of him but fifty meters down the trash-strewn beach. Fritz sprints to the bicycles and exchanges his cap and wetsuit for the black-and-gold striped biking shorts and long-sleeved gold pullover rolled up in the bike's storage pouch. Though the April wind blowing down from the mountains still has a hint of winter, he does not mind his wetness because he knows he will warm up quickly once he starts peddling. Shoes, helmet, and gloves go on in seconds, and he is off with the Iranian only seconds behind him. Bicycling is Fritz's strength. He is already among the leaders when they turn from the access road onto the Autostrada Venezia-Trieste. The road surface is superb, the landscape flat, the wind on his left flank. Automobile traffic streams the opposite way in the lanes not reserved for the bicyclists, but Fritz is accustomed to exhaust fumes.

Suddenly the Iranian is even with his rear wheel and screaming. Where did he come from? "We get you, *Scheisskopf!*" he yells in English. Fritz can see the other Iranian a hundred meters farther back. Unable to call to mind a suitable Iranian insult, he instead calls on his legs for more power and slowly pulls ahead. When they reach the fifteen-mile mark, Fritz is still part of the lead group. The two Iranians have fallen back but are within sight. The one who had matched him in swimming is now lagging behind his compatriot.

He should not have kicked so much in the water, thinks Fritz triumphantly. He unzips the provision bag attached to his bike and withdraws a cannoli, made the Sicilian way, with fresh sheep's milk ricotta and a taste of Superiore Riserva Marsala pressed exclusively from Grillo grapes. One tastes like another, and then a third. He feels an amazing rush of energy flood his body. He thinks of Toots waiting for him at the airport. Love and cannoli, cannoli and love. The kilometers fly by … fifty, sixty, one hundred. He's wheeling. The Three-Thirteen are no longer in sight.

113

Close enough to the end now to strategize the marathon phase. The cyclists exit the autostrada and pedal uphill toward the town of Gradisca d'Isonzo. Fritz leaps from his bicycle in front of the municipal building. He pauses in its doorway, briefly admires its marvelously baroque broken pediment, and eats his last two cannolis. Confident that his pursuers are far behind, he changes into gold nylon running shorts and a black net singlet, swaps his cycling shoes for running shoes, and starts down the course marked by green and white flags.

Pounding along the Viale Trieste, across the Isonzo river, converging now with the Via Redipuglia: destination Trieste. He lets the fastest runners move ahead until he is isolated between the lead group and the first of the chase group. At Ronchi dei Legionari, the green and white flags lead to the left down the Via Gabriele D'Annunzio. Fritz sees no one watching him and veers right onto the Via Giuseppe Mazzini, then right again onto the Via Aeroporto. He glances back. No one seems to have noticed him leaving the course. The Friuli Venezia Giulia Airport terminal is visible on the horizon. He checks his watch. Five-and-a-half hours. Very good.

He spots Toots in her long scarf standing beneath a sign reading Partenze/Departures. She is waving her hand as if flagging a taxi. He looks in the direction of her gesture. The black-robed mullah and the two Iranian athletes, now in street clothes, are waiting for him. How is this possible? They must have seen through Toots' escape plan and skipped the marathon. Toots disappears through the revolving door as Fritz runs past the rental car return drive. Once inside the terminal, he pauses to get his bearings. There she is waiting to join the sparse line at the security check. She looks at him despairingly. Between them stand the three grinning Iranians.

Abruptly, out of nowhere, uniformed police appear. Carabinieri. They have a dog. They are accosting the Iranians. The mullah is cringing backward to avoid being polluted by the dog. Hope rekindles in Fritz's breast. He walks past slowly enough to hear the word *terroristi*. Toots is smiling her love. Then suddenly he feels a hand on his shoulder. Three Italian policemen have him surrounded. "You will come with us, Signor," says the one with the fanciest hat.

Toots looks on in anguish as the carabinieri walk Fritz back toward the revolving door. She sees a tallish middle-aged man and a young woman with short blonde hair join the group. Both are in civilian clothes. They look American. The tallish man is taking charge. They are putting Fritz in a black SUV. The police shake hands with the man and salute as the car drives off with the civilians and her lover inside. Tears come to her eyes.

"Can I be of some help to y'all, Miss," says a not unpleasant voice right behind her. Toots turns and sees a ruggedly handsome young man. He pulls back the coat draped over his arm to reveal a pistol aimed at her midsection. "It would be best if you come with me, Miss Greeley." When they reach the Fiat waiting by the curb, the man pushes her head down to guide her into the backseat. Another man is waiting inside. She feels a prick on the side of her neck. The world blurs and then blinks out … just before the car door slams on her foot.

"What the hell are you doin', Mitch?"

"Sorry, J.M. I thought she was pullin' her leg in."

"How could she pull her leg in when she's unconscious? Sometimes I think you ain't got the brains God gave geese. Now we got to fix her up."

"I know a doctor here. Fixed my hand when I burned it. Pay him enough money and he won't tell no one."

"That'll have to do. But you gotta be more careful, Mitch. She's a nice girl, and you're gonna be responsible for her once the rest of us go home."

*　　*　　*

After handing Fritz off to the Israelis in return for their delivery of Adnan Yafouri into CIA custody, Joseph and Jessie have flown to Romania to confront the suspected terrorist. The

drive from Bucharest has been picturesque, particularly the final half hour on a private road through a dense forest. Now, after settling into her rooms on the upper floor of a palace that had once been a residence of Prime Minister Nicolai Ceaucescu, Jessie Zayyat has joined her senior colleague in the Great Hall.

"Where's the major?" asks Jessie.

"His aide said he'd be right along," replies Joseph.

Jessie looks up at the enormous crystal chandelier. "This is quite something."

"A perfect symbol of the corruption that communism inevitably leads to."

"You were in the Agency before the fall of the USSR, Joseph. Do you miss the Cold War?"

"I did for a while, but fighting worldwide terrorism isn't a bad substitute."

"They hate our freedoms."

"Just like the communists did. But where the communists were clever but brutal, these terrorists are just single-minded fanatics."

"They hate our freedoms and also our religion."

"That's why it's so important to take guys like this Yafouri out of circulation."

Jessie is fingering the heavy brocade draperies. "I know blue, yellow, and red are Romania's national colors, but they don't go together well in draperies." She unhands the drapery and turns to Joseph. "You haven't had any additional thoughts about those Iranians who were at the airport when we picked up Fritz, have you?"

"No. I mentioned them to the Mossad guys when we handed Fritz over. They said they'd had their eyes on them weeks before Fritz showed up in Venice."

"So just a coincidence."

"Yup, just a coincidence."

Just then the colonel in charge of the interrogation center appears at the door. "Miss Zayyat, Mr. Snow, if you'll come with me, I'll take you to Adnan Yafouri."

As they head down to the basement, Joseph whispers to Jessie. "Don't be nervous. You'll do fine. He's been sleepless for forty-eight hours with earphones on his head blasting out Christmas tunes. By now he probably thinks he's Frosty the Snowman."

They enter a small room with heavy padding on the walls. The detainee sitting at the table is wearing handcuffs and leg irons. Jessie takes the chair opposite him while Joseph and a uniformed guard stand out of his line of sight by the door.

Jessie clears her throat. "*Shu ismak?*"

"*Ismi Adnan Yafouri,*" replies the man.

And so it begins.

ÐETAINEÐ

Toots opens her eyes to an achingly blue Canaletto sky spotted here and there with cottony cloud puffs. She is outdoors lying uncomfortably on her back. Something is wrong with her left foot. It aches. She looks down when her toes refuse to wiggle properly and sees that she is wearing a plaster cast up past her ankle.

"Don't get the cast wet," comes a voice from a distance. "Y'all have to keep it on for four weeks or your foot won't heal right."

Where is the voice coming from? She looks beyond her exposed toes and sees water and sun glare. The she sees a motorboat bobbing about twenty feet offshore. She shades her eyes with her hand. One of her acrylic fingernails has come off. Memory comes rushing back. The man from the airport, the man with the gun, is standing in the boat. A man sitting beside him is aiming a camera at Toots.

"Sorry about your foot, Ma'am," he calls. "It was an accident." His voice carries well in the still air. She hears the cries of seagulls. "Y'all got ten cases of bottled water and four cases of Meals-Ready-To-Eat. Civilian version: Menu C. Heatin' pouches are inside the packets so you don't need no fire. Couldn't very well have you startin' a signal fire could we. Just follow the instructions on the package."

Signal fire? Propped now on one elbow and still shading her eyes, Toots looks beyond the boat and sees the dome of St. Mark's cathedral and the towers of other classic buildings in the far, far distance. So she's almost in Venice. She looks to either side of where she is lying. Piles of metal scrap: pipes, cables, drums, furniture, bashed-in containers. Where the hell is she?

J.M. sees her trying to orient herself. "You're on an island in the lagoon, Ma'am. That's Venice off behind us. Island used to be used for dumpin', but the dump been closed for a coupla years now. Scheduled to be cleaned up sometime in the next five years. But you don't have to worry. We'll come pick you up before then."

Toots finds her voice. "You fucking bastard! Go fuck yourself! When I get off this island, I'm coming to get you."

J.M. smiles. "Well, we'll just see about that. And I'll excuse the profanity, though it is pretty offensive comin' from a pretty girl like you. By the way, you got your iPod and computer in your backpack, and your wallet and passport are in the top zipper pocket. We only took your cell-phone. If anybody happen to find you, which ain't likely since we're pretty far from the regular boat channels and nobody goes fishin' 'round all this junk, you'll have a hard time explainin' what happened 'cause we haven't hurt you none. 'Cept for your foot."

"And my fingernail."

"I don't know nothin' 'bout that, but the foot was an accident. And we got it fixed up."

"What's your name?"

"Name's J.M., Ma'am, and I'm the one responsible if you really plan on comin' after me." Mitch, the other man in the boat, puts his camera in a carrying case and pulls the lanyard to start the motor. "Remember, don't get the cast wet!" The boat is putt-putting away from the island. "Mitch here will come by from time to time to take pictures of you. Make sure you're all right. We'll send them to your daddy." The growing sound of the boat's motor drowns out whatever else J.M. is saying.

Toots watches until the boat is a speck in the distance then grabs the rim of an oil drum to pull herself to her feet. Even at a slow hobble with a pipe as a crutch it doesn't take long to survey the island. She reckons it to be forty feet long by eighteen feet wide, completely covered with scrap and barely above the surface of the lagoon. The cases of water and food are on a sort of platform that has been pulled together at the highest point from pieces of junk.

Find some wood, make a fucking raft, get the fuck out of here, she murmurs to herself. Then she begins to wonder whether there's actually anything wrong with her foot, or whether the cast is a trick to keep her from swimming. The nearest islands are clearly swimmable, but they're tiny and covered with junk too. She puts weight on her foot. It hurts, but does it hurt like it's broken? She can't decide. She puts on more weight and winces. Definitely something wrong. Why isn't there any wood? Or plastic bottles and bags? Everyplace else in the world is buried in non-biodegradable plastic. But not here.

She turns to making an inventory of everything in her backpack. The battery levels of her computer and iPod aren't very encouraging from an entertainment point of view. No wifi. Surprise, surprise. Her black raincoat will do as ground cloth or shelter, whichever she may need.

Presently she realizes she's hungry. The first Meal-Ready-To-Eat pouch she pulls from the cardboard case is labeled Menu 8. It takes a while to figure out from the instructions and diagrams how to get the chemical heating envelope to work. While she's waiting for her macaroni and cheese to warm, she squeezes cheddar cheese spread onto a piece of crispy bread and eats it. Not bad.

Is it her imagination or is the island getting smaller? She looks toward the distant row of upright wooden beams that seems to mark a boat channel. Aren't they shorter than they were? A lifetime on Ass Isle has taught her the signs of an incoming tide. She feels a clutching in her chest. How high does the tide get? Is that why there isn't any wood or plastic? Does the tide carry everything floatable away? She hobbles over to examine the junk on the highest part of the island and finds strands of seaweed. That can't be good news. Pretty soon the whole island will be inundated. Despite the pain in her foot she manages to roll an oil drum into the gap between the makeshift platform holding her supplies and a legless, drawerless desk. *Mount Toots*, she thinks.

As the sun sets magnificently over the Queen City of the Adriatic, Toots accepts that the water isn't going to reach her or her supplies and falls exhausted into a dreamless sleep.

*   *   *

Fritz doesn't know why nothing bad has happened to him, but he's not complaining. The Italian police who took him into custody at the airport had handed him over to men in a black SUV who seemed to be Americans. Just outside the airport, the SUV had slowed to a stop behind a small blue van parked on the verge of the highway, and the Americans had handed him over the men in that vehicle. The black SUV had driven off, and a couple of minutes later the blue van had done the same. However, on reaching a traffic circle it had gone all the way around and taken the road back toward the airport. About this time it had crossed Fritz's mind that maybe he was supposed to have a black bag over his head. Not that he was complaining. Nor had he complained when a swarthy, curly-haired man in the front of the van threw him a shirt and trousers and told him to change out of his running clothes.

The van had pulled up underneath the Partenze/Departures sign where Fritz had so recently seen Toots waving to him. The blonde, crewcut driver and the swarthy, curly-haired man had held his arms in no-nonsense grips as they walked him into the terminal, past some carabinieri, who looked just like the policemen who had arrested him forty-five minutes earlier, and directly to the security check. Credentials had been flashed, and the three of them had proceeded down a priority lane and then through passport control. Hadn't Fritz given his passport to Toots?

Did they have Toots too? He tried to get a look at the passport presented as his, but it was pocketed by one of his escorts as soon as it had been stamped. When they reached the gate, the flight posting had been to Israel, but his escorts had neither confirmed that they were Israelis, nor, for that matter, answered any of the questions he had addressed to them.

Ah, well, thought Fritz, *I've never been to Israel.* And then he had crashed as if his body had suddenly expended its very last molecule of adrenalin.

*   *   *

Now Fritz is awake with only the vaguest recollection of getting on and off the plane, being driven from an airport into a city, or falling asleep on a king size bed in a two-room hotel suite. He pees, admires the bathroom facilities, and decides to brush his teeth and shower. The telephone rings as he is drying himself. The person on the other end tells him he is to be ready to go someplace in five minutes. Go where? No answer.

The drive to someplace takes twenty-five minutes. Fritz gets out of the car and sees a man of moderate height with the well-muscled shoulders and upper arms of an athlete standing at the metal gate closing off the driveway of a modern-looking residence. The man has on a short-sleeved shirt with an open neck and is wearing a yarmulke.

"You must be Fritz," he says with his hand extended in greeting. Fritz returns his smile, shakes his hand, and follows his sweeping gesture to precede him into the house. "You can call me the Rabbi. It's a kind of joke nickname, but there's no need for you to know my real name."

"Whatever you say, Rabbi," says Fritz agreeably.

"We'll go downstairs to my study and talk for a bit while my wife finishes getting dinner ready."

"Lead the way," says Fritz.

The Rabbi descends. "You don't seem very upset over the way you've been treated," he says over his shoulder.

"Getting upset has never benefited me. I take things as they come."

"But you must have some reaction to being shanghaied?"

"Shanghaied?"

"An old term for Englishmen who were drugged or knocked out in seaport taverns and woke up to find they were on the high seas and part of a ship's crew."

"Does that mean I'm part of your crew now?"

"Not exactly, but we kidnapped you for what I hope you will regard as friendly reasons."

Fritz looks around the large basement. Packed bookshelves and a paper-strewn desk and worktable occupy one end. Windows high on the wall let in some dim sunlight. The other end of the room has more bookcases along with racks of free weights and colorful gym pads on the floor.

"You work out, Rabbi?"

"I try to do some every day. And I roughhouse with the kids down here. You won't meet my son and daughter tonight, though. They're at their grandmother's. My associates tell me that you're an athlete too. What's your sport?"

"Nowadays I mostly go in for endurance competitions, but I used to play water polo before I hurt my hip. How about you?"

"Rough sport, water polo," replies the Rabbi. "My forte is Frisbee."

"I beg your pardon? Frisbee?"

"You know, the kind of plastic disc you throw? I don't know the German word for it. It's called a Frisbee in English. My specialty when I was young is now called disc golf."

"Ah, Discgolf. We have that in Germany, but not so much. I played once in Munich. Very difficult to aim the disc."

"When I was growing up as a teenager in the United States, I was so good that my goal was to become a professional. But then I decided to study my religion and travel around urging young people to make *aliyah*."

"*Aliyah?*"

"Emigration to Israel."

"So you're American?"

"I have dual nationality. But we didn't shanghai you and bring you here just to hear my life story. Please sit down. I have some important questions to ask you." Fritz sits on a plastic chair opposite the Rabbi's desk. "Here's my first question, and I want you to take it very seriously. Have you ever heard a donkey talk, Fritz?"

Fritz does not hesitate. "One donkey, yes. Quite a number of times. In Morocco."

"Okay, here's my second question. What language did the donkey speak?"

Fritz thinks. "I would have to say that it spoke donkey."

"By which you mean?"

"I mean that the sounds were donkey sounds, but I could understand their meaning. Not in words exactly, but in my head. It was the same with the old man."

"The old man?"

"In Morocco. Up in the mountains. It was his donkey."

"Were there other people you met in Morocco who could understand what the donkey said?"

"I think only the old man."

"I suppose you and the old man were able to talk back to the donkey."

"Yes."

"What language did you use?"

"Donkey."

The Rabbi looks as though he wishes to pursue the linguistic question further but then switches subjects. "What was it that the donkey said when it talked?"

"To the old man or to me?"

"Both."

"To the old man he mostly answered questions. Pretty stupid questions, I would have to say. A lot of them he just ignored. He never directed any specific comments to me when the old man was around. I'm pretty sure he didn't want the old man to know that I could understand their conversation. But then when the old man was away from the house, the donkey complained to me about how hard it is nowadays for a donkey to find anyone worth talking to."

"You think the donkey realized you could understand him?"

"Of course he did. I'm sure of it. He even knew my name."

"Fritz?"

"Fritz."

"Didn't that surprise you?"

"Yes, naturally. But as I said, I take things as they come."

"What was the donkey's name?"

"Ya'fur."

"Can you think of any reason why you and the old man can speak and understand donkey but no one else can?"

"I've wonder about that sometimes. The old man was a religious person, and whenever the donkey answered one of his questions, it had to do with the settlement of a dispute, or a prediction, or something of that sort. With me, however, it was more like the donkey and I were friends. Personally, I'm not religious, but the donkey referred a few times to some of my religious ancestors, particularly one who was called Wolfgang the Messiah."

"You had mentioned Wolfgang to him?"

"No. He seemed to know my family history."

The Rabbi pauses. "You're sure you're telling me the truth, Fritz?"

"Yes, the truth. Why would I not?"

"Have you told other people about this donkey?"

"When I first came back from Morocco, I did a few times as a humor story. But no one took me seriously."

"No one at all?"

"Only my professor."

"And who is your professor?"

"Doctor Monika Farber of Erlangen University."

The Rabbi nods. "Okay, let's go back upstairs and eat. And don't say anything about the donkey to my wife."

*   *   *

Back in his hotel room after a succulent fricassee of chicken with Moroccan spices, Fritz finds an assortment of new clothes piled on his bed. He thinks about calling the German embassy to complain about being kidnapped but decides that his circumstances might not be believable. And in any case, his circumstances aren't so bad.

The next morning a driver takes him to the north and turns off on a sandy road leading to a deserted beach. The Rabbi is already there and is challenging the gusty Mediterranean winds by throwing colored discs at a skinny bespectacled young man stationed seventy-five meters away. The Rabbi says that his target's name is Ariel Rafi. Fritz waves, Ariel waves back. The Rabbi explains that Ariel is standing in for the metal target basket of a disc golf course. Like the vertical pole holding the basket, his role is not to catch the disc but to let it hit him and drop to his feet.

"Have you figured out why I asked you about the donkey?" asks the Rabbi.

"I have no idea, but I suppose it's connected with why the Iranians and the Americans followed me to Venice. Which, while I'm mentioning it, brings up the question of where Toots is."

"Who's Toots?"

"She's my girlfriend. She was with me in Venice. She was waiting for me at the airport."

"Sorry, I don't know anything about her. But I'll make some inquiries. In the meantime I need to tell you some things about your donkey friend Ya'fur and about the Jews."

"You know about Ya'fur?"

"Just listen. Your Professor Farber went to Morocco and from there to Iran where she told President Ahmadinejad that you heard a donkey talk in a certain village."

"So that's where she disappeared to."

"That is why Ahmadinejad sent his men to kidnap you. He wants you to find the donkey for him. The men belong to a group known as the Three-Thirteen. They're a special unit dedicated to preparing for the return of the Shi'ites' Messiah, who's supposed to ride on a sacred donkey. They almost got you at the airport, but my American associates figured out just in time what your escape plan was and were able to head them off."

"It was Toots' plan. I didn't know I had to escape. I was just escaping to please her. But tell me, why does President Ahmadinejad want me in particular?"

"Because you're the only person other than the old man in Morocco who can identify which donkey it was that you heard talk."

The Rabbi throws an impressive anhyser that catches the wind out over the water and then zooms down to the right and strikes Ariel in the crotch.

"What I'm going to tell you, by the way, is so bizarre that I don't even have to swear you to secrecy. The only people who would believe you, besides your own Professor Farber, are a self-important old Harvard professor named Paul Constantine, perhaps an American evangelical minister named Pastor Steve Klingbeil, and possibly an old man named Greeley who runs a donkey sanctuary in Scotland."

"Greeley! That's Toots' father!"

"Your Toots is Victoria Greeley?"

"Yes. She is very sweet. You must find out where she is and let her know that I'm all right. She'll be very worried about me."

"I'll set to work on that as soon as we finish here. But back to what I was saying. The things I'm going to tell you should never be talked about indoors or where there might be people listening."

"You understand, I'm very concerned about Toots."

"I understand, yes, but please, we have to stick to business." The Rabbi unleashes a tomahawk throw that barely misses crashing hard on Ariel's scalp. "The people I just mentioned to you were part of a conversation once about the Messiah. They were all pretty drunk, but not too drunk to remember such a remarkable evening. Professor Constantine knew everything about donkeys and especially about Islamic messianic teachings; Pastor Steve, despite being an ex-politician and an ex-convict, was fairly knowledgeable about Christian beliefs; and I knew my own Jewish tradition. So we got to trading information, and we agreed that if Judaism, Christianity, and Islam are all true religions—let's just say theoretically—then each religion is going to have a Messiah at the end of times, and each of the Messiahs is supposed to come to Jerusalem riding on a donkey."

"The way Jesus did. I don't know if you know this, but my ancestor Wolfgang the Messiah played Jesus in a Passion Play and had to ride on a donkey. My last name comes from him."

"Yes, I knew that. We have done research on you. But back to what I was saying. No one can be a real Messiah without a donkey, and there are buried traditions in all three religions that predict that the donkey will not only be able to talk to the Messiah but will also belong to a sacred lineage of donkeys, a lineage that might be identifiable by its DNA. In other words, all of the great religious leaders in all three religions have ridden on a donkey that is descended from the donkey of some earlier leader. So that's what got us talking about the three-donkey solution, or better the three-donkey complication. It seemed obvious, at least to a bunch of drunks, that whichever Messiah got to Jerusalem first would establish which religious group had the best right to the city, the Jews, the Christians, or the Muslims. According to our three-donkey solution, the three Messiahs would all come at the same time—because it wouldn't make any sense, if the religions are true, for one to come before the others—and they would more or less race their donkeys to Jerusalem."

Fritz grins. "You guys were really drunk, weren't you?"

"That we were. Personally I don't imbibe, but I was intellectually drunk. The conversation gets more bizarre. Constantine first proposed the three-donkey solution and then later in the conversation decided that his own proposal was wrong.

Instead, he said, there were clear traditions that indicated that every great religious leader who came on a donkey rode on exactly the same donkey. An animal named Ya'fur. By this theory, Ya'fur not only talks and hangs out with prophets and Messiahs, but he is immortal."

"An immortal donkey."

"An immortal donkey. Patently ridiculous we all agreed. But later I looked into it a bit more and found that just as Constantine had said, there was a Jewish tradition that all of the donkeys of the great Jewish prophets were the same donkey. It's in a *midrash* collection called Bamidbar Rabbah."

"What's a *midrash* collection?"

"It's a collection of Jewish religious legends. What it says there is this: '"And Abraham rose up early and saddled his ass," which is a quote from Genesis. 'This is the ass on which Moses also rode when he came into Egypt; for it is said, "And Moses took his wife and his sons, and set them upon an ass." This is the ass on which the Son of David'—that's either Jesus, if you're a Christian, or the Jewish Messiah—'also shall ride; as it is said in Zechariah, "Humble, and riding upon an ass."' When I found this, I tucked it away in my memory because even though it made no scientific sense, since Abraham, Moses, and Jesus lived centuries apart, it fit exactly what Constantine had proposed in his one-donkey solution."

"According to Toots it's also what he is writing in his book."

"Constantine is writing a book?"

"That's what she told me. I don't remember exactly what she said, but I remember it had an immortal donkey in it."

"Really? Does he give its name?"

"I have no idea. But Toots would know. She's been editing it."

"Sounds like we have to find Toots."

"That's what I've been telling you."

The Rabbi makes one last throw and beckons to Ariel to come in.

Ariel joins them. "Hi, I'm Ariel."

"Fritz." The two young men shake hands. "How often does this guy take you out for target practice?"

"This is only the second time. I'd be happy to do it more often, but I'm usually out of the country. I just came home now for your debriefing."

"You're another donkey specialist?"

"No. I'm a spy. I work in Iran."

Fritz is taken aback. "Don't you have to kill me now that you've told me?"

"I hope not."

The Rabbi intervenes. "Ariel is one of Israel's biggest secrets, and the one best known to our enemy. He is what you might call a spy with permission. When he is in Iran, he goes by the name of Jamsheed and serves as a junior aide to President Mahmoud Ahmadinejad's Chief of Staff, Esfandiar Rahim Mashaei. Both of them know he's a spy and use him to send us misleading messages. We do the same thing in the other direction. The obvious question, therefore, is to ask why Ahmadinejad would let a known spy into his inner circle. We think the answer is because he is actually a Jew."

"Ariel is actually a Jew? Or Ahmadinejad is actually a Jew?"

"Ariel is obviously a Jew. I'm talking about Ahmadinejad. Most people in Iran who hear about his being a Jew think it's just a dirty rumor. But we suspect that either it's true, or maybe Ahmadinejad himself may not know for sure whether it's true or not. So having a spy around who works for the Mossad may make some kind of crazy sense to him. All we know for sure is that Ariel insinuated himself into the president's circle right after the rumor began."

"How did the rumor begin?"

"With a historian who is also one of Iran's leading anti-Semites and Holocaust deniers. He hates Ahmadinejad, but whether he made up the rumor because Ahmadinejad is in actual fact a crypto-Jew, or because his hatred made him want to tarnish his reputation, we don't know. The story he tells is that Ahmadinejad was born in Garmsar, which is a town about fifty miles from Tehran on the edge of the desert. This historian claimed in print that many Jewish families settled in Garmsar and under pressure from Muslim fanatics fraudulently converted to Islam. They became crypto-Jews. That's the kind of family Ahmadinejad comes from. Again, according to this guy."

Fritz interrupts. "Isn't this the same Ahmadinejad who wants to wipe Israel off the face of the map and is building nuclear weapons to make it happen? How can it make sense for him to be a Jew?"

"When you look at it from that angle, it doesn't make any sense at all. Or maybe when you look at it from any angle. But that doesn't mean we should ignore it, or that Ahmadinejad is ignoring it. Because the rumor is not impossible. Let me give you a parallel example. We know that in 1839 the governor of a big Iranian city called Mashhad forced the city's Jews to convert to Islam and adopt Muslim names. For over a hundred years they acted just like Muslims in public and shared all their attitudes, but they observed the Sabbath at home and secretly taught their children Jewish traditions. Then lo and behold, after the Iranian Revolution the community emigrated to Long Island and resumed their Jewish identity, complete with intense hostility toward Islam and the Islamic Republic.

"Now we don't know exactly what happened in Garmsar, but the claim is that Ahmadinejad's original family name was Saboorchi. Some people think that the name refers to his forebears being weavers who worked with a kind of thread called *saboor*. The suffix *–chi* just means someone who does something. Some others think that it goes back to the editors who finalized the Talmud in Iraq fifteen hundred years ago. They were called the Saboraim. As for me, I'm putting my money on *saboor* being a variant of Zaboor, the name the Quran gives for the Psalms of David. This way a Zaboor-*chi* could be something like a psalm-singer. And once you go that far, you might as well go all the way and speculate that Ahmadinejad is actually a descendant of King David and hence, like Jesus, of the right lineage to become the Messiah."

"This is all very confusing. Are you suggesting that Ahmadinejad himself is …"

"That he's the Messiah? The Mahdi? The Hidden Imam? The Master of the Hour? Just waiting to hook up with the sacred donkey Ya'fur before revealing his true identity to a savior-hungry world? No, I'm not suggesting that at all. Absurdities like that belong in comic books. But that doesn't mean that the notion of Ahmadinejad as the Mahdi hasn't occurred to some of the fruitcakes in the Three-Thirteen. I don't know how much you know about Shi'ism, but the Hidden Imam, their Mahdi or Messiah, disappeared over a thousand years ago and is supposed by the believers to be alive but hiding out away from people. This is absolute gospel among Iran's Shi'ites. So where has he been all this time? In the Bermuda Triangle? Some idiots believe this. You can google it. But how about this instead: Maybe he's been at home among his Shi'ite followers the entire time. At home, but unrecognizable: observing, acquiring a deep understanding of human affairs, waiting for the right moment.

"Suddenly there's a religious revolution in Iran. Shi'ite faith becomes central to national identity. Twenty-five years later, out of nowhere, an obscure, ferret-faced veteran of the Iran-Iraq War sweeps into the presidency. He thumbs his nose at the Americans. He mortally threatens us Israelis. He defies the world by building an atom bomb. Meanwhile, Muslims everywhere have been champing at the bit to welcome their Mahdi ever since the turn of the Muslim year 1400 at the time of the revolution. Why should it come as a surprise if a handful of Iranian nutcases, 313 of them to be precise, conclude that Mahmoud Ahmadinejad will soon reveal himself as the Master of the Hour? Their job is to help fulfill this destiny, and Esfandiar Rahim Mashaei, the man Ariel here works for when he's in Tehran, takes on the role as the leading Ahmadinejad-*parast*. That's 'Ahmadinejad-worshipper' to you. All

Messiahs come with advance men, you know. So in this version of
the rumor, Mashaei is Ahmadinejad's John the Baptist."

Fritz looks baffled.

"You're not following this, are you?"

"No, you're confusing me with all this Shi'ite stuff. What does
Ahmadinejad being a secret Jew have to do with anything?"

"That's the crucial question. And we don't know the answer.
If, like Ariel here, you were in the Mossad, my country's allegedly
peerless intelligence service, wouldn't you just salivate at the
thought that a Jew had become the president of the country
that threatens our very existence? Or if you were one of the
approximately 200 million idiots in the Middle East who believe
in every conspiracy theory that comes around, wouldn't the idea
of Ahmadinejad being a Jew make perfect sense to you?

"One version of the conspiracy story goes this way: Israel
wants to destroy the Islamic Republic of Iran because its leaders
want to kill the Jews. How do the Israelis know the leaders want
to kill the Jews? Because Iran's president, Ahmadinejad, denies
the Holocaust and says Israel is going to disappear. Clearly code
words for killing the Jews. But Iran's president is actually a secret
Jew. And what a tricky Jew! Is it possible that he's denying the
Holocaust and being nasty about the Jews just to give Israel and
the United States an acceptable excuse to attack Iran first and
destroy the Islamic Republic. That would make Ahmadinejad
the ultimate Israeli mole, the hero who wards off the second
Holocaust. What do you think?"

"Utterly ridiculous," says Fritz.

"The more ridiculous the more believable in Middle East
conspiracy circles. Besides it may be true."

"But what about the talking donkey?"

"You tell me. Did you really hear a donkey talk?"

"I've already told you I did."

"Then anybody who wants to be the Messiah has to get his
hands on that donkey. Whether the Iranians are just preparing for
the return of their Hidden Imam or fantasizing that Ahmadinejad

himself is the Mahdi, they need the donkey. And that means they need you."

Fritz contemplates what he has heard. "If what you say is true, Rabbi, doesn't it mean that if the Christians and the Jews want their Messiah to come instead of the Shi'ites' Mahdi, they also need me to identify Ya'fur for them?"

"Yes. Unless you yourself are the Messiah." The Rabbi gives Fritz a quizzical stare.

"Me? No. I told you, I'm not even religious. I don't know why I could understand Ya'fur, but I'm certainly not Messiah material. What Messiah ever played water polo? Besides which, the world may never be ready for a German Messiah no matter what religion he belongs to."

"I had to ask."

"I understand."

*   *   *

"I just feel so inadequate," says Jessie. "I've tried all the techniques I've been trained in, and Mr. Yafouri still isn't talking."

Joseph brings her a can of Diet Sprite from the stash they brought with them from Venice. "Don't take it personally, Jessie. Interrogation is an art, and you're still a beginner. I'm just sorry I don't know Arabic. I'd like to give him a try myself."

"Do you think I'm in the wrong career, Joseph? I didn't feel at all good interrogating him,"

"It's not like you didn't get anything out of him, Jessie. We know the names of all his friends and contacts, and we know his travel history."

"But only one flight out of thirty-five was on Ukrainian-Mediterranean Airlines. And we still haven't found out for sure what 313 means. If in binary it's the number of a bank account, we still don't know which bank it is or whose name it's under. I don't know why the Israelis haven't gotten back to us on that."

"It's not our problem any more. If they come up with something, they can send it on to Afghanistan after Yafouri is transferred there. They've been interrogating Arabs at the Bagram facility for almost ten years. High-level al-Qaeda people. No offense, Jessie, but they've had a lot more experience than you have. And their techniques are probably not quite so by-the-book."

"But you see, Joseph, it isn't just that Mr. Yafouri hasn't confessed anything. I've also begun to think that maybe he's not a terrorist."

"Well, you can put that thought right out of your head, Jessie. We have it on the authority of our Mossad friends that he's the real deal. Who knows more about terrorism than they do?"

"I know you're right, but it keeps coming back to me that Ya'fur was the name of Muhammad's donkey. And those other letters, U-F-A-I-R, I found out on the Internet that they spell the alternate name of his donkey, Ufair."

"Whoa, don't go down that road, girl. Connecting dots doesn't include inventing a great big dot way the hell off the map."

"I know. I know. I'm just so depressed. What if the donkey names are a code of some kind? We'd be missing it."

"A code for what?"

"I don't know. An action they're planning maybe. Like we use code names for military operations."

"You think Operation Ya'fur?"

"It's a possibility. Connects with the life of the Prophet. That would appeal to *jihadis*."

"So how would you check it out?"

"Get NSA to do a search of phone calls and e-mails mentioning Ya'fur and Ufair and the number 313."

"As simple as that?" Joseph mulls it over. "I suppose you're right. You could check it out that way."

"I think we have to try, Joseph. If an Operation Ya'fur went down, we'd look like dunces for not seeing it coming. Of course,

I know we have to keep going on Mr. Yafouri. But we could do both, couldn't we?"

"No stone unturned, Jessie. If your hunch pays out, I'll make sure you get all the credit. You have some home leave coming. Why don't you fly back to DC and check things out with NSA. Just don't make it too obvious what you're doing. And make sure you don't mention any donkeys. I can hold the fort in Munich for a couple of weeks."

The next morning, unaware that his earnest but not very skillful interrogator is already winging her way to the U.S., Adnan Yafouri hears his leg irons clink as he shuffles blindly behind a guard across an expanse of pavement. The sack over his head conceals everything, but the sounds tell him he is at an airport. The guard guides his manacled hands to a narrow metal railing and tells him to climb the steps. Someone pushes his head down to keep him from banging it on an airplane doorway. Belted into a seat with a guard beside him, he ignores the amplified voice reciting safety instructions in Romanian, Russian, and English.

Why is this happening to him? He answered truthfully everything the woman asked him, even though most of her questions made no sense. Now he is flying somewhere, and it is probably not back home. The faces of his wife and children come to mind, and he weeps inside his sack.

ÐOUGLAS GREELEY
WRITES AGAIN

Baleine artfully maneuvers the rented Lincoln Town Car through the late rush hour crush on the Washington Beltway. At her insistence—"I don't want to sit next to some old white guy. He might have cooties."—Constantine is riding in the backseat and awakening from a restorative nap.

He looks out at the stream of automobiles. "Are we almost there yet?"

"We're not going to get there tonight. You made us start too late. We hit the worst of the traffic."

"That's all right. No rush. Find us place to eat and pull over."

Ten minutes pass. "Denny's all right with you?" Baleine is already pulling into the parking lot. "Sign says free wifi. We can catch up on our e-mail."

"By which you mean you don't want to have a conversation with me."

"By which you can believe anything you like. But I'm going to check in with my uncle and see how Baby Dog is doing. He doesn't like it when I go of town."

"Your uncle?"

"No, Baby Dog."

Waiting for his chicken fried steak to be served, Constantine finds a new e-mail from Douglas Greeley.

Dear Paul,

I'm afraid I have some bad news. As if being held hostage here on at Ass Isle weren't trial enough, Toots has been kidnapped. I received today a video of her sitting alone on a junk-covered island somewhere. I am attaching it. As you will see, there is nothing in the background to indicate what the body of water is. Just two more islands. They must have been used as dumping places. The video starts with a picture of the *International Herald Tribune* showing the date so I know it was taken just two days ago. The poor little girl. She looks so forlorn even though she is giving the cameraman a rude gesture with her middle finger.

I don't know what to do, Paul. Perhaps you can suggest something. I've spoken to the police, but they have no more idea than I do about where she might be. Except they're pretty sure she's not in Scotland.

Please, I beg of you, if you hear anything at all about her, let me know immediately. I don't believe I could survive anything dire happening to her. She has been my companion and solace for the last dozen years since her mother died. She even chose not to go to university in order to stay with me and the donkeys. I know they miss her and worry about her as much as I do.

Also, I finally got through entering all the corrections she had made to the last chapter of your book. I don't think they're quite as good as the earlier chapters. You'll find it in an attached file.

Sincerely,
Douglas

CHAPTER FIVE

A propos of the note at the end of the last chapter, I have to talk about some major changes in my quality of life between the time of Jesus and six hundred years later when I hooked up with Muhammad. They don't all have to do with horses, but horses are a good place to start.

First of all, let me confess a prejudice. I think horses are as dumb as bricks. In fact, I suspect that's why humans became so taken with them. I know that the usual line is that they have elegant lines and bond with their riders, who are usually characterized either as noble knights or romantic cowboys. But originally they didn't look all that different from us donkeys, or at least from the half-asses that lived in the same region they did. Shorter ears, but since when is that a virtue?

While my fellow donkeys were eking out difficult lives in the desert, great hordes of horses were wandering around Central Asia in a sea of grass. There weren't many people around because the grass was so deeply rooted that they couldn't grow much of anything except in the mud along some rivers. But the people that did live in the area didn't think twice about going out and killing a horse whenever they had a hankering for some meat. There was certainly no shortage of horses, and the herd never seemed too upset when one of the group went missing.

What changed all this were new customs that seeped in from the west, the area north of the Black Sea. People there had learned to harness oxen to plow up the sod and to support themselves by planting crops. When the people traveled, they used the same oxen to pull wagons, which were a pretty new invention at that time, about six thousand years ago. Well, the horse eaters were amazed when the oxen people began to move into their territory. They managed to get their hands on some oxen and wagons of their own. But since cattle weren't native to Central Asia, they became items of value. Worth stealing.

To make a long story short, cattle stealing became a way of life for some of the horse eaters. And as the wagon builders learned how to make lighter wheels that had less friction, it became possible to hitch up horses to do what the oxen did, even though the horses were nowhere near as strong as the oxen. When that happened, the horse eaters, who were gradually turning themselves into horse herders, picked up an idea from the cattle people. Gods, they thought, traveled through the skies in wagons pulled by animals. The sun and the moon looked like wheels. Since each of the divine carts was pulled by two animals—cattle, horses camels, geese, goats—they developed a kind of fetish for two-animal teams. Or two-something anything. Light and dark, night and day, good and bad, male and female, husband and wife, you name it.

The horse herders borrowed these ideas. They didn't think them up. But they pushed it to the next level. The gangs of cattle rustlers developed little two-wheeled carts that were light and flimsy enough for a couple of horses to pull, and they convinced themselves that a rustler riding a chariot was like a god riding through the heavens. The fact that the way they were hitching the horses to the chariot, a technique they borrowed from the cattle people, didn't work all that well didn't bother them. It was more important for a chariot rider to drive a team of horses that was divisible by two than to experiment with harnessing each animal separately, which was the more efficient way to do it.

Now what you're thinking is that as a donkey, I shouldn't have had much interest in these things, or even have known about them. But when gangs of brutal chariot rustlers came charging into what had up to that time been donkey territory, they not only set up their own kingdoms, but they created this romantic image of the majestic horse as a symbol of royal grandeur. As you can imagine, a donkey like me, who for thousands of years had seen his fellows treated as mystic symbols of masculinity, felt royally dissed. Even the Egyptians went gaga over the idea of hundreds of stallions galloping across a battlefield dragging their little chariots behind them. It made no difference that half the chariots flipped over, or lost a wheel, or got stuck. It was such a fad that even when the smarter generals decided that riding on horses would actually be more effective militarily than driving chariots, the aura of the racing vehicle persisted. And still persists to the present day. What do NASCAR vehicles have under their hoods? Horsepower.

But I digress. At the time we donkeys had no choice but to accept a huge demotion in status. Because of me and Ufair, of course, we held our ground in the area of religion, but as a species we were doomed to being considered humble and given the worst jobs. And some of our randier studs even deigned to screw lady horses so that the horse owner could get himself a mule. As if a mule weren't just as dumb as a horse.

Adding insult to social injustice, the idea got spread around, I suspect by Egyptians who still were into the Set-Satan-Lord of the Underworld thing, that it was donkeys who were stupid, and by extension, anyone who worshipped a donkey was doubly stupid. I don't know if they were paid off by the horse breeders or what, but perfectly respectable writers began to spread ridiculous stories. First, as I mentioned earlier, they said that the Jews carried the severed head of Moses' donkey around with them in their sacred shrine. And then they spread the really disgusting rumor that Jesus was half a donkey because his mother had intercourse with an ass demon. In fact, with Set himself.

Jesus showed up in cartoons as a man with a donkey's head wearing a toga with a caption saying he was half an ass. Some people treated it all as a joke, others took it more seriously. But it all contributed to the growing idea that donkeys were stupid at best and demonic at worst, when in fact—and here I'm excluding myself and Ufair because we're special—as a species we're remarkably bright and have a natural talent for reverence and psychologically supportive relations with humans. And proportionally speaking, we have bigger dongs than horses.

All of which leads me to my relations with Muhammad. I had been living in Arabia for quite some time because that was one place where donkeys still had a reputation for making spiritual connection with prophets. I'd hang with one minimally talented prophet for a bit, then move on to another and another. None of them even came close to being a heavy hitter.

Then I began to get a sense of who Muhammad was. Clearly a man with a spiritual gift, but one that rode on horses and fought battles. Even Moses, brutal as he was, never pretended he was a general. Eventually Muhammad took over the oasis I was residing in and we came face to face. He immediately grasped that we could converse so he asked me what my name was. Being still a bit unsure of how fully he realized his own spiritual powers—after all, he rode on a horse—I gave him an evasive answer. "I'm Yazid ibn Shihab," I said. "Allah brought forth among my ancestors sixty donkeys, none of whom was ever ridden on except by a prophet. Today, none of the descendants of my grandfathers remain but me, and none of the prophets remain but you. So I expect you to ride me." As a kicker, I threw in an anti-Jewish bit because I knew that Muhammad had been having trouble convincing the Jews that he was a prophet. "Before you, I belonged to a Jewish man. I caused him to stumble and fall a lot so he used to kick my stomach and beat my back." To this Muhammad replied, "I will call you Ya'fur." So then I knew we were meant to be together because he knew my real name. I said, "I obey." Then he tried something clever with me in return. He said, "Do you want females?" What he was asking was whether I wanted to sire some foals since I was supposedly the last of my line. When I said no, he understood that the last-of-the-line story was crap. I was the one and only eternal Ya'fur, and he was the one and only Muhammad. (In actual fact, I did like to sire foals, but they were ordinary donkeys like their moms.)

From then on he rode me constantly and generally stayed away from his horses. I saw the angel Gabriel when he revealed God's words, and I got to know Muhammad's family. He even sent me on errands. I would bump my head against someone's door, and when he came out and saw me, he would realize that Muhammad wanted to talk to him and follow me to where he was. In return for the favors I did for him, Muhammad outlawed the eating of donkey meat, though the local hunting lobby required that he make an exception for the wild Arabian half-asses. When he asked me whether he should extend the ban to horsemeat, it gave me special pleasure to say that I couldn't care less whether people ate horses.

Though things went well between us, and Muhammad was interested in the stories I told him about earlier prophets, there was one fly in the ointment. Late in the Prophet's life, the governor of Egypt, in response to a letter Muhammad had written asking him to convert to Islam, sent a she-mule as a gift. Her name was Duldul, and she was just as dumb as a horse. Nevertheless, the next time a big battle loomed, Muhammad gave in to the horse fanatics in his army and agreed to ride Duldul into battle. I could understand how it happened because even though people by then had accepted the notion that Muhammad and Ya'fur were a team, they couldn't know how close we really were. So they argued that a steed that was half a donkey and half a horse would give him the best of both worlds.

As it turned out, Muhammad won the battle against heavy odds, and Duldul was inundated with praise. Since it was the Prophet's last big battle, Duldul was still in the limelight when he died a couple of years later. A big deal was made of her being inherited by Muhammad's cousin Ali so I decided not to make a fuss. I just wandered off by myself one night. I heard later that a story went around that I dove into a well and drowned myself, either because of grief or so that no later prophet could ever ride me. But that wasn't true.

How did Muhammad stack up against Abraham, Moses, and Jesus? Well, he certainly had a better sense of humor. In fact, he had an infectious laugh. And even though his wives didn't always get along, he handled his family affairs better. No child sacrifice, no slaughter of kinfolk who disobeyed him, no celibacy. Though no one knows what Jesus would have been like when he turned forty, which was Muhammad's age when he first received a revelation, I'd have to say that Muhammad was a better rounded human being than his famous predecessors. Was he my favorite Prophet? I'm not willing to say. We haven't reached the End Times yet.

Constantine finishes reading the chapter revision and starts in on his chicken. After a few bites he says, "It seems Douglas Greeley's daughter Toots has been kidnapped. You remember who the Greeleys are?"

"Of course I do. Don't be an idiot. Give me the computer."

"You have your own computer."

"Give it to me so I can see his e-mail."

Constantine slides his iBook across the table and butters a dinner roll. "Nothing we can do to help from here."

Baleine reads and then replays the video of Toots on the island.

"Your dinner's getting cold."

"Don't bother me, I'm thinking."

Constantine uses the last of his dinner roll to swipe up the last of the sauce on his plate.

"Venice," announces Baleine. "Greeley's daughter is stranded on an island in the Venice lagoon."

"The Venice lagoon? How in the world can you tell that?"

"Baleine never explains her magic, but she'll make an exception out of sympathy for Toots' father. The girl went to Germany, and the video was shot only two days ago. Not enough time for her to fly all over the world and get in trouble."

"Maybe she got in trouble and then flew."

"Just keep quiet. You can't very well take a tied up girl through passport control at an airport. So Baleine assumes that she's still in Europe. Then there's a time stamp on the video: 6:00 PM with the shadows slanting away and a little bit down. So the camera, which is in a boat—you can see it bob up and down—must be pointed east. But there's no shoreline. Just these little junky islands up close and maybe possibly a very low bigger island farther away. That's it. No hills, no mountains, not even any buildings that I can see. And no boats. So that means if there's shipping or docks, they're all behind the camera or out of sight off to the left or right. Unless it's not a seaport. But that wouldn't explain the junk. Only a big city, probably with some industry, is going to produce that much scrap metal. Which they've decided to dump instead of recycle. So that doesn't sound like northern Europe. Danes, Swedes, Finns, Germans likely keep their islands nice, recycle. Not Poland and the Baltics maybe, but their seaports don't face east."

"You're sure about that?"

"Can't you keep quiet? Baleine's teaching you something. So how far are scrap dumpers going to carry that heavy stuff from shore? Not very far. So we can assume that there is a seaport behind the cameraman's back and that it's probably a city that can be recognized. Or else why would it be hidden from us?"

"Maybe it's an island in a lake."

"An obvious idea that Baleine has already thought about. What's the chance that only metal—no wood, no plastic, no cardboard, just metal—gets dumped on that little island? Not much. If they separated out the metal, they'd be doing recycling, which they obviously don't care about. This means there must be a reason we can't see no light stuff. Now you look at how the whole island is only a foot or so above the water. Shows that there's probably a tide that comes in and floats the wood and stuff away. Lakes don't have tides. So what we are left with is a seaport in southern Europe with a recognizable skyline looking east over a bay full of islands with no mountains or shoreline visible. East coast of Spain or Italy your best bet. But look here." She pivots the computer screen for Constantine to look at. "This is the frozen and enlarged video frame that shows the *International Herald Tribune* with the date at the top. What do you see? Your old eyes, probably not much. But Baleine's can read three headlines. Two about Silvio Berlusconi, and one about his wife. That spells *Italian News Section*, and *Italian News Section* spells Venice, Italy."

"My word. All of that from a video clip."

"Baleine is a detective."

"Yes, she certainly is. Couldn't it be Syracuse in Sicily?"

Baleine's face becomes cloudy. "Now why you want to say something like that?"

"Just a thought. But really, Baleine, remarkable work. After we've had dessert I'll write Douglas Greeley with your idea. Let him take it from there. But now, I'm inclined toward the strawberry shortcake. This is the season."

KRUMLAKE FARM

North of Richmond, over breakfast at an Applebee's just off I-95, Constantine springs a surprise he's been phrasing in his head ever since waking up, studying himself in the mirror, and forming the suspicion that Baleine's company may be making him physically smaller. "You probably don't know it, Baleine, but I'm a bit of a detective myself. For example, I've found out from sources I can't divulge that your real name is Marie Adelaide Millefeuille."

"So."

"Your parents are Haitian, but you were born and brought up in this country."

"What of it?"

"Your father is a nurse anesthetist."

"My father is dead."

"But that's what he did when he was alive."

"Any idiot can find things on the Internet. You probably also found out that they took my father's license away and kicked me out of my aromatherapy training program."

"No, I didn't know that. Some committee of old white men unjustly charged your father with malpractice, I suppose."

"No, he was justly accused of recreational sale of prescription drugs … with some innocent help from his daughter. Uppers, downers, hallucinogens, dissociative anesthesia agents. Never touched cocaine or marijuana. Also, no conviction. Just the license revocation. It's on the Internet."

"Alas, I have to confess that I don't know how to use the Internet. Thank you for the compliment, though. What I do know how to use is connections, in this case the person who vetted your credentials in President Summers' office when you worked for him."

"Baleine never should have told you that. Proves she can make mistakes."

"It's good for all of us to admit our mistakes. What about the rest of your family?"

"What about yours?"

"Well, I have two sisters and a ..."

Baleine waggles an admonitory finger. "Ts, ts, ts—that was rhetorical. Baleine was telling you to shut your mouth."

"Oh." Constantine sighs and returns his attention to his biscuit and sausage gravy.

Back on the road again, Baleine says, "I transferred some relevant files from your computer to mine last night and read through your donkey chapters this morning while you were dawdling around putting on your makeup or whatever. I have two things to say. First, ditch your own chapters and go with what that Toots has written. Girl has flare. At least by comparison. Second, I don't see where people of color fit into your story."

"People of color? Of course they fit in. A couple of billion of them are either Christians or Muslims."

"But they weren't when your donkey was doing all its stuff. That's all white person crap. What about Buddhism? What about Hinduism? What about Voodoo?"

"Voodoo?"

"Don't go dissing voodoo unless you want to see Baleine's bad side."

Constantine ponders the notion of Baleine having a worse side. "Would I be right, Baleine, in guessing that you were not brought up a Roman Catholic?"

"That's a technical matter. But Baleine's family also believes in *luos*."

"What's a *luo*?"

"Sort of like a god. In voodoo, for example, your Set-Satan person is a *luo* named Baron Samedi. He lives on the border between life and death. Everyone must respect him. He wears a black suit, a black top hat, and white gloves, and his face is a white skull."

"Your point being?"

"Don't get fresh with Baleine. My point is that with Baron Samedi there's no desert, no red color, no animal, and certainly no male organ fetish. These are all white guy things."

"That may all be true, but what I've written in my book is what's in the historical record. Everything. I can support it all."

"Even the part about there being an immortal donkey?"

"Of course that's made up. Authorial license. By support I don't mean everything is literally true. I just mean that there are old writings that can be interpreted the way I'm interpreting them. That's what historians do. And as for what you call a male organ fetish, I've exercised good taste in leaving out the material that you would probably find the most offensive."

"What's that?"

"I wouldn't want to lead Baleine down a dark path."

"Leave that to Baleine."

"Okay. But remember, you asked. When you have time, read *The Golden Ass* by Apuleius and *The True History* by Lucian. I may not know much about the Internet, but my assistant showed me how to find the full texts of classic works on-line. You may find them offensive, but they are both classics, which makes reading them a better expenditure of your time than reading private files stolen from my computer. And a more ethical exper well."

Baleine scowls.

The next three hours pass in stilted silence the Town Car onto a gravel road below a r saying Krumlake Farm. After half a mile they round a curve and see a large white frame house fronted by a wide verandah harking back to the pre-AC era. Baleine takes one look at the obese, red-faced man who opens the screen door of the house as they drive up and decides to stay in the car.

The professor crunches his way across the gravel and climbs the steps. "Howdy! I'm Ray Bob Krumlake," says the man. "What can I do you for?"

"How do you do. My name is Paul Constantine. I'm a professor at Harvard University." Hands grip and shake. Krumlake wins the firmness competition. "I'm interested in your work on breeding a red heifer. I know I should have called ahead and made an appointment, but I only realized a half hour ago that I was going to pass close to your farm. I'm on my way home from a speaking engagement at Furman University down in Greenville."

"Well welcome, Professor. Always happy to talk about my animals. Come on inside. I've got the AC on. Turned warm early this year. How's the weather up north?"

"It's been a cool spring so far."

Once inside, Ray Bob inclines his head toward Constantine in a confidential fashion. "I don't mean to be inhospitable not insistin' that your colored gal come inside and have some lemonade with us, but she is one scary lookin' woman. She be all right waitin' out there?"

"She'll be fine. I hired her from an agency. My sore back won't let me drive long distances, and I don't fly if there's any other way to get where I'm going."

"Feel the same way myself. Gout's my problem. Makes my big toe so sore sometimes I can hardly hobble around. Gout and poor sleepin'. Sit up in a chair half the night."

"I have the same problem. Not the gout, but the poor sleep." Constantine decides not to prescribe for Ray Bob the weight loss cure that his doctor has fruitlessly pressed on him.

J.M.!" calls out Ray Bob in a louder voice. "Come in here and meet Mr. Constantine. He come down here from Boston to ask about our red heifer. And bring some lemonade."

The swinging door to the kitchen opens to admit a stocky, muscular young man with freshly buzzed white sidewalls and a tray of glasses.

"This is my son, J.M." There is a twinkle in Ray Bob's eye. "You say you're a professor, Mr. Constantine. So tell me if you can guess what the J and the M stand for. I ask everyone this. Go ahead and give it a try."

Having neglected to inform Ray Bob that he and Baleine have already discussed at length the members and connections of the Krumlake family, Constantine furrows his brow in grave contemplation. "I would guess," he says at length, "that the J and M stand for John Matthew."

"Jumpin' Jehosaphat! How you figure that out?"

Constantine smirks on the inside. "Your last name is Krumlake, which happens to be an anagram of Luke and Mark. And I know a man who goes to the trouble of breeding a red heifer must be a man of deep Christian faith. So I figured John and Matthew would finish off the four disciples."

"You hear that J.M.? Ain't that somethin'! Mister, you've just earned yourself a dinner on me at Stamey's. Best barbecue in North Carolina. Still smoke their own pork shoulders the old fashioned way in a brick pit over hickory coals. J.M. and I were about to head out so when you're finished with your lemonade, we'll get goin'."

The Town Car follows J.M.'s pickup over to Battleground Avenue. "How you and the cracker getting on?" says Baleine.

"Eating out of the palm of my hand."

"You tell him where you work?"

"Even rednecks have heard of Harvard."

"The marine his son?"

"His name's J.M. Is he a marine?"

"Has a bumper sticker says, KILL 'EM ALL, LET GOD SORT 'EM OUT. That was the U.S. Marine slogan when they invaded Haiti."

"I'm sure it wasn't an official slogan."

"And take a look at that sticker in the back window up behind the gun rack." Constantine squints but can't read it. "It says: THIS CAR BRAKES FOR PREGNANT WOMEN AND CHILDREN UNDER FIVE."

They follow the pickup into Stamey's parking lot. "Ray Bob said he would be happy to have a sandwich sent out to you."

"No, I'll just stay here. Clean my gun. Strop my razor."

At a loss for a response, Constantine gets out of the car and follows the Krumlakes into the restaurant. The tables are packed with diners. A five-foot in diameter clock face ornaments the dining room for no apparent reason except, perhaps, to hasten customers through their meals and thus to free up tables. He orders the large chopped pork plate with slaw, hushpuppies, and sweet iced tea.

"Now then," says Ray Bob as they sip iced tea and wait for their food. "What do you want to know about our breeding a red heifer?"

"To tell the truth, Mr. Krumlake …"

"Call me Ray Bob. Everybody does."

"All right, Ray Bob. I'm Paul. The fact is I've read a lot about you, and I already know pretty much all I need to know about your heifer. It seems you've done a really impressive job. First genuine red heifer in a thousand years."

"The real thing too. Not like that one in Missouri that's more a one-time mutation. My daughter Christine is a whizz scientist, and she spliced a red hair gene into our Naomi so she'll have all red calves once we breed her."

"Your daughter must be really something."

"That she is."

"But I'll tell you, Ray Bob. What I really want to find out about is whether you also have a donkey genetics program."

The One-Donkey Solution

Ray Bob's porcine eyes fix Constantine with a beady stare. "Now why would you be askin' about donkeys?"

"Does the name Ya'fur mean anything to you?"

Ray Bob sits back and lets the waitress serve the meals. The three men dig in without further conversation. The food is scrumptious.

Being the first to clean his plate, Ray Bob resumes the conversation. "Now I'm going to insist that you have some of the cherry cobbler with ice cream."

"I couldn't eat another bite, Ray Bob."

"Then you can try the cobbler without the ice cream. You're in for a treat." He hails the waitress. "Honey, two cobblers with ice cream for me and my boy and one without for Mr. Constantine." Turning back to the professor, he seems uncertain where to begin. "Mr. Constantine, I've got nothing against the Jews. You wouldn't happen to be a Jew, would you?"

"No, I'm not."

"Okay, then. I've been completely aboveboard with the Jews. I've told them that I want to help them rebuild their temple for only one reason, to pave the way for Jesus Christ to return in glory and for the true Christians, like me and my boy here, to be took up to Heaven in the rapture. You know what I'm talkin' about with the rapture?"

"Yes I do. I'm quite familiar with the Book of Revelation."

"Good. Then you know that durin' the final days of tribulation, 144,000 Jews see the light and turn to Christ. That's 12,000 from each one of the twelve tribes, including the so-called lost ones. That big group gets saved and goes to Heaven. But the rest are damned. That's just a fact. No prejudice involved in it at all. But from one slant, some people might say I'm helpin' the Jews to bring on the end of the world, at which time they're gonna be royally screwed. Unless they're part of the 144,000, of course. Some people think this is at the very least unfriendly. But I got rabbis who are behind me all the way. To their way of thinkin', Jesus ain't never comin' back in glory because he was nothin' more than a rabble rouser and a criminal when he come the first time. So once they get their red heifer, all they gotta do is blow up those Arab buildings on the Temple Mount—that Dome of the Rock and that other one—sacrifice and burn my red heifer, purify everything with her ashes, and build a new temple. Lookin' at it from their point of view, someone might say that they're takin' advantage of me 'stead of me takin' advantage of them. If you take my meanin'." He holds up his hand. "Hold on. Don't say nothin'. I can see you want to get off the red heifer and move on to the donkey part. And you're very sharp even to know there is a donkey part. I didn't know myself 'til J.M. joined the marines and got hisself taught Arabic. Maybe I should let him go on from here. J.M.?"

Constantine turns his attention to J.M., who for the first time looks engaged in something other than chewing.

The waitress puts the cobblers on the table and leaves. J.M. clears his throat. "As Papa said, Mr. Constantine, I learnt Arabic in the marines and got real good at it in Iraq. They assigned me to community affairs so I used to talk to the old guys in the neighborhood. Naturally, me and them all bein' pretty religious, we got to talkin' about the end of the world and Jesus comin' back and all. Came as a big surprise to me that them Moslems believe almost the same things as we do about Jesus, except that they believe that after Jesus comes back and kills the Antichrist—what they call the Dajjal—he passes the leadership on to a Moslem Messiah they call a Mahdi."

"Them Moslems ain't all terrorists," puts in Ray Bob with a cheerful wink. "They understand Jesus a helluva lot better than the Jews."

"Where the donkey comes in," resumes J.M., "is that Jesus rides on a donkey when he comes back. And so does the Dajjal. And so does that Moslem Mahdi. Donkeys all over the place. And I'm cool with that, because everything in Revelation is symbolic. Not like your red heifer in the Torah. Back in Torah days, when God said a red heifer, He meant a red heifer. Not even a single black or white hair. But Book of Revelation and the Koran—or even more, them Moslem stories that ain't in the Koran—they're more modern. They use symbols. So a donkey don't have to be a real donkey, ya see. 'Cept that they also talk about how Mohammed's donkey was related to Jesus' donkey and Moses' donkey and Abraham's donkey. All named Ya'fur. Now I'm not one to believe that a donkey can live for thousands of years. But then I hear from this Eye-ranian dude livin' in Iraq that the Eye-ranians got a project goin' to find the donkeys related to Ya'fur by screenin' their DNA. I think, that's the kind of thing Papa and my smart sister Christine are into."

Ray Bob can't hold still. "I'm so proud of my boy. I tell the elders in our congregation about what J.M. learned, and the head of our church, Pastor Steve Klingbeil—he's also my son-in-law, married to my Christine—immediately takes an interest. He says that if there is such a donkey, a Ya'fur, alive somewhere, whether there's a whole family of 'em or only one, then whoever finds it is gonna have a big leg up in gettin' ready for the End Times."

Constantine can't keep still. "Can you spell that out for me, Ray Bob? What do you think is going to happen in the End Times?"

"Sure. It's like this. If the Jews—and like I said, I got nothin' against the Jews—but if the Jews find Ya'fur, then maybe it's their Messiah who comes at the end, 'stead of Jesus comin' back the way he's supposed to. And if the Eye-ranians find Ya'fur, then maybe their Mahdi gets to be the one. So as Christians, Pastor Steve says we have a duty to be the ones to find Ya'fur and keep him ready for Jesus. Hidden in a secret place, needless to say. Like maybe here on my farm."

"And that's why you started the Donkey Genome Project? To look at DNA samples of all the likely donkeys and see which ones aren't normal?"

"You got that right. Christine's idea. Everything on the up and up. We pay good money for them samples. But we gotta keep a low profile about who we are and why we're collectin' samples so when we do find Ya'fur and bring him to the farm, no one else will know where to find him. Bunch of J.M.'s marine buddies, good church-goers every one, doin' the collection work."

"Do you know about the Iranians who are doing the same thing, the Three-Thirteen?"

"Not a whole lot. But we see them as an opposin' team so we keep track of 'em. Even had a run-in with a few a coupla weeks back."

"What if the Jews find Ya'fur first? Another opposing team?"

"You talkin' about the Mossad? That Israeli secret service? Yeah, we heard about them too from some of our rabbi friends. Would you believe there are some rabbis who like us better'n they like the Israel government? Frankly, what they tell us about the Mossad isn't much. Seems there's a possibility that the Mossad is workin' with the Three-Thirteen, but we don't know why. Nevertheless, be that as it may, since we're talkin' about the Messiah and the end of the world and all, it stands to reason that someone's gonna take home all the marbles. Pastor Steve, me, and J.M. and his buddies are set on Team Jesus bein' the winnin' side."

"This is all so very interesting. I just have two last questions. Why did you look at donkeys in England, of all places? And have you found Ya'fur?"

"Superior intelligence gatherin' answers the first question," says J.M. "We got boys in the service in Iraq that acquired some confidential information from a Three-Thirteen Eye-ranian. Got it the hard way, but I won't go into any unappetizin' details. He said Eye-ran has some sort of guru who's had a vision of Ya'fur surrounded by people talkin' English. Given where the world's donkeys are, this don't seem to make much sense. But on the other hand, those donkey homes in England have collected livestock from all over the Middle East and North Africa and the islands in the Mediterranean. So as soon as Pastor Steve learned that the Three-Thirteen were headed for England, he told us to get on our horses and go there too. Turned out, we got there first 'cause we didn't have to wait for visas. As for the second question about the Ya'fur, the answer so far is no, we don't know just where it is."

Ray Bob reenters the conversation. "Fact is, Mr. Constantine, finding the Ya'fur is what we expect you to help us with. We just been waitin' for you to show up. Expected you yesterday, but I guess you got a late start."

"What are you talking about?" says Constantine anxiously. "I don't know anything about any donkey. Everything you've told me has been news to my ears." He glances toward the exit. "But my goodness, Ray Bob, J.M., this has been just fascinating, and the food was out of this world." He rises from his seat.

"You bet it was fascinatin'," says Ray Bob rising with him. "You asked your questions, and we answered every one of them completely honestly. However, as the man says, if I tell you exactly what you want to know, then I might have to kill you."

"Come again?"

"Just foolin' with you, Mr. Constantine."

J.M. pushes a grim face forward. "Or should Papa say: Professor Paul Constantine, who's writin' a whole book about Ya'fur? I told you about our superior intelligence operation. Well, we know who you are, we've read your book, and we scouted you out up there at Harvard. Now we'd like your help, and we're pretty sure we have ways to get you to give it."

"Don't put it that way, son. You're scarin' the man. What J.M. is tryin' to say is that we're gonna insist that you and your colored gal stay down here as our guests until we got Ya'fur safely stowed away. And as J.M. says, Pastor Steve is expectin' a whole lot of cooperation from you in that endeavor."

Constantine casts a panicky glance through the glass door into the parking lot. Baleine is standing beside the Lincoln Town Car. The expression on her face reads murder, but her hands are clasped on top of her shiny lacquered hairdo while two young men standing at a safe distance keep rifles trained on her.

Hope drains from Constantine's heart at the sight of Baleine defanged. "Will we be guests at your house, Ray Bob? Or should we stay in our motel? We wouldn't want to be a burden."

"In your motel to start with. We got plannin' to do, and my house ain't very soundproof."

"I only have reservations for two nights. Will that be enough?"

"I don't expect it will, but we can take care of that. The manager belongs to Pastor Steve's congregation so I'm pretty sure he'll agree to turn off the phones in your rooms to guarantee your privacy. And of course we'll have to impound your computers and cell-phones."

Ray Bob has Constantine's elbow fixed in a tight grip and is walking him out the door. "Y'all come back again," calls the waitress. J.M. stops at the register to pay the check. Constantine and Ray Bob step out into the sunshine.

"I'm disappointed you didn't ask about one thing," says Ray Bob.

"What's that?"

"The beast the Antichrist rides on, which the Moslems are probably right in thinkin' is a donkey rather than a dragon like in Revelation. J.M. give you hint when he mention the symbols. You see, what Pastor Steve thinks is that that evil donkey has already put the Antichrist in power. And that's how we know Jesus is about to return. The evil donkey is the Democrat Party, and Barack Hossein Obama is the Antichrist. What do you think of that?"

The Plot Thickens

CIA headquarters, Langley, Virginia: Jessie Zayyat on home leave to recharge her batteries and get her head back on the right track is talking to the secretarial assistant to the Deputy Chief of Operations. "Sir, do you know when I might expect a report from NSA on international telephone and e-mail traffic containing the keywords Ya'fur and Ufair and the number 313?"

He looks at her with sincere concern. "Soon."

"I filed the request a week ago. It should be here by now."

"We've had organizational changes since you were last stationed here, Jessie. Queries don't go directly to NSA any more. They now go to OIAF, the Office of Inter-Agency Facilitation. It's important to keep close track of what agency is doing what. In your particular case, since the words were not already on the NSA list of terrorist watchwords, the OIAF had to get authorization from WANAB. That's also new. It stands for Words and Names Authorization Board. They run requests past a federal judge to make sure that national security concerns outweigh possible impositions on the freedom of speech of American citizens. As we scale up the War on Terror, it's important to make our lines of authority and reporting clearer than they used to be."

"You're saying we're doing our job better now?"

"Not only better but also four percent faster according to the trend-lines in this month's Homeland Security Efficiency Survey."

"Thank you, sir. I just want to connect the dots."

"As do we all, Jessie. I'm sure you'll get the information soon. In the meantime, I can tell you that some of the higher-ups have noticed your good work. That Yafouri you nabbed began to talk after his first week at Bagram. He's already mentioned the operational names of the three top al-Qaeda chiefs in Yemen. New stuff we haven't had before. They're drilling down now for more."

"What were the names?"

"I shouldn't tell you without filing an NTK form …"

"NTK?"

"Need to Know. But since you were part of the operation that landed him and you did some of the interrogation yourself, I think I can break protocol and tell you. The names are Abu Kalb, Abu Kinzer, and Abu Himar."

Jessie digests the intelligence. "Sir, has anyone considered that the names might be fake? In Arabic Abu Kalb means Father of a Dog; Abu Khinzir, which I assume is what you're pronouncing Kinzer, means Father of a Pig; and Abu Himar means Father of a Donkey."

"It'll all be checked out, Jessie. It's probably significant, though, that they're consistently using animal names."

An hour later a message from the National Security Agency shows up on Jessie's computer informing her that all international communications over the past ten months involving the words Ya'fur and Ufair have been directed to the same personage, a Professor Paul Constantine at Harvard University. A few keystrokes and up pops Constantine's Wikipedia entry. *Lots of donkeys*, thinks Jessie. A sixteen-character password and a few more keystrokes and she is examining his bank and credit card activity. She does a search on an unusual name. *Hmm. Why would a Harvard professor hire a private investigator?* She e-files a Local

Police Contact Form and twiddles her thumbs for twenty minutes until approval comes through from her section's LPC officer.

"Hello? Am I speaking with the Boston Police Homeland Security liaison office? My name is Jessie Zayyat ... yes, I'm keying in my password now ... Okay? I need any information that might have come to your department over the past month about a professor at Harvard named Paul Constantine and a private investigator named Baleine Tontonmacoute. I assume that's a professional name and not a real name ... no, not Paul Constantine, Baleine Tontonmacoute." Jessie waits, listens, waits some more, listens some more. "Why would a woman detective pick a first name that means Whale? ... I see, she's big ... and the last name is the name of the terror squads that worked for Papa Doc Duvalier in Haiti ... I see, she's Haitian and she's scary. What about her qualities as a private investigator? What sort of jobs does she do?"

The words "best in Boston" run repeatedly through Jessie's mind as she begins to read a series of e-mails containing the words Ya'fur and Ufair. Why does a donkey specialist need a top-notch private investigator? Two hours later Jessie has discovered the answer.

*   *   *

Toots puts a medium size stone in a Ziploc bag left from her lunch and throws it into the water. She scratches the time, tide level, and wind direction onto the formica desktop she is using to keep her log. She watches the movement of the bobbing bubble of plastic for an hour. Once again, no indication of a current that might float her to Venice or one of the built up islands she can see in the distance. What she needs is a strong northeast wind, an incoming tide, and enough daylight to see where she needs to go once she reaches paddling distance.

She finishes another gallon of water and recaps the plastic bottle. She looks to make sure the man who takes videos of her is not approaching the island and pulls her concealing black raincoat back from her raft, a six-by-four-foot sheet of slightly bent aluminum with plastic bottles wired to its bottom through screw holes in its edges. Seven more bottles and she should have the buoyancy she needs to make her escape. Then she's going after that asshole J.M..

*   *   *

Paul Constantine and Pastor Steve are sitting by themselves in Ray Bob's living room. "I know you told Ray Bob and J.M. you couldn't help them find Ya'fur, Paul, but I don't think that's quite true."

"It's absolutely true. You know me, Steve …"

"Pastor Steve."

"Okay. Pastor Steve. You know me. You heard my lecture when we were at the Hydra conference. I'm just an old fart collector of donkey lore. I live in an ivory tower. Even if there were a Ya'fur in the real world, that's a world I know nothing about."

"So you don't think Ya'fur is real? Remember, we've all read the chapters of your book."

"I just made up what's in the book because it fit the lore and was fun to write. Do I really believe there's an immortal talking donkey somewhere that's going to bear the Messiah into Jerusalem? No, I absolutely do not. My book is just spinning a legend. It's like a novel."

"That doesn't mean that other people don't believe what you write, Paul. What would you think, for example, if I told you that I and Ray Bob and our whole congregation are as sure that the Ya'fur is real as we are that every word in the Bible is true?"

"Because you're holding me prisoner, Pastor Steve, I'll just say that you are misguided if you believe that. And whoever had the idea of using DNA to identify a special donkey was misguided too."

Pastor Steve looks peeved. "Let me put it differently. What would you say if you heard that Monika Farber—I'm sure you remember her—has a graduate student who actually heard a donkey talk when he was in Morocco. Would you say Farber is misguided?"

"I don't know if I would or not. Farber may be too nasty to be misguided, and I don't think she has any religious feelings at all. So I guess if she's really saying something like that, she's probably doing it to dominate some poor religious cluck she wants to humiliate. Or else maybe her student is nuts."

"Do you think it's likely that Farber would be taken in by a nutty student?"

Constantine considers the question. "No. She's the one who takes people in. Who has she told the story about her graduate student to?"

"President Ahmadinejad of Iran."

"You're joking."

"No. It's God's truth. We've confirmed that the student is real. His name is Fritz Messiassohn, and he did spend time in Morocco. And we also know that Ahmadinejad's agents almost got their hands on him in Venice. But the police intervened."

"I presume those are the agents called the Three-Thirteen. I talked to some of them during a trip to Scotland."

"So you do know what's going on in the real world."

"I know the Three-Thirteen are your rivals in collecting donkey DNA samples. At least that's what they told me. But I didn't know that Farber had anything to do with them."

"Now you do."

"Then tell me, Steve … Pastor Steve, if you believe this German student has really heard the Ya'fur animal talk and knows where he is, why didn't you kidnap him yourself? Isn't that part of J.M.'s job description,"

"Truth us, we were a step too late. We didn't know enough then about who Fritz was so we picked up his girlfriend instead."

Constantine sits up in his chair. "You picked up his girlfriend? Toots? Toots Greeley? You kidnapped her? You bastards. She's a very sweet girl, and her father is desperate to find her."

"So I found out from reading your e-mail."

"You've been reading my e-mail? You, a so-called man of the cloth? That's totally immoral and illegal."

"You seem to forget I did prison time before I became a minister. And you should have given more thought to keeping your affairs private when you decided to use your last name as your password. It took Ray Bob less than three minutes to figure it out. Ray Bob, of all people. You should take lessons from that black girl who drives for you. Ray Bob says that everything on her computer is deeply encrypted. Even Christine couldn't figure out how to get into her files."

"Her name is Baleine. She believes in voodoo."

"Does that tell us how to read her files?"

"I'm just saying."

"Forget it. She's not important. Let's get back to your e-mail. This morning you got a most interesting message from an old acquaintance we both made at Hydra."

"Not Farber."

"No. The Rabbi. Here's a print-out of it."

Dear Professor Constantine,

You may not remember me. We met a few years ago at the ass conference on Hydra. I was the specialist on Jewish ass lore. I am writing you now because of a most unusual situation that has arisen. It involves what on one memorable evening you called the one-donkey solution to the problem of competing Messiahs. There is a possibility that as silly and impossible as your theory unquestionably is, it might be true that a single messianic ass exists. Whether it is or not, our intelligence sources tell us that the Iranian government has become convinced that there is such an animal and has launched an operation to capture it in Morocco. If they succeed in this, or even if they only believe they have succeeded, some analysts in my country fear that they will then claim that their Mahdi is about to return and use that as an excuse to attack Israel with nuclear weapons. The same analysts maintain that even ordinary Iranians are religious fanatics and Jew-haters who need only a spark to ignite a new Holocaust.

The reason I am writing you about this is twofold. First, I have heard about the book you are writing about the Ya'fur and I would like to read it. It may have some clues that will help us resolve this mess. Secondly, through the help of some international friends we now have in our custody the one person who claims to have heard a donkey talk. He is a German, and he encountered the donkey in Morocco. He heard about your book from his girlfriend, who is the daughter of the Mr. Greeley who was with us on Hydra. Her name is Victoria, but she goes by Toots. The German says you know her, and he is eager to find out where she is and to be put in contact with her. So if you have any information on this score, please let me know. The German's cooperation seems to depend on his receiving reassurance on this matter.

With all good wishes.

The Rabbi

"Do you see where this is headed, Paul? We have Toots, and we know that you know that because you got a video from her father showing her stranded on an island somewhere."

"How do I know that the video you saw on my e-mail didn't give you the idea of saying you have Toots? How do I know you really have her?"

Pastor Steve pulls a small box big enough to hold a finger out of his pocket. Constantine tenses as he teases it open. Nested in cotton is a magenta-and-black checked acrylic fingernail. "Proof enough for you? Or do you need a whole finger?"

"Oh my God! And Fritz?"

"You'll just have to take the Rabbi's word for it that the Israelis have Fritz. As for Farber, she's working with the Iranians. Logically what's going to happen is that both the Three-Thirteen and the Mossad will go to Morocco to find the Ya'fur. Which leaves us Christians out. And that's no good. So the better plan is for you to write to the Rabbi and offer to trade the Greeley girl for Fritz. We'll have J.M. and his boys take her to Morocco, and they can make the trade there. Once we get Fritz, we'll have the upper hand in finding Jesus's donkey."

"You don't really think that getting your hands on that donkey will persuade God to send Jesus back, do you? The Iranians may be that simple-minded, but good Christians like yourself should have more sense."

Pastor Steve slaps his knee. "I remembered you were sharp, Paul. You got that just right. Let those Iranians think what they like about what might happen if they get hold of the Ya'fur. My plan is a little different."

"In what way?"

"You should be able to figure it out from your own book. Were Abraham and Moses and Muhammad Messiahs?"

"No, they were men who had visions of God."

"Let's call them prophets for short."

"All right."

"And how many evangelical preachers today talk about having visions of God?"

"I don't know. A lot probably."

"A whole lot. So what do you think will happen when we get hold of Ya'fur? Jesus hotfooting it to North Carolina to pick up his donkey before going to Jerusalem is a long shot. But my wife Christine knows everything there is to know about cloning. In point of fact, a mule already has been cloned. Happened back in 2003. Its name was Idaho Gem. You can go back and read about it in *Science* magazine."

"You're going to clone Ya'fur?"

"Christine is. Then we're going to let a chosen few preachers know about how we've got a clone of Abraham's donkey. You have any idea what that will be worth? No preacher worth his salt is going to be able to compete without having one of our donkeys."

A feeling of outrage grows in Constantine's chest. "You're going to use Ya'fur just to make money?"

"Don't act so shocked. You're not a religious man."

"No, but you're supposed to be."

"Religion and politics are just two more ways of getting what you want, Paul. Found that out in prison. I want money, always have."

"Do Ray Bob and J.M. know about your plan?"

"No, and they wouldn't believe you if you told them about it. After Christine takes the cells she needs for the cloning, they'll keep the real Ya'fur here on the farm and never know what's going on in the lab. Couple of years pass, we start selling Ya'furs to some of the megachurch preachers, Ray Bob and J.M. won't know a thing about it. A faithful congregation is like a state legislature. It only raises questions about what the executive branch is doing when the newspapers rake up some corruption story."

"Is that why you ended up in jail?"

"My first wife ratted me out to a reporter. I'll tell you the story sometime. But for now we're going to work together."

"Other than writing to the Rabbi and proposing a swap of Fritz for Toots, what else do you expect me to do?"

"That should be obvious. You're going to write a chapter in your book about how every true man of God has been elevated by connecting with Ya'fur. There's got to be a lot of examples you haven't talked about." Examples come flooding into Constantine's mind. "You stay on down here until you finish the book. Then I'll see to it that it gets published a few months before the first Ya'furs go on the market. It being written by a Harvard professor who's not even religious himself will make it sell like hotcakes."

Outrage courses through every fiber of Constantine's professional being.

"And you can have a hundred percent of the royalties because my return will come from selling the animals."

His outrage is suddenly on hold. "Royalties?"

"Hell, Paul. I can do better than that. You can have one hundred percent of whatever the book earns in excess of the cost of printing, paper, and binding."

Constantine's fibers stop quivering. "I can't work in a motel."

"No one expects you to. Once we become partners, you'll move here to Ray Bob's house. There's plenty of room."

"Can my driver go back to Cambridge? She costs me an awful lot."

"Can't allow that. There's no telling who she might talk to. But she can stay here in the house too, and I'll see to it that she gets paid."

BALEINE WRITES

"Rabbi, is Professor Constantine a good man or a bad man?"

"What do you mean?"

"I mean, is he the sort of man who really cares about whether an innocent woman who came to him for help lives or dies?"

"I don't think I can answer that, Fritz. I only knew him for a few days at a conference. What I remember is that he's pompous, pedantic, vain, and self-absorbed. But that describes a lot of older professors. Whether it reflects his inner philosophy is hard to say."

"Let me put it differently. This is a man who has just written to you to say that he's being kept under a kind of house arrest by crazy evangelical Protestants who are holding Toots prisoner on an island somewhere. He says they want to exchange her for me so I can identify for them the donkey I heard talking in Morocco. And on the basis of what he's written, without a shred of corroborating evidence, you've come up with this plan to fly me and your Frisbee target Ariel to Morocco where we're supposed to make the exchange in some tricky way you haven't determined yet."

"The details of the exchange are Ariel's job."

"And the kicker is that this mission is supposed to end up with you and not the Protestants getting the donkey."

"That's the best case scenario. But the plan is a work in progress. I hadn't expected the evangelicals to be involved, but we can be flexible. Ariel's a master of flexibility. You do want to rescue Toots, don't you? If not, we can forget about the Protestants and just go for the donkey."

"Rescuing Toots means more to me than anything."

"Then it does for us, too."

"Am I supposed to believe that? So far as I can see, the payoff for you comes when I identify the damn donkey, and you can steal it or buy it. This whole Toots story could just be made up."

"Not by me. You read Constantine's e-mail. But I guess what you're asking is not whether Constantine is a good man or a bad man, but whether I am a good man or a bad man."

"Maybe. Personally, I couldn't care less who gets the donkey. I just want to save Toots. I owe her that. But what if we get to Morocco and there's no Toots?"

"Then you don't have to find the donkey. No Toots, no donkey. You're the only person who can hear the animal talk. No one can trick you on that."

"Except the old man. He talks to the donkey."

"The old man will be out of the way. That's part of Ariel's job."

"So I could just point to any old donkey and say that that's the one?"

"I don't think so. If Ya'fur exists, the Iranians and the evangelicals are probably right that its DNA is different from other donkeys. So once the evangelicals release Toots and you gratefully identify a donkey for them, they're likely to keep you close while they send a tissue sample back to their lab and get confirmation that it's a breed apart. Constantine said they have a good DNA facility there in North Carolina. That means that if you lie about the donkey, as you will have to do since you're giving the real Ya'fur to us, you'll just have to find a way to get free of them before the report comes back from North Carolina."

"Do you think I can count on Constantine helping me out over there?"

"I would guess not. Tenured professors at fancy universities are not known for being other-directed. Even if he could help you, I think he would only do it if his personal interest were involved."

"How about your friends in the Mossad. Can't they rescue me if I get in trouble?"

"Alas, no. I'm not even telling them about your mission. Just as Ariel gives us a channel into certain Iranian intelligence secrets, the American evangelicals have moles in Israeli intelligence. Any sign that we're out to get Ya'fur for ourselves, they'll put the word out. If a few key senators start fretting that the Jews are stealing Jesus' donkey, our political support in the United States will take a hit. We can't afford that. Israel can do anything it wants to Arabs, even Christian Arabs, but American Christians are off limits. They would go ballistic. We've spent centuries beating back propaganda attacks by anti-Semites, and I'm not going to give the Jew-haters grounds for a new attack."

"Even though you do in fact plan to steal Jesus' donkey."

"That's my personal goal. But as you said, who ends up with Ya'fur is not your concern so long as you get your Toots back. In this matter, Ariel is acting as my personal agent. Not as a member of the Mossad."

"Are Ariel's loyalties as slippery as they seem?"

"He's a remarkable young man. We call him the chameleon. He is whatever he needs to be wherever and whenever a situation arises."

"Is this supposed to encourage me?"

"His obligation to you is to free your girlfriend. That's all."

"I heard you use the phrase 'no-donkey solution' when you were talking to Ariel. What does that mean?"

"You must have misheard. If there is a Ya'fur out there somewhere, it must be immortal. So there can never be a no-donkey solution."

*   *   *

Baleine is standing at the door of Paul Constantine's bedroom in the house at Krumlake Farm. "Time for you to talk to Baleine. We were in that ratty motel, and now we have nice bedrooms here in Ray Bob's big house. What's going on?"

"I had a talk with Pastor Steve, Baleine. He is a dedicated Christian and took pity on us. He told Ray Bob that we should henceforward be treated as guests rather than as prisoners."

"Even though our car and cell-phones are gone."

"That's just temporary."

"Is my computer being gone temporary too? I see yours on that dressing table. How did you get it back?"

"I explained to Pastor Steve that I need my computer for some writing I'll be doing. I told him he and Ray Bob could continue to monitor my e-mail. You don't need your computer."

"Don't you tell Baleine what Baleine needs." She fixes the professor with a baleful eye. "Something's not right here. Tell me you sent the e-mail to Mr. Greeley telling him where his daughter is."

Constantine hesitates. "To be absolutely truthful, I forgot. That strawberry shortcake I was eating pushed the idea right out of my mind. When I finally did remember, Ray Bob had already taken our computers away. Besides, it was only a guess."

Baleine's gaze becomes a sulphurous glare and she suddenly appears to expand in height and girth until her wrathful form completely fills Constantine's visual space. "Baleine's guesses are never wrong. But despite her lifetime of experience, Baleine does sometimes fall for old white guy tricks. So Baleine is asking you now, under pain of her transforming from your bodyguard to your worst nightmare, are you a good old white guy or a bad old white guy?"

Constantine trembles from his voicebox to his toes. "I'm a good old white guy, of course," he says weakly.

"And are you committed to rescuing Toots from these crazy crackers?"

"If I can."

Baleine scrutinizes his cowering form. "Fine. I accept that for now."

"You do?"

"I do. But from now on Baleine has her eye on you. Besides, I want you to read something I wrote the morning we came here while you were dawdling over your toilet. You'll find it on your computer in the folder with your book chapters. It's a chapter for you to add to your book."

"What's the file name?"

"It's called 'The Black Ass of Baron Samedi'."

ThE BLACK ASS OF BARON SAMEDI

It was a dark and stormy night. The times they were Roman. A ship smashes to bits on the rocky coast of Greece, and a handsome young African slave named Lucius is the only survivor. When he recovers his strength, he makes his way to a nearby home where a buxom maid named Xena gives him bread and wine and makes him a pallet on the floor.

In the afterglow of an evening of lovemaking, Xena tells him that the mistress of the house is a witch and a shape-changer. Lucius is intrigued and persuades Xena to hide him where he can see into the witch's room. While he watches, the witch comes in and opens a window. She extracts a small vial from a jeweled chest on the mantel and drinks from it. An owl promptly soars into the room on silent wings. It alights softly on the witch's arm. In the blink of an eye the witch is absorbed into the shape of the owl and they fly off as one into the night.

Lucius sits tight in his hiding place until nearly daybreak when the owl returns. It snips a rose blossom from a vase of flowers with its beak and eats it. Instantly the witch reemerges from the body of the owl and the bird flies off. Lucius feels his heart surge. Having been captured by Libyan slavers and kept chained for weeks on his way to a slave market, he longs to fly free like a bird.

When the witch leaves the house the next day, he enters her room and takes the vial from the chest. As soon as he drinks from it, he hears a clattering noise at the door. He opens it and is surprised to see a black donkey.

"I was expecting an owl," says Lucius.

"The witch is from Athens, and the owl belongs to Athena. But you, Lucius, are from Africa, not from Greece. Your animal must be an African animal. So here I am. I am the black ass of Baron Samedi, whom the Egyptians call Set."

"Do you have a name?"

"My name is Ufair. You will keep your name after you get on my back, but otherwise we will be as one."

Apprehensively, but with a tingling of hope, Lucius straddles the black donkey's back. Instantly he feels his body being absorbed into the donkey's shape. His mind now senses the mind of Ufair as if they are more-than-identical twins. While he is pondering his new situation and wondering whether to avail himself immediately of the nearby bouquet of roses, a racket arises in the courtyard. Screams and the clanging of swordplay reach his large and acutely sensitive ears. Moments later a band of robbers bursts into the house. Though sensing that Ufair is unconcerned, Lucius sees corpses sprawled outside the door and fears the worst. He brays loudly in alarm.

His fear is allayed, however, when he finds that the robbers count themselves lucky to have found a donkey to carry away the loot they are ransacking the house to collect. So off Lucius goes, in the guise of Ufair, to become the beast of burden of the robber band.

The following days are filled with thieving and murder. Never having known white people during his childhood, Lucius is amazed at their villainy. He resolves to escape, and soon an opportunity presents itself when he is left alone with the slatternly woman who cooks and cleans for the robbers. No realizing that the donkey can understand her, she exclaims aloud that since black donkeys are the best of all lovers, she intends to avail herself of his presence. When she removes her clothes and teasingly approaches Lucius with a rope and halter, he brays loudly and charges past her out of the hideout.

Once he has put a safe distance between himself and the lustful woman, he stops to recover his composure. Then he hears the voice of Ufair inside his head. "You must not be concerned, Lucius. All white people feel sexual longings for black donkeys. But that is their problem, not yours. Your problem is that they treat black donkeys as lowly animals and beat and kill them."

"What am I to do?" replies Lucius. "If I stay a donkey, they will beat me and kill me. But if I eat roses and regain my human form, they will put chains on me and make me a slave."

"All that would be true if you were not in the company of Baron Samedi's black ass. My hoity-toity brother Ya'fur would ignore you entirely since he has become famous for bringing religious exaltation to white people. But Ufair spells the downfall of white people. He strips away their illusions and makes them see their injustice in their treatment of dark people. When they realize the truth, it is something they cannot bear."

"I didn't see you revealing any truth to those robbers. Their woman would have had her way with me."

"Have patience, Lucius. First I want you to see what the world is really like."

The next morning a band of priests with shaven heads comes walking along the road carrying a large wooden statue of a goddess. "What's this?" says the head priest when he notices Lucius. "A donkey with no owner about? What say you, lads, about acquiring this animal to carry the Virgin Queen of Heaven?" The others enthusiastically second the head priest's proposal, and soon Lucius is being led down the road with the garishly painted statue strapped to his back.

Presently they come to a village. One priest produces a double flute, another a drum. The rest begin a frenzied dance. They whirl and stomp and howl the holy name of their Virgin Queen of Heaven. At the climax of their ritual several of them flourish knives from beneath their robes and slash their arms and legs. The villagers that have gathered to watch the performance are awestruck by the pounding music, the flowing blood, and the priests' climactic screams. When the head priest passes among them with a bronze bowl, they freely toss in coins and receive an orotund prayer in return.

Back at their camp, Lucius watches the slashed priests bind up one another's cuts and curse their wooden goddess in no uncertain terms. But when the head priest returns from a trip into town for food and wine, their bad spirits give way to carousing. And then to fornication as the priests drunkenly strip off their robes and join together in every sort of sexual act. Wary from his experience with the robbers' woman, Lucius keeps his distance from the priests' orgy. Yet eventually he sees their lascivious gazes turn in his direction. "Not again," he thinks. But soon there is no doubt. As scarred and bandaged arms reach out for him, he edges backward and then bolts from the camp.

"Once again you didn't do anything to protect me, Ufair," says Lucius when he is safely away.

"Have patience," says Ufair.

The next person to claim the services of a wandering donkey is a caterer named Plato. He and his brother Socrates furnish banquets for the rich families of the city and put Lucius to work carrying great baskets of food and drink. To make sure his business is profitable, Plato keeps a careful count of everything that is prepared. Unfortunately for Lucius, this gimlet-eyed scrutiny soon detects that the donkey has been snacking on the hors d'oeuvres. Ufair has sternly advised Lucius to quell his human tastes and satisfy himself with grass and straw, but Lucius is so homesick for human form that he cannot resist a tray of baked cheese puffs and another of stuffed mushrooms.

Though chagrined at being found out, Lucius is pleased to discover that his un-asinine tastes amuse the brothers. They inform their wealthiest patron, Pericles, and he insists on inviting Lucius to a banquet as part of the entertainment. Though Lucius feels out of place reclining at table with the rest of the guests, he very much enjoys the food and wine. Ufair's voice in his head says, "Do not be distracted, Lucius. Notice how unkindly the guests are treating the servants. Look in particular at how they are goading and humiliating Pericles' African slave."

Lucius takes note of everything Ufair tells him, and is momentarily distressed to see the African woman stripped of her clothing. But he cannot focus fully on these petty cruelties because a beautiful woman named Sappho, the sister-in-law of the host, keeps tweaking him in a private place and giving him sneak peeks at her own private places.

In the days that follow, against Ufair's repeated advice, Lucius and Sappho become lovers. Lucius, who has not yet learned to fancy female donkeys, is thrilled to bring a long sexual fast to an end. Sappho is similarly thrilled to bring something long to her end.

Alas, news of their torrid affair leaks out. Just as Pericles had been amused by the idea of inviting a donkey to a banquet, now he is amused by the idea of a donkey mating with his oversexed sister-in-law. To turn his private amusement into a riotous spectacle, he offers to stage a gala public event. Lucius will parade into the arena to great fanfare and meet with an African slave woman at a bed in its center. There they will engage in sexual intercourse, and at the moment of climax, executioners will step forward and cut off the heads of both fornicators. Pericles is sure that people will talk about such a show for years to come.

When Ufair tells Lucius that he is slated to spend his last humiliating moments as a public spectacle, Lucius again berates him for not using the powers he has claimed to have. "Have patience," says Ufair.

The day comes. Lucius is tugged through the gate of the arena by a rope tied around his neck. Jeering citizens pack the stands. Before him he sees the frightened slave, who is exposed naked except for a garland of roses around her neck. Seeing a glimmer of hope, Lucius trots forward boldly to the raucous applause of the crowd, which misinterprets his sudden enthusiasm.

As soon as he gets to the woman, he extends his muzzle and bites off a rose. Instantaneously he feels his body begin to separate from the donkey form of Ufair. Moments later he stands proudly forth as a man … but a naked black man surrounded by hundreds of onlookers. A voice in the crowd screams, "He's a wizard! Stone him! Stone them both!" Other voices take up the cry.

"Now is the time," says Ufair in a voice that only Lucius can hear. "Now I lift the veil from their eyes and make them realize that they are about to stage a beastly public murder of two innocent Africans. Guilt will destroy them as it did Sodom and Gomorrah."

As he speaks, cries of dismay begin to be heard in the crowd. Some people sob and tear their hair. Some prayerfully fall to their knees to seek forgiveness. Some pummel themselves with their fists. Some become deranged by the confrontation with their own evil thoughts and attack their neighbors. Chaos spreads. People flee and are trampled. The city poises on the brink of self-destruction.

Amidst the pandemonium, no one notices Lucius and the slave woman don clothes and exit the arena riding on Ufair. A ship captain, barely able to contain his guilty sobs, comes up to Lucius and the woman and offers to return them to Africa. As they are leaving to follow him to the port, Ufair speaks to Lucius one last time.

"My brother Ya'fur brings tears of gladness to the eyes of the faithful—so long as they are faithful to a religion he approves. I bring tears of anguish to the unjust oppressors of the world's downtrodden, regardless of their religion. So which of us is the good donkey, and which the bad?"

UFAIR

Paul Constantine has his feet up on the verandah railing and is tilted back in a rocker when he finishes reading Baleine's story. He stares off at a stand of hickory trees beside the gravel drive. The heavy air is hot but bearable. Cicadas are buzzing. Presently Ray Bob steps through the screen door to join him. He holds the door open for a brightly smiling Baleine who is following him with three glasses of lemonade on a tray. Ray Bob settles himself in the neighboring rocker. Baleine sits demurely nearby on a straight chair.

"Professor, I want to thank you for bringin' Marie here to visit me. Fine young woman. Tells me she was raised in Haiti and learned a special kind of aromatherapy practiced by old voodoo women. She gave me one of those inhaler things a coupla hours ago supposed to give me energy and I feel just great. She also guessed that my weight problem is mostly portion control so she's startin' me on a different inhaler to reduce my appetite."

"What's in the inhaler?" asks Constantine.

"For appetite control," replies Baleine sweetly, "it's the essential oils of lemon, which reduces acidity; orange, which calms the stomach; bergamot, which regulates appetite; patchouli, which brings peace and acceptance; ylang ylang, which eases anxiety; and a special Haitian ingredient that my teachers won't permit me to divulge. You take a deep breath, exhale it all, and then put the inhaler deep in your nostril and take three deep breaths in a row while pressing the button on the bottom. Repeat for the other nostril."

"How come you don't know about this, Professor?"

Baleine smiles sweetly. "Why, I never told him about my aromatherapy, Mr. Ray Bob. The limousine agency I work for doesn't permit me to conduct any business with clients except driving. I'm not even allowed to mention my other occupation or hand out business cards."

"Well, that's a damn shame, Marie. If you don't mind me sayin'. The Professor here tells me he's like me, has trouble stayin' asleep and gets up in the night to sit in a chair. He could use that sound-sleep inhaler you're fixin' to give me."

"Why maybe he could." Baleine emits an improbably girlish laugh. "But don't nobody tell the limousine company that it was my idea."

"What's in the insomnia cure, Bal ... Marie?"

"Well now that you ask—and I wasn't the one who brought the subject up, mind you—I'll tell you. It has rosemary to encourage deep breathing, comfort, and balance; lavender, which calms, refreshes, and relaxes; vetiver to reduce mental hyperactivity; chamomile for deep comfort; and two special Haitian ingredients. What my teacher says is: 'When you breathe in lavender, vetiver, rosemary and chamomile, your breath deepens, your eyes feel heavy, and your thoughts drift away to a dreamy world of comfort and renewal.'"

"Amazing. To think we've spent so much time together on this trip, and I never knew."

Baleine takes a sip of her lemonade. "Marie doesn't boast about her accomplishments."

*　　*　　*

"All right," says Constantine when Ray Bob eventually leaves them alone on the verandah. "Much as I want you to tell me what's going on with your so-called aromatherapy ..."

"I don't know what you're talking about. Everything Marie says is true."

"... I'd rather we discuss your black donkey story. To begin with, it's ridiculous. Apuleius' and Lucian's stories are classics: witty ribald stories about metamorphosis, a human turning into an animal. Metamorphosis was a very popular concept in ancient times. But in your parody, Lucius doesn't turn into an ass, he merges with an ass. You missed the whole point."

Baleine's scowl has returned. "He doesn't merge with an ass. He merges with Ufair, who for some reason you decided to barely mention in the chapters you wrote."

"That's because Ufair is unimportant in the sources I relied on. That's the difference between what you wrote and what I wrote. I had sources. You're just making up a story."

"If Ufair is so unimportant and doesn't show up in what you call sources, why is he in the book at all? I've heard you go on about your three-donkey solution and your one-donkey solution, but in your own story you have two donkeys."

"It's because of the evil Dajjal. The Muslim version of the Antichrist rides on a donkey. That *is* in the sources. But so does the good person who kills the Dajjal, either the Mahdi or Jesus depending on which version of the story you follow. He fights with him and runs him through with a spear. So there we have two donkeys on the cosmic stage at the same time."

"In that case, you should say something about the other donkey. But you don't."

"I don't because I can't. The stories in the sources are too absurd. The donkey of the Messiah, which I'm calling Ya'fur, acts just like a donkey. But according to Muslim tradition, the Dajjal will come riding on a donkey that has a distance of a mile between its two ears. Or in another version the Dajjal's animal will be a huge white donkey that can cover a mile in a single stride. If I put stories like that in the book, it will reduce the whole thing to fairy tales."

"As if it isn't already. Do the Jews and the Christians have the same bad donkey?"

"No. If they did, I wouldn't have a problem. Jewish legend talks about an evil person named Armillus, who is supposed to conquer Jerusalem and persecute the Jews until the true Messiah defeats him. But no donkey. Unless the story of Armillus being the offspring of Satan and a virgin connects him with Set. But it's more likely that that's an anti-Christian reference to the image of Jesus as the offspring of Satan and a virgin. As for the Christians, they have a whole raft of beasts and dragons in Revelation, but no donkey. The most sober text about the Antichrist is in Paul's Epistle to the Thessalonians where he is described as a 'man of sin' who will sit in the temple of God as if he were God and work signs and perform lying wonders by the power of Satan until the coming of Lord Jesus kills him. Again, no donkey."

"So Ufair is just there for the Muslims."

Constantine reflects. "For the Muslims, yes. But also for balance. Good donkey, bad donkey."

"The good donkey that the nice white people who expect to be saved believe in being humble and normal, like a real donkey, and the bad donkey being a monster."

"Yes, you could say that. Non-Semitic sacred donkeys do tend to be monsters. Take the Zoroastrians. In their tradition there's a good donkey that's as big as a mountain and has three legs, six eyes, one horn, and nine testicles. And the Tibetan Buddhists believe in a ghastly blue goddess named Palden Lhamo, who protects the Dalai Lama. She looks horrible, drinks blood from a skull, and had a saddle made from her son's skin after she killed him. She rides on a donkey. The Tibetans also have a less solid tradition that the ferociously anti-Buddhist king Langdarma was the reincarnation of a donkey who felt that his noble owners had neglected it."

"You do know the most worthless shit, don't you?"

"Wait. I'm not done with the Buddhists. This one's great. The type of Buddhism called Pure Land Buddhism teaches that a Buddha called Maitreya will someday appear as a Messiah. He doesn't have a donkey, but someone figured out that if you write his name in Hebrew letters and then add up the numerical value of those letters, you get 666, which is the number of the Antichrist in Revelation. Isn't that cool?"

"You done?"

"I think so."

"Then let me tell you what I think about all this bullshit, leaving aside the fact that you made most of it up. First, you feel that there has to be a good donkey-bad donkey balance."

"Yes, if there's a cosmic good donkey, there has to be a cosmic bad donkey. The philosopher Giordano Bruno thought so too in the sixteenth century. He was burned at the stake for ..."

"That's enough. It's Baleine's turn to talk now. What you and your so-called sources call the good donkey is only good for some people. Obviously it's bad for others because anyone who doesn't believe in the donkey's Messiah goes to Hell. So it stands to reason that for cosmic balance your bad donkey must actually be good for some people. What I'm saying is that that would be all those people who weren't members of the Messiah club when the good donkey story started going around. Need I say that those people were primarily people of color. So instead of good donkey-bad donkey, we got a yin-yang of donkeys. What your book needs to explain this is a story that shows the bad donkey standing up for colored people and not being a monster. So that's what I wrote. Put it in your book. You don't even have to use Baleine's name."

"But you made so many changes to what Apuleius and Lucian wrote."

"I kept the basic story. Anyway, they're both old white guys. Baleine doesn't care about them unless they pay her."

After decades of wrangling with fellow scholars, Constantine knows when to sound a retreat so he can return to the fight another day. "I'll think about it."

"You do that."

"Now back to the aromatherapy. What was that all about?"

"That's about our escape from here."

"What escape? We're not prisoners, Baleine. That was a misunderstanding. We're guests now, and I, for one, am enjoying getting to know Ray Bob's southern country ways immensely."

"You got Stockholm syndrome. You know what that is?"

"Of course I do."

"You're getting rid of the distress caused by being held prisoner by developing love and sympathy for Ray Bob and Pastor Steve."

"That's preposterous! I don't love Ray Bob and Pastor Steve."

"You sure do. Three old white guys together. It's like you belong to a club. Once we escape, you'll realize that."

"When are we going to escape?"

"When the time is right."

"You thinking of letting me know a little in advance?"

"Nope. You'll know soon enough when it happens."

*   *   *

In Tehran Monika Farber offers her toes for her new *seegheh* husband to caress. Major Farhad Yazdi, who will be commanding the Three-Thirteen mission to Morocco, is more than eager to please her. "The news from the president's office is better than we had expected, my Chickie. It is confirmed that my student Fritz is in the hands of the Israelis, but he is refusing to cooperate with them unless they rescue his girlfriend."

"Is she the short girl our men saw being abducted from the airport in Venice?"

"That's the one. It was American agents from the DGP who took her, but there is reason to believe that she is still in Venice. A DGP agent has been observed taking repeated motorboat trips out into the lagoon. If they're keeping her on an island, we should be able to grab her and trade her for Fritz."

"Do you need Fritz so very much?" says the Major plaintively.

"Don't be pathetic, Farhad. This isn't personal. We all need Fritz. He is the only sure way to guarantee the success of our mission."

ESCAPE FROM JUNK ISLE

Jessie's dream is transpiring in a Seventh-day Adventist church. A gray-haired minister, who looks like her grandfather, but also like the CIA Deputy Director of Operations, is sermonizing from the pulpit.

"I would like to examine the people who were there when Jesus rode into Jerusalem. In our examination, I would like to classify these people into two groups. The first group I call the Palm Branches. The Palm Branches are those Christians that are green with energy, that when things are going well, they are there to reap the benefits and even praise the Lord. But when Jesus is out of their sight, they fall to the ground, turn brown, and wither away. The second group I would like to call the Donkeys. The Donkeys are those who are like the donkey that Jesus rode. These are those who are humble to God's will and can be unmovable when Jesus is in their hearts. The Donkeys are those that do not see God, yet act upon His commandments in their lives. The Donkeys are those that enter into glory with Jesus in their hearts."

Jessie is aware of a young girl beside her on the pew. Her clothes are soaking wet, and she is shivering. Black hair dangles over her face in dripping strands. It is the secondary school yearbook face of Victoria Greeley. Jessie reaches out to comfort her, but the pew is somehow flooded and the girl is drifting away. Her mouth moves imploringly, but Jessie cannot hear her words. In the last glimmer of her dream as the ring of the bedside phone awakens her Jessie feels a yearning to be a humble donkey for Jesus. She reaches out and picks up the phone.

"This is Zayyat."

"Jessie, your Where's Waldo search has come through. They're pretty sure the girl you're looking for is on some little island in the Venice lagoon."

Jessie had submitted her emergency-locate request, or ELR, to the CIA WW desk four days before. Quick work. "Can we get satellite confirmation?"

"Hopefully. WW figured the location out from shadows, time codes, landscape, and tide data. Brilliant work. To get satellite reconnaissance you'll need to file a SatCon 1290 form."

"I've got the form ready. I just need the WW information."

"I'll text it to you."

"As soon as you can."

"It's already 11 AM in Italy, Jessie, so they probably can't get anything until tomorrow. Also there's a weather front moving in that could black out the area."

As soon as Jessie has completed and faxed the form, she calls Joseph in Munich.

"Joseph, this is Jessie."

"You sound sleepy. Maybe you need a cup of coffee. A little caffeine to get you going in the morning."

"Very funny. I'm calling about that girl I mentioned to you. Victoria Greeley."

"She's the spunky little video star giving the finger to a cameraman on an island somewhere?"

"The same. The WW desk thinks they've found the island in the Venice lagoon. I want you to go down and pick her up. She's in danger, and she knows things we need to know."

A long pause. "Not like you to be giving me an order, Jessie."

"Please, Joseph! Please rescue her! I'm on my knees praying for her. And for heavens sake, don't tell the Israelis what you're doing. I'm sure they've been playing us on the Adnan Yafouri thing. They gave us Yafouri and asked us in exchange to pick up Fritz Messiassohn as a minor favor. Turns out Messiassohn was the real package. Adnan Yafouri is a set-up. Probably just as innocent as he claims."

"The operational names he gave us for the Yemeni al-Qaeda sure didn't check out. But he may just be a hard nut to crack. The boys in Bagram want to ship him on to Guantanamo to let the real pros work on him."

"Stop that if you can, Joseph. But not before you get to Victoria Greeley."

"Can you fill me in on the big picture? Are Greeley and Messiassohn terrorists?"

"No, they're both good guys. More importantly, they're also material witnesses. An operation is going to go down soon in Morocco, and we need them to explain it to us." Jessie's fingers are crossed.

Joseph pauses before replying. "Sounds like you're onto something important, Jessie," he says at last. He sounds convinced. Jessie uncrosses her fingers. "More important, at least, than your donkey thing." Joseph's barking laugh is even harsher over the phone than in person.

"We should get SatCon on exactly where the girl is sometime tomorrow. So just get yourself on down there."

Jessie scans her work files to see if there is anything new on Professor Constantine and the Boston detective. No fresh credit card charges in Greensboro. The rented Lincoln has shown up wiped clean of fingerprints in long-term parking at Piedmont Triad International Airport. Constantine's last out-going e-mail still the one to an Israeli called the Rabbi proposing to swap Victoria Greeley for Fritz Messiassohn in Marrakesh.

She's already at Langley when the travel office opens. The secretarial assistant to the Deputy Director of Operations expedites a Government Travel Request. Being still technically on home leave Jessie decides she is not required to file a plan and get authorization from the CovOpPro board. She looks at the flight options the travel office gives her and checks her watch. Just enough time to race home, pack, and get to the airport for the 9:00 PM Air Maroc flight to Marrakesh.

*   *   *

Joseph Snow's flight into Venice circles for half an hour before the dense clouds signaling the approach of a bizarrely out-of-season storm lift enough to permit a landing at Marco Polo Airport. He didn't bring an umbrella, but it isn't actually raining yet when he bustles into a car waiting to take him to the central police station.

A few steps behind him, a svelte businessman in a gray Gianni Campagna suit who was on the same connecting flight from Rome is met by two tieless men with week-old beards. They look at the sky and the choppy water of the lagoon and argue for a while in Persian before deciding to risk the 25-minute water taxi ride to the center of the city.

*   *   *

Toots is sunburned, dirty, and tired, but she is finally ready. She has tested her raft by weighting it with metal scrap and pushing it into the water at the end of a 15-foot cable. She has laminated and overlapped her empty meal pouches and glued them together into a waterproof sleeve using sticky black gunk seeping from a steel canister. The sleeve holds her computer, iPod, passport, and wallet. She ties the sleeve tightly around her midsection.

The moon has pressured her to finish her preparations. It was full last night so the next tide will be as high as it gets. Now she just has to wait for the tide and hope for a good northeast wind to carry her out toward the current that she has calculated will carry her raft to the city. For the hundredth time she mulls over the question of whether to remove her cast. Her foot still won't bear much weight, but she suspects that the cast itself is causing the pain, not a broken foot. She half wishes she had more experience of broken limbs so she could appraise the pain more professionally. If it becomes necessary, she will go into the water and propel the raft by kicking. But she hopes that the paddle she has improvised from Venetian blind slats will suffice.

At noon her excitement begins to mount. The dark cloudbank that has been looming over the hills to the north all morning is finally closing in, and a steady breeze that she can almost call a wind has begun to blow from the northeast. Two hours until high tide. She smiles and fantasizes about being free. *I'll go after that son of a bitch J.M. and kill him*, she thinks. *He is so dead.*

Toots welcomes the rain. Getting wet was always part of her plan, and the air temperature is in the balmy 70's.

In a tiny piazza across the Grand Canal from St. Mark's Cathedral the tourists sitting under café awnings on the south side scurry indoors. The wind is driving the heavy drops at a slant, and the waiters are getting soaked furling the billowing canvas. Having wisely decided to drink his afternoon beer on the sheltered north side, Mitch Roland laughs at their antics. Then he notices that two men at a nearby table don't seem amused. Two Marine tours in Iraq, the first in Anbar Province, have sensitized him to dark bearded men who seem out of place. He puts money on the table to cover the beer and saunters casually out into the rain. The men at the other table rise and signal for their check. Mitch turns a corner and starts sprinting along the narrow pavement beside a canal. There's a man in a tailored suit up ahead walking slowly holding a newspaper over his slicked back hair. If Mitch can get past him, he will be screened from the men he hears racing after him. Just a few more steps. Suddenly the man in front of him turns around. He is holding a gun. *Oh shit*, thinks Mitch. Solid buildings flank him on his right, an armpit-high wall on his left. He skids to a stop on the slippery paving stones and clasps his hands on top of his head. *No point getting hurt.*

The Three-Thirteen agents walk him quickly to a staircase leading down to the canal. A motorboat is waiting. "Take us to the girl," says the one in the tailored suit.

"I don't know what you're talking about," says Mitch. Excruciating pain as an icepick is driven into his left bicep and then pulled out.

"We don't have time to talk. We know you're DGP. Take us to the girl, or you will become ... what do you call it? ... a pincushion."

Mitch believes him. "Head for the Grand Canal and turn right. Once we pass the Arsenal it's a long way across the lagoon."

The man in the suit gives instructions to the boatman in Italian and gets backtalk in return. The wind is stiffening, the rain coming in sheets. The suit hands the boatman a rolled wad of money and shows him his gun. The boatman utters some imprecations, but turns to his job. The motorboat moves off slowly and slows still more when it hits the heavy chop of the Grand Canal. *We'll never make it to the island*, thinks Mitch.

*   *   *

"I assure you, Signor Snow, there is nothing we wish more than to cooperate with your famous CIA and make a search of the islands." The speaker is the Comandante of the Carabinieri. "But there is a flood coming. The wind, the rain, the tide: this is going to be a difficult day. Not something we ever expect to see in the summer season, but the weather has done such strange things in recent years."

"Surely you have boats that can handle heavy weather."

"Assuredly, Signor Snow, but on such days we hold them in reserve for rescues and emergencies."

"Dammit, this is both a rescue and an emergency! Do I have to call the Interior Minister?"

The Comandante shrugs dramatically. "Perhaps if you knew which island she is on. There are many small islands."

"It's covered with scrap metal."

"Alas, many are. You spoke of a satellite picture."

"We're never going to get one in this rain. We'll just have to search each one. You have the video. Can't you make an educated guess?"

"Ah, the video. In truth, Signor Snow, we can make an educated guess. And we have done so. Our guess is that with this strong northeast wind, when the tide is at its maximum, the girl's island will be three feet under water in a strong current heading out to sea. Pfft! No girl. She'll be gone. I'm very sorry."

*   *   *

Toots doesn't need to push the raft into the water. It rises with the tide that floods the island and heads out into the current without her even having to paddle. *That J.M. is so dead*, she thinks as the distance between junk island and the wooden channel markers narrows. She feels the wind pushing strongly against the back of her raincoat. The markers are almost at hand. She had hoped to be able to see where the channel headed once she got this far, but the storm conceals anything more than twenty feet beyond the front of her raft. On clear days she had made out a long, low island in the far distance. That was to be her target. But it now dawns on her that if she can't find the island, she might be swept out of the lagoon entirely and find herself adrift and storm-tossed on the Adriatic Sea. She grips her paddle but can't decide in which direction to apply it.

A sudden jolting confluence of two currents spins the craft around, and two of the plastic gallon bottles beneath the raft break free with a rasping sound. Lacking the floats, the raft's rear right corner dips down into the water causing it to rotate clockwise. Toots throws all her strength into fighting the rotation with her paddle but can only slow it. She no longer has any idea where she is in relation to junk island. The waves have become larger. Fear seizes her as the thought creeps insidiously into her mind that she might indeed be on her way out to sea.

Time passes. One minute? Two minutes? She doesn't know. She hears a sharp crack and sees that the metal around one of the screwholes through which the cable holding the main group of plastic floats passes has snapped off and is dragging in the water. The raft starts to spin more rapidly while at the same time pitching wildly up and down with the waves. Toots feels to make sure the waterproof sleeve with her computer and passport is still tied around her midsection. *At least they'll be able to identify my body*, she thinks.

Minute by minute the surge of the sea intensifies. Then a strange, mechanical groaning sound joins the noise of the wind and the rain. It grows louder and louder, sounding, she fears, like a ship bearing down on her. She can see almost nothing, but suddenly it makes no difference because she has lost her grip at the top of a violent pitch and plummeted into the water. Where is the raft? She catches a fleeting glimpse of it spinning rapidly away from her. She tries to kick in that direction, but the disintegrating cast on her foot and the package tied to her abdomen are dragging her down. She is sinking …

… and now she is rising again as something massive, hard, and solid pushes inexorably upward beneath her feet. A metal wall with an angled top pointing upward like the gable of a roof rises slowly out of the water. With a strength born of desperation she grabs the top edge of the gable and rides its rise. To her left and right the steel wall stretches as far as she can see. When it finally stops moving, she is entirely out of the water and beyond the reach of even the highest waves. It dawns on her that what she is clinging to must be a flood barrier closing off the Venice lagoon from the sea. Still buffeted and half blinded by the strong wind and driving rain, she clambers over the gabled edge until she has one hand and one knee firmly lodged on either side. Keeping her body pressed to the metal she finds she can creep forward despite a sharp pain in her foot beneath the remaining sodden fragments of the plaster cast. She tries to remember whether she may have once read about a Venetian flood barrier, and if so, where it might be located. Logically, if the wall she is perched on prevents flooding, it must reach dry land in either direction. She decides to crawl along the gable to her right.

*   *   *

"In a flood like this, Signor Snow, bodies occasionally wash up on the surge wall along with other debris. We can send a boat to look for the woman before we let the engineers lower it again to the seabed."

"That won't be necessary, Comandante. Miss Greeley was only useful to us alive, and since she's not an American citizen, it would be best to leave the problem of her body to the British consular service. In fact, it would in the best interests of all concerned if no one learns about my visit here."

The Comandante looks dubious. "But my report, Signor."

Joseph pulls a wallet out of the breast pocket of his suit and extracts from it a sheaf of bills. He slowly counts 100 Euro notes onto the Comandante's desk. When he gets to fifteen, he pauses.

"Perhaps, since there is no proof that the girl was ever on our island, there is no need to file a report."

"You have been most understanding, Comandante."

Joseph rings Jessie as soon as he leaves to tell her the bad news, but her phone is turned off as she wings her away toward Marrakesh.

*   *   *

"In a flood like this," says the Italian boatman, "bodies occasionally wash up on the surge wall along with other debris. We can look." The man in the gray suit and the two other Three-Thirteen agents, Ebrahim and Babak, have taken refuge from the storm with their boatman in a beach café on the narrow barrier island known as the Lido di Venezia.

"That won't be necessary, Giuseppe," says the man in the gray suit. He pulls a wallet out of his breast pocket and extracts from it a sheaf of bills. He counts five 100 Euro notes onto the table. "You did your best." He adds two more bills. "It would be best if no one hears anything about our transaction, or about what happened to the American."

The boatman nods, pockets the money, and takes his leave. The worst of the storm has headed off south into the Adriatic, but it is still raining. He stops to buy some cigarettes and thinks about how best to tell his story about the crazy Iranians who tossed an American man into the lagoon at the height of the flood.

Back in the café, the Three-Thirteen first share their positive emotions about killing the DGP agent named Mitch in revenge for the murders of Asef, Moosa, and Said in Scotland. Then they turn gloomily to debating their next steps. "If there is any chance she is alive, we must pursue it," says the man in the gray suit. "Otherwise, Tehran will want proof that she is dead."

"Do we just wait around until her body is found?"

"Let us think more positively, Ebrahim. If she is truly the key to the holy return of the Master of the Hour, it is possible that a miracle has saved her. We must pray for that. And supposing a miracle has happened, what will she do?"

"Go home," says Ebrahim. "But slowly because the American Mitch broke her foot."

"What before that?"

The three men ponder the question. "She will want to tell her father she is alive," ventures the youngest of the group. "She will telephone."

"No, Babak," says Ebrahim. "Asef reported that he threw away the mobile phones on her father's island and cut the land line."

"Then she will e-mail him," says Babak.

The men resume thinking. Babak sneaks looks at his senior colleagues to see if they are about to say anything. Eventually he is moved to speak. "I'm sure you both remember this much better than I do, but didn't Asef report that he installed a keystroke logger on the woman's computer so she couldn't contact the police by e-mail without him knowing it? Asef was technically skilled."

"What's a keystroke logger?" asks the man in the gray suit.

"It's a kind of spyware program. It's what a hacker uses when he wants to find out what someone is doing on his computer without that person knowing it. It secretly broadcasts every keystroke the person makes to the hacker's computer."

Ebrahim looks at Babak suspiciously. "How do you know this?"

"Be quiet, Ebrahim," says the man in the gray suit firmly. "Babak, do you think they still have this … "

"Keystroke logger."

"… keystroke logger in Tehran?"

"That's easy to find out. They have wifi in here." He takes out his laptop and quickly logs in to a dedicated Three-Thirteen server in Tehran. His pride in showing his elders what he can do fights a mental battle with his worry that showing advanced computer skills might mark him as a rebellious youth. Both feelings, however, give way to excitement when he clicks open the folder containing the reports sent from Ass Isle by Asef and then a sub-folder marked 'Greeley key-log archive'. The files inside are labeled by month. May, the first month, shows much activity and contains all of the e-mails sent by Toots while still on her father's island. Babak opens the June file. A few e-mails in the first week and then nothing … until one hour ago!

The man in gray reads the new e-mail aloud in English translating each sentence as he goes into Persian for the benefit of Ebrahim:

Dear Daddy,

I am writing you from Venice where I am safe and sound after the most awful experiences. I have been kidnapped, marooned, and almost drowned, but I'm still alive with no worse damage than some sunburn, a few scrapes and bruises, and an aching foot that may be broken. I won't try to go into any details, but it's all about that donkey Ya'fur. Fritz says he heard it speak when he was in Morocco. Can you believe that? I can't. But it's why everyone is after him. I am longing to see you, but I haven't had a chance yet to make travel arrangements. At the moment I'm at a Starbucks on the Lido beach in Venice. I'll let you know about my flight home as soon as I can make a reservation.

If you know what has happened to Fritz, tell me, even if the news is bad. I saw him being kidnapped, but not by same people who grabbed me. It is all very confusing. You can also tell Professor Constantine to keep on digging into the DGP. They are the ones who marooned me, and they deserve to die.

I love you so much. Please give my love to the donkeys.

Toots

"She gives her love to donkeys?" says Ebrahim.

Babak is googling Venetian Starbucks outlets. "She's only two blocks from here!"

The man in the gray suit wears an expression of tearful reverence. "We prayed for a miracle," he says, "and the Master of the Hour has granted us one." He holds up his hands in the open-book gesture of Muslim supplication. The other two make the same gesture, and the three of them in unison offer a prayer in acknowledgement of God's omnipotence.

Somewhat drier and much revived by a mocha frappuccino and chocolate biscotti, Toots looks out at the street. The rain has stopped, and the waiter has given her instructions on how to get to the ferry dock. When she stands up, a sharp pain shoots up from her foot. The plaster cast had totally disappeared during the endless, painful crawl along the flood barrier. She props herself against her chair and grabs the pole of a beach umbrella that she has been using as a walking staff since climbing down from the flood barrier at the Lido shore. With her computer back in its waterproof sleeve and tucked firmly under her arm, she pushes open the door and steps onto the sidewalk.

A man in a rain-spotted but meticulously tailored gray suit is standing at the open door of a taxi, either just arriving or just about to leave. He looks pityingly at Toots and says in English, "Would you like to have this taxi, Miss?"

Toots thanks him and awkwardly manages to get herself and her aching foot into the back seat. The man in the gray suit slides in beside her while another man opens the door on the other side and seizes her arms. Before she can speak or react, a cloth bag descends over her head.

Oh shit, not again.

MARRAKESH

The donkey prods the old man with his nose. It is not yet dawn. The old man wakes. "Is it time, Donkey?"

"Yes," says Ya'fur. "They are coming."

"You are certain?"

"Do you need to ask?"

The old man gathers his few belongings and pulls his brown burnoose over his sholders. "All my life," he says wistfully, "I have wanted the Ouled Muhammad and the Ouled Hassan to work together."

"It is finally happening. You can take satisfaction."

"But they are working together to steal you away from me, Donkey."

"It always ends some way. I will go with them, and you will find two other tribes that need a holy man."

The old man wipes a tear from his wrinkled cheek. "How can I be a holy man without you, Ya'fur?"

"You'll see. The donkey waiting for you outside looks just like me. Just pretend to listen to it from time to time. If the people think you can understand it, it will be almost the same as having me with you."

"But your wisdom."

"You will discover your own wisdom."

They are standing outside the stone hut that the old man will never see again. He mounts the stolid gray donkey waiting for him. "Will the Ouled Muhammad and the Ouled Hassan be all right, Donkey? I care about them."

"As all right as people ever are. The sheikhs will sell me for so much money that they will be able to buy big houses and new young wives in Marrakesh. Their children will take drugs and drive fast cars. But here in the mountains the rest of the Ouled Muhammad and the Ouled Hassan will have many years of peace before they find a new reason to quarrel." The old man looks content. "You had best go now. They will be here soon."

Ya'fur watches the old man ride off as the first rays of the sun stab over the eastern ridge. Then he turns to a pile of straw and eats his breakfast while he waits to be stolen.

*   *   *

Ariel has stowed Fritz in a shabby two-star hotel overlooking the giant Marrakesh market square, the Djemaa el Fna. The skinny, intense young Israeli whose penetrating eyes are framed by squarish black-rimmed glasses has not proven so companionable or as good a conversationalist as the Rabbi, but Fritz has come to appreciate his chameleon skills and envy his command of Moroccan Arabic. He accepts that the life of a secret agent on a mission is a demanding one and is willing to cut Ariel some slack. But on the whole, his preference would be to sort through a tray of unpolished gemstones or, the best option currently available, stare out the window at the teeming market stalls. Fritz is concerned that he has heard nothing of Toots. The Rabbi's "no Toots, no donkey" has become his anchor, but he worries that it may be snagged on an uncharted seafloor.

Idling away time waiting for Ariel to return to the hotel, Fritz makes a mental inventory of the businesses he can see in the market lanes: leather goods—used books—shoe-shiners—public scribes—transvestite dancers with week-old beards—child tumblers—black dancers stomping to a beating drum—water-bearers in red costumes with bells on their hats—African women selling coconut meat and shell necklaces—a man with a bronze flute whipping monkeys to make them perform—snake handlers accompanied by musicians—blind chanters with tin cups—story tellers—religious exhorters—a vendor of decorated ostrich eggs and plume fans—strolling hashish dealers—scammers enticing people into a game with a seemingly looped string—shooting galleries—spice merchants—nut sellers—child boxers whose manager urges bystanders to bet—a hedgehog seller—beggars—cripples—idiots—patent medicine hawkers—a woman with an automobile windshield for sale—

"We're in business!" Ariel announces as he bursts into the room. "I've closed the deal with J.M. and his boys. He's having the vehicles serviced today, we head for the mountains tomorrow."

"What about Toots?"

"He's being cagey, but I did my best. He will fly her in by helicopter once we get to the old man's village. He says he doesn't want the two of you meeting before then. Thinks you'll conspire."

"Does he have a helicopter?"

"I talked to the pilot and saw his license."

"So why don't we all just fly in, get the donkey, and fly out?"

"It's a rental. No donkeys on board. Besides, the pilot says he won't know where to go until J.M. sends him a radio signal to home in on. One mountain village looks just like another from the air."

Fritz sighs. Getting to the old man's village is not an easy trek. "How much does this J.M. know about you, Ariel?"

"Enough, but not too much. So far as he knows, I'm just a facilitator sent by the Rabbi to make the exchange of you for Toots happen. We're in agreement that from now on, my job is to follow his plan."

"J.M.'s plan? His plan is to drive a few hundred miles up into the mountains and buy a donkey from an old man. Right? Doesn't he realize that if a person really has a talking donkey, he's not going to sell it? And particularly not to a foreigner who's not even a Muslim?"

"He has a Plan B, but he's counting on you being able to persuade the old man to sell."

"Of course I can be persuasive. The old man will never suspect a thing. I lived with him for three months, ate his food, drank his tea and never once offered to buy his donkey. Now, four years later, I show up with a wallet full of cash, two Hummers, a truck pulling a horse trailer, and five guys who look like soldiers."

"Six, counting me."

"You don't look like a soldier, Ariel. You look like a bookkeeper."

"I'll take that as a compliment. As for you, I'm sure you still look like the starry-eyed innocent wanderer the old man knew and trusted four years ago. Except for that tattoo on your neck. You should have something done about that."

"I don't mind it."

"As for J.M. and his men, if the plan goes right, the old man won't ever see them, or me, or the vehicles. You show them where to set up a camp out of sight of the village. Go in the rest of the way on foot, just like you did when you first went there. After a happy reunion with the old man, you say you're tired of walking and offer to buy his donkey. He sells it to you. You ride it back to the camp and swear on a stack of bibles that it's Ya'fur. That's when J.M. will radio the helicopter to fly Toots in. You'll get a few minutes for a warm reunion. Then J.M. will turn her over to me, and I'll fly with her back to Marrakesh. Once there she'll be free. I can put her up in a hotel to wait for you, if that's what she wants. Or I'll pay for her to fly to Scotland, or anywhere she likes."

"Why are they turning her over to you instead of me? What's that all about?"

"That's the best deal I could get. You get to see Toots, make sure she's okay, do a little kissy face. But no walking off into the sunset until they send off Ya'fur's tissue sample and get his DNA checked out."

"Which will take days. Maybe weeks."

"Plenty of time for you to shake free of them. Remember, you're not going to want to be around when they find out that they've gone to all this trouble for an ordinary donkey."

Fritz works through the plan in his head. "Maybe it will work after all," he murmurs with a tentative nod. "It wouldn't have a chance if Ya'fur were actually involved, but the old man shouldn't object to me buying a different donkey from him. There are plenty around. And he'll believe me when I tell him I'm tired of walking. He'll probably just give me a donkey."

"Now you're getting in the mood! But don't come back with a donkey too soon. Make them think you've been haggling. That's what they expect Arabs to do. We can do this, Fritz."

"J.M. thinks so too, right?"

"Absolutely. It's his plan. I'm a good negotiator. First I told him his plan was stupid and full of holes. I told him that a better plan would be to promise a lot of money to the tribal sheikhs in the area to get them to steal Ya'fur. People like that have been stealing each other's donkeys for centuries. But then I let him persuade me that using locals couldn't guarantee that the donkey they deliver is the right one. You have to have boots on the ground if you want real results, he said. So I finally gave up and told him that his plan was better than mine."

"But your plan actually is better."

"Of course it is, but we won't know that for sure until we get there."

*   *   *

Jessie has isolated herself in her hotel room and has been weeping intermittently for two days, ever since receiving Joseph's phone call on her way from the airport into Marrakesh with the news of Victoria Greeley's death. She can't understand the flood of emotion engulfing her. Every time she tries to pull herself together, Victoria's drowned body resurfaces in her mind. She had tried so hard to save her! God damn Joseph for being too slow!

She was just a helpless little girl whose life was torn from her by powers beyond her reckoning. Jessie hadn't actually known her, of course, but she had come to think of her as the little sister she never had.

What to do now. There is still the DGP strike team out there in the city somewhere. Probably the same people who marooned Victoria on the island. She thinks about finding them and calling in a Predator airstrike to take them out. Report their deaths as collateral damage in a counter-terrorism action. The thought of collateral damage brings Victoria back to mind. A fresh flow of tears soaks into her pillow. *Without Victoria, what's the point of it all? Maybe I should go home and quit the Agency*, she thinks. *But if I quit because it hurts so much, won't I be just like a green palm branch that withers and turns brown when times get hard? I do want to be a humble donkey for the Lord, but how can I when my heart is broken?* Victoria's sweet innocent face, this time pale, wet, and dead floats back into her consciousness.

*　　*　　*

"Fucking assholes abandoned me on that fucking island!" screams Toots in a tent in Algeria near the Moroccan border. "I'm going to kill them!"

Monika Farber beams supportively. "That's the way to feel, Toots! Let it all out. Think about the pain they deserve to feel before they die."

"They broke my damn foot!" A state-of-the-art walking cast with a fiberglass sole has replaced the old-fashioned plaster one lost in the flood. "They were going to fucking trade me for fucking Fritz! Like I'm a used car or something."

"They most certainly do deserve to die, Toots. But stay focused. You hate them because they attacked your father's house, put your donkeys in danger, broke your foot, and stranded you on the island. Trading you for Fritz is just politics."

"But it's humiliating to be traded."

"Humiliation doesn't support as satisfying a rage as genuine pain and fear. Besides, as I've told you, my plan is also to trade you for Fritz."

"I know, Monika. But you asked me first."

"I did, yes. But that was a formality. If you had said no, I would have traded you anyway. We're not the DGP, but we are the Three-Thirteen, or at least my male escorts are. You have good reason to hate us, Toots. We are the people held you and your father hostage in Scotland."

"But your people were nice, and Asef didn't kill me and Daddy when the DGP attacked the way he should have."

"Nevertheless, we kidnapped you in Venice, we flew you here ..."

"With Negar sitting beside me, a very pleasant woman guard."

"... and soon we will swap you for Fritz. The only value you have for us is as a device for getting him. These are all bad things, and I apologize for them."

"You don't have to apologize. Maybe I should hate you guys, but what I really hate is the fucking DGP."

"I assure you, killing them will feel very satisfying."

"Look, Monika, I know you're not what anyone would call a nice person. Fritz has told me things. And I know I'm a prisoner and a pawn. But Fritz also says that you treat him with respect."

"And I will continue to do so once he comes over to us. Someday he will get his Ph.D. I am loyal to my students."

"I also respect the fact that you're the only woman in this ridiculous farce and that you're not some creepy religious nutcase."

"Now you're being too considerate. Don't go soft on me, Toots. Hold on to your anger. Rage purifies. Violence heals. You're right that I'm not a religious nutcase, but the people I'm working with, including my dear temporary husband Major Yazdi, are precisely religious nutcases."

"How can you stand being part of their ... their fantasy?"

"I can stand it because they are all at my mercy. Even the cool and calculating President Ahmadinejad and his henchman Mashaei. Have you ever wondered why there are no female Messiahs?"

"No."

"It's because we women are the Antichrist, Toots. If ever a Messiah comes—and it may well happen someday now that we know that Ya'fur is real—he will kiss the feet of some woman. You might not be able to predict who will be among the saved and among the damned, but that you can bet on."

"Are you that woman?"

"Perhaps. Time will tell."

Toots is impressed. "When you exchange me for Fritz, can I trust you to give me what I need to kill those DGP fuckers?"

"Toots, I will be right beside you when you pull the trigger."

"They are so dead."

*   *   *

Joseph's second call reaches Jessie on her room phone at her hotel in Marrakesh. "Jessie, I don't know whether you're going to love me for this, or hate me, or both, but Victoria Greeley is alive. NSA intercepted an e-mail from her father to someone named Paul Constantine mentioning the word Ya'fur. Apparently you put the word on the WANAB watch list."

Jessie's heart is beating so hard she can barely speak. "Alive? What did the e-mail say?"

"It was a forward of a message she sent her father from Venice. She somehow survived that terrible flood."

"That's incredible!"

"You might even call it a miracle. I was there. The storm was unbelievably bad."

"Where is she now?"

"She told her father she was coming home, but here's the bad news. I just got word from Italian immigration that after she landed in Rome on a flight from Marco Polo, she connected with a flight heading for Algiers. Not only that, but the people traveling with her had Iranian passports."

"Then they're all probably coming to Morocco." Jessie's mind is back in professional mode.

"Why would they do that? Do you want me to come down there and give you a hand, Jessie? I feel kind of out of the loop."

"No. I've got things under control." Jessie already has a map out and is tracing her finger over the vast expanse of sparsely patrolled deserts and mountains along the Algerian-Moroccan border. "But you could get onto the Algerians and see if you can find out where the Iranians went after they got to Algiers. My guess is that they're on their way to Tindouf. It has an airport, and there's a big Polisario camp not far away. I've been studying up on this, Joseph. The Polisario are guerrillas from Western Sahara, which Morocco occupied militarily after the Spanish colonial authority withdrew. Algeria supports them, and they regularly send cross-border missions against Moroccan assets. If the Iranians who kidnapped Greeley are planning on doing something in Morocco, getting the Polisario to help them across the border would make a lot of sense."

"Why would the Iranians be planning an operation in Morocco, Jessie? I really could help you more if you would connect some of the dots for me."

"I'll have to call you back on that, Joseph. And by the way, why did the NSA intercept intel come to you instead of me? I was the one who asked for Ya'fur to be flagged."

"They tried you first, but your phone is turned off and you're not responding to e-mail. You didn't leave the name of a hotel with the travel office either. This is the seventh one I've tried. It's not right to drop off the radar, Jessie. You got good training so you know that."

"Sorry about that Joseph. You're absolutely right. It was an oversight. Won't happen again."

"I have to ask, Jessie, is everything okay? You sound stressed."

"Everything is just fine, Joseph. But I've got a lot of work to do. Get back to me soon with that Algerian travel info. Got to go now. Thanks for giving me the good news." *And no thanks for not trying harder to rescue Victoria in Venice, asshole*, thinks Jessie as she hangs up. The Iranians doing a better job of finding Victoria than the CIA. Unthinkable. She turns on her computer, logs in, and begins to fill out forms, one for a satellite photograph review of the Tindouf border area covering the past four days and another requesting stand-by authorization for real time reconnaissance.

The Road South

The setting sun lengthens the shadows in the dusty, empty streets of the Moroccan mountain town of Tafraoute. Two Hummers and a Dodge Dakota with 6-speed manual transmission towing a Sundowner two-horse trailer pull up before the reddish gingerbread façade of the Hotel Saint-Antoine. They have crossed the Atlas Mountains and are now in the Anti-Atlas range. Except for the last couple of hours on a narrow and dangerous road, it has been a fairly easy day-long trip from Marrakesh via Agadir.

Ariel, accompanying J.M. in the lead Hummer, has recounted selected and almost true adventures from his life in garrulous detail. In return, J.M. has offered to introduce him to Jesus Christ … several times.

Fritz has dozed much of the way in the rear of the Dakota extended cab, effectively cut off from the conversation of Weston and Sparky, two of J.M.'s boys, sitting up front. Thus he has missed a detailed update on the American sports scene complete with colorful commentary and witty repartee. Having been down the road to Tafraoute more than once in years past, he has satisfied his interest in the passing landscape by raising his head to the window from time to time to check where they are. A quick look at arid, boulder-strewn hillsides, mud-brick villages surrounded by terraces of almond trees, and goats perched incongruously on tree limbs, and then back into snooze mode.

Better rested than his fellow travelers and more at ease in the less-than-exotic surround of the hotel restaurant, Fritz zestfully pings a fork against his wine glass after a spicy couscous dinner and insipid *crème caramel* dessert. He unfolds a detailed terrain map across the three metal tables they have pulled together to accommodate the party. A thick red marker line snakes away from the road outside Tafraoute and into an area of progressively higher elevation tints.

"I'm going to give everyone the details in case we get separated tomorrow or a vehicle has a breakdown. Eight kilometers out of town you will find a dirt road on the right. It's just after a triangular yellow sign, also on the right, showing an S-curve. We take that road and keep on it for forty-one kilometers. Check your odometers. Donkey tracks branch off from time to time, but you don't want to take the wrong one. The one we want goes off on the left between two big argan trees. You should spot these pretty easily. There'll be a lot of goats in them. They love to eat the nuts. Once we're on the donkey track, it will be slow going. Be prepared to detour around some of the bigger rocks. But we should still make it over the third pass with plenty of daylight. The place we're headed for is called Sidi Ben Adam, but you will probably not encounter anyone so don't think you're going to be able to ask directions. It's scarcely a village, just the sheikh's house, a well, a few almond trees, and a half dozen stone huts. A half mile or so before we get there—I can't give you the exact distance from the turn-off—we'll come to a granite outcropping or protrusion about twenty meters tall and maybe six meters thick. It will look almost like a thick, tapered chimney from the direction we'll be coming. It will be on the left. Don't miss it. That is where we will camp. It's the last point on the track where no one in Sidi Ben Adam can see or hear us. According to the plan, we don't want the sheikh—sometimes you've heard me call him the old man—to know anyone's around until tomorrow. In the morning, I'll go on foot to say hello to the sheikh and remind him of our time together. It'll take a good deal of time. We'll drink a lot of tea, talk about the weather and what's been going on in the village since I left. But eventually we'll get down to business. I can't say just when that will be, but be ready. Once I have the donkey, I'll ride it out, you'll put it in the trailer, and off we go. Anyone have any questions?"

There are no questions.

"That was super," says Ariel later when he is together with Fritz in the room they are sharing. "You made it sound like you were absolutely on top of the plan. I talked to J.M. afterward. He was impressed. They all were."

"You didn't think you were the only big talker on this trip, did you Ariel?"

"I tip my hat to you."

*   *   *

Two hundred miles to the south, Major Yazdi and Monika Farber have already crossed the desolate Algerian-Moroccan frontier. Their company consists of a Western Saharan guide from the Polisario Front guerrilla movement, who is their expert on local geography and avoiding border patrols, along with five battle-hardened Three-Thirteen agents from Iran's Revolutionary Guards Corps. Plus Toots. They are camping in the desert beneath a half moon. Toots limps over to join Monika in watching the soldiers perform the evening prayer toward Mecca.

"It is so peaceful out here."

"Unless you're fighting for a homeland seized by the Moroccans, like our guide, or fighting to crush the Polisario guerrillas, like the Moroccan border guards who are somewhere out there in the night." Farber is whittling an acacia wood switch with a clasp knife and thinking of using it on her husband.

"I worry about my father. I don't know whether he got my e-mail from Venice or not."

"He may have replied. When we trade you for Fritz, we'll give you your computer back, though it probably won't be of any use to you until you get to Marrakesh."

"Do you think there will be a fight with the DGP?"

"It's hard to say. Neither side wants to risk hurting Fritz, so no one wants to risk hurting you. A Fritz with Toots is a happy Fritz. And a happy Fritz is a Fritz that is willing to identify Ya'fur."

"Couldn't you just order him to? He's your student. Also, you're very forceful."

Farber laughs. "I've discovered that Fritz does only what he wants to do. Oddly enough, you he finds very attractive, but toward me he is utterly oblivious. I mean sexually."

"Why did you make him get the tattoo?"

"I make it a practice with my advanced male students. The pain and the public labeling as one of my men normally creates a bond. But with Fritz it had no effect at all. It's just a picture on his neck. I sometimes think he does want a doctoral degree, but not if it means submitting to me the way my other students do. If he wakes up one morning and decides that continuing his studies no longer interests him, I'm sure he won't hesitate to walk away."

Toots raises her head to look at the first evening stars.

"You should give some thought to what I'm telling you about Fritz, Toots."

"What do you mean?"

"I mean it was Fritz's passion for your body got you into this mess, and he has most nobly committed himself to getting you out of it. Even to the extent of sacrificing his own freedom, which he cherishes more than life itself. But this proof of his love does not necessarily mean that he will be willing to spend the rest of his life on an island in Scotland taking care of donkeys."

The twilight specter of one of the company's seven white riding camels passes jerkily in front of them. To prevent wandering its right front leg has been tied in flexed position forcing it to hobble on the remaining three to graze on the sparse vegetation.

"Are you giving me advice on my love life, Monika?"

"I'm not without experience in that area."

"But I'm not at all like you. I'm not looking for a submissive man."

"Just one who is willing to spend his life on Ass Isle. As my friend and teacher Dominique Raven taught me, love and submission are hard to distinguish. The difference, she says, is that love starts in the heart, migrates to the penis, and then metamorphoses into a chronic ache. Submission follows the opposite path."

"What is that supposed to mean?"

"I'm not sure. I'm still trying to figure it out. But Dominique knows a lot about sex."

The two women presently retire to their shared tent. The men unroll blankets and sleep in the open air. Early the next morning the sounds of the camels being rounded up and loaded wake Toots from a solid sleep. Monika Farber has already risen. The riding camels are couched down and fitted with the combat-efficient *rahla* riding saddles typical of the Western Sahara region. Bulky loads of provisions and weapons make the saddles of the two brown baggage camels almost invisible. A third baggage camel, fitted with a conventional North Arabian *shadad* saddle, is reserved for Monika and Toots. Like the guide, the animals are courtesy of Polisario operatives in Rabouni, the guerrilla base camp outside Tindouf. President Ahmadinejad has personally sent a message promising to return the favor, and the Polisario Front needs all the international political help it can get.

Soon the small caravan is on its way toward the looming Anti-Atlas mountain range. Approached from the Algerian side, the village of Sidi Ben Adam is not far off. They should be there by early afternoon.

*   *   *

The DGP trip into the mountains has been as slow as Fritz predicted, but it has gone without a major hitch. Camp is established in the shadow of the granite outcropping, and the vehicles are refueled from jerry cans. As Fritz looks on with apprehension, J.M.'s men unload M16 rifles, armored vests, and night vision gear from one of the Hummers. Sitting on a flat boulder next to Ariel, he nods toward the weapons, and asks, "What's with the weapons, Ariel?"

"They're taking precautions. Call them Plan B precautions. Word has it that an Iranian military team may be trying to beat us to Sidi Ben Adam."

Fritz tries and fails to suppress a feeling of alarm. "Word has it? What word? Whose word?"

"I really don't know."

"Then you'll have to find out quick if you expect me to go with you to meet those Ouled Hassan and Ouled Muhammad sheikhs who stole the old man's donkey and confirm that it's the real Ya'fur."

Ariel ponders his alternatives. "Okay. The word J.M. has about the Iranians is a deliberate leak from the Mossad to the DGP headquarters. He was informed just before we left Marrakesh."

"And he quickly went around the suq buying American military supplies?"

"All right, you got me. The guns were already part of the equipment. For if/maybe use only. You have to appreciate that J.M. and his team are ex-Marines. They like having guns."

"And the Mossad would like to see the DGP and the Three-Thirteen get into a firefight. Is that it?"

"The confusion would help us."

"Who's us, Ariel? Does us include me and Toots? Or is it just you and the Rabbi? What side are you on?"

"I can't talk to you about this, Fritz. You're getting worked up over nothing."

"You don't have a choice, Ariel. No Toots, no donkey. No talking about Plan B, no donkey. No donkey, and everyone but me goes back to square one."

Ariel is squirming. "I got my instructions from the Rabbi, Fritz. You know that. And the Rabbi has promised that one way or another Toots will be set free. That's solid. You can trust that. It's what happens after that that gets complicated."

"Are you talking about the no-donkey solution?"

"That's just a phrase."

"It's a phrase I've heard the Rabbi use with you. What does it mean? According to Toots, the book by Professor Constantine says that Ya'fur is immortal. And personally, I think he's right. So the no-donkey solution can't mean killing it."

"I'm really not at liberty to talk about this."

"Fine. Just let me know when you are at liberty. I don't have anything to do for another hour. Isn't that when the sheikhs get here with Ya'fur? I think I'll just rest until then and try to remember what a talking donkey sounds like, though my memory on this seems to be fading."

Sparky, J.M.'s cook, has gotten the butane stove going and the odor of simmering puttanesca sauce pervades the camp. A fair-skinned black man named Haywood lifts the lid of the pan and gets his hand rapped with a wooden spoon. J.M. and Weston laugh. Then from back along the track comes the distant sound of tinkling bells, at first almost impossible to hear but growing louder. J.M. stands up and puts his hand on an M16.

"Everybody stay calm," says Ariel loudly. "Animals wear bells in these parts. It's probably just some locals. Fritz and I know Arabic so we'll walk back down and see who it is. If they're headed for Sidi Ben Adam, we'll tell them we're from the government and they can't go there. Everyone is afraid of the government, and dressed the way we are we look like government. If it's anyone else, we'll tell them the same thing and make them take a detour."

Ariel leads the way back along the donkey track. J.M. looks wary. "If you're not back in half an hour, we'll come looking for you," he calls.

"Do that, J.M." shouts Ariel in reply.

"I still can't remember how to speak donkey," says Fritz when they are out of earshot.

"All right. I get it. I'll tell you everything I know about the no-donkey solution."

"I doubt that."

"Just listen to me. When the Rabbi gets Ya'fur, he's going to hide him someplace where no would-be Messiah can get to him, at least not in our lifetimes."

"You mean no would-be Messiah who isn't Jewish?"

"Jewish, Christian, Muslim, it's all the same. The Rabbi's line is: no donkey, no Messiah. Of course it's obvious he doesn't want there to be a Christian or a Muslim Messiah, but he doesn't want a Jewish Messiah either. He says—and I agree with him—that the sorts of Jews who get excited these days about the Moshiach are bad for Israel. Not all of them, but a lot. Right-wing zealots. If they think the Moshiach is on his way, they're likely to blow up the Dome of the Rock so a new Temple can be built in Jerusalem. And that will start a war that Israel can't win."

"Where's he going to hide Ya'fur?"

"He didn't tell me. All he said was that it will be in the U.S. As far away from Jerusalem as possible."

They can see now a group of six men dressed in turbans and burnooses, the sheikhs of the Ouled Muhammad and Ouled Hassan. Following a prior arrangement with Ariel, they are standing around the gnarled tree that Fritz has picked as the rendezvous point. The walk from the camp has taken less then ten minutes. When they approach, Ariel exchanges some words with the thievish sheikhs and then turns to Fritz. Fritz has expected to be confronted with a donkey, but instead there are seven, six of them presumably the ones the sheikhs have ridden on to get to the meeting. All donkeys don't look alike, but Fritz hasn't seen Ya'fur in four years. Is he the one farthest to the left?

No, he's the one in the middle. "Hello, Fritz," says Ya'fur genially. Ariel and Fritz have agreed that Fritz must show no sign of understanding the donkey's sounds and should even look away from any donkey that vocalizes. "I thought we'd meet again." Fritz looks over the assemblage of donkeys and then glances at

Ariel. He nods toward Ya'fur and then turns to walk away. "I'll see you one more time in New York City." Fritz struggles against the desire to respond but keeps on walking.

Ariel takes a can of spray paint out of his pants pocket and sprays a large blue circle on Ya'fur's side. After a few final words with the sheikhs, he hands the principal leader from each tribe a thick envelope. Then the sheikhs and the seven donkeys turn and head back down the mountain. Ariel and Fritz watch them go for a bit, but mindful of J.M.'s half-hour warning, they turn and retrace their steps toward the DGP camp. The smirk on Ariel's face betrays a mood of scarcely contained exhilaration, but he says nothing.

"How much did you give them?" asks Fritz.

"Ten percent of what I promised. They'll get the rest from an associate when they get to Tafraoute. He'll put Ya'fur in a horse trailer there and drive him to the coast."

"Who's your associate?"

"None of your business."

"What happens at the coast?"

"None of your business."

"No, I guess not." As they walk on in silence, Fritz thinks, *I've never been to New York City.*

*   *   *

On authorization from Washington, Jessie has shifted her base of operations to the Marrakesh headquarters of the Royal Moroccan Gendarmerie. A few sentences of polite introductory conversation suffice to establish a viable level of communication between her basically Egyptian schoolbook Arabic and Moroccan dialect. When Jessie feeds in the codes to activate a computer link with Langley, sharp aerial images appear on the screen. Neither Lieutenant Fasi nor his computer technician Yassine, the two Moroccans who have been detailed to assist her, have ever worked directly with high-resolution satellite images like the ones now being transmitted. Jessie feels a twinge of CIA pride at their excited oohs and aahs but keeps them moving quickly from one image to the next. Interpreting shapes seen only from above is tricky, but both the lieutenant and Yassine have experience reading aerial photographs so they work expeditiously through the images archived from the previous four days.

"There," says Yassine pointing. "That group. Those aren't nomads or smugglers. Those are guerrillas. The one in the lead is a Sahrawi. Polisario."

"How can you tell?"

Yassine seems at a loss for the proper words. The lieutenant says, "The seven white camels are *méharis*, fast riding camels. Smugglers have no use for them. They use baggage camels like these other three." He uses a mouse to zoom in. "And see there? They have military weapons. Smugglers don't need them and get in trouble if they're caught with them. As for the leader, he wears his turban in the Western Sahara style. That means he's a Polisario guerrilla."

"Two of them are women," says Yassine.

"Which two?" asks Jessie staring intently.

"The ones riding together on the *shadad*. They don't know how to tie the turban." The front rider is tall, the one behind much smaller, perhaps just a girl.

"Yassine is right," murmurs Lieutenant Fasi. "I hadn't noticed that. What are women doing out there?"

"Zoom in closer. I want to see if the short woman has an injured foot."

"Maybe," says Fasi. The image becomes a blurred smudge. "That may be a bandage on her left foot. It doesn't look quite like her right foot."

"Can you tell where they're headed?"

"We'll need to look at some later images to tell that."

After five more images the lieutenant and his technician confer in dialect and bring a large terrain map up on the computer screen next to the one with the satellite pictures. Jessie waits while they look back and forth at the map and picture.

"Yassine isn't from that region, but he's been through it a number of times," says Fasi at last. "He says that the direction they are following doesn't go anywhere. Just to a little village called Sidi Ben Adam. It's on the map. From the village they might get on the track to Tafraoute, which is a sizable town. But if that's where they are headed, they could have taken a much easier route."

"Then Sidi Ben Adam must be their target," says Jessie under her breath.

After thanking the two men and asking them to keep themselves on call for further reconnaissance, Jessie retreats to the office of the regional commander and makes three phone calls. The first is to the Deputy Director of Operations in Langley requesting final authorization to carry out real time surveillance of Sidi Ben Adam starting at daybreak. The second, under the Deputy Director's authorization, is to an Agency technician on a nondescript merchant ship moving slowly along the Moroccan coast in international waters. As soon as the call is finished, the technician opens a crate, wheels out a Predator drone aircraft, and starts through a prep list. The third call is to a consular officer at the British embassy in Rabat informing him that an injured British woman is stranded in the high mountains and is in need of emergency helicopter evacuation. She tells the officer that she will get back to him with precise coordinates at first light.

SIDI BEN ADAM

J.M. has assigned Weston and Haywood the midnight to 0400 watch. At 0300 Weston slips quietly back into camp and shakes J.M. awake. "We've been scouted. Half an hour ago. Two of them. Could have been locals, but I don't think so. Acted more like military though they made more noise than we would. Did something to the road half a click up. Couldn't tell what, but my guess is either a claymore or an IED."

"Did they see you?"

"Might have. You never can tell."

A slight sound just outside the tent draws their attention. Haywood pops his head in, and the two others crawl out to join him in the open air.

"What's out there, Woody?" asks J.M.

"They're camped on the far side of the village. Six armed hostiles and two women. They got a bunch of riding camels plus a couple others with extra gear, maybe heavier weapons."

"What about the donkey? Did you see the donkey?"

"See the donkey? Are you kidding? There gotta be twenty donkeys down there, man. They must have searched around and picked up every donkey they could find."

"Sounds like the old man split. If he was there, they'd have found out which donkey is his."

"I don't think there are any people in the village. I didn't hear or see anything around the houses. Eye-ranians must have to told 'em all to clear out."

"Looks like they're fixin' for a fight," says J.M matter-of-factly. "So let's make a plan and get it on."

*   *   *

Dawn has still not broken. J.M. summons his crew and reads from the Bible using a flashlight:

"St. Matthew, chapter twenty-one, verses one through seven: 'And when they drew nigh unto Jerusalem, and were come to Bethphage, unto the mount of Olives, then sent Jesus two disciples, saying unto them, Go into the village over against you, and straightway ye shall find an ass tied, and a colt with her: loose them, and bring them unto me. And if any man say ought unto you, ye shall say, The Lord hath need of them; and straightway he will send them. All this was done, that it might be fulfilled which was spoken by the prophet, saying, Tell ye the daughter of Sion, Behold, thy King cometh unto thee, meek, and sitting upon an ass, and a colt the foal of an ass. And the disciples went, and did as Jesus commanded them, and brought the ass, and the colt, and put on them their clothes, and they set him thereon.'

"Brothers, what the disciples did for Jesus the first time 'round is what we're goin' to do for him today. Almighty Father, bless our mission this day and keep us safe from harm. In Jesus' name. Amen."

"Amen," echo his men.

"All right, everyone listen up. The civilians and the truck stay here. I got the ignition keys, Ariel, so don't be gettin' one of your sneaky ideas. We got vehicles. They don't. That's our advantage. But we can't just charge into Dodge because the track may be mined. Woody scouted another track three clicks north from here that will take a Hummer and get us close to the village. That's what we'll use. We move quiet, come in from the north, take 'em by surprise if possible. If they see us comin', we dismount and fan out. Weston and me take the up-slope, the rest of you the down-slope. If they move the donkeys, we head 'em off as best we can. Be careful where you shoot. We don't want any donkey casualties. Questions?"

J.M.'s men need no further guidance.

"What do Fritz and I do?" asks Ariel.

"You stay here with the truck and the trailer. Here's a radio. If you see anyone comin', press this button and talk to me. But I don't think you will. There aren't enough of 'em to hold us at the village and also get behind us. Still, you gotta be alert. When we've done whatever we gonna do, one of us will come down and get you."

The DGP strike team give their equipment a final check and mount up. Fritz watches the Hummers depart sitting in the open rear end of the horse trailer dangling his feet. He looks at Ariel. "This is Plan B?"

Ariel nods and boosts himself up beside him in the trailer.

"Was this always the plan?"

"Only if the Iranians showed. We weren't positive of that."

Within three minutes the Hummers have disappeared into the dawn, and their engines can no longer be heard. Fritz stares after them and then turns back to the scrawny Israeli facilitator.

"Tell me the truth, Ariel."

"Always."

"J.M. doesn't have Toots, does he?" No reply. "You didn't talk to any helicopter pilot in Marrakesh. He isn't going to fly Toots in here so she can be exchanged for me, is he?" No reply. "What was J.M. planning to do once I found out? You know I meant what I said: no Toots, no Ya'fur."

"Plan C is to threaten to shoot you to make you tell which donkey is Ya'fur. Plan D is to shoot you and then shoot the donkeys. Their thinking is that if Jesus' immortal donkey is one of them, it will stand up again after it's been shot. Marine slogan: Kill 'Em All, Let God Sort 'Em Out."

Fritz buries his face in his hands. "Why did you all lie to me? The Rabbi, J.M., you. I've cooperated with everyone and only asked for one thing in return. I've already identified Ya'fur for you on your solemn promise—even more, the Rabbi's promise—that Toots would be freed. That was the real Ya'fur with the sheikhs. He talked to me. Said we were going to meet again in New York."

Ariel brightens slightly. "So now you know you're going to live through this. That's good."

"But it doesn't change the cheating. If I were a violent man, Ariel Rafi, I would kill you where you stand. But what good would it do?"

"The plan was always a work in progress. Exchanging Toots was originally an integral part of it."

"When did Toots stop being part of it?"

"When we found out that the DGP didn't have her. J.M. did in fact kidnap her at the airport where we nabbed you. We know that for sure. But then they lost track of her."

"Lost track of her? What kind of idiot loses track of a hostage? Didn't they have her locked up?"

"J.M. doesn't know what happened. The man who was guarding her turned up drowned in the Venice lagoon. I don't even know when J.M. learned that. I only found out about it in Marrakesh the day before we left. The Rabbi telephoned me. When I confronted J.M., he admitted it, and we negotiated a new plan."

"So you're saying, Ariel, that you could have just left me in Marrakesh since you knew that without the trade for Toots I wasn't going to cooperate. But you didn't do that because for the Rabbi to get what he wanted, I had to come up the mountain to identify Ya'fur. Is that it? You'd already made the deal with the sheikhs to steal the old man's donkey and it was too late to change it? I'm speechless, Ariel. I'm really beyond words. Toots has gotten loose and is free somewhere, but you're still leading me around like a goat on its way to the butcher."

Fritz's disclaimer of violence has not prevented the distinctly unathletic Ariel from quaking with fear. "Toots ... "

"Toots what?"

"Toots may not be entirely free."

"What do you mean, not entirely free?"

"The Iranians may have her."

"What Iranians?"

"The ones over the hill in the village. It's only a possibility. A leak from an intelligence source in Tehran."

Fritz stands and pulls Ariel out of the horse trailer by his shirtfront. "Let's go." Fritz is dragging him by the arm.

"What are you going to do to me?"

"You're coming with me."

"Where."

"To the village. To rescue Toots."

"But J.M. said the track might be mined."

"That's why you're going to walk twenty feet ahead of me."

*   *   *

Toots wakes to a dull throbbing ache in her left foot after a night sleeping in the open. The previous day's ride had made her butt sore but was kind to her foot. Standing up now and hobbling a few steps on her cast she realizes that it was the limping around after they got to the village that had been too much. But what choice had she had? The Three-Thirteen were being pretty rough in roping and rounding up every donkey they could find, and she was the only one who knew how to calm them down. Also, watering them and talking to them, easing their fear away, had reminded her of her own donkeys and taken her mind off everything else that was happening, including the renewed ache in her foot.

The first light of the new day banishes idyllic thoughts of Ass Isle from her mind.

Two men are lying with their weapons in long shallow holes scooped out of the dirt. The Polisario guide and two other Iranians, mounted on their *méharis*, are in the midst of the donkey herd, which is again becoming restless and agitated. The fifth Iranian comes running up to Major Yazdi with a scouting report.

Toots hobbles up beside Monika to get a translation. "What's he saying?"

"He says the DGP are coming. They have two army vehicles."

"How many are they?"

"Five apparently."

"Is there going to be a fight?" Toots sounds eager.

"I hope not. The plan is to swap you for Fritz and then get away with Ya'fur, not to fight a battle."

"But how does anyone know I'm here?"

"Ahmadinejad's people in Tehran have been leaking the information like mad. If the DGP don't know you're here, they're pretty dense."

"So Fritz knows too?"

"I should think so." Just as Toots is wanting to hear more, Monika breaks off to listen to Major Yazdi explain the situation on the ground. She asks questions, nods, and looks where he points while Toots champs at the bit. At last she finishes and the Major moves off to talk to the men on camels.

"What was all that? What's going to happen?"

"Calm down. I'll tell you. The scouts sent out by the DGP have presumably discovered that we don't have any vehicles and realized that they have the advantage if they use theirs. That's why my smart husband sent out two men last night to pretend to plant a bomb on the path into the village." Monika points to a worn path winding down a slope and ending among the stone huts. "As you can see, if the the DGP tried to drive in that way, they would have the shelter of the huts and be between us and our escape route back to the Algerian border. By forcing them to take a different track and come from the north, Major Yazdi has made sure that we and the donkeys will be between them and our escape route." Toots looks puzzled. "I know you're thinking that we're just as exposed from either direction. But think about it this way. It's true they can shoot at us, but the guns they're using shoot bullets that travel for about two miles. If the donkeys are behind us, they can't shoot without a risk of hitting Ya'fur. Unless they're absolutely convinced that he is immortal and can't be killed."

Toots gets it. "So the donkeys are shielding us even though they're behind us."

"That's the Major's theory."

"Where does Fritz come in?"

"I honestly have no idea. The scout said there were no civilians in the vehicles that are coming this way."

"Do we even know that Fritz is with them?"

"We think we know. An Israeli I met in Tehran is supposed to be with the DGP. He's a double agent who's had dealings with Iranian intelligence and also works for the Mossad. His name is Jamsheed."

"So you think Fritz is with Jamsheed?"

"That is my guess."

*   *   *

On Jessie's order the Predator drone soars away from its parent ship. The launch technician sees it to cruising altitude and then speaks by phone to an operations specialist sitting at a console in a low, windowless, warehouse-like building outside Ogden, Utah with a joystick in each hand. "Janice, Bitty Bird is flying. You have the control."

"Roger that. All signals coming through clear."

Jessie is at the Gendarmerie headquarters in Marrakesh wearing an earphone with an attached mouthpiece. "Ogden Control? Can you hear me? This is Jessie Zayyat."

"This is Janice at Ogden Control. I hear you loud and clear, Jessie. Bitty Bird should be over the target in ten minutes."

Lieutenant Fasi and his technician Yassine are watching real-time satellite images on their computer screen.

"We're getting a real-time satellite feed here, Janice, but the resolution isn't good enough for us to see the detail that you're seeing. It looks from here like there's a group of hostiles next to a herd of donkeys and some camels outside a village."

"Roger that."

Yassine points to two moving rectangles. "Humvees."

"And there are two Humvees approaching the village from the north."

"I've got them. They've stopped now. The people are dismounting and deploying behind rocks. Are they hostiles or friendlies?"

Jessie thinks. "Let's call them unfriendlies until we find out more."

"There's also a truck with a horse trailer parked a couple of kilometers west of the village. I can see two people in the back of the trailer. Looks like they're wearing American athletic shoes."

"Those are definitely friendlies, Janice. Keep an eye on them. I can't make them out from the satellite."

"You will in a second. They're on the move. Walking toward the village. The one out front is carrying a stick with a white cloth tied to it. No, maybe not a stick. Too thin. I think it's the radio antenna broke off the truck."

"Where's the second one?"

"About twenty feet behind the first."

"Go back to the hostiles. Can you see a very short woman with a bandaged foot?"

"There's a tall woman, but no short ... yes, I've got her. She was behind the tall one."

"Bandaged foot?"

"Roger that. Looks like a cast."

Jessie picks up a telephone and calls the British embassy number. "Hello, this is Jessie Zayyat again. CIA acknowledgement code fourteen-hotel-victor-seven-three-three-three-kilo-oscar. I'm about to transmit the coordinates for the injured British national. She needs help as soon as you can get it there."

"Thank you, Ms Zayyat. I'm hooking you up with a Gendarmerie medevac helicopter standing by in Agadir. Can you give the coordinates in Arabic?"

"No problem. And thank you." Jessie turns the phone over to Lieutenant Fasi and tells him what to do. A few moments later he reports back that an Aérospatiale SA 315B Lama helicopter has lifted off. ETA twenty-five minutes.

Jessie turns her eyes back to the screen. "I'm back, Janice. Tell me what's happening."

*   *   *

Morning stillness still blankets Sidi Ben Adam. A hundred and fifty meters separate the two armed groups, some dug in or shielded by boulders, others standing up boldly in front of the donkey herd. Some of the donkeys are stomping and milling about, but nothing else moves. Suddenly a flutter of white appears at the crest of the path into the village, and a moment later Ariel comes walking cautiously down toward the stone huts, Fritz a short distance behind him. Every Three-Thirteen and DGP eye is fixed on the parade.

Fritz tells Ariel to stop when they are a dozen feet from the Iranian position and comes up beside him. He sees Toots standing with Monika Farber. "Hi, Toots!"

"Hi, Fritz!"

"Professor Farber, it is good to see you."

"It's good to see you too, Fritz."

"Are you the leader of your side?"

"No, my husband is. Major Yazdi. But I'm the only one who speaks English so I will speak for us."

Fritz turns his head toward the north and raises his voice. "J.M.," he shouts, "come on down here. It's time to negotiate."

J.M. stands out from behind a boulder with his M16 held at the ready. He doesn't move forward. "There's nothin' to negotiate, Fritz," he yells. "It's time to finish this."

"No it isn't. Look at where you are. If you shoot, you're going to kill donkeys. Do you want that?"

"Some things can't be helped."

"Yes they can. Now come down here and talk to me. You owe me that."

J.M. looks over his shoulder and says some words to his men, then begins a slow walk into the village. He stops as far from Fritz and Ariel as they are from the Iranians. "This close enough?"

"It'll do."

"That's the asshole who kidnapped me!" screams Toots.

"It was nothing personal, Ma'am," says J.M.

"You broke my foot and set me out to drown!"

"I'm sorry about your foot. It was Mitch that broke it. Mitch is dead now. He was a good man, but not too sharp."

Fritz is content to listen to the interplay between the two.

"It wasn't Mitch that put me out on that island. That was you. I almost drowned."

"I'm sorry about that, too. Nobody expected a flood this time of year. I suppose you want to kill me."

Monika interrupts. "Yes, she does, and she has every right to. But that is not why we're here. We both want the same donkey, but only Fritz can identify it. Agreed?"

"Agreed."

"And Fritz won't identify the donkey until Toots—Miss Greeley—is released. Agreed?"

"Agreed."

"As it stands, we have collected every donkey in the vicinity. The old man was gone when we arrived so we don't know which one was his. You, on the other hand, don't have any donkeys at all. We also have Toots, and you don't. So logically, we win. We take Fritz and the donkeys away with us, and we leave Toots here. Maybe with a gun. She's been practicing."

"Your logic don't hold up if we kill y'all."

"No, but are you and your men prepared to herd twenty donkeys down the mountain to the nearest town and at the same time drive your vehicles?"

"We only want one donkey. Fritz'll tell us which one and we'll be on our way."

"But that won't happen unless we give you Toots, which we aren't going to do."

"Then I guess we got a stand-off."

Major Yazdi, who has been standing patiently by Farber's side, asks her what is happening. While she summarizes the negotiation in Persian, J.M. and Fritz stare at each other.

"J.M.," says Fritz while the Persian discussion is continuing, "are you a good Christian?"

"I am that, but I am also a soldier."

"As I see it, you are getting set to violate a whole bunch of commandments. 'Thou shalt have no other gods before me.' You're acting as though Ya'fur is a god. 'Thou shalt not kill.' You're planning to kill everyone. 'Thou shalt not steal.' You're planning to steal Ya'fur. 'Thou shalt not bear false witness.' That means lie. But you lied to me. 'Thou shalt not covet thy neighbor's ass.' No comment needed."

"It's Jesus' donkey for when he comes back in glory."

"Do you think Jesus can't find his own donkey? What kind of a Messiah would that be? J.M., will you get down on your knees and pray with me?"

"Are you a Christian?"

"How could I not be a Christian. I am the person who can talk to Jesus' donkey. Pray with me, J.M." Fritz sinks to his knees and puts his hands out to J.M.

J.M. hesitates and then puts his rifle on the ground, walks forward, and kneels beside Fritz. Fritz grasps his hands and looks up.

"Heavenly Father, who is the beginning and the end of all things, I beseech you to look on your faithful servant J.M. and bless him with your forgiveness. And grant to me the grace to forgive him for the trespasses he has made against me. And grant to Toots the grace to forgive him the trespasses he made against her. He strove mightily and with a pure heart, and his sins were those of a soldier. So bless him, Father, and make your light to shine upon him. Amen."

"Amen," says J.M. "But I still want my donkey."

*   *   *

"Are you sure they're praying, Janice?"

"Well, I can't hear anything, but they sure look like they're praying. Now they're getting up. The unfriendly is taking his gun and heading back to his position."

"Enough of this. Time to let them know they're on candid camera. What can you do that won't kill any people or animals, Janice?"

"I can take out the truck and trailer. No one's anywhere around them."

"Then do it now."

"Roger that." Janice depresses a joystick button. Five thousand miles away a rocket ignites beneath the wing of the Predator and streaks toward a target two kilometers away. "I can confirm a direct hit."

"We can see it. Nice explosion. Good job, Janice. Take Bitty Bird on home. We've made our point, and I don't want to leave a bigger footprint than I have to."

Lieutenant Fasi hangs up the telephone he has been talking on. "The medevac helicopter is almost there."

*   *   *

In Sidi Ben Adam all heads, including the donkeys', turn toward the immense billow of flame and smoke rising over the crest of the path to the village following the bang-whump of the Predator's rocket exploding.

232

Time to get out of here, thinks Major Yazdi. He gives a hand signal to his men to mount up.

How did they get behind us? thinks J.M. He gives a hand signal to his men to return to their Hummers.

Clever idea, thinks Monika. *No horse trailer, no way they can get a donkey off the mountain.*

I wish I had a gun, thinks Toots.

What the fuck was that? thinks Fritz.

Fritz was right. I'm not the only big talker, thinks Ariel.

The flutter-whirr of an approaching helicopter interrupts all thoughts and draws most human eyes to the apparent direction of approach. Some of the donkeys become skittish as the small Red Crescent-marked craft lands near the herd.

Fritz looks at Toots. "I think that's your ride, Babe." Toots hobbles painfully toward him her arms stretched wide. He hugs her briefly and then steers her toward the medevac doctor who has stepped down from the helicopter. "I will see you again in better times. I have to go with my professor now."

"I love you, Fritz."

"Ariel, you speak Arabic. Go with Toots in the helicopter."

CONSTANTINE WRITES

While he waits for Pastor Steve to arrive, Paul Constantine sits in Ray Bob's recliner and rereads with uncritical satisfaction the final chapter he has drafted for *Ya'fur, the Messianic Donkey*.

After Muhammad it was all small fry for a long time. The only big hitter was his cousin Ali, but he rode around on that dumb mule Duldul. Occasionally I would hook up with someone who would try to make a noise about being the "Master of the Ass", but they were men of very little potential. The most promising one, a gimpy old Tunisian schoolteacher named Abu Yazid, almost captured an empire in the early 900s. But he made one mistake. After riding me for years and becoming a famous preacher as a result, he decided to switch to a stupid horse during a crucial siege.

Needless to say, I abandoned him immediately. His army was defeated, and his headless body, stuffed with straw, was exposed to the insults of a ravening mob. Good riddance. Anyone with spiritual gifts who prefers a horse to a donkey deserves what he gets. It was not all negative, though. Abu Yazid gave me a new land to explore: North Africa. What a lovely place. Steep forested mountains, rugged seacoasts, bustling walled cities, and a dozen different flavors of desert. I liked the region so much that I have stayed there ever since.

The greatest, and also the cleverest, of the saintly people I met in North Africa—this was a couple of hundred years later—was Ibn Tumart. He was rigid like Abu Yazid and took unholy delight in going into a marketplace to break musical instruments and wine jars. His reputation preceded him, but we didn't actually meet until one of his followers presented him with two gifts: me and a horse. Ibn Tumart took a look at the horse, took a look at me, took another look at the horse. I guess the horse was a fine specimen of its type, though I have prejudices. I wasn't letting on yet that I could follow his thoughts. I was testing him.

Finally he turned to his most faithful disciple and said, "Abd al-Mu'min, the horse is for you. I will take the donkey."

Music to my ears. We worked together for quite a while after that, and he generally followed my advice. For example, when some Berber-speaking Moroccan mountain people were having a hard time learning Arabic prayers, I was the one who suggested that he teach each of them one Arabic word and then line them up in the order in which the words were recited in the prayer. When he said go, they spoke their words one after the other, and that was the prayer. It was hilarious. Everyone loved it. That was how they learned to pray.

I did not, however, recommend that he announce that he was the Mahdi. He had the right spiritual qualities to be a Messiah, but the time wasn't right. All in all, it's better for a man with spiritual gifts to be a preacher or a prophet than to be a Messiah. As it turned out, calling himself the Mahdi didn't hurt Ibn Tumart. His disciple Abd al-Mu'min eventually established a great kingdom in his name that stretched all the way into Spain. But technically speaking, the Mahdi is supposed to come at the end of time. So Ibn Tumart jumped the gun.

After Ibn Tumart died I stayed on in Morocco. There were dozens of holy men there. They called them *marabouts*, and each one had his little following. I'd spend some time with one, then some time with another. But as I roved around I heard more and more stories about a place called Europe, where I had never been (though Ufair had). When I got to Morocco, it was politically linked with Spain. Then later, when the Christians took over up north, Morocco became overrun by Muslim and Jewish refugees. What I divined from eavesdropping on the conversations of these refugees, and later confirmed by listening to Spanish, Portuguese, and English soldiers and freebooters who made their way to Morocco, was that Europeans loved horses and despised donkeys.

In Spain, for example, when the Christians convicted some poor soul of heresy, they would put a tall pointed hat on his head and parade him around on a donkey. The hat was supposed to be a demeaning symbol of the donkey's penis. As if having a big penis were shameful! It made me long for the good old days in Egypt when maleness was properly respected. There was also an English writer I heard tell of who wrote a play in which a beautiful queen is given a love potion in her sleep. As soon as she wakes up, she becomes enamored of a stupid oaf who has magically been given the head of a donkey with huge ears. It was like the humorous old story by Apuleius, complete with roses, except that when Apuleius told it, the young man who was transformed into a donkey was of noble birth, and his love affair with a noblewoman was good clean fun. For this Englishman and his audience, however, it was obvious that having long ears—you know what they stand for—meant that you were clumsy and stupid.

The irony was, that despite all their anti-donkey sentiment, I could tell that the Europeans were desperately in need of me. I could sense the presence of men with spiritual gifts a long way away, and it was just sad that they were all lacking the inspiration that I alone could give them.

One poor soul, an Englishman named James Nayler, did his best, but it failed miserably. He rode into Bristol on a donkey while his followers sang "Holy, holy, holy" and spread their cloaks in the mud. All very Jesus-like. For this the English authorities flogged him, pierced his tongue—not a fashionable thing in those days the way it is now— and branded a B for blasphemy on his forehead. His followers went on to form a sect called the Quakers, but the peril of pretending to be the Messiah and riding on the wrong donkey was there for all to see.

It hadn't always been that way. Centuries earlier in the Middle Eastern lands I was more familiar with, people just assumed that a man on an ass was likely to be a prophet. How times had changed. In North Africa, only soldiers rode horses. But in Europe, so far as I could tell, it was horses, horses, horses all the time. To symbolize maleness, they even invented a crazy legend about a horse with a long horn protruding from its forehead. Or else they made maleness a smutty joke, like having their children play "pin the tail on the donkey." Wink, wink, nod, nod.

One of the saddest stories involved a Jew named Sabbatai Zevi. Like Nayler he accepted a mumbo-jumbo theory that the Jewish Messiah would appear in a certain year and lead his people back to their homeland. Though I never met him, I could sense from afar that he had a great spiritual calling. When he finally declared that he was the Messiah, Jews from all over Europe made ready to embark for the land of their forefathers. And I am convinced he would have made good on his claims if I had been with him. But alas, he had no donkey to reassure and advise him when the Ottoman Sultan had him arrested. He converted to Islam, and his movement collapsed, except for those few who also converted. Sabbatai's oversight was eventually recognized. Four centuries after his death, a tiny sect of his followers formed around the teaching that his failure to recognize the divine voice that spoke through Balaam's donkey caused his downfall. But by then it was much too late.

As I pondered the things I was learning about Europe, one part of me wanted to head north and help the spiritually gifted, who seemed to be particularly numerous among the people called Protestants. But another part of me cautioned that it would be folly to depart the donkey-friendly lands of Islam. Understandably, my greatest wish was to somehow multiply myself so I could serve in many places, but I didn't know of any way to do that. So I stayed on in Morocco, hoping against hope that someday I would be transported to a land of virtuous Protestants and there be multiplied so that I could become the companion of the greatest of their preachers.

The crunch of gravel under the wheels of Pastor Steve's Mercedes marks the clergyman's timely arrival just as the author is pondering whether he has laid it on a bit too thick at the end.

"Hot out there!" exclaims Pastor Steve dabbing his brow with a carefully ironed linen handkerchief.

Constantine holds the door open. "Come into the air conditioning. It's good to see you. Can I get Marie to bring you a lemonade before we sit down?"

"Thanks, Paul, but I just drank one in the car coming over here. Wasn't as good as Marie's, of course, but it did the job."

Pastor Steve usurps the big recliner Constantine has been sitting in leaving him to take a seat on the sofa. Much as the professor wants to know what Pastor Steve thinks about his manuscript, he doesn't wish to seem overeager. "I hear J.M. is coming home."

"Yep. Ray Bob's out at the airport fetching him. Gives us a chance to talk, just the two of us, about your new chapter." Constantine inclines forward in anticipation. "Basically, what you got here, Paul, is a good start." Constantine sags back and steels his mind for criticism. "You get the message across, specially at the end. But it doesn't have the same feel as the other chapters. Doesn't read as well. The others have a popular feel. This one is more academic."

"It's a draft, of course," says Constantine defensively. "I do a lot of revising."

"I'm sure you do, but I'm just saying it'd be more effective if it read more like what you wrote about Lucius and Ufair, that Black Ass of Baron Samedi chapter. That was a hoot." Pastor Steve holds up his hand to nip Constantine's startled reaction in the bud. "Now, now. I know that I wasn't supposed to see that chapter. When Marie showed it to me, she told me that you weren't sure it should be in the book at all since it takes an old story by Apuleius and changes it around a lot. But that's just the professor in you, Paul. Those old Greeks and Romans are long gone. Everything they wrote is in the public domain. You can do what you want, switch it around any way you like. Nobody's going to sue you. The fact is, the Lucius and Ufair story is what people want to read. Marie likes it very much, and I do too. So I think you should just make up your mind to include it."

"Well, if you both like it so much."

Pastor Steve misses Constantine's caustic overtone. "That's the spirit! Now then, let's go on. I think maybe we could use a little less on the Jews and a little more on the Protestants. What did Calvin and Luther and our other early leaders say about donkeys?"

"Nothing good. They were the sort of typical European horse-lovers Ya'fur talks about. Luther said several times that a Catholic and a donkey are indistinguishable. Calvin got angry once at another theologian and said, 'I care as little for this fellow's words as I care for the hee-haw of a donkey.' And Thomas Müntzer, who was more like today's evangelical preachers than either of the other two, called the people who disagreed with him 'donkey fart doctors of theology.' None of this, needless to say, belongs in Ya'fur's memoirs."

"Uh-huh, I see. So maybe that's not the way to go. But you still need some stories that are more colorful than what you've got. That thing that happened to that Nayler was pretty hard to take."

Constantine is sneering on the inside. "In 1993 some members of the Chabad Lubavitch sect in Brooklyn thought their leader, Reb Schneerson, was going to announce he was the Moshiach so they went to Israel to find a white donkey for him to ride on. Is that more colorful?"

"That's that Jewish stuff again. You know so damn much, Paul, I'm sure once you think about it you'll be able to come up with some good Protestant stories."

"How's this? In 2010 Pastor Manny Ojeda in Columbus, Indiana gave a sermon about Jesus entering Jerusalem. He divided the people who were there into palm branches and donkeys. He said the palm branches are good Christians only while they are green, which means when times are good and everyone has a job. But the donkeys of the Lord are always good and humbly do the Christian thing without asking why."

"Hmmm. A little better. Not much about Ya'fur, though."

"The preacher is a Seventh-day Adventist."

"I've got no problem with that. Still Protestant. Better than being Jewish. Anyway, you work on it. You'll come up with something good. You got plenty of time. Christine tells me that the cloning isn't going to happen overnight, and apparently J.M. and his boys came up empty in Morocco."

"I'm sorry to hear that."

"Only a temporary setback, I'm sure. We'll end up with Ya'fur one way or another."

The swinging door to the kitchen opens a crack to reveal a three-inch sliver of Baleine in a flowered apron. "Professor? Mr. Paul? Can I talk to you in here for just one moment?"

"I'm talking with Pastor Steve now, Marie. Can't it wait?"

Baleine glares at him. "Of course it can, Mr. Paul," she says sweetly. "I'm so sorry I interrupted."

"Oh, go on in the kitchen and talk to Marie, Paul. I have to call Ray Bob anyway and see whether J.M.'s got in."

Baleine holds the kitchen door open and pulls Constantine forcibly into the back pantry out of earshot of the living room. "Did I hear him say that J.M. didn't get Ya'fur?"

"If you were eavesdropping, you did."

"Then you should excuse yourself and go upstairs and pack your things. We're leaving tonight."

"Why? I've still got some business to do with Pastor Steve."

"The reason why is because I am being paid to be your bodyguard, and I say so. Your being here was supposed to guarantee that Toots got traded for Fritz. It sounds like that didn't happen."

"We don't know what happened."

"No, but J.M. does, and he'll be telling Ray Bob and Pastor Steve all about it as soon as he gets them alone. What I've seen of J.M., my guess is that he'll be looking for someone to blame everything on. And that's what old white guys are for."

"But that wouldn't be fair. I didn't do anything."

"How's J.M. going to know that? He's been out of the country, and his daddy doesn't run a very secure lockup. But why am I explaining anything to you? Just get your old white ass ready to leave."

Constantine is upstairs putting scattered items in his toilet kit when he hears another car drive up and Pastor Steve greeting Ray Bob and J.M. He goes downstairs and meets them coming into the house.

"Hi, J.M.!"

"Howdy, Professor." He looks past him at Baleine standing in the kitchen door. "What's the colored gal doin' in the kitchen, Papa?"

"Now you don't gotta be like that, J.M. Marie here may have a helluva a scowl sometimes, but she's a real sweet gal. She can cook, and she knows all about that aromatherapy. Gave me one dose for holdin' my appetite down and another for my sleep problem. I tell ya, I don't know when I've felt so good. But nobody but me cares about that. What Pastor Steve and the professor want to hear is what you told me in the car about how things went in Morocco.

"It didn't work out so good. Come down to us and some Eye-ranians tryin' to find the same animal. They come in by a shorter route from Algeria and got there first. Had all the donkeys rounded up ready to go by the time we arrived. We had the tactical advantage and woulda blowed 'em away in a shoot-out. But then the horse trailer and truck we left at the camp exploded.

Figured some Eye-ranians musta got 'round behind us so we had to bug out of there. Once I got a look at the truck, though, I saw that it was a missile that took it out, not the Eye-ranians."

"A missile?" says Constantine.

"No question. Seen plenty of blown up stuff in Iraq, and I can read the signs. Short-range air-to-ground."

"Whose missile was it?"

"Well, not Moroccan, that's for sure. They didn't even know we was in the country. And not Eye-ranian. They don't have good stuff like that. So that leaves the CIA, so far as I can figure." Pastor Steve and Paul Constantine wear identical expressions of perplexity. "And that means someone's been tattlin' on us."

Constantine senses that it is time to change the subject. "What about the girl. Was she exchanged for that German student?"

"I don't want to get into that right now. It was screwed up from the start and didn't get no better. The Eye-ranians got the German, but I think he may have been workin' for 'em all along. The girl got flown out on a medevac copter. Had a hurt foot."

J.M. stares at the carpet. No one seems to know where to take the conversation next. Baleine chooses the opportunity to announce that dinner will be ready in ten minutes if anybody needs to make himself comfortable.

Dinnertime talk is desultory and ends abruptly when an agitated J.M. pleads travel exhaustion and skips the pecan pie. Pastor Steve stays for the pie but then takes his leave. Constantine tells Ray Bob he needs to work on his writing and goes upstairs.

When Baleine finishes cleaning up in the kitchen, she comes into the living room to say goodnight to Ray Bob. "Mr. Ray Bob, I have a new sleep inhaler for you to use. I changed the formula a little. It should be even more relaxing than the first one I gave you. That one was almost empty so I went into your bedroom and took it back to refill it. I hope that was all right."

"That's just fine, Marie. And that was a delicious dinner. You make a wicked pecan pie. You should stay down here when this if over and let your boss go back up north by himself."

"Remember, three big sniffs in each nostril when you're ready to get into bed."

Three hours later the nighttime calm is broken by screams, shouts, gunshots, and barking dogs. Baleine taps on Constantine's door and then opens it.

"Time to go. You got two minutes."

"Is this our escape?"

"What do you think?"

"I think it's awfully noisy for an escape. Don't escapees usually sneak away and then hear the hue and cry break out after they're safely away?"

"That's one minute gone." She shuts the door.

In the hallway the noises are louder, and it's apparent that the screaming and commotion are coming from Ray Bob's room. The gunshots have stopped. J.M.'s voice can be heard trying to outshout his father's frantic cries. Constantine follows Baleine down the stairs and out the front door. The dogs are already barking so their passage across the driveway sparks no added response. Baleine produces keys to J.M.'s pickup. As she maneuvers down the gravel drive without headlights, Constantine looks back past the empty gun rack. No one is following them. In five minutes they are on I-85 speeding toward Raleigh.

"What happened back there?" asks Constantine.

"A staged diversion is what happened. Standard escape procedure."

"Who staged the diversion?"

"Ray Bob, obviously."

"Ray Bob? Really? So he wasn't actually holding us hostage. J.M. was the one we had to worry about. Good old Ray Bob came through for us. I could have predicted that."

"Good old Ray Bob sniffed a massive dose of ketamine through his inhaler when he went to bed. Woke up totally crazy."

"What's ketamine?"

"A horse tranquilizer. Part of the stuff that got my daddy in trouble. Just one of the essential oils I carry around in my cosmetics bag. No one ever looks at a woman's cosmetics. Ketamine causes numbness, out-of-body feelings, hallucinations, suicidal thoughts, and general psychosis. Judging from the sound of things, Ray Bob woke up screaming, grabbed his gun and started shooting. That made the dogs bark and brought J.M. running in shouting. Classic diversion."

"So Ray Bob wasn't helping us."

"Not deliberately, he wasn't."

"What will happen to him? When will the stuff wear off?"

"Depends on how much he sniffed. I imagine he'll be in the hospital for a couple of days. Or weeks."

The view from Tehran

In a corral at Rabouni, the Polisario guerrilla camp outside Tindouf, twenty donkeys are variously standing, eating, walking around, or lying down. Two Three-Thirteen soldiers are mounting a relaxed guard, their rifles supplemented by coiled lariats. An occasional Polisario soldier stops by to look with curiosity at the animals. All that risk just for donkeys?

Elation mixed with relief had overtaken Major Yazdi's men as soon as they recrossed the frontier undetected by Moroccan border police. Major Yazdi, however, has held off his personal celebration until he has personally seen the last donkey into the corral. That done, he is now on the phone to Tehran to report mission accomplished: Fritz—acquired; donkeys—acquired; casualties—zero. One job remains, to identify which of the donkeys is Ya'fur.

Only Monika Farber has learned the truth, that Ya'fur is in the hands of the Israelis and that none of the donkeys in the corral can satisfy President Ahmadinejad's need. She and Fritz are leaning disconsolately on a wooden gate overlooking the milling herd.

"You're sure the donkey you identified for the Rabbi is the real Ya'fur?"

"Of course I'm sure. It talked to me. As clearly as I'm talking to you. It said we would meet again in New York City."

"I doubt you'll ever make it to New York once Ahmadinejad finds out the Israelis have him. He'll probably have you executed."

"Won't you protect me?"

"He'll probably have me executed too."

The two look morosely at the animals. Then Fritz brightens. "You know what, Professor? I'll protect you." Monika looks at him askance. "It's just dawned on me that Ahmadinejad isn't going to hurt me."

"Why not?"

"Because he's going to let me go to New York. That's where I'm going to meet Ya'fur. Ya'fur has spent thousands of years inspiring the world's greatest prophets so a random future appointment like that isn't something he's going to be wrong about. We'll just explain to Ahmadinejad that there'll be another a chance to capture Ya'fur there."

"In New York?"

"In New York. Here's our argument: Why did you send a mission to Morocco? Because you believed that if the Three-Thirteen could get me in their custody in trade for Toots, I could find Ya'fur and positively identify him. Dealing with the DGP and trading me for Toots were the only operational obstacles. Now those obstacles are gone. J.M. and his boys have presumably gone back to America, and you released Toots. Out of gratitude I'm now willing to help you get Ya'fur back from the Israelis, who have him in their possession only because they lied to me when they promised me they could free Toots. Send me to New York, and I'll get Ya'fur back from them. Send my disciplinarian professor along with me, and she'll make sure I get the job done. How does that sound?"

Monika thinks before responding. "I don't suppose Ya'fur mentioned just when he was going to meet you again."

"No. That could be a problem."

"Another problem is whether Ahmadinejad will believe that you're really on his side. You're not a Shi'ite."

"Doesn't the same doubt apply to you, Professor? You're not a Shi'ite."

"True, but it's going to complicate things when you confess that you gave Ya'fur to the Israelis and didn't tell either us or the DGP until we almost went to war."

"That was because I still thought the Israelis could produce Toots, not because I was on their side. I don't even know if being on a side actually means anything when it's the coming of the Messiah you're talking about. People aren't going to vote on whether to be saved or not saved. Professor, did you think you were picking the Shi'ite side when you went to Iran?"

"No. I went because I found out Ahmadinejad was looking for Ya'fur, and I knew—or I knew that you knew—where to find him. I was thinking of making a mark in history and wrapping Ahmadinejad around my little finger rather than bringing history to an end."

"So you're not personally a believer in the return of the Hidden Imam."

"I'm an across-the-board non-believer, Fritz, not a believer. And the coming of a Messiah at the end of the world is at the top of the list of things I don't believe in. Besides, if it actually did happen, no matter which religion the Messiah was partial to, I'd be sure to end up in Hell along with most of my family."

"Then we're in almost the same situation. Christians, Jews, Muslims, for all I care they can flip a coin to see who gets to have a Messiah. What's different between the two of us is that I don't see myself going to Hell. Being on speaking terms with Ya'fur has to have some benefits."

"You make a good argument, Fritz. President Ahmadinejad is a shrewd man. He may actually send you to New York. If I were like Professor Constantine, I would unfairly take full credit for your intellectual development. But we still have some hurdles to cross here. My brave husband is expecting you to tell him which of these donkeys he went to so much trouble to bring back from Sidi Ben Adam is Ya'fur. If you don't, or if you say you can't, I happen to know that he's authorized to shoot you. Then he'll fall back on the DNA technique: take samples from all the donkeys in this corral and let the scientists in Tehran determine which one is not a real donkey."

Fritz shrugs. "So? I will just fake an identification. Eventually I'll have to confess that I gave Ya'fur to the Israelis, but that can wait until we're in Tehran."

"That's not a good plan, but it may be the only one."

"What's wrong with it?"

"What's wrong is that if you lie once in saying that you can talk to one of these donkeys, Ahmadinejad will think you're lying again when you say you're supposed to meet the real Ya'fur in New York. How will that not sound like a trick to get him to pay your plane fare to the United States? Why not throw you in prison until Ya'fur sends a note saying he's waiting for you at the Empire State Building?"

Fritz stares out at the donkeys. "What choice do I have?"

"None. But don't count on me to vouch for you. For all I know, you're conning me too."

"Con my professor? Never."

Monika grins. "You're such a smart-ass. Stop talking and go in there and pick a talking donkey. I'll go so far as to assure Major Yazdi that you're being honest. He knows better than to disbelieve his wife and court her wrath. But once we get to Tehran, you're on your own."

Fritz sighs and straightens his shoulders as if he is presenting himself before a firing squad. He lifts the loop of rope holding the corral gate shut and walks inside. The Three-Thirteen guards are now watching closely. *Don't pick the first one*, he thinks. *Look them all over.* He walks with a slow pace and scrutinizes each donkey face. Gray? White? There's a black one. Another big gray.

"Hello, Fritz."

Fritz freezes in place. He looks to where the donkey voice is coming from. It's the black donkey. "That's not you, Ya'fur, unless you can change colors."

"Ya'fur's in the Canary Islands. I'm Ufair, his brother."

"Ufair? What are you doing here?"

"Helping you get to New York." Ufair's tone lacks the warmth of Ya'fur's.

"You know about that?"

"Of course. You'll meet Ya'fur there at the end of September."

"I will?"

"Don't question me, Fritz. It's annoying. Just identify me as the talking donkey. I'll pass the DNA test, and that will keep you out of trouble."

"But do you want to be taken to Iran? Is that part of what you see in the future?"

"Don't worry about me. If I ever go to Iran, it will be on my own terms. As for this pathetic pen, I can leave anytime I like. And when I go, you can be sure that whoever is around will get hurt."

"What's going to happen with me and Ya'fur in New York?"

"No questions. Just get on with what you're supposed to be doing."

Fritz looks around and sees the guards and his professor looking at him strangely. He walks back to the gate of the corral.

"Was that donkey language you were talking?" asks Farber.

"I guess it was."

"I've never heard a human utter anything like it. It was a great act."

"It wasn't an act. That black donkey is Ya'fur's brother, Ufair. He says his DNA will prove that I fulfilled my commitment to identify a talking donkey. He also says that I'm going to meet Ya'fur in New York at the end of September."

*   *   *

As on three occasions in the past, the venerable Zoroastrian sage Sohrab Jahangir Mehta converses with his distinguished Iranian visitor in the reception parlor of the one-story stone house he occupies with his faithful servant in the Parsee Colony section of Quetta. His well-trimmed white beard reaches the middle of his chest, and he wears a squarish black skullcap. Otherwise he is dressed in a white European dress shirt and pleated woolen slacks. As the Pakistani city closest to the southern border of Afghanistan and a refuge for Taliban fighters, Quetta is no longer safe for the Parsee Zoroastrians so only a handful of souls remain in Parsee Colony. Nor is it much safer for President Ahmadinejad's Chief of Staff Esfandiar Rahim Mashaei, which is why he has traveled there from Karachi's Jinnah International Airport in an armored SUV with heavily armed bodyguards in two accompanying pickup trucks.

Tea, candies, and fruit have been served, and expressions of warmest wishes and deepest respect from and to Iran's president have been conveyed and reciprocated. Mashaei has followed these rituals with a detailed account of the report that President Ahmadinejad has received from his Morocco mission, including a subsequent communication from the Polisario at the Rabouni camp saying that the men guarding the captured donkeys have killed one another in a meaningless gunfight and that the animals have all escaped.

"I have two things to say," the ancient seer replies in a tremulous and broken voice. "First, you misunderstood what I told you when you first visited me. Or perhaps I didn't make myself clear. The voices I hear in my vision of the sacred donkey Ya'fur are in English. But the accents are American, not British. Second, I need to warn you about the donkey named Ufair mentioned by the German Fritz. He is not the donkey of the Mahdi. He is the donkey of the Dajjal. According to the old stories, no matter how black and evil he looks, once the Dajjal mounts him every hair of his body will play a beautiful and seductive melody. Everyone who hears it will become entranced and follow the Dajjal into the Fire. Your President is lucky that Ufair caused the guards to butcher one another so he could escape from captivity. But if he should ever encounter him, he must not listen to him."

"I don't understand. The Mahdi and the Dajjal come at the same time. How can anyone who sees the one not see the other?"

"Many will see the Dajjal and his donkey and still go to the Garden, Mr. Mashaei. It is those who listen to the music of Ufair who will be lost in the Fire."

*   *   *

Iran's President and his Chief of Staff—Mahmoud and Rahim in the privacy of the presidential residence—are mulling over a just received rumor.

"How far can we trust anything we hear from young Jamsheed, Rahim?"

"He's our ear into the Mossad."

"And their ear into us. We use him when we want something known, and they surely do the same."

"However, in this case, Mahmoud, I think there is reason to believe him. Here are my reasons. First, the German woman tells us that the Israelis have Ya'fur. Neither of us trusts her, of course, because she is a manipulative whore. But on the other hand, she did succeed in bringing her student back from Morocco as she promised. Second, her student, Fritz Messiassohn, reports that Ya'fur spoke to him and predicted that he would meet him again in New York. Neither of us trusts him, of course, because no one can prove that he's actually able to talk to Ya'fur. On the other hand, our geneticists have now tested some hairs from the black donkey that Fritz claims to have talked to in Algeria and confirmed that it is definitely not an ordinary donkey."

"But the black donkey itself has now vanished."

"It seems so. I'm still waiting for clarification of the report we got from the Polisario. The first report was that something touched off a fight between Major Yazdi's men and the Polisario guerrillas, who were helping them guard the donkeys. Everyone on both sides is dead now, including Major Yazdi, and the donkeys have dispersed into the countryside. The Polisario leadership believes there was a curse on the donkeys."

Ahmadinejad smiles grimly. "There seems to a curse on everything we try to do, Rahim."

"Third—if I may go on—Sohrab Jahangir Mehta, the Parsee seer, tells me that the voices he hears around Ya'fur speak with American accents and that he sees you personally standing with Ya'fur and feeding him an apple. Neither of us can fully trust him, of course, because he may just invent stories to gratify me. On the other hand, if Ya'fur is going to be in New York, then the people around him will be speaking English with an American accent. So that part of the Parsee's vision will have been proven right."

"So that's the background for Jamsheed's rumor."

"Yes. Jamsheed reports that the Israelis are planning to donate Ya'fur to President Obama at the end of September, and President Obama is going to put it in the National Zoo."

"The end of September. I'll be in New York at the end of September for the United Nations General Assembly meeting."

"The Israelis and Americans are doing this deliberately to insult you, Mahmoud. They know how much we have struggled and sacrificed to prepare for the return of the Hidden Imam, and they want to thumb their noses at us."

"Don't get excited, Rahim. They've been thumbing their nose at us for years, and what has it gotten them? A sore nose. We know that eventually Ya'fur must come to us."

"But we can hasten the day, Mahmoud."

"You think we can do that by taking the two Germans with us when we go to New York? They can get the donkey?"

"We know that an opportunity will arise because Fritz is going to be close enough to Ya'fur to talk to him. It's just a question of seizing the moment."

"Will the Germans cooperate?"

"Fritz will do what the Farber woman tells him to do, and she will do whatever you ask her to do. That was her commitment on our day of shame."

"We don't talk about that day, Rahim."

"I know. It is completely forgotten."

THE VIEW FROM ASS ISLE

"Watch the colt suckle, Jessie. See it's face muscles move? That's the rhythm that works best in milking a jenny. It's not like a cow. Your hands have to be more sensitive. And keep you fingernails away from her teat. I wear fake fingernails to remind me of that. The jenny wants to feel like she's suckling her baby. That's why it's good to have her baby standing nearby."

Jessie squats beside the donkey and reaches for her teats. The donkey walks away. "You could at least hold her head, Toots."

"Is she trusts you, I won't have to. She needs to get familiar with your smell."

Jessie stands up and brushes a bit of straw off her hand. Levis and a sweatshirt become her better than the drab pantsuit that is her standard Munich attire. Her hair is pinned up under a cap. "I'm sure I'll get the hang of it. I earned a marksman rating in training, and that requires good hands."

"How in the world did you get into the CIA?" asks Toots as they walk back toward the house. They take a circuitous route to avoid the crime zone barriers around the site where the St. Andrews police have dug up the bodies of Asef, Moosa, and Said.

"Simple. I did well in college. As an SDA I don't have any bad habits. I got a government fellowship to take Arabic for my language requirement. I want to keep my country safe. And the pay is good even for someone who majored in English."

"I never went to university."

"I know. You told me you decided to live with your dad and help him care for the donkeys after your mother died. That was a very loyal choice."

"But you know, even if Mommy hadn't died, I might not have gone. I don't have the right skills."

"Don't say that, Toots! Of course you have the right skills. Since I've been here I've read the book chapters Professor Constantine wrote and compared them with the edited versions you and your father sent to him by e-mail. You're a wonderful writer. You're twice the writer he is, and writing is the most important skill to have in college."

Toots smiles. "The professor does write terribly. But he knows so much and reads so many languages. I could never do that."

"You don't have to. Not even if you want to become a professor. Nobody wants to be another Professor Constantine these days. He's a fossil. And he's in a league by himself when it comes to useless knowledge."

Scaffolding erected to facilitate window replacement and gunshot repairs to the house façade blocks the front door. The two women walk around through the dry, late-summer grass toward the kitchen entrance.

"I know I've told you this before, Jessie, but father and I are both enormously grateful to the CIA for paying to repair the house. And to you for getting the social and veterinary services agencies to visit daddy while I was gone. He was very shaken up after the DGP invaded the island. He needed the help."

"Don't mention it. I just put in a request to CD-DACP and got the right people to sign off on it."

"What's CD-DACP?"

"The Collateral Damage—Damage Assessment and Compensation Program. The War on Terror causes so much damage and civilian loss of life that compensating victims has become one of the Agency's major activities. What I reported was that if we had simply detained Fritz when we picked him up at the Trieste airport instead of handing him over to the Israelis, you wouldn't have been put through all your misery."

Toots looks doubtful. "That isn't really true, though, Jessie, is it? The house got shot up in a fight between the DGP and the Three-Thirteen that you didn't know anything about. And J.M. would have stranded me on that island no matter who had Fritz."

"Don't fret. No one's going to check up on all that. I've become something of an Agency star for connecting the dots and figuring out all on my own that Polisario guerrillas had crossed over into Morocco to stage a terror attack. Taking the initiative and ordering a Predator strike to chase them back to Algeria again is being touted as a big, bold move, particularly since it didn't kill any random civilians."

"No one's going to check up on that story either, I presume."

"The only one who might is Joseph. You know, my boss. But he would be too embarrassed. He would have to talk about sacred donkeys and Messiahs, and he would sound like a religious nut. As a Mormon, that's the very last impression he wants to give."

"Did you actually tell him the whole truth?"

"Of course. He's my boss, and I'm a loyal employee. SDAs don't play fast and loose with the truth. But rather than reprimand me, he signed off on the CD-DACP application for your compensation. He's always considered me too religious, but if he says anything to that effect, it will sound like he didn't mentor me properly. And let me tell you, nobody wants to be called up before the CIA's Mentoring Review Board."

"Can you stay in the CIA if they get the idea that you're a religious fanatic?"

"I can't answer that without violating security protocols. But I am giving some thought to changing careers after this is all cleared up."

"Really? To what?"

"I'm seriously considering donkey rescue."

"Brilliant! But don't quit until I've gotten my free trip to the States. Being officially debriefed by the CIA will be something I can tell my grandchildren about."

"As soon as things are shipshape here, I promise you I'll bring you to the U.S."

"I'd like to visit Professor Constantine while I'm there. I want to find out what he has to say about my editing."

"Easily arranged. Let's aim for late September."

PEOPLE OF THE WORLD, L.P.

Tall, blonde, and handsome Sargent Peabody Gibbs III scored a near perfect 178 on his LSAT, which was enough for Stanford Law School's admissions committee to overlook his lackluster Harvard grades. A year later, he was in an internship program with the top-tier New York firm of Webster, Bachelor, and Craven, and after graduation he became a full-time associate. So where, he wonders, has he gone wrong?

He has plenty of billable hours so his compensation is on a par with his peers in the firm. He has a gorgeous wife, a cute daughter adopted from China, a big house in Cold Spring Harbor, a 30-foot boat on Long Island Sound, and membership in an exclusive golf club. But instead of representing Google or Microsoft or Bank of America, here he is in the sunny Canary Islands surveying a palm-bordered beach from the lounge of the Hotel Reina Isabel in Las Palmas and waiting for a dubious Israeli contact whose name he doesn't even know. All of this on behalf of People of the World, L.P., a shadowy business whose sole concern seems to be the importation into the United States of a single donkey.

Sarge sees a compact, youngish man in a gray chalk-stripe suit and a black skullcap carrying a sleek computer case enter the lounge and speak to the hostess. He stands as the man walks briskly to his table.

"Hi, I'm Sarge Gibbs," he says as he extends his hand.

They shake vigorously. "Pleased to meet you, Mr. Gibbs. I'm the Rabbi. It's a joke name. I'm not really a rabbi. But it will do for our purposes."

"Order you a drink, Mr. Rabbi?" Sarge signals a waiter in an iridescent blue vest.

"Orangina," says the Rabbi to the waiter.

The two men sit down.

"Tell me how our project is faring, Mr. Gibbs."

"Sarge."

"Sarge. Will there be any problems sending the property to the United States by September?"

"None that Webster, Bachelor, and Craven can't handle. As you may know, the United States has very strict rules on importing hoofed animals. They cannot easily be brought in from any country that has a history of foot-and-mouth disease. By good fortune, however, the Canary Islands have no such history even though we're only 100 kilometers off the coast of Morocco, which has had the disease. So as long as the animal or animals in question were born and bred here on the islands, quarantine problems are minimal."

"No problemo. I will furnish you with affidavits from the donkey's owner and from the Spanish Ministry of Health, which has colonial authority here, that the donkey is from a long line of pure-bred Canary Islands stock."

"Affidavits should do the trick." Sarge is uneasy. "Just between us, though, is the donkey really from here? I'll tell you, Mr. Rabbi, it doesn't make any sense to me that anyone would go to all the expense this is going to cost you just to fly one donkey to the United States."

"Where else would the donkey be from? You think it might have been smuggled here from Morocco in a fishing boat in the dead of night?"

"For example. It makes no difference to me personally, you understand, but I must stress that even the inadvertent introduction of a livestock disease into the United States is punishable by law. And I mean severely punishable."

"That will not be a problem. The donkey is in robust health. In fact, it's probably the healthiest donkey in the world."

"Would it be appropriate for me to ask what purpose the import of this donkey is meant to serve?"

"Quite appropriate. After all, you are going to be our public and legal face. People of the World, L.P. plans to give the donkey as a gift to President Barack Obama. It's a symbol of the Democratic Party, and the partners are eager to see the President receive it on behalf of America's children and donate it to the National Zoo. Then, at such time as a Republican makes it again to the White House, People of the World will make a parallel donation of an elephant."

Sarge mulls the information over. In a polite and judicious tone reserved for his most powerful and esteemed clients, he says, "Surely, Mr. Rabbi, there are rules and limits on what a President can accept in the way of gifts. Value limits, for example. And this is not to mention Mr. Obama's personal inclinations in this matter. Presidents have owned dogs, and have even accepted dogs as gifts. But giving a donkey to a sitting Democratic president, particularly one noted for his reserve and decorum, may not be easy."

"Don't worry about that, Sarge. We are hard at work on those matters. People in high places talking to people in higher places, if you know what I mean. I think we can pull it off. And when we get the go ahead, we will be depending heavily on you to handle all of the legal details and to present the gift to the public in the most favorable light."

Sarge is feeling a tingle of excitement. "When the gift is made, will I be photographed with the President? Maybe appear on television with him?"

The Rabbi grins. "You can count on it, Sarge. I guarantee it."

Sarge raises his glass. "I'd like to drink to that."

The Rabbi obliges with a loud clink.

"You don't happen to play golf, do you, Mr. Rabbi? I mean, it isn't against your religion, is it? They have a splendid course here."

"The only golf I play is with a Frisbee. Have you ever tried your hand at disc golf?"

"No, can't say that I have. I was on the championship intramural Eliot House Ultimate Frisbee team in college, though."

The Rabbi grins. "You're kidding!"

"Nope. God's truth."

"Then why don't you come with me tomorrow. There's an Ultimate Frisbee club on Tenerife that welcomes visitors. It's just the next island over. I'm a bit of a fanatic so I'm all set to go." The Rabbi picks up his computer case from beside his chair and unzips it. Slotted alongside a white laptop is a similarly white throwing disc. "I never travel without my favorite Frisbee."

"Then you're on."

"Meet in the lobby at nine?"

"I'll be there."

*   *   *

Three days later the Rabbi is addressing a dozen senior Israeli officers in a confidential seminar at Haifa University, the training school of choice for intelligence officers specializing on Middle Eastern affairs.

"Everything we have talked about is now in place. The donkey is hidden away. Our geneticists have confirmed that it is entirely unlike any donkey known to science. Now all we need is a descendant of King David with the appropriate spiritual gifts to manifest himself before the Jews of the world as the Moshiach." There is an uneasy stirring in the room.

"That's a joke, gentlemen. Given the quality of our political leadership, what possible need could we have for a genuine Moshiach?" The stirring does not subside.

"That's another joke. Let me put the situation in scriptural terms. When King David was dying, he told the prophet Nathan, who had anointed him king after Saul, to put his son Solomon on his, David's, mule and take him to the high place to be anointed as the next king. Not to be pedantic, but 'mule' here refers to the cross between a true donkey and a Syrian onager, also known as a hemione or half-ass, rather than our mule of today, which is a cross between a donkey and a horse. The Bible repeats the story three times word for word, which makes two things crystal clear. First, the 'mule' of Solomon's father was necessary to make the succession to the kingship legitimate. This is what the Christians harp on when they claim that Jesus both rides on an ass and is descended through Mary from King David and thereby is qualified to be anointed Messiah and King of the Jews. And second, it was a prophet named Nathan, basically a spiritual bureaucrat, who saw to it that it was David's son Solomon who got to ride the mule. If you're up on your Bible, you'll remember that Nathan had come out against David's other son Adonijah after he prematurely declared himself David's successor. But Adonijah didn't have his father's mule. If this, then, is our scriptural model for the advent of the Moshiach, it looks like the bureaucrats—that's us, gentlemen—get the job of taking care that the messianic donkey goes to the right person."

"Who's to say who the right person is?" comes a hoarse voice from the end of the room.

"Let me correct myself. I should have said that we have the job of making sure the donkey doesn't go to the wrong person. I suspect that the right person eventually arranges for his donkey by himself, at least in a spiritual sense. Some day the world will find out, but with any luck it won't be on our watch. In the meanwhile, what's for sure is that we don't want the Iranians to have the donkey. Some of them are convinced that their Mahdi is going to show up any day now, and getting their hands on a genetically bizarre donkey might be the tipping point prompting them to do crazy things, like nuking Tel Aviv. And we don't want the evangelical Christians to have it either. A lot of them already think that Jesus is about to return, and I don't need to remind you that messianic Christians are only friendly toward Jews when they think that they need them to facilitate Christ's return.

"Then last but not least, we don't want our own zealots to feel that the Moshiach is on his way. Look how worked up they got about reports of a genetically pure red heifer. A weird donkey could inspire some hothead to blow up the Dome of the Rock, and then we'd have another war with the Arabs on our hands, this time with the Iranians putting their oar in, so to speak. So while it was good that we got our hands on the donkey before the Protestants and the Iranians did, that donkey now happens to be the hottest of hot potatoes. The last thing we want is for that potato to be situated here in Israel."

"But that doesn't explain why we should want the Americans to have it," comes the same hoarse voice.

"The reason for the Americans having it—and I'm talking about ordinary Americans, not the evangelical extremists— is that they won't have a clue as to what it really is. However much their political elite may invoke God and publicize their churchgoing, they invariably ignore the strictly religious views of the evangelicals. Once we give it to President Obama, it will be safely socked away in the National Zoo where nobody can get their hands on it."

The hoarse-voiced skeptic, a bespectacled general of great renown in the world of covert operations, now leans forward and states his case.

"Personally, I think it would be best for us to give it to Ahmadinejad, and to let him know that he's getting it courtesy of Israel. Three things could happen: One, since some of us believe he's a secret Jew, maybe its spiritual powers and his gratitude for the gift would turn him back into being a good Jew. I'm not saying he himself is potentially a Messiah, but we're told that lots of people who have had this donkey have done good things as a result even if they haven't risen to the level of a Messiah. Take

Richard Bulliet

Abraham and Moses for two. A spiritually reformed Ahmadinejad might stop building the bomb, admit he was wrong about the Holocaust, and give up supporting Hamas and Hezbollah.

"Second possibility, maybe having the donkey would drive him around the bend, make him crazy, make him think he really is the Mahdi, or that the Mahdi will show up almost instantly. If that happened, he might do things that are so fanatic and so nutty that the United States would decide it can afford to take out the Islamic Republic militarily without suffering in world opinion. There's obviously nothing wrong with that outcome.

"Or third option, maybe it would make the Shi'ites in general so fanatic about their Hidden Imam being about to return that all the Sunni Muslims who are frightened of Iran and have a history of hating Shi'ism would come around to supporting us. The Saudis, the Egyptians, and the Jordanians are already half way there. Again, not a bad outcome."

"Those are all good points," says the Rabbi. "But you have to remember that Muslim theology also talks about the *khar-e Dajjal*, the donkey of the Antichrist. This character, the Dajjal, is really bad news. He's demonic, but he is deceptively alluring and gathers an enormous following before he is killed ... by Jesus no less. We wouldn't want some Iranian demagogue to use the donkey to gain vast popularity throughout the Muslim world. Enough popularity, for example, to bring Shi'ites and Sunnis together against us. This may not seem probable, but when you're dealing with a genuine spiritual being, as I am convinced we are with this Ya'fur, you can't take that chance. And the Sunnis don't want to take that chance either. That is why the ones you mention, the Saudis, the Egyptians, and the Jordanians, along with the Gulfis, have already signed onto our proposal to send the donkey to America. The story we'll sell to the Americans will be ass backwards, if you'll pardon the expression. The idea of giving a donkey to Obama, we'll tell them, comes not from Israel, but from rich, friendly Sunni Arabs. Israel is just signing on casually

264

as a friendly gesture. Of course, we'll let our friends in congress know that we really think it's a terrific idea."

Heads nod around the room. The tenor of the murmurs is positive.

"What if Obama won't accept it?" says the general in retreat.

"How can any American president say no to something that both Israel and the oil sheikhs agree on? Congress being what it is."

*   *   *

In an austerely contemporary conference room featuring vaguely pear-shaped stainless steel wall art and a panoramic view of midtown Manhattan's East Side, Sargent Peabody Gibbs III calls the partners meeting to order. "Why don't we start by going around the table and introducing ourselves. I'm Sarge Gibbs. I'm the General Counsel of People of the World, L.P."

"I'm Gretchen Priebe," says a tweedy woman with a giant Starbucks cup seated to his right. "I represent one of the People of the World partners."

"Which one would that be?" asks Sarge.

"I'm not at liberty to disclose that, Mr. Gibbs. I'll simply refer to him as my Principal."

The next four lawyers similarly identify themselves as agents for unnamed principals. Sarge laughingly suggests that the unnamed individuals be designated Principal A, Principal B, Principal C, and so forth in the order in which their attorneys have introduced themselves. Everyone agrees, and the meeting is off to a good start. The seventh person at the table, a tall, thin black man with a Clark Gable mustache, introduces himself as Randall Ace, temporarily serving as the deputy to President Barack Obama's Chief of Staff.

"My presence here is off the record," says Randall Ace.

"No record is being made of this meeting," replies Sarge. "It's only exploratory. Just getting to know one another."

"Then let me stop the exploration in its tracks by assuring you on the highest authority that the President of the United States does not want a donkey, won't accept a donkey, and will not discuss anything related to a donkey."

Sarge smiles benignly. "Good place to start. Gets the tough questions out on the table in a straightforward manner. Thank you, Randall."

Pierpont Maxwell, the chubby but elegantly outfitted lawyer representing Principal C, chimes in. "Yes, an excellent place to start. In fact, why don't we all just forget about the donkey for the time being and concentrate on the big picture. Let us say, purely hypothetically you understand, that my Principal rules a country that produces a million barrels of oil a day and sells half of it to the United States. He never presses for higher prices, and he spends the bulk of his oil proceeds buying American goods and services. And American weapons. He admires President Obama, he was moved by the President's speech to the Muslim world in Cairo, and he wants to express this personal admiration."

"To make things even clearer, Randall," says Gretchen Priebe,
• "let's expand Pierpont's example and hypothesize, just for the sake of illustration, that all of the People of the World partners are in similar situations. Their esteem for President Obama is without limit, and they want to express that esteem. However, a token of that esteem in the form of a gift to the President of any monetary significance would surely be taken the wrong way and properly be rejected. By the same token, the expenditure of a few billion dollars more on American warplanes and weapons, which is something well within the realm of possibility, would inevitably provoke congressional anxiety about the security of Israel, the balance of power in the Middle East, and so forth. And as for what President Obama might actually wish for, like some coordinated multilateral change of foreign policy to be more supportive of the use of American force in the Muslim world—for example, a simultaneous extension by several countries of the hand of friendship to the new regime in Iraq—this would be politically

unfeasible for some of the partners at the domestic political level. So that is why a purely symbolic gift, one that endorses not just the President, but also his political party, which none of us would deny is a party that the Arabs have not always admired, makes an appealing alternative."

"Nobody ever gave Bush an elephant," observes the elderly lawyer in the white suit, blue shirt, and plaid bowtie representing Principal E.

"But there's no reason why that couldn't happen after the next election," says Sarge.

Randall Ace looks unmoved. "If you want to express your appreciation of the President, what about your Principals making some concrete gesture toward Israel to help his peace initiative along? Maybe allow Israeli airliners to cross Arab airspace, or free up trade with Israeli companies, or accept that there will have to be significant territorial adjustments if a settlement with the Palestinian Authority is going to be reached."

Sarge beams. "Hold that thought, Randall. I want to invite someone to join us." He goes to the door and invites in a compact man wearing a yarmulke and a chalk-stripe gray suit. "This is the Rabbi. He's not a real rabbi, but that's what we will call him."

"Hi, guys!" says the Rabbi as he nods to the lawyers around the table.

"I would like the Rabbi to lay out the position of Israel on the matter at hand. I think you will all find it very interesting."

"Thanks, Sarge. In a nutshell, both our political and our security leadership are happy, I can even say delighted, with the plan to give President Obama a donkey. I guarantee you no friend of Israel in Congress will say a word against the idea, and no Israel-friendly think tank or political action committee will do so either."

"Does that include the Republicans?" asks Randall Ace suspiciously.

"A few Republicans may complain initially that the gift is partisan since it involves the symbol of the Democratic Party, but Sarge Gibbs here, representing People of the World, L.P., will privately promise them that there will be a parallel gift of an elephant as soon as the Republicans regain control of the White House. The elephant, needless to say, will get much more publicity than the donkey. And also live longer."

"What about the impact of public opinion? Gifts from oil sheikhs have a way of backing up on us."

"The Rabbi's talking about the insider information loop, Randall," says Sarge soothingly. "Publicly the question of who the People of the World, L.P. partners are will never come up because the gift will be announced as coming from the 'people of the world' without the capital letters. People of the World, L.P. won't even be mentioned. The publicity releases will show a rainbow of happy faces saying, 'Thank you, Mr. President, for bringing peace to the world.' If some hard-ass reporters want to press deeper, they'll discover the partnership, but it will be described to them as an altruistic convergence of anonymous philanthropic souls from many different countries united in their desire to praise President Obama. Aside from legal representatives like ourselves, no names will ever surface, I assure you."

Randall Ace seems to be softening. "Suppose the President accepted it as a gift from the people of the world to America's children and put it on display in the National Zoo? Like a Chinese panda. That might insulate him from charges that it is a Democratic Party publicity stunt."

"Perhaps declare that it's a specimen of a rare ass species rather than a domestic donkey," chimes in Gretchen Priebe.

The Rabbi grabs the idea and runs with it. "Excellent! What a wonderful addition to the story. Asses once ran wild all across North Africa, but then they went extinct except in the far eastern part of the Sahara, basically Sudan, Egypt, and Somalia. But this ass will be coming from the Canary Islands, where, in point of fact, asses were historically unknown until they were introduced from the Moroccan mainland. But who's going to know that? We could say that this donkey is one of a nearly extinct species of native Canary Island donkeys, long thought to be entirely gone but recently rediscovered. Looks just like a regular donkey, but it's actually one of a kind. Release a statement from animal geneticists to confirm it. That way President Obama is furthering the cause of protecting endangered species, and it becomes entirely incidental that the animal is the symbol of the Democratic Party."

"People of the Canary Islands Muslims or Christians?" asks Randall Ace. "It wouldn't be wise for the gift to have a Muslim overtone. Nothing against Muslims, of course, but you know how the talk show hosts blow things out of proportion."

"It's a Spanish colony," the Rabbi replies. "All the natives were wiped out or died of disease after the Europeans came in the sixteenth century. So it's heavily Catholic. We could make it even more Christian, however, by tying it in with St. Francis of Assisi. There's a story that when St. Francis died, his donkey wept."

Pierpont Maxwell representing Principal C becomes animated. "What a good thought! On St. Francis' feast day, some churches stage a Blessing of the Animals. In New York it's at the Cathedral of St. John the Divine at Amsterdam Avenue and 111th Street. The donkey could be blessed there by a priest and then presented to Obama."

"When would that be?" queries Ace.

"The feast day is October 4th, as I recall; but there's another St. Francis day a couple of weeks before that."

"That's roughly when the U.N. General Assembly meets, isn't it? The President would be coming to New York anyway to speak to the U.N. If he did that on a Monday, this could be a public relations event for the day before."

"I think we have a plan," says the Rabbi.

"We need someone with big pop credentials to write a song," adds the lawyer in the white suit.

heehaw

The visitor smiles benignly. Baleine scowls. Her pit bull looks up from its basket. "Child, tell the Professor that Father Pancho Sanchez is here to see him."

"Do you have an appointment?"

"No. But he will want to see me."

"The only person he's told me he wants to see is a short woman with magenta-and-black checkerboard fingernails. That wouldn't be you, would it?" Baleine's interlocutor is a short, fat man dressed in a black clerical suit and white clerical collar. The crumbs clinging to his jacket betray recent consumption of a muffin, or, considering their abundance, several muffins.

"Bless you, Child, and your lovely scowling face. When have I ever encountered such a ferocious countenance combined with such a pure soul? You can't keep your goodness from shining through, can you? As for the Professor, he will want to see me because I know something important about a very special ass."

"You think I haven't heard that line of bullshit before? Just because he is a Professor of Asinine Studies doesn't mean he has the time to shoot the breeze with every donkey freak who finds his way to this office."

"Of course he doesn't. But I'm talking about a very, very special ass."

"Do you have a card? I can give it to the professor, and he can contact you if he thinks your ass is special enough."

A laugh bubbles through the priest's smile. "Touché. A well turned phrase indeed, Miss Scowly Face."

"That would be Miss Tontonmacoute."

The priest's amusement grows. "Tontonmacoute? As in the dreaded Haitian security police under Papa Doc Duvalier? Another good one! The perfect *nom de guerre*. What fun you and the Professor must have sharing gibes and puns. I think I could stay here all day and just enjoy conversing with you. You don't mind if I sit here by your darling puppy, do you? Morbidly obese men of my advanced years seek every opportunity to sit down." He takes a seat next to Baby Dog's basket.

"I'm actually very busy, Father, so I suggest you pick your elderly, obese, white ass up again and be on your way. You're not going to be seeing the professor, and I'm not going to spend all day talking to you."

"Suppose I told you I was working with the FBI?" Baleine shakes her head. "The New York City Police?" Her head keeps on shaking. "The ASPCA?"

"In your dreams. Forget it, Father. No is no. And if I have to throw you bodily out of this office on your fat clerical ass, my conscience will be so clean that it won't even cross my mind to ask whether I've committed a sin the next time I go to confession."

"Is that a fact? Tell me, then, Miss Dreaded Haitian Policewoman, what sort of deed do you feel you would have to confess?"

"Letting you in to see the professor contrary to his instructions. That sort of deed."

"What if I told you I know that there is a secret plan to give President Obama a donkey and that there are people who are prepared to use violence to prevent it?"

"Brrrr. That's very spooky. You can see me all shivering. The professor will definitely want to hear about that."

The priest struggles to rise from the chair. "So?"

271

Baleine rubs at a smudge on her computer screen with a tissue. "He just won't want to hear about it from you. Particularly as you are stating your knowledge as being of the 'what if' variety. Like 'what if' you're from the FBI or the ASPCA?"

The priest is unfazed. "The 'what if' is just a turn of phrase. What I'm saying is that I do know concretely of such contemplated violence."

"Oh, my goodness! Just like that? You know? Maybe God told you? Do you think that anyone, without an appointment, can just walk through that door, tell me they know something sensational, and make me jump to attention? If I did that, I would hardly be carrying out my orders to keep dingbats out of the professor's hair, would I?"

"No, you would not."

"Then in view of the many chores that are weighing me down, don't you think the most considerate thing would be for you to leave your business card and go away?"

"That lovely scowl again. I'll tell you what: I'll give you a name and you can decide whether the Professor would be interested enough to chat with me. John Matthew Krumlake."

"J.M., huh." Baleine mulls over the situation. "I guess you better see the professor."

After listening to the conversational give-and-take through his bead curtain, rooting now for Baleine, now for the priest, Constantine is primed to make the acquaintance of the rare man who has pierced his Haitian firewall. He stands and extends his hand as the priest waddles through the curtain.

"Hello, I'm Professor Paul Constantine."

The priest has short, thick fingers, but his grip is firm. "How do you do, Professor Constantine. I am Father Pancho Sanchez of the High and Exalted Ecclesiastical Household of Ass Wardens."

It takes Constantine a few seconds. "HEEHAW for short?"

"Bravo, you got it! So few people do. Our actual name is just the Ecclesiastical Household of Ass Wardens, but we like to tack on the extra HE for the fun of it."

"I have never heard of your organization."

"Nor would you now if matters had not progressed so rapidly toward a possible crisis. My organization works in secret. May I sit down?"

The professor beckons him to the rush-bottomed ladder-back chair beside his desk and subsides himself into a German-engineered professorial throne.

Father Sanchez sits tentatively and then more firmly as he accepts that the chair is strong enough to support him. "I'll start at the beginning, if you will allow me, and proceed to the end."

"My ears are long and they are pricked."

"How delightful. Does your office banter come from you? Or from your charming receptionist? Or from the chemistry between you? Never mind. Let me get to my story. As a Professor of Asinine Studies you have doubtless heard of James Nayler."

"George Fox's partner in the founding of the Quakers. Arrested in October 1656 for blasphemously riding a donkey into Bristol."

"Very good. Now keep that moment in history in mind and let us move on to Nayler's contemporary, Sabbatai Zevi."

"The Jewish false messiah in Turkey."

"The same."

"He didn't have a donkey."

"Don't anticipate me, Professor. I'll get to the ass in time. Both men were inspired by the kabbalistic calculation that the Jews were destined to return to the Land of Israel in 1666."

"I know all that," says Constantine impatiently. "But I repeat, no donkey."

"Agreed. So what we have is a seventeenth century pan-European wave of messianic expectation in which some people who felt like messiahs sensed that an ass is essential, and others didn't. Just as today some evangelical Protestants think Jesus needs an ass to return on, and some don't. Same thing with the Jews and with the Muslims and their Mahdi. But I'm getting ahead of myself. Let's go back to the seventeenth century."

"When the Holy Father in Rome, Clement IX of blessed memory, learned about the messianic turmoil that was overtaking the Protestants and the Jews, he established a secret commission to determine the Church's position on the sacred ass question. Clement died in 1669 after a most humane papacy of only two years. But the Commission continued to follow his directive and eventually concluded that there were two sacred asses at large in the world and that at any given time there existed a handful of individuals who possessed some sort of consciousness of them. Their work culminated in the authorization of a secret body called the Ecclesiastical Household of Ass Wardens. The dual charge of the wardens is to always know where the two sacred asses are located, and to leave them scrupulously alone. The Commission decided, you see, that the time and the place of the End Times ought to be determined by the coming together of the Messiah and his ass without the interference of mortal intelligence or planning."

"What you are saying, then, Father Sanchez, is that you and the other ass wardens, past and present, are able to distinguish a sacred donkey from an ordinary donkey? How do you do that without DNA testing?"

"We don't know. It is a mystery of the Holy Spirit that settles upon the few of us who follow this calling. We pray, and we know. We can sense the location of the asses as precisely as a GPS tracking system."

"In that case, where is the sacred donkey right now?"

"You would trick a fat old priest, Professor? Shame on you. As I mentioned, there are two sacred asses, not one. The one named Ufair is currently walking eastward across the Algerian desert. He is just south of the oasis town of Laghouat."

"I'll have to take your word for that. What about Ya'fur?"

"Ya'fur is adapting to confinement in a fenced garden in Westchester County. The garden is behind the main house on the 100-acre estate of the honorary consul of the Persian Gulf sheikhdom of Qatar. It arrived by helicopter two days ago at Igor

I. Sikorsky Memorial Airport in Stratford, Connecticut after entering the country at JFK Airport in a private aircraft that had taken off from Las Palmas Airport in the Canary Islands. It traveled to the consul's home in a horse trailer."

No it didn't, thinks Constantine in confusion. *It couldn't have.* Memories of an inebriated evening in the taverna on Hydra flash into his mind. *There are no sacred donkeys. I invented them. I write about them.*

Father Sanchez is looking at him with compassion. "You don't believe, do you? Even if at some level you know it's true. I didn't believe either, Professor Constantine. I had heard the stories from my predecessor, Father Francis. But my faith in the godhood of Christ Jesus and the unerring guidance of Holy Mother Church had a limit: No immortal asses. Father Francis understood. He said I would have to wait for the gift of the Holy Spirit. For years it didn't come. I served the wardens at their headquarters in Salamanca but was not one of them. Their bank account was always flush, and their food and drink were excellent. I thought they were spiritually a bit loopy, but I was happy to attend upon them. Then one night I awoke from a dream, though I thought I was still in the dream. I was watching an old man riding his ass toward a small mountain village, and I knew with certainty that the scene was in Morocco, and I knew exactly where it was in Morocco. The village of Sidi Ben Adam."

Constantine feels profoundly uneasy. "I don't dream. My knowledge about Ya'fur and Ufair is certain only insofar as it accurately reflects what I have read in books. And I have no reason to believe that the authors of those books had access to some cosmic proof. My story of the asses is purely my invention, a hobby I have been indulging in for many years."

"And yet it is true. Isn't that a wonder? One person can talk to Ya'fur, another can sense his precise location, and a third can be inspired to invent the truth and yet not be able to recognize it. May the Lord be praised."

"May the Lord butt out of my scholarly life." Constantine looks about his surroundings to check for signs that he is hallucinating a conversation with a fat Spanish priest. *Maybe I'm suffering a transient ischemic attack.*

"Let's change the subject, Professor. You need some time to think about things. The reason I have come to you is that the wardens are not permitted to take any actions with respect to their charges. If you wish, you can consider my claim to know where the donkeys are a mere delusion on my part. But I am not deluded in believing that J.M. Krumlake, acting at the behest of his father Ray Bob Krumlake and Pastor Steve Klingbeil, is planning to hijack the ceremonial presentation of an ass to President Obama at the Blessing of the Animals to be held at the Cathedral of St. John the Divine in New York City. I have this on the most reliable authority."

"Conspiracy to steal a donkey is not a crime. Let him do it."

"The rules of my brotherhood dictate just this course of inaction. No police, no FBI, no Secret Service."

"But you've come here to tell me what is going to happen. Why is that?"

"Because you are Ya'fur's biographer. In your mind, I grant, simply the teller of tales about an imaginary beast named Ya'fur. But in the reality opened up to me by the Holy Spirit, you are a witness to history. It is surely not by chance that you are closely acquainted with the conspirators. Hence it would be a tragic loss for the history of 'imaginary' asses, which is the day-to-day mission of my order, if you were not present to witness Mr. Krumlake's hijacking of Ya'fur at first hand."

Though still in doubt about his own lucidity, Constantine weighs what Father Sanchez—or the Father Sanchez he is, or may be, imagining—is saying. If there is a plan to give a donkey to the President, and J.M., whom he knows to be determined, violent, and religiously delusional, does derail the ceremony, it would make a stunning concluding chapter for *Ya'fur, The Messianic Donkey*. And the news coverage would make it a bestseller. The royalties and fame would outclass anything he might get from publishing with Pastor Steve, whom he knows can't tell good scholarly writing from a Haitian harridan's fairy tale.

Father Sanchez gives him time to think. "I'm simply suggesting that you make plans to come to New York in a couple of weeks."

"I might do that."

"Splendid. In that case, I will see to it, once the plan to give Ya'fur to President Obama becomes public, that your name gets mentioned as the best expert consultant for the event."

"So I might meet the President?"

"I should think so. Unless this entire conversation has been as much a figment of your imagination as you think the donkey of the Messiah is."

The telltale sound of the outer office door opening catches Constantine's ear. He listens for Baleine's challenge to the intruder. He hears nothing. *Aha, I am hallucinating*, he thinks. Then suddenly the bead curtain is pulled aside and a diminutive figure enters the inner office.

"The girl with the magenta-and-black fingernails," announces Baleine portentously.

Constantine and Father Sanchez rise. Constantine has half a notion to smother Toots in a hug and half a notion that neither the priest nor Baleine should witness him doing it. The more decorous half wins out.

"Father Sanchez, this is Victoria Greeley."

The priest grasps her hand between his own pudgy ones. "How pleased I am to meet you, Child."

"The Father was just leaving."

"Indeed I was. The professor and I have completed our talk." He turns to the bead curtain, which Baleine is still holding aside. "I hope to see you in New York," he says as he disappears into the outer office. Constantine does not reply.

When the priest has gone, Constantine turns his attention to Toots, who looks to be entirely real. "Did you just see a big fat priest in here?"

"Yes. He had crumbs on his chest. But I've come here to tell you my adventures and talk about writing. That is, if you're up to it. You look distracted." *Could Ya'fur really be real?* thinks Constantine. "I could come back at another time."

"If you would. I don't mean to be rude, Toots, but I'm undergoing something of a shock."

WAITING FOR YA'FUR

"Welcome gentlemen, lady. This is our final partners meeting before the transmission of the gift. We will start with two reports and then take up any new business that might arise. Our first report is from Randall Ace, who has done so very much good work on the political side to make this happen. He will tell us about the public relations program. Then the Rabbi will go through with us the nuts and bolts of how things will proceed on September 29th."

Sarge Gibbs leads the warm applause for Randall Ace, who nods in response and then touches a key on the laptop before him to project a large image on a wall-sized screen. He gives everyone a few seconds to read.

> ## WORLD TO HAND
> ## OBAMA HIS ASS
>
> BY PETER BLUE
>
> Washington insiders report that 'the people of the world' will present a rare breed of donkey to President Obama during the occasion of his visit to New York to address to the General Assembly of the United Nations. The presentation will be part of the annual Blessing of the Animals ceremony at the Cathedral of St. John the Divine in Morningside Heights. The ceremony is held annually in conjunction with the feast day of St. Francis of Assisi on October 4.
>
> White House aide Randall Ace characterized the president as accepting the gift on behalf of the children of the United States. As part of the administration's policy of protecting endangered species, the animal will be housed in the National Zoo in Washington, D.C.

"This is the article that appeared today in the *New York Post*. I picked the *Post* to break the story because it is Republican and because it has caustic headlines. I thought we should know at the outset whether the story is going to be given a negative spin. Or rather, how negative the spin it will inevitably receive from the opposing camp will be. And I also gave it to the *Post* and because it wallows in trivial human-interest stories. Looking at the result, I think we can breathe a sigh of relief. No mention of the donkey as the symbol of the Democratic Party. No mention of the propriety of the President receiving a gift of this sort. No effort to figure out what the phrase 'people of the world' means beyond what is in the headline. This doesn't mean we're out of the woods, of course. *The New York Times* and the *Washington Post* will dig a little deeper. But my guess is that they will just fold the story into the bigger story of the President's speech to the General Assembly on the 30th. Basically make it no more than a calendar note."

"What about Congress?"

"Thank you, Gretchen. Good question. Notification has been sent to the committees in both houses concerned with foreign affairs, conservation, and agriculture. No one has asked for an oral briefing. I also had a word with the staffers who attend the faith-related caucuses, and with a few individual staffers who support the animal rights agenda. They all seem very happy with the idea of the President making a personal appearance at the Blessing of the Animals."

Sarge looks around the table. No hands are raised. "Okay. Thank you, Randall. Now we'll hear about the details from the Rabbi."

"Thanks, Sarge." The image on the screen changes.

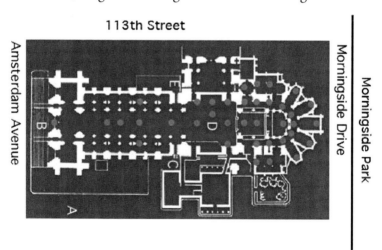

"What you're looking at is the plan of the Cathedral of St. John the Divine. The letter A indicates the driveway where the animals and their handlers assemble for the procession. The handlers wear loose white gowns so they are easily identified. B is the main entrance to the cathedral at the top of a long flight of stairs. The animals go through that entrance and are led down the nave between rows of seated spectators. C, over here on the south side, is a side entrance where the President and his party will enter after all of the spectators are seated but before the procession of animals begins. The President, Mayor, Manhattan Borough President, and other members of the official party will be seated in chairs just inside entrance C and somewhat to the right, quite a distance from where the general public will be seated. This is at the insistence of the Secret Service. The animals will be assembled in a broad open space between those chairs and the pulpit, which is a stone affair that arches up like the prow of a ship. The priest will deliver a very brief homily from the pulpit and pronounce a blessing. Then Sarge, in his pretty white dress" (everyone chuckles) "joined by the priest, will lead the donkey over to the President, who will stand and accept the animal on behalf of America's children. This will be a photo op so it will take a couple of minutes. When that's done, the President's party, along with Sarge and the donkey, will exit through the side entrance. A motorcade will take the President over to his hotel at the United Nations, and the donkey, with police escort, will travel in a trailer to a temporary holding area on Staten Island for later transfer to the National Zoo. Are there any questions?"

The chubby lawyer representing Partner B raises his hand. "What does E stand for on the drawing?"

"That's an emergency exit for the President in case entrance C should be compromised. It goes into a parking lot, which will be locked and empty, and then out onto 113th Street."

Gretchen Priebe's hand goes up. "Will you yourself be there, Rabbi?"

The Rabbi grins. "I can only imagine what the Press would make of an Israeli in a yarmulke being a member of the President's party at an Episcopalian ceremony."

"But you are part of People of the World."

"Not formally. Nevertheless, I have made arrangements to be there as a member of an ecumenical group of animal lovers nominated by the Cathedral. We will be sitting near exit E, opposite the President with the animals in between."

"But that means you will not be near enough to help out if the President has any questions about the donkey or about us."

"Don't worry about that, Gretchen," puts in Sarge. "We've arranged for America's greatest authority on donkey symbolism, Professor Paul Constantine, Harvard's Professor of Asinine Studies in their Department of Symbology, to be with the President's party."

"Is that a proper use of the word 'asinine'?" asks the lawyer in the white suit and bow tie representing Partner E.

"Alas, yes," replies the Rabbi.

*   *   *

At the end of their second meeting, which was indeed devoted to Toots telling adventure stories and Constantine defending his prose style, the two of them agreed to train down to New York together in the Business Class coach of Amtrak's Acela from Boston. A third member of their party has turned out to be Jessie Zayyat, who wins a smile from Constantine by saying how much she enjoyed reading his Ya'fur book.

"You must be someone special, Toots, to have your own CIA escort."

"Toots is the one who's special," says Jessie.

"Jessie spent a whole week with us in Scotland. She adores the donkeys, and father fell in love with her."

"He calls me his second daughter."

"Beware of old men looking for second daughters," replies Constantine with a wink.

"Takes one to know one," says Toots.

"Touché."

"Mr. Greeley tried to get me to sample his whisky, but I was brought up Seventh-day Adventist and don't consume alcohol, caffeine, or tobacco. It was our only disagreement."

"Seventh-day Adventist? I know of an interesting sermon about donkeys by an SDA minister."

Toots holds up her hand. "Jessie and I don't want to hear about it. We're going to sightsee and shop and not think about donkeys all weekend. I'll have my fill of talking about them when I go to Washington on Monday."

"What about the Blessing of the Animals? Aren't you going to that? The People of the World are giving President Obama a donkey. You must have read about it. I've been selected to be the President's donkey-advisor."

"I think he has enough donkeys advising him already," says Jessie.

"Actually, we *are* thinking of going, but for the whole thing, not for the donkey in particular. We'd have to get there early in the morning; but if we don't carouse too much, you might see us there."

"I'll keep her from carousing, Professor."

"If you do go, I doubt I'll see you," says Constantine. "I'll be sitting in the south transept with the presidential party. In case the President wants to ask me any questions."

"Jessie's been told that the best thing to do is to stand out on the front steps and watch the animals parade in so you're right. We probably won't see you."

"Well if you do stand outside, keep your eyes open for my receptionist, Baleine. She should be outside with Father Sanchez, the fat priest who was with me in the office when you first stopped by."

"Why are they going to be there?"

"It's a secret."

"Oh, come on."

"They're going to be on the lookout for one of your acquaintances."

"A friend?"

"Not exactly." Constantine smirks.

"Don't tease. Who is going to be there?"

"Guess. You both know who he is. He probably won't show up, but there's a rumor that he's coming." The two women look at each other in puzzlement. "All right, I'll tell you. It's J.M. Krumlake."

"Good heavens no!" exclaims Jessie. "You know what he did to Toots?"

Toots nudges her. "Do you have a gun, Jess? Maybe this time I can kill him."

"Carry a gun on an Amtrak train? Permission to do that would take at least a week."

"I'm kidding, Jessie. But Professor, what makes you think J.M. might be at the ceremony?"

"It's just a rumor. But I've asked Baleine to keep her eyes open in case he becomes obstreperous. There might be something amusing for me to write about to close my book."

*   *   *

President Mahmoud Ahmadinejad has a map of Manhattan spread out on a low marble table. He and his party, including Monika Farber and Fritz Messiassohn, have taken over the Fifth Avenue residence of the Islamic Republic of Iran's United Nations ambassador. But at the moment he is alone with his Chief of Staff. "I've looked at this map, Rahim. We're on the eastern edge of Central Park, and the cathedral where they are going to give away Ya'fur is just here, almost on the western edge. It is so close to Columbia University that it is practically on its campus."

"You won a great victory over American arrogance at Columbia University, Mahmoud. That president—I can't remember his name—addressed you with such rudeness that everyone in the world sympathized with you."

"They sympathized with me because I was a guest being insulted by my host, not because they listened to anything I had

285

to say. The Columbia president's insults were repeated around the world. My words were forgotten, except for my remark about homosexuals, which nobody understood."

"No one remembers that anymore, Mahmoud. Whenever you are in New York to attend the General Assembly, people pay attention to you. But ever since the Columbia speech, they pay you twice as much attention. That is why I say you won a great victory."

"It makes no difference. We move on. Tell me what the plan is for gaining control of the donkey."

"It's still not set. We know two things. The first is that Ya'fur told Fritz he would meet him. The second is that the Parsee in Quetta said he saw you personally standing with Ya'fur and feeding it an apple."

"Do you believe that?" Ahmadinejad's eyes brighten.

"He says he saw you, and he has no reason to lie to me."

"You still haven't mentioned a plan."

"Actually, when I take those two things into consideration, I come to the conclusion that Ya'fur is going to come to you."

Ahmadinejad is amused. "To get an apple from me?"

"I was thinking more about Fritz being here. If we keep him in the residence, the only way Ya'fur can meet him is by coming here."

"Don't you think it is odd, Rahim, that a German is able to talk to Ya'fur? He's not even a Muslim."

"I don't know what religion he is. But Professor Farber tells me that a few men in every century enjoy the spiritual gift of conversing with Ya'fur ..."

"If you can believe her."

"... but do not choose to become prophets."

"Why is that?"

"She says it is either because they cannot decide between being the Mahdi and being the Dajjal, or because being a savior may not be a very rewarding occupation."

"Is that a joke, Esfandiar? Is that dreadful woman making a joke out of this?"

"Not a good one."

"Watch out for her, Rahim. She is a destroyer of men."

*   *   *

Pastor Steve is sitting in the corner of Ray Bob's hospital room reading the *New York Post*. "Here it is; it's official. Just like Senator Lamar told me, this group People of the World is going to give Obama a donkey. Considering no one claims to know who People of the World are, it's nothing short of amazing that the Arab-lovers and the Jew-lovers are all agreed on this. I wonder how many of them know that it's Jesus' donkey. Typical Israeli intelligence operation. Out there for everyone to see if they just take a look, but they pull it off anyway."

"They're not gonna get away with it this time, Pastor Steve," says J.M., who is kneeling at his father's bedside. He leans his head forward so that he can talk directly into Ray Bob's ear. "Papa, it's J.M. I know your anti-seizure medicine is keepin' you from sayin' anything, but I want you to know that I've got a plan, and it's a good one. Back in Falluja and Ramadi we always talked about watchin' each other's ass, and a lot of us didn't come back. Well that kind of feelin' for the guys you go out on patrol with doesn't end just 'cause you leave the service. Particularly for those of us who have Jesus in our hearts and follow him in our everyday lives. Coupla old buddies from Iraq are in the NYPD now. I got in touch. They agreed to help me even though it might get 'em in trouble. No way Barack Hossein Obama is gonna get his hands on Jesus' donkey. I swear that to you, Papa. So you just rest and get better. I'm prayin' for you every day. Pastor Steve is prayin' too."

*   *   *

"Dudes! Did you read about Obama and that donkey?" Richie Stevens shouts to be heard over the din of the Blue Donkey Bar at Amsterdam Avenue and 80th Street. "Blessing of the Animals! Going down in a couple of days just a mile from here."

"Two more pitchers, boys?" says the waitress to the thirsting table of college students.

"Is a pig's ass pork?" shouts someone in response. The rest of the table make affirmative hoots.

Richie is still shouting. "What the Blue Donkey Bar should do is get a blessing for its own donkey."

"I didn't know they had a donkey," says a pie-eyed Franklin Liu.

"They don't, asshole. Blue Donkey's just a name."

"But they could have a donkey," offers Lynda Weisman. "My aunt and uncle over in Jersey have a donkey on their farm. We could sign up at the cathedral on behalf of the Blue Donkey Bar and bring it over in my uncle's truck."

The intoxicated consensus among Richie and his friends is that Lynda's impressive rack and truly spectacular ass make her every remark worth listening to.

"That sounds like an idea," declares Richie pounding the table with an empty mug.

"Maybe we could get our picture taken with Obama," adds Franklin.

the blessing of the animals

Traffic noises rouse Constantine early in his hotel room. He lumbers to the bathroom to pee and examine his visage in the mirror. He realizes that he should have gotten a haircut and an eyebrow trim. He returns to bed and remote clicks the television from one morning show to another. Everyone is covering Obama and the Blessing of the Animals.

Martin Meister is holding a Fox News microphone in gloved hands. "It's chilly out here, Alice, but the animals and their handlers are beginning to assemble. Nobody seems to mind the cold, but you can see that there's a pretty stiff breeze blowing the handlers' gowns. Everyone I talk to is happy and excited. There are dogs and cats of all shapes and sizes, of course, but some larger animals too. I've seen a cow and a horse. But the elephant, camel, and World Donkey aren't here yet."

"Tell us about the cathedral, Martin."

"Right, Alice. Behind me you're looking at one of New York City's great monuments, the Episcopalian Cathedral of St. John and Divine on Morningside Heights. It's the world's largest cathedral built by traditional stonework, and it's still not finished after more then a century of work. Take a look at those twenty-plus steps leading to the great portal with its bronze doors. They're already filling up with spectators, and they will be completely

289

jammed by nine o'clock, leaving just an aisle for the animals to pass through. It will be interesting to see how the elephant, camel, and other animals do climbing stairs."

"Do you think a pet goose can go up stairs, Martin?"

"Ha-ha. Good question, Alice. Maybe it will be carried. We should find out in a couple of hours."

"When does President Obama arrive?"

"According to the schedule that has been handed us, worshippers and spectators will be admitted at nine-thirty, Alice. President Obama's party will enter later by a side door. That's scheduled for ten forty-five. The ceremony is set to begin at eleven. After the President accepts the World Donkey, he will leave by motorcade for the American U.N. Mission at attend diplomatic meetings."

"Sounds like a traffic nightmare for the Upper West Side, Martin."

"Indeed it will be, Alice. After eight-thirty only official and police vehicles will be permitted on the streets around the cathedral. That includes Amsterdam Avenue and 110th Street, which of course are major thoroughfares. Drivers take note. As for Morningside Park, which is across the street opposite the back of the cathedral, it has been completely cordoned off south of 116th Street. But I don't expect there will be too many disappointed softball players and picnickers this early on a chilly Sunday."

Constantine clicks off and checks the bedside clock: 8:25.

The clock reads 8:46 when he finishes his shower and shave. He takes his freshly pressed three-piece navy blue suit out of the closet and lays it on the bed next to a pale blue shirt and bold pink necktie. Conservative as befits a Harvard professor who is going to sit near, and perhaps even talk to, the President of the United States, but not devoid of liveliness and humor—the message of the necktie.

He is mildly surprised, indeed somewhat irked, to find the Rabbi sitting in the back seat of the limo that picks him up right at nine. They haven't met face to face since the long ago Hydra conference, but the e-mail negotiations over exchanging Toots for Fritz renewed their contact. Though informed that the Rabbi is somehow involved in the day's ceremony, Constantine feels that the limo should be for him alone. After all, he is the one who is going to join the presidential party. The Rabbi is only a spectator.

"Great weather," the Rabbi remarks as they head up Third Avenue.

"Too chilly for my taste."

Silence. *Has he no more conversation?*

"Paul, if the President should ask about donkeys, I don't think he needs to be told anything about Ya'fur and the Messiah."

"Do you think I'm an idiot?" *Let him chew on that answer.*

*   *   *

In Sunnyside, Queens, on the other side of the East River, J.M. arises after a fitful night on the couch in his policeman friend Justin's apartment. He reads the Bible for half an hour and then goes over the uniform he has borrowed from Justin's partner, whose place he will be taking: tight dark blue trousers with a gold stripe up the leg, dark blue shirt with large NYPD badges on the shoulders, double-breasted leather jacket with brass buttons and more badges. It will be nippy; Jack Frost has come early. He gets a towel from the kitchen and buffs up a shine on the black riding boots. He will enjoy wearing those. No so much the light blue plastic helmet with the black chinstrap. Justin will give him a nightstick and an unloaded gun when they leave for the cathedral. The short lasso is his own. He practices wrapping it loosely around his waist to make sure he can get to it quickly and that it will not be too bulky beneath the jacket. He had urged Justin, unsuccessfully, to ask his commander for permission to carry the rope openly since the event would feature livestock. Justin's response? No need to attract attention. J.M. will simply have to find an opportunity to redeploy the rope once he gets to Morningside Heights.

Richard Bulliet

*   *   *

Toots and Jessie have located Baleine. Baleine and Toots are bonding over tales of incessant and unwarranted harassment by men. Baleine completely understands that a girl should not be taken hostage again and again and again, much less be marooned on an island with a broken foot. Toots completely understands that the employer-bodyguard relationship should not require listening to pedantic mini-lectures on the possible relationship between the donkey's big penis and its undeserved reputation for stupidity.

Jessie and Toots have spent the night in a midtown hotel. Baleine is crashing with her brother in the Bronx. The brother, a security guard at Columbia University, has attended the Blessing of the Animals ceremony in the past. Over breakfast, Baleine has heard about the immensity of the cathedral and the crush of spectators. Now she asks Toots and Jessie to save her a place at the top of the steps to the great portal. She has to pick up Father Sanchez, and then she'll join them.

The fat ass warden has taken the subway from the Franciscan convent he is staying at. The Number 1 Broadway Local to 110th Street. Baleine meets him as planned at the Starbucks a block from the subway station.

"This is a great day of remembrance," says the priest. "St. Francis loved and blessed all animals."

"I don't think that white dude put enough cinnamon in this Skinny Dolce Latte," says Baleine.

"We had best leave. Your friends may be having a hard time saving us a place." They head for the door; the cathedral is a block away. "I assume you'll recognize J.M. when he shows up. I've never even seen a picture of him."

"I'll recognize him, all right, Father. Recognize that cracker anywhere."

*   *   *

292

Sarge Gibbs is feeling more than a bit foolish in a flimsy white gown that flaps in the steady breeze off the Hudson River. He is keeping his distance from the wrangler who trucked the World Donkey down from Westchester in the wee hours of the morning and is still managing him. The wrangler will hand the lead rope over to Sarge when the procession begins. Sarge has been told that the donkey is docile and easily led, but other than his family's succession of pet Labs and, twice, his wife's riding horse, he has never touched an animal bigger than a pussycat. Were it not for the promised money shot of him posing with President Obama, he would have fobbed the presentation off on someone else. He is reassured that in a pinch he can summon the Rabbi, who will be seated fairly close to the place where the presentation will be made, but he is still apprehensive.

A voice from behind makes him start.

"You ready to go, cowboy?" It's the White House aide Randall Ace looking very New York in a black suit and turtleneck with a laminated ID hanging from his neck on a lanyard. A Bluetooth device covers his right ear.

"Piece of cake, Randall. Call me donkey wrangler *extraordinaire.*"

"Terrific. Here's the final plan. When you get to the end of the nave where the church widens out, an acolyte in a black gown and a white cotta will lead you and the donkey to the right hand side of the animal enclosure away from the pulpit. He'll put you about twelve feet from where the President is sitting at an angle that will let the TV camera get a good shot of the President with you and the donkey in the background. The priest will deliver his homily and then offer a prayer of blessing for all of the animals. After that, he will say, 'Now we have a special ceremony,' and walk over to the President's party.

"The acolyte will prompt you to make sure you don't miss the cue. You will lead the donkey over to the President, who will then be standing up with the priest beside him. You will hand the rope to the Secret Service agent standing to the right of the priest.

That's to your left. Don't make a mistake on this because if you hand it to the agent on the president's left, it will partially block the television shot. Then you say your line, the President shakes your hand and says a few personal words, and you take a couple of steps back and to your left. The President turns to the camera, makes some very brief comments about reverence for animals and the need to slow the pace of extinction. Everyone in the world takes a photograph. Maybe the President will invite you to pose with him, but that's his choice. Then he and his party leave with the donkey. After that, as soon as the Secret Service signals the priest to announce that the audience is free to rise, you'll be all done. Except for looking at your picture with the President on every front page and television screen tomorrow morning."

Sarge experiences a moment of anticipatory rapture.

Randall gives him a look. "You good to go, Sarge? Looking a bit strange there."

"*No problemo,*" replies Sarge, snapping back to reality.

*   *   *

"They're coming," says Baleine, who has gained a foot-and-a-half in height by climbing onto a stone footing beneath the row of sculpted saints that funnels visitors to the cathedral's bronze doors.

Jessie strains on tiptoes to see the parade. At eight inches shorter, Toots doesn't have a chance. Then a gap fortuitously opens between two portly women recording the event on cellphones, and she can just see the bottom of the stairs.

"Tell me when Ya'fur is coming." In her line of sight, an elephant led by a man in white begins to climb the stairs.

Fifty yards away, J.M. and Justin maneuver their horses onto the sidewalk to control the spot where the animals emerging from the driveway next to the cathedral make a right-angle turn to go up the staircase. J.M. has spotted six other mounted police operating in pairs, but he has kept his distance without difficulty and no one has noticed him. His lasso is coiled in his right hand.

An elephant and a camel plod past. He senses some tension in his mount, but it is well trained and easy to control.

Jesus' donkey is making the turn from the driveway onto the sidewalk and heading toward the foot of the staircase. The tall blonde man holding his lead looks jumpy. With Justin and his mount shielding him from the view of the policemen stationed out on the street and farther down the sidewalk, J.M. knees his horse slightly forward and skillfully drops the noose of his lasso over the donkey's head. As he turns his mount to the left the rope comes taut. He feels a brief counter-tug from the lead in the hand of the donkey's handler, but the pull of J.M.'s lasso is stronger. The tall blonde man loses his grip and careens backward with a look of surprise and horror on his face.

With Justin maneuvering in front to clear the way, J.M. eases his horse forward into the packed crowd of spectators with Ya'fur following docilely behind at the end of his rope. There are many confused looks and a muffled call of distress from the donkey's escort, but the crowd knows that NYPD mounted policemen rule the streets of New York. In a matter of seconds, J.M., Justin, and Ya'fur are clear of the crowd and heading briskly down the sidewalk toward the corner of 113th Street. Still on the sidewalk, they make a right turn in the direction of Morningside Drive. It is clear sailing ahead. The block-long cyclone fence shutting off the construction and parking areas on the cathedral's north side has made an active police presence on 113th Street unnecessary.

Back on the cathedral steps, Father Sanchez has given up on getting a view. Suddenly he mutters, "Something's wrong."

"What do you mean 'wrong'?" says Toots.

"The donkey's gone," reports Baleine at almost the same moment.

"What do you mean 'gone'?" says Jessie.

Baleine hops down from the stone footing. "It was about to do the steps, and then it wasn't there. I couldn't see what happened because there were a couple of mounted police … and … omigod, one of them looked like J.M.! He's here!"

"Where's Ya'fur, Father?" demands Toots.

"I can't tell you where he is. As an ass warden, I can't interfere."

"Can you tell me where he's not? Like, is he not going into the cathedral?"

"He's not going into the cathedral."

Baleine lets loose a frighteningly loud and intimidating shout. "GET OUT OF OUR WAY, PEOPLE! SICK WOMAN COMING THROUGH!" The nearby spectators take a look at the heavy, ferocious-looking black woman shouting at them and instantaneously make a path for Baleine, Toots, and Jessie to run diagonally northward down the steps.

Baleine has her cell-phone to her ear. "Professor! We have a problem. J.M.'s done it. He's kidnapped Ya'fur! He and another guy are dressed as mounted police. I'm after them, but I can't see them on Amsterdam. I think they turned down 113th."

Despite his determination to observe the ass warden code and remain passive no matter what transpires, Constantine stands up and waves both arms at the Rabbi sitting opposite him in the north transept beyond the pulpit. A Secret Service agent promptly moves toward him with his hand reaching into his jacket. Seeing that he has caught the Rabbi's attention, Constantine thrusts his arm forward with his finger pointing at the side exit behind the Rabbi.

"You will have to sit down, Sir," says the Secret Service agent gripping the elbow of his raised arm painfully. As Constantine resumes his seat, he sees the Rabbi rise and slip discreetly past seated dignitaries toward the aisle.

Baleine reaches the corner. She is still talking into her cell-phone. "I see them! They're on 113th about halfway down toward the park."

"There's nothing I can do, Baleine," says Constantine. The elephant leading the procession is halfway down the nave. The spectators on both sides are on their feet applauding and snapping photographs.

The Rabbi darts through the north exit and into a parking lot. He looks around to get his bearings and spots the gate in the cyclone fence that opens onto 113th Street. He jogs in that direction while phoning.

"Randall Ace," comes the voice in his ear.

"Randall, it's the Rabbi. Something may have happened to the donkey. I'm checking it out." He closes his cell and sprints forward.

Randall Ace steps confidently into the animal enclosure area just as the elephant enters. An official personage on what is doubtless an official errand. He insinuates his way unnoticed up the animal-choked passage in the center of the nave. A camel, three horses, two cows … Ah, a donkey. He falls into step with a white-gowned youth leading a gray donkey and startles him with an arm around his shoulder.

"Who are you!?"

"Just keep walking. I'm with President Obama." He holds up his dangling ID. "The President may need your help. The World Donkey isn't in the line. Slight indisposition apparently. If it doesn't show up in time, you and your donkey are going to have to fill in. No drama. No one will know the difference. Just do what I tell you. I'll stay with you all the way."

"But this donkey represents the Blue Donkey Bar. It's on Amsterdam."

"What's your name?"

"Richie. I go to Columbia."

"Okay, Richie. Tomorrow, after this is all over, you'll get to tell a whole posse of reporters about the Blue Donkey Bar and how you got to meet President Obama. Then for a little while you'll be Columbia's most famous student ever. But that's for tomorrow. For right now, you have to do everything I tell you. When I take you up to the president, you hand the rope to the Secret Servant agent to the right of the president and say, 'Mr. President, I present this rare donkey to the children of America on behalf of the people of the world.' Practice that in your head. 'Mr. President, I present this rare donkey to the children of America on behalf of the people of the world.' After that, the President will shake your

hand, you'll get your picture taken a few million times, and it'll
be over. But no story about a substitute donkey. And absolutely
no mention of the Blue Donkey Bar. Understand?"

"Yes, sir. What's my line again?"

The Rabbi peers down the street through the locked gate of
the parking lot. At the corner to his right he can make out a horse
trailer with NYPD blazoned on it and two dismounted policemen
in riding boots trying to lead a donkey up a loading ramp. He
steps back, takes a run at the gate and leaps. Stabbing his fingers
through the fencing, he finds a foothold on the gate's chain lock.
He climbs upward and swings first one leg and then the other over
the top of the gate. Dropping lightly to the ground, he looks again
toward the end of the block. One man is now on either side of
the donkey with an arm around its rear end clasping his partner's
hand while the other hand grips the vertical handles on the back
of the trailer. The donkey is stubborn, but it is beginning to give
way to their combined force.

The Rabbi strips off his suit coat and extracts a white Frisbee
from a specially sewn pocket in its lining. He turns his head to
sample the stiff breeze from the west then turns back to estimate
the distance down the sidewalk: a hundred yards sloping slightly
downward with gingko trees close in on the left and continuous
cyclone fencing on the right. He takes two steps, leans deeply to
his right and whips off a mighty forehand throw. Starting just
inches above the pavement, the whirling disc climbs slightly as it
zooms arrow-straight toward the trailer. Coming in unseen over
the shoulder of the near side policeman it strikes the donkey a
sharp blow on its right ear. Hee-haw! Ya'fur brays with alarm,
kicks his hind legs to dislodge the hands forcing it into the trailer,
and jumps from the ramp. The Rabbi immediately loses sight of
it as it speedily trots south on Morningside Drive.

Ya'fur passes a pair of ivy-covered stone pillars flanking a
steep stairway into Morningside Park. A bit further on he pauses
at a similar entrance just opposite the cathedral's apse. Instead of
stone steps, an asphalt path slopes toward a broad treeless lawn.

Running behind on foot, J.M. and Justin lose sight of the fleeing donkey when it passes between the stone pillars and enters the park. When they reach the entry, the animal is nowhere to be seen. But policemen with drawn weapons are closing in on them from both up and down Morningside Drive.

Back in the cathedral, Randall Ace ushers Richie Stevens through his fill-in role after leaving him in the hands of the acolyte for a long enough time to update the Secret Service and the President's aides. The smiling President graciously receives the gift from the people of the world and gives Richie the photo-op of a lifetime before heading out to his motorcade.

Scarcely has he exited the building, however, when the President yells to his staff in a harsh voice that no one can remember ever having heard:

"WHO STOLE MY DONKEY!?"

*   *   *

In the Iranian ambassador's residence on Fifth Avenue, President Ahmadinejad sits despondently on an overstuffed sofa beside his Chief of Staff. He looks at his watch. A bowl of apples, oranges, and figs is untouched on the marble table in front of the sofa, but the teacups have been used. A few aides cluster silently at the door of the ornately formal reception room.

"The donkey of the Master of the Hour is now in American hands. How could that happen? You assured me, Rahim, that there would be an opportunity to stop the ceremony, but now it is too late. The Germans lied. Your Parsee lied."

"I don't know what more we could have done, Mahmoud."

"Your Three-Thirteen have failed me, Rahim. We have all failed the Hidden Imam. What right do we have to rule if we cannot prepare for his return?"

Professor Monika Farber and Fritz Messiassohn are sitting silently on straight chairs at the side of the room.

An aide enters and goes over to whisper in the Chief of Staff's ear. Mashaei's eyes open wide.

"Something has happened, Mahmoud," says Mashaei excitedly. "It's on the news. After Obama left the cathedral, the police closed down all the streets in the area and began searching the park behind the cathedral. A rumor is being reported that the donkey has escaped."

Ahmadinejad brightens. "Ya'fur escaped? Little Ya'fur has defeated the Mossad and the CIA?"

"It's only a rumor, Mahmoud. We will just have to wait to find out more. There is still a chance that Ya'fur will come to us."

"If you will allow me, gentlemen," interjects Monika from across the room. "If Ya'fur has chosen to become lost, neither you nor the police will be able to find him. Only Fritz can do that." Fritz pricks up his ears at the sound of his name embedded in a Persian sentence. "You must send him to that park immediately."

"What if he meets Ya'fur and doesn't bring him back?" asks Ahmadinejad. "Why should we trust either of you?"

Mashaei speaks into his master's ear. "If Fritz finds the donkey, Mahmoud, Ya'fur's prediction will have come true. So maybe the Parsee's will come true also, and you will feed an apple to the Mahdi's steed. We have acted on faith this far, let us take this one more step."

"You do have faith, Rahim."

"I do, Mahmoud. We must pass through the dark to get to the light."

The President looks at the German professor. "Explain to him what he must do. Tell him that if he finds Ya'fur but does not come back here with him, there will be harsh consequences. There is no traffic moving where he is going so he must run."

In running shoes, shorts, and a dark blue singlet borrowed from the ambassador's cook, Fritz peruses a map of Manhattan. The route to Morningside Park could not be simpler. Only a little more than two miles and almost all of it through Central Park. An aide gives him a New York Yankees baseball cap. Fritz leaves the residence, crosses Fifth Avenue dodging between gridlocked cars, and enters the park on the run.

MORNINGSIDE PARK

Toots springs from the table at the 111th Street Starbucks and rushes out the door. "Fritz! Fritz!" she shouts at a jogger on the far side of Broadway. "Fritz! Over here!"

Fritz hurdles the low bushes enclosing the Broadway median strip and rushes into Toots' embrace. She leads him inside and introduces him to Jessie, Baleine, and Father Sanchez. The Rabbi he already knows.

"What are you doing here, Fritz?" says Toots.

"They heard at the Iranian mission that Ya'fur had escaped. Professor Farber sent me to find him and bring him back, but I have no idea how to do that. The police have closed Morningside Park. I don't dare speak to them because of my accent and my tattoo. They will think I'm a terrorist. So I ran all around the park and looked at it from the opposite sides of the surrounding streets. I don't see how a donkey could hide there very long. I think Ya'fur must already have been taken somewhere else. The park is nothing but a cliff with the cathedral and Columbia University at the top and playgrounds at the bottom. There are some trees here and there, but no real forest or thick bushes. There is even a duck pond fed by a waterfall that seems to come out from underneath the cathedral. Which seems very strange because there isn't any stream up here to provide the water."

"My brother told me about that," says Baleine. "Once upon a time, Columbia University planned to build a gymnasium to oppress black people."

"How can a gymnasium oppress black people?" asks Fritz.

"It was being built on the face of the cliff. The plan was for white boys to enter up top and play in their white boy gym, while black neighborhood youth entered at the bottom and played in a black folks gym. All of it on public land, of course. Given to Columbia by the old white guys who ran the city."

"What does this have to do with a waterfall?"

"Don't interrupt Baleine. She hasn't decided yet whether she likes you. As I was saying, when they got to digging a hole, cutting down trees, and turning the nice rocky cliff into a sheer wall of stone—that is to say, when they actually started ruining a public park—the people of Harlem rose up in revolt. Columbia surrendered and gave up the plan for the gymnasium, but they had to cover up all the damage. They turned the hole for the gym's basement into a duck pond, and the pond water pumped up to the top of the cliff made the waterfall. Your basic Disneyland, but my brother says people like it anyway."

Toots puts her hand on Baleine's arm. "This isn't getting Fritz any closer to finding Ya'fur, Baleine."

Fritz shrugs. "That's okay, Toots. I've given up looking. I'd like to just disappear now, but I only have a tourist visa. When I don't come back with Ya'fur, the Three-Thirteen will wait for me to leave the country and then hunt me down."

Father Sanchez has been listening thoughtfully to the conversation. "It is really true that you can hear the donkey talk and understand him?"

"Yes."

"You can!?" exclaims Jessie. "The CIA is never going to believe this."

Father Sanchez beams. "Sensing Ya'fur even once is enough. I've felt it. It means you are an assman. Like me, but different. I belong to the Ecclesiastical Household of Ass Wardens. It is my gift from the Holy Spirit that I always know the whereabouts of both Ya'fur and Ufair." Jessie's mouth is hanging open in astonishment. "For me to tell laypeople where either donkey is would violate the ass warden code. But you don't exactly fit the definition of a layperson, Fritz. So please, the rest of you, go somewhere else so I can talk privately with Fritz."

The Rabbi, acting as if nothing extraordinary is transpiring, ushers Baleine, Toots, and Jessie out onto Broadway, which is barricaded and empty of traffic.

"What's the Ecclesiastical Household of Ass Wardens?" asks Jessie.

"It's what the Roman Catholic Church decided to do about the donkey of the Messiah," replies Toots. "Namely, nothing. It's an organization that knows but doesn't tell. Professor Constantine explained it to me."

Back inside Father Sanchez ponders how the ass warden code applies in the present circumstances. He comes to a decision. "Here is what I can tell you: Ya'fur is not moving."

Fritz's expression brightens. "In that case, Ya'fur isn't being trucked to some unknown location as I thought he probably was. Is he in the park?"

"I would like to tell you, Son, but I don't believe I can go that far."

"That's cool. Anyway, I can't get into the park."

Outside the Rabbi speed-dials a number on his cell phone.

"Randall Ace," comes the voice in his ear.

"Randall, this is the Rabbi. I have someone with me who may be able to find the donkey. But he needs access to Morningside Park. I'm taking him to 113th and Morningside Drive. Let the police know."

"Will do. Whoever it is, tell him this is urgent. No Drama Obama, who never loses his cool and never gets angry, is foaming at the mouth about his donkey being stolen. Don't ask me why. It just came across to him as the ultimate insult. If we don't get it back, we're going to have our asses handed to us. No pun intended."

"I'll keep you posted." The Rabbi closes his phone and gestures through the window to Fritz, who takes his time bidding a warm goodbye to the priest. The look on his face when he steps out the door is the opposite of the dejection he had displayed on entering.

"Fritz, let's go. They'll let you into the park."

"Good. I still don't know how to find him, but I'm sure he's there."

"Let Ya'fur find you."

"Remember, donkeys don't like stairs!" cries Toots as he and the Rabbi cross Broadway.

A policewoman in a day-glow green vest walks the Rabbi and Fritz to the park entrance on Morningside Drive where donkey was last seen.

"Good luck," says the Rabbi.

Fritz passes between the ivied stone pillars. To his right is a cascade of staircases leading down to the softball fields on the flat. Remembering Toots' admonition, he turns left onto a path bordering a grassy lawn. At the far end of the path, the lawn the gives way to trees, bushes, and then another steep downward staircase. He stops the looks around. The roar of gushing water reaches his ears from somewhere close by. He steps over the iron railing beside the path and follows the sound into the trees where he finds an artful array of boulders heaped up to disguise the outlet pipe from which the artificial waterfall is spurting. The cliff is sheer, but the waterfall descends only a dozen feet or so before bouncing off a jutting rocky shelf and dispersing for a further foamy fall into the duck pond far below. Fritz scrutinizes the point where the falling water splashes onto the first shelf of rocks. Is that a donkey he sees crouched behind the torrent?

"I've been waiting for you, Fritz."

"Ya'fur?"

"It's time for us to leave."

"Aren't you getting wet?"

"I'm a donkey, Fritz. I've been standing out in rainstorms for centuries. And worse than rainstorms. Climb down and get on my back."

"I don't think the police will let us out of the park, Ya'fur."

"Once you are on my back, we can go anywhere and no one will see us."

"Is that true, Ya'fur?"

"You'll find out."

Fritz clambers awkwardly down the rocky flank of the waterfall and picks his way across wet, slippery boulders to get behind the sheet of water. In adventure movies, he recalls, it's always pretty dry when the heroes go behind a waterfall. And there's usually a tunnel into a secret realm. But now he is thoroughly drenched and buffeted by the force of the water."

"Get on," says Ya'fur.

Unable to straddle the donkey in the confined space, Fritz sits on him sideways. Ya'fur rises and with Fritz desperately clutching his mane to keep from falling off maneuvers with surprising agility down the rocky, torrent-splashed, scree to dry land at the side of the duck pond. Away from the falling water, the park is a halcyon urban refuge. A sign cautions users to stay out of the pond. Another posts a warning about rat poison. A dozen Canada geese waddle past a clump of reeds growing out of the greenish water.

Feeling unbalanced sitting sideways, Fritz shifts to a straddling posture. Ya'fur ambles on and approaches an exit onto 110th Street. A policeman stares straight at them from six feet away but obviously sees nothing. They pass more police, some of them with leashed dogs, but everyone is oblivious.

"They really can't see us or smell us, can they?"

"Not unless I let them," replies Ya'fur.

After a two-block stretch behind police barricades on 110th Street, they cross the broad thoroughfare of Central Park West and pass between another pair of stone entry pillars into the manicured wilderness of Central Park.

"Have you noticed the people we've been passing?" asks Ya'fur as they walk at a slow pace among clusters of bicyclists, and joggers.

"They all look incredibly happy. Even the dogs."

"That's because we are passing. Or more accurately, because you are passing. I am just a donkey."

"But who am I?"

"What would you like to be, Fritz? A Messiah? Have everyone love and worship you? Establish a new moral order? Change the course of history?"

"No, Ya'fur, I don't think I'm cut out for that. All I really like to do is work out, sort through gemstones, have sex, and sometimes read history books. Making the world happy doesn't figure much in my view of myself."

"Don't pass over this opportunity lightly. Every orgasm, if you chose to indulge yourself that way, would have five stars. Women would kneel before you and wash your feet with their hair."

"We don't go in for that so much nowadays."

"You could better every athletic record. Become the uncontested champion of champions."

"And spend years trying to prove I'm not using steroids? I don't think so."

"Are you sure you don't want to help your fellow man? People everywhere seem to be feeling a need for a Messiah."

"To be honest with you, Ya'fur, I don't think the world is ready for a German messiah."

"Fair enough. I see your point. But how about going the other way? Become a demonic destroyer, an Antichrist."

"A German already tried that."

"I see."

"It didn't work out so well."

"I never knew your Herr Hitler. Ufair may have known him. I'm not sure. Ufair and I are only occasionally in touch."

"I met Ufair in Algeria."

"I know. I asked for his help. Now I owe him one."

"Do you know where we're going?"

"To see the president of Iran I assume. He is supposed to offer me an apple."

showdown on fifth avenue

Fritz and Ya'fur are crossing the North Meadow softball diamonds and approaching the Reservoir. "You haven't asked me what I thought of Jesus."

"Am I supposed to?"

"It's what's normally in people's minds when they think about a messianic donkey. Jesus, or Moses, or Muhammad."

"I guess I'm shallow. I don't really care what you thought of them. I read a professor's version of what you must have thought, but it didn't mean much to me."

"What was it like?"

"Glib. More showing off what he knows about donkey history than conveying anything spiritual."

"Actually, I wouldn't tell you if you did ask."

"You're not one of those bray and tell donkeys?"

"It's not so much that. It's more that my relations with the people I can talk to aren't very profound. After all, I'm a donkey."

"Then why did you ask me what I thought about being a Messiah."

"That was more of a questionnaire to see where you thought you were headed. Any answer you gave would have been all right with me."

"What if I had told you that we were going to Mexico instead of to the East Side?"

"We would still have to go to the East Side first. I have a rendezvous with Mahmoud Ahmadinejad."

"Why?"

"Because a Parsee seer said I did. I don't tell seers what to see, but if they are genuine, what they see comes to pass."

"Do you know what is going to happen once we get to the ambassador's residence?"

"No. The Parsee didn't see past Mahmoud's apple."

They are standing on the corner opposite the Iranian residence. The walk signal appears, and the donkey and his rider cross the avenue amidst a bunch of pedestrians with beatific looks on their faces. When they get to the door, Monika Farber comes down the front steps and takes hold of the dangling lead rope.

"You can see us?" asks Fritz as he slips down from Ya'fur's back.

"Of course. Why shouldn't I?"

Fritz turns to the donkey. "Professor Farber, allow me to present the donkey Ya'fur."

"Hee-haw," says the donkey.

Monika peers at the animal. "You're sure this is Ya'fur?"

"I've never been so sure of anything in my life."

"Then let us go inside and break the good news."

The donkey negotiates the three steps awkwardly and follows her lead into the building. They come to a stop at a staircase in the narrow entry hallway. Monika ascends the stairs by herself at a dignified pace. She is wearing a beatific smile that accentuates her natural beauty. At the door of the reception room she encounters an array of beaming Iranian faces: "Your Excellency, President Mahmoud Ahmadinejad, I am pleased to inform you that the sacred donkey Ya'fur is standing in your entry hallway having come to this residence of its own free will."

Tears form in the smiling president's eyes. "We've waited so long," he says softly. "For a thousand years. But now it is happening in my time. I am overwhelmed. Think of it, Rahim, today Ya'fur, tomorrow the Master of the Hour." With Esfandiar Mashaei and the Iranian United Nations ambassador two feet behind him, he steps forward and extends his hand to the professor. "The old rules will not apply in the new era, Doktor Monika. You have my heartfelt thanks, and the thanks of every Iranian and every Shi'ite in the world." They shake hands in a courtly fashion.

The solemn moment is abruptly broken by the static pop of a powerful bullhorn being turned on. From the street comes a voice so amplified that some of the Iranians cover their ears.

"Attention inside the Iranian residence. This is Barack Obama, the President of the United States. President Ahmadinejad, you have stolen my donkey. I want it back."

*   *   *

Paul Constantine's limo is dawdling in heavy midtown traffic on the West Side Highway, but he is too irritated and dejected to care. When the President of the United States called out, 'Who stole my donkey?' the one—the only—person who could have helped him out was the Professor of Asinine Studies at Harvard University. But did anyone call out for Paul Constantine? Did anyone lead him to the President? Did anyone hear his pleas that he was an expert on donkeys? No. Pushed to the side. Given hard looks by Secret Service agents, especially the one who had forced him to sit down when he was signaling the Rabbi. Ignored and humiliated. He had stood by powerless and hopeless as the President's motorcade roared down the cathedral driveway and turned onto Amsterdam Avenue.

What a sad position for the world's greatest authority on sacred donkey history, he thinks. The bitter scene plays over and over in his mind. An officious black functionary named Somebody Ace pushing him into a limo as if he were a caterer being sent home after a party. Tears of frustration fill his eyes. It's almost more than a person can bear.

Adding to his annoyance is the sight of the limo driver with a Bluetooth device in his ear talking while he drives. *That is both insensitive and illegal,* he thinks. His grief demands silence.

"Professor?" says the driver, handing him the earpiece. "Someone wants to talk to you."

Constantine can't figure out how to attach the gadget to his ear so he just holds it close. "Hello?" He looks at the back of the driver's head. "Can anyone hear me on this?"

Then he hears a voice. "Professor Constantine, this is Randall Ace. There has been a development. The driver will take you immediately to rejoin the President's party on Fifth Avenue. Turn on the television in the back of the limo. All of the channels are covering it. I'll update you as soon as you get here."

Constantine turns on the television. It's the same Fox News reporter from the morning show. "To put it in a nutshell, Alice, two political asses are in a bizarre face-off on opposite sides of Fifth Avenue."

The anchor is chuckling. "That's a good way to put it, Martin. One more thing. How did the donkey get from Morningside Park to the East Side? Was it kidnapped by Iranian terrorists? Are the authorities preparing for further terrorist actions?"

Constantine switches to CNN. "... here with the President's party at the exit of the 86th Street transverse onto Fifth Avenue. Traffic on Fifth Avenue is being diverted from 90th Street down to 79th, and the police have pushed the crowd away from the confrontation area. As you can see in our helicopter shot, Fifth Avenue is totally empty for several blocks north and south of 84th Street, where the Iranian residence is situated. There is a solid phalanx of NYPD and Secret Service personnel shielding President Obama's vehicle on the west side of the street. I doubt that any Iranians, even from the roof of the residence, can actually see the President, who is back inside his vehicle after having gotten out to make his non-negotiable demand that the Iranian leader, President Mahmoud Ahmadinejad, return the World Donkey. The primary concern, as always, is for the President's safety. But the President is overruling his security people and is said to be extremely angry."

Constantine's heart soars. The President of the United States needs him. Looking out the window at the Hudson River he suddenly notices that the driver is still heading south, away from the drama on the television screen. "You're going the wrong direction," he yells at the driver's back. "I'm supposed to get over to the Metropolitan Museum."

"I'm following our escort, sir," replies the driver. For the first time Constantine notices that there are NYPD patrol cars before and behind the limo. The Harvard Professor of Asinine Studies getting a police escort in New York City to meet with the President of the United States. It can't get much sweeter than this.

The limo pulls into the entrance drive of the 30th Street heliport. Randall Ace opens the door. "This way, Professor Constantine. The helicopter is ready to take off."

A crewmember straps him in and within moments they are in the air. A few dizzying minutes of flight and then a descent onto a patch of lawn just north of the museum and behind the security line guarding the president on Fifth Avenue. Randall Ace delivers Constantine from the flying machine into the hands of two Secret Service agents. The Rabbi, Baleine, Toots, and her CIA friend from the train are standing behind the row of police some distance away. For the first time, it occurs to Constantine that he has no idea what he is going to say to the President. An earlier comment by the Rabbi resurfaces in his mind. "If the President should ask about donkeys, I don't think he needs to be told anything about Ya'fur and the Messiah." What had he replied? "Do you think I'm an idiot?"

Constantine experiences the next few minutes as a blur that he will have a hard time recalling. The President gets out of his car and shakes his hand. An aide, whom he is probably expected to recognize, briefs him on the situation. The people who have been indentified in the Iranian residence, in addition to President Ahmadinejad, his Chief of Staff, Esfandiar Mashaei, and the

Iranian ambassador himself, are a German professor named Monika Farber and a German student named Fritz Messiassohn. Maybe the aide says more, but Constantine stops listening after hearing the name of his nemesis, the Teutonic vixen Farber.

"The donkey is in the building?" he hears himself asking.

"Yes, that is confirmed," replies the aide.

Who knows what the mechanism is of a flash of inspiration? First he has no idea what to say, then suddenly an idea is there and fully formed. "Mr. President," says Constantine, "give President Ahmadinejad the donkey. Say the word *peeshkash* and tell him that the donkey is his. Among Iranians, if a guest admires something in a person's house, particularly something very nice, it is fitting and proper, but not necessary, for the host to say *peeshkash* and spontaneously give it to him. The action takes the receiver of the gift by surprise and places on him an extraordinary burden to reciprocate."

"But I don't want to give him my donkey," says President Obama bluntly.

"I understand that, Mr. President. But what you may not know is that some Iranians, including Mr. Ahmadinejad and Mr. Mashaei in particular, entertain fanatic delusions about this particular donkey. They believe that the donkey in the residence is a sacred animal, and that it is destined to be the mount of the Hidden Imam when he returns from occultation. They believe that it is the same donkey that carried Muhammad and that carried Jesus. They think it's immortal, and that it can talk, at least to a few chosen people."

"You're not putting me on, Professor?" says the President with a look of utmost skepticism.

"I assure you, what I'm telling you is true. They're idiots, but that is what they believe."

"I've heard of this Hidden Imam. Some of my intel people tell me Ahmadinejad is crazy and that for him the coming of the Hidden Imam requires the destruction of Israel."

"The actual argument, Mr. President, is that Ahmadinejad is so convinced that it is his destiny to pave the way for the return of the Imam that he would destroy Israel to hasten the Mahdi's coming, even if it meant the destruction of Iran in an Israeli nuclear counter-strike. With all due respect for your intel people, however, belief in the return of the Hidden Imam has nothing to do with killing Jews. Theologically, the Imam is a peaceful leader who presides over a millennium of peace and justice that precedes the end of the world. That being so, giving Ahmadinejad the donkey might completely change Iran's relations with the United States. You've heard the idea of trying a carrot on the Iranians instead of a stick? Well, bizarre though it may seem, this is the biggest carrot a lot of Iranians can imagine."

"All because the so-called Hidden Imam is going to ride that particular donkey."

"Correct."

"Or so Ahmadinejad believes."

"Or so he believes."

"What about you? I'm told you're the top American authority. Do you believe this donkey is the sacred one?"

Constantine works to calm himself. *Why aren't I following the Rabbi's advice? I am about to tell the President of the United States the stupidest thing he has ever heard from a non-Republican.* "Yes, Mr. President, I believe it is."

"Then why should we give it away? Why shouldn't we keep it?"

"Because ultimately the donkey itself chooses who to be with. That's the way it has always gone."

The President looks Constantine appraisingly in the eye, then asks for his bullhorn. He steps forward until he is right behind the security line. He is tall enough to see the deserted avenue before him and the Iranian residence beyond.

The bullhorn is deafening. "Hello inside the Iranian residence. This is the President of the United States again. If the President of the Islamic Republic of Iran will come to the door of the

314

residence so I can talk to him directly, I have a message he will want to hear."

Presently the door opens and the short, slight figure of Mahmoud Ahmadinejad appears in the doorway.

"Mr. President," says Obama, "you have not always been made to feel welcome in this country. But during the meeting of the General Assembly of the United Nations, you are here as a guest on American soil. I am sure you will agree with me that it is inappropriate for a guest to take something that belongs to the host."

The U.N. ambassador has appeared beside Ahmadinejad in the doorway carrying another bullhorn. His face is close to Ahmadinejad's ear as he translates the President's remarks into Persian. The two converse for a few seconds. Then the ambassador puts the amplifier to his mouth. "President Obama, this is the Iranian ambassador speaking. My President tells me that the donkey came to the residence of its own accord. We Iranians did not steal it. But now it is standing on what is legally Iranian soil."

"Let us not have a needless confrontation on that point, Mr. Ambassador. I want to say something that will make this easier for all of us. I know how much you value that donkey. So as a host to a guest, I say to you *peeshkash*. The donkey is yours. It was a gift to me. Now it is my gift to you."

The ambassador translates the President's words. The discussion between them is animated and prolonged. The figure of Esfandiar Mashaei appears behind them in the doorway as a third participant. The conversation ends and all three men look across at President Obama. The ambassador again puts the bullhorn to his mouth.

"On the instructions of my President, and on behalf of the Iranian people and all people of the Shi'ite faith, I wish to thank you, President Obama, for this wonderful gift. In return, President Ahmadinejad hereby commits his government to putting all of the Islamic Republic of Iran's nuclear fuel enrichment facilities

under the full control of the International Atomic Energy Agency
as a sign of our commitment to live peacefully with the peoples
of the world."

Obama calls over a man in a military uniform and speaks to
him briefly before he responds. "I thank you, Mr. President, from
the bottom of my heart. And the American people thank you.
But I must caution you, Mr. President, that the entire world is
watching and listening to our conversation and will expect you to
live up to your word. That means full and unimpeded inspection
of all of your country's nuclear facilities."

"That is assumed," replies the ambassador without further
consultation.

Standing beside President Obama, Constantine says softly,
but loud enough for him to hear: "The donkey must choose."

Obama considers the advice and then speaks again into the
bullhorn. "Before we end this historic meeting, Mr. Ambassador,
I would take it as a sign of good will on the part of the Iranian
government if the donkey could be brought out to the street. Some
of my advisors believe, and say that you also believe, that ultimately
this donkey will choose its own course. I have relinquished my
claim to the donkey in a gesture of friendship. And you, President
Ahmadinejad, have graciously and generously responded. The
exchange between us as human beings is completed. But now I
ask that you take the final step of letting the donkey decide."

The translation and ensuing debate in the doorway of the
residence lasts for several minutes. Then the humans step away
from the doorway, and Ya'fur appears. Fritz is holding his lead
rope. As soon as he has led the animal down the three steps
leading to the sidewalk and out onto Fifth Avenue, Fritz drops
the lead and walks across the street to where Toots is standing at
the entrance to Central Park. They kiss.

Ya'fur stands still facing toward the south. Minutes pass.
Ahmadinejad appears again at the doorway and calls out in a
friendly voice: *"Beeyaw khar-e jun. Beeyaw Ya'fur."*

"Come, dear little donkey. Come Ya'fur," translates Constantine for Obama's benefit.

"Ya'fur?"

"It's the donkey's name."

Ahmadinejad is now on the sidewalk. He has in his hand an apple and some sugar cubes from the fruit and tea service in the reception room. "*Seeb daram, khar-e jun. Beeyaw.*"

"I have an apple, dear little donkey. Come."

President Obama stands motionless.

The donkey moves its head and looks at the Iranian president. Ahmadinejad comes up to it and gently puts a hand on its mane. The donkey delicately takes the apple from his other hand and chews it. "*Besyar khoob, Ya'fur. Beeyaw ba man.*"

Constantine translates again. "Very good, Ya'fur. Come with me."

President Obama is standing very still observing the scene aloofly.

Without noticeable provocation, the donkey turns from Ahmadinejad and starts to walk toward Obama. The police line parts, but Ya'fur turns north instead of south. Fritz is waiting. He turns and looks into Toots' tear-streaked face.

"You know I have to go with him," he says tenderly. Then he turns back to Ya'fur. "Is it time?"

"Yes, it's time." Fritz mounts Ya'fur's back, and the pair immediately vanish from sight.

As the donkey and his rider move off into the park, the police, officials, reporters, and bystanders congregated on the sidewalks look at one another in puzzlement. Mixed with the puzzled looks, however, are smiles of the sweetest beatitude, as if they are all children who have just been praised by their favorite grandparent. Or blessed by God.

"Where are we going?" asks Ya'fur.

"You don't know? I thought Mexico. I've never been to Mexico. I hear the people down there are very devout."

"I thought you would say Mexico," says Ya'fur.

SOMETIME LATER

Sometime later the Scottish postal service delivers a parcel to the Greeley residence on Ass Isle. It contains two copies of *Ya' fur, The Messianic Donkey*. One is inscribed to Toots, the other to her father. Jessie opens Douglas Greeley's copy and scans the Acknowledgements. "He doesn't mention you, Toots."

"I told him he didn't have to."

"If he were a gentleman, he would have anyway."

Toots is looking at the Table of Contents of her own copy. "I see Baleine's chapter on The Black Ass of Baron Samedi is included. Does he thank her?"

"He says, 'I am grateful for the research assistance of Marie Adelaide Millefeuille.' Isn't that Baleine?"

"I think so."

Toots takes her father's book indoors to give to him after his nap and then comes out again. Jessie has the other copy under her arm. In high rubber boots and thick woolen jackets, the two women head off to muck out the donkey sheds on the south side of the house. Jessie takes Toots' hand. Toots smiles.

"You do know that I don't fancy women romantically, Jessie." Toots nevertheless keeps her friend's hand in a warm grasp.

"Oh Heavens, Toots. I should hope not! Perversion creeps me out. I want to live here as your sister and as your father's other daughter. You can sleep with anyone you like other than me."

"Spoken like a true donkey of the Lord," laughs Toots.

"I'll take that as a compliment," says Jessie.

"You think you can care for Daddy and handle the donkey chores here if I take a couple of weeks off to visit Mexico?"

*   *   *

Pastor Steve is sitting with Ray Bob in his living room when the caregiver comes back from picking up the mail. Though he has lost thirty-five pounds and is looking more fit than he has in twenty years, Ray Bob is still a little unsteady on his feet and quick to tire.

Pastor Steve unwraps the book and peruses it. "Let me read you this from the Acknowledgements, Ray Bob. 'My thanks go also to Pastor Steve Klingbeil for encouraging me to finish a project that was languishing, and to Ray Bob Krumlake for offering the hospitality of his home as a retreat for a harried writer.' I think that's real considerate, don't you Ray Bob?"

"Does he talk about J.M.?" Ray Bob's speech is slightly slurred.

Pastor Steve looks at the index. "Yes indeed. He's here in the last chapter. Mentions him on quite a few pages."

"I should take the book with me next time I go see him in Butner. It might cheer him up."

"How's he doing there? It's supposed to be a fine correctional facility. Is he settling in?"

"I think so. He only has to do a couple of years for impersonating a police officer. They dropped the other charges. He says they have a good Bible study group."

*   *   *

President Ahmadinejad has moved on. A chief executive cannot afford to waste time over plans that do not work out. When he thinks about Ya'fur, which he does not often do, he recalls the gentle feel of the donkey taking the apple from his hand.

Esfandiyar Mashaei has arranged to have a beautifully caparisoned horse standing at the ready every day of the year at a certain point in the Tehran suburb of Rayy. Some traditions report that it is the spot where the Master of the Hour will first appear when he returns. Care of the horse has been assigned to the Three-Thirteen.

The two men still meet regularly to discuss official business, but a coolness has developed between them. Concerned that he is growing apart from his Chief of Staff, the President takes advantage of an unusually warm fall day to invite him for tea in the garden behind the presidential mansion. Just the two of them. As they sip their tea and look at the few remaining leaves on the slender fruit trees, a black donkey suddenly ambles through the garden gate.

"I am Ufair," it says. "We have business to accomplish."

*   *   *

After a year and a half of interrogation, special rendition, and incarceration, Adnan Yafouri is released from Guantanamo. Thanks to a CD-DACP settlement arranged for by Jessie Zayyat during her final week at the Agency, he is entitled to generous compensation—if the Syrian government will allow him to keep the money.

*   *   *

Paul Constantine had expected to be elated by the highly publicized publication of his book. But an uncertain memory haunts him. The "Showdown on Fifth Avenue," as the press labeled the confrontation between the two presidents, is blurry in his mind, as it is in the memories of everyone who was there. But he seems to be the only person who clearly recalls seeing Fritz and Ya'fur ride off into the park. More troubling, he thinks he heard Ya'fur say, "I thought you would say Mexico." What was that all about?

THE END

ACKNOWLEDGEMENTS

I began forty years ago to collect information about the messianic and sexual symbolism of donkeys. The scholarly tome I anticipated writing on the subject would have been fully annotated with appreciations of the many friends and colleagues who brought unusual sources or studies to my attention. Settling on a fictional rather than a non-fictional vehicle for bringing my studies to a climax took away the opportunity of thanking individuals for specific nuggets of information. But collectively their contributions were greatly appreciated. I can only ask the reader to take my word for it that almost every bit of lore in this story is based on a concrete text, personal observation, or other source.

As for the five friends whom I have caricatured, sometimes outrageously, in inventing some of the characters in the story, they know who they are and have privately forgiven my trespasses against them.

I would like to thank the following for their valuable comments on the first draft: Zeev Maghen, Nathan Stroupe, Hossein Kamaly, Barak Barfi, Jahan Salehi, and Nerina Rustomji. There would never have been a final draft, however, were it not for my son Mark's painful to listen to but invariably sound editorial interventions.

CPSIA information can be obtained at www.ICGtesting.com

225945LV00001B/87/P